THE LAST ROMAN:
HONOUR

JACK LUDLOW

Allison & Busby Limited
12 Fitzroy Mews
London W1T 6DW
allisonandbusby.com

First published in Great Britain by Allison & Busby in 2014.
This paperback edition published by Allison & Busby in 2015.

A CIP catalogue record for this book is available from
the British Library.

10 9 8 7 6 5 4 3 2 1

ISBN 978-0-7490-1446-9

Typeset in 10.5/15.5 pt Sabon by
Allison & Busby Ltd.

The paper used for this Allison & Busby publication
has been produced from trees that have been legally sourced
from well-managed and credibly certified forests.

Printed and bound by
CPI Group (UK) Ltd, Croydon, CR0 4YY

To Roy and Trish David,
the creative and academic
heart of Nantwich

CHAPTER ONE

Fighting on the Persian frontier was about containment, which had frustrated Flavius Belisarius ever since he arrived. Just eighteen summers in age yet in command of a half *numerus* of light cavalry, he thirsted for the kind of fight in which reputations were made and deeds attained of which people would speak in decades and centuries to come: he wanted glory and with the impatience of youth he wanted it right away.

This attitude he maintained while serving alongside men who had experienced proper battle, soldiers far from happy at the prospect that conflict on a large scale might break out once more. Many had previously faced the might of the Sassanid Persian Empire and were wary of doing so again. The Romans had enjoyed little success against an enemy that generally outnumbered them and one that could rapidly gather its forces given the frontier was closer to their heartlands.

If Sassanid Persia sent forth a heterogeneous army, made up of many different tribal groups, then that too applied to the troops raised and paid for by Constantinople. Centuries had passed since Rome could field an army made up of its own citizens or indeed men recruited from within its own territories. The empire relied on mercenary barbarians to fight its battles, and given the Emperor Anastasius was a parsimonious ruler, such troops were numerically too low in the uneasy times of peace and late to arrive in proper quantities when real danger threatened.

The mainstay of the policy of containment was the great fortress at Dara, a massive effort at construction begun after the last conflict, one in which the Romans had been forced to buy a truce by paying a huge sum in gold to the Sassanid King Kavadh. Dara was a stronghold designed to ensure that no such bribes would ever be needed again but it was not a springboard for attack: likewise enterprising officers were discouraged from poking at the Sassanid hornet's nest lest some small action provoke a less containable response.

'It is like fighting with one arm tied behind your back.'

This opinion was imparted to the eunuch Narses, the man who commanded the force of which Belisarius was a part, sent out from Dara to patrol borderlands that were porous and always under threat of raids by small bodies of tribal forces in search of easy plunder. The forward screen had seen smoke hanging in the sky, which often indicated an incursion; the fact that had still been rising suggested it might still be in progress.

Flavius Belisarius had been strongly for Narses to cross into Persian territory and cut off the raiders from their homelands so they could be properly chastised. This meant annihilated and their bones left to rot, which would serve as a warning to others. Narses, who carried the greater responsibility, while acknowledging the temptation, had demurred at this. He feared the possibility of the kind of retaliation that could get out of hand, for the imperial edicts were perfectly clear: hold our territory but do not provoke.

Thus the Romans marched straight for the column of smoke, even the cavalry, which could have ridden to seal the route of escape, so surprise was sacrificed. However engaged the raiders were in their robbery and rapine none could miss the signs of such a force marching across a dry and arid landscape, especially the clouds of dust sent up by the horses' hooves.

Frustration that had been barely disguised now came near to boiling over. Narses would not release Flavius to at least get amongst the enemy as they began to retire, waiting until they were well away from the burning homesteads of a fertile valley before initiating the chase and that came with a parting command.

'You know where the border is, Flavius Belisarius. The marking posts you cannot miss. Do not cross it at a peril from which your high and mighty connections will struggle to protect you.'

That was maddening; worse was the quality of the unit he led. The establishment of a *numerus* was set at three hundred fighting men, yet there was not a unit in the imperial armies that had that as its true strength. Flavius was deficient by a full quarter of what should have been his command and, in addition, the provision of horses, the main source of mounted effectiveness, was far from perfect. Any kind of sustained and disciplined movement was constrained by the variety and fitness of what was being ridden.

Personally well mounted, nothing more than a fast canter was possible lest he wished to find himself isolated with only a rump of support; in short, most of those Flavius led could not keep up with him. So much for high connections, he thought, recalling the barbed comment of a commander keen to remind him that support in Constantinople was no guarantee of survival in the face of failure.

Such thoughts were banished as the first of the short marble pillars marking the frontier came into view. His enemies had been well enough ahead of him to get across that first and what had been headlong flight ceased; such raiders knew of the restrictions on Roman actions as well as those who laboured under them. Perhaps if they had not jeered and bared their buttocks they would not have brought on such a furious response.

Flavius slowed his mount and issued a series of shouted commands to get his men into some form of order. To those observing them, far enough inside their home territory to be safe from the best cast spear, it must have looked like a display of useless impotence and they were vocal in their ridicule. Their loud jeers were stilled as, a hundred paces from the borderline, the man who led their enemies called for the horn to be blown that initiated an advance.

The shocked raiders failed to react fast enough to secure their escape; those on horses, the leaders, who had remained mounted, fled at speed, pursued by Flavius and those of his own cavalry on horses of matching quality, some fifty in total. But most of the marauders had been on foot and, having jogged for over a league while carrying that which they had plundered, they were now too short of wind to even scatter properly before the Romans got amongst them and slaughter ensued.

Concentrating on his own quarry Flavius was not witness to what ensued. He was riding flat out, his eye on a pair of marauders who, by their richer accoutrements, in reality decorated helmets and fine cloaks, could be the leaders of the raid. He had his reins in one hand and a spear in the other, this as he shouted commands he was unsure would be heard, to get his subordinates to select a target and pursue it to the exclusion of anyone else.

'None to live,' was his last bellowed command.

A full gallop could not be maintained for long even on a fine animal and between his thighs Flavius could feel his horse beginning to tire. Yet if that applied to him it did so equally to those he was pursuing and the gap was closing as their mounts, harder worked by the trials of the day, visibly flagged. Always proud of his ability to cast a spear, Flavius took one of the riders ahead in the middle of his back as, raising himself from his hunched position to look over his shoulder, he presented a worthwhile target.

The way the man reared up as the spear sliced through his cloak, added to the scream that went with it, alerted his companion to the proximity of the fellow who had cast it. He too looked backwards as the mortally wounded rider alongside him slid out of his saddle to hit the ground. In doing so he obviously concluded that flight would not save him so he suddenly hauled hard on his reins and in a display of outstanding horsemanship, riding an animal that had reared up to send foaming flecks in all directions, he spun it round on its rear hooves to face the charging Roman.

The action, so sudden, caught Flavius off guard. Only by slipping a foot out of a stirrup and ducking along the outer flank of his own mount did he manage to avoid the swinging blade that would have removed his head. His assailant, sensing he was going to miss his main objective, sought to drive down with the sword in order to maim the horse, an act that removed a major portion of his mount's flying tail.

Flavius swung round in order to engage, his newly drawn sword out and ready, and for the first time, as they closed, he could look into the face of his opponent, to see a pair of startlingly blue eyes set in pallid skin that indicated the fellow might be Circassian. This registered along with the realisation that his opponent would likely be a doughty fighter for he came of a race of grassland dwellers allied to Sassanid Persia, famed for their horsemanship as well as their fighting skills.

Time for further speculation disappeared as one sword blade clashed against another as the two horsemen hastily passed each other by. Flavius too was a highly proficient rider, just as well, for he had been afforded a scant interval to wheel again and face a renewed onslaught from an enemy who was able to spin his horse with greater speed.

To fight with swords on horseback imposes dangers that do not exist on foot; the mounts, regardless of what the man in control wishes, do not always obey in a way that provides safety. They are as affected by the excitement of battle as their riders and they see themselves in contest with one of their own, so they buck continuously and as their shoulders barge or hooves collide, or when they seek to land a bite, there is an inevitable reaction.

It was Flavius's round shield that made the difference. Hooked over his saddle horn he managed to get it into play by hauling his mount away from the fight for a fleeting instant. This meant the next swing of his opponent's weapon was deflected by the hard leather and the metal boss, the feel of the heavy blow jarring up his arm. Having cut into the surface of the shield it took effort for the blade to be freed and that gave Flavius a chance to come under the rim and jab at his enemy's belly. That the point of his sword caused a wound he knew, but it was not deep enough to prove telling and again the action of the horses broke fighting contact.

Closing once more, Flavius concentrated on those blue eyes, they too fixed on his, for it was not bodily movements that a good fighter guards against but the flicker that alerts to a movement and its direction. All around men were acting likewise, with the clang of fighting blades echoing across the flatlands on which battle was taking place, with both Flavius and his opponent assailed by the ringing and screaming coming from other equally desperate contests taking place all around them.

Was it that which had caused his man to be distracted? Flavius was never to know, all he could say with certainty was that the Circassian let his attention become distracted for a moment. Brief as it was it proved enough to allow Flavius to strike, his sword swinging in a high arc that forced his opponent into a desperate act of defence that proved his undoing. With his blade stuck aloft he was too slow to get it down and stop the immediate thrust that followed, one that took him at the point of his neck, and because there was a swing to that too, had cut into his unprotected gullet with force enough to inflict a deep wound.

The Circassian's free hand came off the reins by which he had exercised some control over his mount, to clutch at blood spilling through his fingers, leaving his horse free to pursue its own contest. It raised itself to kick out at Flavius's mount, spinning slightly to get in a set of hooves. His already wounded opponent would have been skewered if the Roman's horse had not reacted, but the way it shied took Flavius's sword down on the enemy arm, into which it sliced deeply to render him defenceless.

The kill that followed was odd, for it seemed the fellow gave up and surrendered to a fate he knew was coming. His shoulders seemed to slump and if his lips moved it was not to cry for mercy but perhaps silently to pray. Even so his eyes never left sight of the blow that finished him, a flat slicing sword that swept in as wide an arc as Flavius could manage to practically remove the fellow's head from his trunk.

His mount span away of its own accord to canter clear. Not that it retired far, only a few paces, as slowly, like his companion before him, the dead enemy slipped to the ground spouting blood from his severed neck. The man who had killed him did not wait to watch, he kicked his own horse into motion in order to close with the nearest continuing fight, able to come up behind an engaged enemy and cut him down with a blow that sliced open his kidneys, the shock allowing his original opponent to finish him off.

The rest of the fighting was over very soon, leaving an area littered with bodies seeping blood into the dry earth. One or two severely wounded horses were lying on the ground and kicking their legs in distress, while others without riders either stood with heads bowed or trotted in confused circles. Exhaustion hit Flavius and he was not alone; all of his still-mounted men were hunched over haunches and a look at the field of the fight showed that not all the bodies were those of their enemies, which made no difference to the orders he could only issue in a near breathless voice.

'Every dead body to be laid over a saddle, every wounded mount to be finished off and their bodies roped so they may be dragged back to Roman territory.'

The looks he got from men as drained as he were full of disbelief. What was this young madman talking about? It took time to dawn on slower minds. Hardly yet a fully grown man in anything but his way of behaviour, the tyro who led them had the wit to save them from a folly and imperial retribution they were only now beginning to sense. Seeing his orders put into practice, Flavius cantered back to the ground just beyond the border pillars where an equally grim slaughter had taken place.

There, too, the earth was stained with blood, while the vultures were beginning to circle overhead awaiting the departure of humans so they could feed. There would be big cats as well as the carrion eaters sniffing the wind and sensing blood and Flavius had no desire that they should be denied their needs. His only concern was where they would gorge.

He would despatch a messenger to Narses to say that the pursuing cavalry had caught the raiding party within the confines of the empire, a lie and one the man selected to deliver it was obliged to rehearse with his commander several times before being sent on his way.

'Narses is bound to ask, indeed he will scarce believe it to be true, so add that once he has freed himself from the need to assess the damage this raid has caused, I invite him to come and observe.'

'And if he says he will do so, Your Honour?'

Flavius produced a weary grin and ran a hand though his black and sweat-matted hair. 'Then you may see my head stuck on a pike above one of the great gates of Constantinople.'

There was no humour in the response, from a person who understood fully what was at stake. They had collectively broken an imperial edict and one that was no mystery to even the lowest ranker, so the chosen messenger knew he was equally at risk.

'Might fall to us all as a fate.'

'I will take any blame that comes from this and I have enough influence in the imperial palace to suspect it will be accepted as so. If it does not spare me I believe it will save you and the rest of the men.'

'Might not believe another, Your Honour.'

'Do you believe me?'

That got a shrug to an earnestly posed question. 'You're given to honesty, we all talk of it.'

'I thank you for that.'

'Let's hope then, Your Honour, that I can lie as well as you can tell the truth.'

The task the fellow left behind was far from easy to fulfil, dead weights being a burden to tired men, but they toiled on till the sun was low so every cadaver, human and equine, ended up on the western side of those imperial markers, spread out to make it appear as though that was where they had died, the Romans being in receipt of a proper burial.

Eyes were cast anxiously to the east but no one appeared; thankfully, it seemed Narses was too occupied to check on the tale he had been fed. In the fading light the last act was an examination of the true place of slaughter. The field was soaked with blood, as would be the place where he had fought himself, so a silent prayer for rain was not amiss, nor a hope that there was insect and scavenging life enough to remove such traces.

The number of vultures now circling was in the dozens and as the sky took on a dark-blue tint to the west, Flavius had his men remount their somewhat recovered horses and, with the booty they had recovered, set off to rejoin the main body.

The operation, a sweep across a defined area of the borderlands completed, Narses led his men back towards the great fortress of Dara, still a place of masons and engineers skilled in constructing defence works formidable enough to hold off anything Sassanid Persia could send their way. It sat above on a trio of hills that gave a commanding view of the surrounding plains. Within the walls lay several wells, which fed huge cisterns so the water supply was secure and could not be cut off. The storerooms were so large that food and fodder for a two-year siege was stockpiled and maintained, time enough for the empire to mount an operation of relief should Dara be invested.

Flavius Belisarius oversaw the weary mounts handed over to the grooms who would care for them. The men were sent to their barrack rooms, those with wounds diverted to the place where they could receive treatment. He next ensured his men would be fed and the food he saw delivered to the tables at which they would consume it, he having tasted it to ensure it was edible.

Satisfied that his duties were complete he made for the officers' quarters where he could strip off his armour, breastplate and greaves, as well as clothing made filthy by a week of campaigning, and enter the baths where he could wash and be afforded a massage. He was on the stone slab, with the hands of the masseur kneading out his aches and pains, when one of his fellow junior officers came by to deliver a message. In his absence an order had come from Constantinople calling him back to the capital.

'A personal order and one that brooks no delay, from no less than the *comes excubitorum* himself. Our general was so impressed he nearly sent out messengers to fetch you back.'

'Have you not heard?' came a voice from another stone

table. 'Flavius is a hero who can fly and so swiftly that his enemies are rendered unable to move by the sight of him above their heads.'

A third voice responded with faux wonder. 'So that's why they let themselves be slaughtered within the bounds of empire.'

There were those amongst the officers garrisoning Dara who resented his connections within the imperial palace, influence that had got him his present posting at such a young age. Men were bound to be jealous in a world where such links provided the route to promotion and wealth. The allusion to the recent fight and that last remark indicated Narses had chosen to accept the story rather than believe it, no doubt to cover his own back as the overall commander. Yet he had seen it as sensible also to let his doubts be known to others.

It was a febrile world in which he lived, but that was a fact known to him for many years now. The next question was obvious. Why did Justinus, *comes Excubitorum* and one of the most powerful men in Constantinople, in command of the body that guarded the person of the Emperor Anastasius, want him back in the capital?

CHAPTER TWO

There was a great deal about the capital of the Eastern Roman Empire for Flavius Belisarius to dislike; the sheer teeming mass of humanity was easy to resent as his horse sought to push its way through the crowds that filled the streets, all jostling and refusing to give way as they, in no discernible order, moved simultaneously in two directions on foot, in carts, with the occasional palanquin or mounted worthy. Also, if a military barracks in high summer was not a scented place, Constantinople was many times worse, given it needed heavy rain to wash the filth, both human and animal, from its streets and into a sea often rendered deep brown by the effluent.

Worst of all was the utter lack of regard or respect for a

fellow citizen, a natural belligerence in the eyes of those he fought his way through until he reached the Triumphal Way and the open space before the great imperial palace, one so huge not even the population of the city could render it full, where he could dismount.

Flavius had been inducted three years previously into the military unit responsible for the bodily security of the Emperor and it was men of that body who stood guard at the gates leading into the maze of buildings that constituted the seat of imperial power. As befitted the successors to the Praetorian Guard, they were beautifully accoutred in gleaming and decorated armour, archaic in its design, breastplates and helmets flashing in the strong sunshine, as were the points of their spears.

Their commander, Justinus, after a year of training, had sent him to the eastern borderlands to hone his soldiering skills and in doing so he had donned the equipment of the units with which he had served, equipment that now showed the wear of two seasons' campaigning. His padded garment was worn, the surface nearly worn away in parts and lacking any decor. Added to that he had upon him the grit and muck of weeks of travel which, to these finely clad sentinels, made him look like some kind of vagabond.

Naturally haughty anyway, common soldiers of such an elevated body were not inclined to give any form of greeting to an officer from another unit that came even close to respect. Flavius had also been gone two whole years, time in which the composition of the Excubitors had changed enough to render him unknown to many of those now acting as guards. So his enquiry to be let through to attend upon the *comes*, if not greeted with mirth, was not taken as anything even bordering on serious, while the response was delivered to a point just above his head.

'Best if you apply in writing, young sir, and if His Excellency approves of you coming to see him he will issue you with an authorisation to enter the palace.'

Flavius replied in an even tone, partly because of his equable nature but also because of the weariness of the traveller. As if to underline he would brook no delay he held out his reins so that his equally tired mount could be taken care of, an offer declined with a shudder of indignation as it was caught at the edge of the guard's vision.

'I am here at his express command, fellow, and I tell you that if I will not resort to temper in the face of your refusal to let me pass, I cannot speak for Justinus. He may be a commander known for his consideration but he is also famous for his attention to the behaviour of his men and not shy of the whip.'

The eyes dropped for an instant to take in the face, as if to acknowledge a commonly known truth, only to be raised again. 'If I face such wrath it will be for letting you pass.'

'Then I ask that you at least take my name to the guard commander?'

'To say what?'

'That Flavius Belisarius of the Excubitors is returned.'

That brought the eyes down to stare, to take in the grubby padded coat and the filth that encrusted it, the man's tone so full of astonishment as to render any respect to his rank absent. 'You, an Excubitor?'

'I admit to failing to appear as one but I am still part of

the imperial guard, so I order you to take my name to your officer.'

'Best comply,' said the second guard, stood only two paces distant, who had hitherto remained silent.

The reluctance of his companion was obvious, he having taken a position that he had no wish to relinquish. 'You go, then.'

The man declined to move; he merely yelled out the alarm and that brought out of the barrack room under the gatehouse a whole file of running Excubitors, many fiddling with old-style breastplates that had been loosened for comfort. From his cubicle inside the gate it also brought forth their officer who, looking like thunder when he could observe no reason for apprehension, strode right up, passing his now parading guard detail, to stand between the two sentinels.

'What in the name of Christ risen is going on?'

'The prodigal returns, Domnus Articus,' Flavius said, lifting off his helmet, 'that is what is going on.'

That got a close if unfriendly look, one that slowly changed to recognition as he saw that the face before him was familiar, though last been seen with the spots of puberty still showing. Now it belonged to a grown man, and if unblemished, had been rendered very dark by exposure to the sun and the growth of a trim beard.

'Is it you, Flavius?'

'In the flesh.'

'Then the Sassanids did not manage to kill you?'

'They tried.'

Domnus stepped forward making as if to embrace

Flavius, only to stop and look him up and down. If the men on guard were polished in their accoutrements, then as an Excubitor officer Domnus was positively sleek. Flavius laughed at his fears, that some of the muck on his body might take the sheen off an old comrade, a fellow who had been inducted into the unit at the same time as he.

'Wait till I have bathed and changed, my friend.'

'That I will, Flavius,' Domnus replied, before turning, clearly intent on berating the sentinels. That was cut off by the man to whom they had barred entry.

'Your men did a fine job, Domnus, don't you think?' That stopped their officer and he turned halfway back. 'Can't allow entry to any dusty fellow, regardless of who he claims to be.'

The two guards, still seeking to stay rigid, did react, but in such a way it took a very acute look to spot it, no more than a grateful flick of the eyelids. Domnus intended to chastise them and he was not to be entirely deflected, though Flavius suspected his tone was more moderate that it would have been without his intervention.

'This man is an officer in the imperial military yet I do not see your spears at the salute.' Both tips shot forward in unison as the shafts were presented on rigid, extended right arms. 'Better, but late. Come, Flavius, let one of my men see to your horse, for I know our general will be eager to see you.'

'Not like this, I think.'

'No, it will be a long time since he smelt the likes of you.'

The *comes Excubitorum* had many duties, the primary

one to ensure that his emperor was never at risk of assassination, but his responsibilities extended to guarding all the high officials in a palace spread over a great area. Justinus took his duties very seriously, and was therefore always, throughout the day, on the move to ensure all was as it should be. When Flavius, bathed and properly dressed in clothing taken from the chest he had left behind two years previously, presented himself at the apartments his mentor occupied, he did not find his patron present, only his nephew.

'At last, Flavius!' Petrus Sabbatius exclaimed. 'I feared that you had got lost or murdered by thieves on the way.'

When you have not seen someone you know well for two years it is natural to look for changes and this Flavius did, though he could discern nothing meaningful when it came to Petrus. He still had a thin frame and face as well as that habit of canting his head to one side when thinking, while his reddish hair was yet untidy. Not a man to smile often, Petrus was doing so now, exposing his unevenly spaced teeth.

'Not killed by the Persians?'

'That I never thought would happen. Is not there a guardian angel ever on your shoulder?'

'He would need to be with you on my side.'

If that was delivered with a smile, there was an undercurrent of spleen to it. Two years previously Petrus, ever the schemer, had put him in mortal peril in pursuit of a political goal that he had declined to share with the person who might have paid the price to see it completed or fail. If they had never discussed it, Flavius knew that if he had died in its execution that would have been, for this natural courtier, a price worth paying to achieve success, namely the removal of someone he saw as a potential future rival to both himself and the man he served.

To say Petrus was his uncle's right hand was literally true; Justinus was a bluff and honest soldier where his relative was the opposite. He could neither read nor write, therefore he depended on his nephew to both compose his orders and to a large extent see them executed. If the bond between them was strong it was often strained as Petrus pursued goals that were disapproved of by a man of an upright disposition, objectives the nephew insisted were designed to aid and protect his uncle in a polity ridden with intrigue and infighting as courtiers jockeyed for power and the affluence that went with it.

'You will have written the orders for my recall?' Petrus nodded; he even had access to the signature stencil Justinus used to sign his orders. 'So what does Justinus have in mind for me?'

The nephew just smiled, but it was not one of humour, more of supremacy. About to speak again, Flavius was cut off by the entry of the general himself and his opening words, as well as the surprise in both voice and face, spoke volumes.

'Lord, Flavius, what has brought you home?'

About to reply that it was obviously not at his personal command, he flicked a glance at Petrus to get a very slight shake of the head, added to an expression that told him to be cautious and it was he who spoke.

'Has it not been too long since he was with us, Uncle,

and was his deployment not for a fixed term?'

'Was it?' Justinus enquired, looking slightly confused, before breaking into a wide grin, one nearly as wide as the arms with which he stepped forward to embrace Flavius. 'Well I am glad to see you, boy.'

'Are we not all glad to see him,' Petrus added, if less fulsomely.

The hands of Justinus were on the shoulders now and he was looking hard into the face of the youngster. 'I swear you are the spit of your father, God rest his soul.'

That had the young man drop his head and move his thinking from the very obvious fact that it was not Justinus who had recalled him but Petrus, a notion that presaged something that might be both unpleasant and dangerous. The memory of how his father and three brothers had died because of downright treachery haunted him enough to overwhelm that immediate concern, the reaction not missed by Justinus.

'Forgive me if it causes you discomfort but I mention it only to praise you. I knew your papa when he was the age you are now, with the pair of us not long joined the imperial army. What a set of rogues we were—'

'Have you eaten, Flavius?'

His uncle stopped as Petrus butted in, wishing to cut off a flow of reminiscence of the kind he had heard far too often; old soldiers never seemed to tire of their tales of camp life and fighting, as well as what they got up to elsewhere.

'Well,' said Justinus, 'we shall all dine together and you can tell us of your exploits on the border.'

A swift response came from the nephew, to whom the

tales of young soldiers were no more enthralling to him than that of their elders. 'I have another arrangement, Uncle.'

Justinus looked pained. 'I can guess in what kind of company.'

Petrus merely shrugged; it was an ongoing dispute that had obviously not been tempered in the time Flavius had been absent. Justinus sought for his nephew the same as his parents. Born of a mother who had risen from humble stock to wed a nobleman, it was possible he could marry into the patrician class and become connected to one of those ancient families that had filled the high offices of state for centuries and had deep prosperity to prove it. There were many of that class, if not all, who saw the brood to which Justinus belonged, his wife Lupicina included, as Thracian peasants and barely sought to temper their condescension.

Petrus did not care but his uncle and father did, sure that it was the only way to secure the future success of a bloodline ascended to eminence only by the military prowess of the present *comes Excubitorum*, who had risen through the ranks to become a successful and much lauded general. In his elevation to his present senior position, Vigilantia, sister to Justinus, had risen on his cloak tails and had made for herself an advantageous marriage. She was keen to embed the family in the higher ranks of the populace.

Their great hope was not in the least interested, openly stating that he found the scented daughters of the patrician class vapid and dull and besides that he was only ever considered marital material by those families on the way down. Either that or they had daughters already passed over for a lack of comeliness or with some obvious physical flaw.

Torture for Petrus was to sit and dine in the surroundings of such a family, where no chance was avoided to remind the guest of their centuries of high birth. The fathers and brothers would go out of their way to show both learning and erudition by quoting classical texts, as if scholarship compensated for having no worthwhile position in the imperial bureaucracy.

'Tonight,' Petrus exclaimed, standing up, 'I will forgo my usual pleasures. How can I not stay to break bread with Flavius newly returned?'

The youngster looked at Justinus then, to see if he had taken that at face value, which Flavius had decidedly not. Petrus was not one for hearty male companionship either, only truly happy in the company of hard-drinking Excubitor officers, low life and whores, more at ease in the brothels and taverns of the dock area than the villas of the upper orders. If he was forgoing that there would be a reason other than manners.

'That is as it should be,' Justinus responded forcefully, proving that if he was a good, nay brilliant soldier and as upright as a man could be, he lacked perception when he was being teased by his close relative. Flavius was again treated to another wide grin that followed by a hearty military slap. 'Look at you, boy, skin and bone on army provisions. You need feeding up!'

Later, as they dined, Petrus made a good fist of hiding his boredom, there being no subject to air other than the military one. If he became fully engaged at all it was when Flavius began to talk of Dara and the progress of the building of the fortifications. Anastasius had personally chosen the site, only three leagues from the Sassanid fortified city of Nisibis, the forward base from which King Kavadh had previously launched his attacks on Roman territory.

'Which is what we should do, Uncle, use Dara as a base for aggression not just defence. Otherwise it is a waste of our treasure.'

'Anastasius wants peace,' Justinus replied, with a tone of weariness that suggested it was a statement not entirely to his liking. 'And nearing his ninth decade you can see why that would be. He is not one to waste money, as you know, but this to him is a saving on buying off the Sassanids every ten years with talents of gold. He hopes, with such a strong fortress that the Sassanids dare not pass by, to make the game not worth the candle.'

The response was very animated for a man normally very much in control of himself; Petrus positively spat back. 'They only attack when Kavadh runs out of the funds he needs to bribe his tribal leaders and keep them from seeking to depose him. What do we do? Pay up and keep him alive as a threat.'

'And if they did depose him would his successor be better?'

'Then kill the whole snake if cutting off the head will not do.'

'To eliminate the Sassanids we would need an army ten times the size of the one we can muster, Petrus, and even then we might not succeed, and could we hold that which we take?'

'Rome cowed Persia once and Alexander ruled there.'

'Then that,' Justinus exclaimed, seeking to inject a

lighter vein, 'is what you need, another Alexander. It is well to remember when you speak of Rome what happened to Crassus, not Trajan and Pompey. Crassus lost an entire army and his own life fighting Persia and if Trajan and Pompey did better, neither sought to keep what they had won.'

'Perhaps if they had?'

'Then we would have even more trouble on our border than we have now. Enough, sad to say, I must leave you two young folk to talk, I have to do my nightly rounds.'

Petrus did not speak until Justinus had said his farewells, which included the admonition that now Flavius was back they would have to return him to Excubitor duty. Again the expression on the face of Petrus was of more interest, as he gave his uncle a look that bordered on disappointment, very brief and soon replaced by blandness when he realised Flavius had observed it.

'Perhaps I will take Flavius to meet some of my friends.'

'Spare him.'

'What, Uncle, a fellow just back from the wars? If he is anything like the other Excubitor officers, then he is in need of the comfort only a woman can provide.'

'Not the kind of woman to whom you will introduce him,' Justinus barked over his shoulder as he departed.

'Precisely the kind.'

Petrus said this softly, as he indicated the servants who had attended upon their meal should leave them alone. Then he leant forward to refill the goblet that sat before Flavius.

'Why have you brought me back, Petrus? Clearly Justinus did not initiate it.'

'Believe me, it was for a purpose.'

'Which is?'

'My uncle trusts you.'

'Justinus trusts many people.'

'Not always a wise course, even for a man of an artless nature. But put that aside and ask yourself what is coming here in Constantinople. Anastasius is fading, he has more ailments than his strength can resist. When he dies, and that could be this very night, then who will become emperor and what will become of my uncle?'

'Do you not mean what will become of you?'

'I admit to the concern. What is necessary is to ensure that whoever assumes the purple is in some way indebted to Justinus, so much that he may even rise to a position greater than that he now holds.'

'Tell me, Petrus, do you think Justinus could have stayed as *comes Excubitorum* without you to aid him?'

'Secretaries are nor hard to come by.'

'I did not have you down as a man given to self-deprecation. He has held his position with your aid and he will need that whatever he aspires to.'

'The problem with my uncle, Flavius,' Petrus replied bitterly, 'is that he aspires to so very little, so I must do so on his behalf.'

In the silence that followed, Flavius had the feeling that try as he might he would never be able to see into the mind of the man he had just dined with. If Petrus said he had an aim there was ever the feeling that much lay beyond it and undisclosed. What he said next did come as a surprise.

'In order to protect him from his own lack of ambition,

or indeed a need to secure his back, I require that you aid me. Thus I engineered your return.'

'Me!'

'I am engaged in some very delicate negotiations that I hope will secure a bright future for us all. To proceed I need with me someone who can make sure that I am not a victim of the secret knife yet who will not disclose to anyone what is said and to whom.'

'And I am that person?'

'Yes, Flavius, you are, and before you protest let me say what is important. I believe it to be true and in doing so I will be putting my life in your hands, for there are any number of people vying for the diadem and if I can see how fast our emperor is fading so can they, not least his own discredited nephews.'

Having been part of the military disgrace of the best of them, Hypatius, Flavius could only nod; the other two, Pompeius and Probus, were held to be so unsuitable for high office as to be a laughing stock, though Flavius silently admitted to himself, as Petrus kept speaking, a serious look on his face, that such things were beyond the comprehension of a mere junior officer.

'There is one courtier who not only aspires to decide on the wearer of the purple but seeks my aid to gain the throne for his man and the price of that aid will, of course, be paid for in consideration for us.' Seeing Flavius's eyebrows go up and in conclusion, Petrus added. 'If my uncle prospers, so will you.'

To avoid alluding to the evident fact that Petrus cared more for his own advancement than that of himself or perhaps even his own relative, Flavius ask the obvious question. 'Who is this aspirant?'

'One thing at a time, Flavius. Can I rely on you to aid me?'

'You can rely on me to do anything that will protect your uncle, a man who has shown me nothing but kindness.'

'One day, perhaps,' Petrus sighed, 'you will hold me in the same light as that paragon.'

Tempted to deny the possibility, Flavius just smiled.

CHAPTER THREE

To go from being a fighting soldier to a member of the elite imperial unit required such a degree of change that Flavius, for several days, felt lost. He had been greeted warmly by those he knew from his original induction into the Excubitors, sensing that only a few, as had many on the frontier, resented his connection to their commander. Yet everything in the palace was so different and not just because of the sheer number of functionaries that staffed the various bureaux that ran the empire.

As a breed these were so very different even from the civilian officials at Dara, having about them a guardedness that even manifested itself in their way of movement. Few came striding through the endless corridors with the confidence their eminence should provide. Most were silent and wary, the worst adopted a sort of slinking way of walking, accompanied by many an over-the-shoulder look as if they feared immediate arrest, which made Flavius wonder how much they were stealing or taking in bribes, these being the methods, and it was no secret, by which such people enriched themselves.

He had to assume the atmosphere was more troubled than normal given the Emperor was fading, albeit lingering by rallying in a way that increased the tension. There would be all sorts of conspiracies and manoeuvres being initiated, alliances made and broken, with many a pledge examined to seek to find if it was true or false. To meet any eye other than that of a fellow soldier was to feel as if one was being weighed as an asset on a set of unknowable scales.

Who are you, what are your connections, should I acknowledge you or guard against you? That was the commonplace, yet to accompany Petrus down those same pillared corridors was doubly instructive, he obviously being someone whom these functionaries reckoned to either guard against or to seek to impress and he was not slow to relate the reasons why.

'Friends are necessary, enemies more numerous and care is required when the man promising to aid you is secretly preparing to bring you down. It is hard to rise in imperial service, Flavius, and too easy to fall, and when you do there is no bottom.'

There was a pause as Petrus nodded a greeting to a gorgeously clad fellow passing in the other direction, followed by several slaves carrying baskets of scrolls.

'You are a soldier and like my uncle you take death, even a painful one, to be the risk of your chosen path. Many of those we pass have crawled on their knees or paid out in gold to attain a position at court only to find they are surrounded by others who will embrace them just before they betray them. It frays even the stoutest nerves.'

'I sense you thrive on it.'

'It is a sport in which I take pleasure, that is true.'

'So you do not fear death either?'

'Disgrace, Flavius, that is what all here fear, even the soldiers, and then there is beggary if you are blinded. Great fortunes are to be made but there are dungeons below where you can be forgotten, cells where the rats can eat at your toes for decades.'

Petrus stopped and hauled on Flavius to do likewise. 'Just make out we are deep in conversation.'

'Why?'

'I need to be sure we are not being watched.'

'Talk? What about?'

'Tell me of that fight you had when serving under Narses?' Seeing the younger man's eyes open with surprise, Petrus added. 'It cannot shock you that I know of it.'

'Did you have me spied upon?'

'Flavius, I esteem you and trust you but please take no offence if I say you are scarce worth that. I did, however, need to know that you were alive, or if not—'

'Which would require you to correspond with someone.'

'Regarding the situation on the border, I did with several and your well-being was supplemental. Now tell me how you pulled off your little charade for it interests me?'

As he did so, Flavius was far from sure Petrus was really listening. Placed as they were in a long and well-frequented corridor it seemed he spent more time flicking glances to those who came and went by the pillar near which they stood, some to be ignored when close, others to be acknowledged with a nod.

'Narses is a good soldier but too cautious. He could have seen it as I did but chose not to—'

The interruption was physical and, for a man of such slight frame, surprisingly strong. Petrus dragged Flavius deeper into the gap between two pillars then along behind them to a small doorway on which he rapped a tattoo. It was opened quickly and the youngster was bundled into a chamber that lacked a window and was lit only by guttering candles. It took a moment to sense the other person present and time for the eyes of Flavius to adjust and take in his physical features, even longer to make out the face.

'Amantius,' Petrus said softly.

The voice that replied was restrained and hoarse. 'It is past the appointed time.'

'Better a wait than we and our purpose should be discovered.'

The man was either bald or he shaved his head. Maybe it was the indifferent light but his eyes seemed sunk into a head that appeared as well-defined as a skull, with prominent cheekbones and a substantial lantern jaw.

'Let me introduce my companion, Flavius Belisarius, whom you will observe is a member of the Excubitors.'

'Not a very elevated one.'

'If a man of higher rank were here, Amantius, given

what we are about to discuss, he might see it as his duty to stick a sword in our vitals. For what we propose to do you need the aid of the junior officers of the *Excubitorum*, for it is they who are close to the common soldiers and they who will be able to marshal them to our aid as well as convey to them the promise of great reward.'

'And to protect me and my candidate?'

'That too.'

The man stepped a pace forward, which increased the light that shone on him. He was not of any great height and had a narrowness to his body that matched that of Petrus. His eyes were on Flavius and unblinking, the youngster thought trying to see into his soul, and when he spoke it was to confirm that was his purpose.

'I will need to place much faith in you and your like.' When Flavius did not respond, only holding steady the mutual gaze, the bald man nodded. 'You stay silent, no protestations of constancy or reliability. That is good.'

'For to do so would sound false,' Petrus added, which got a hearty nod. 'It is however necessary, Amantius, that my young friend knows who you are and what offices you hold.'

'They are many. All he needs to know is that the advantages of my positions provide the means by which I will succeed in rewarding the men who guard the Emperor, when they allow the man I have chosen to assume his mantle.'

Flavius had to fight hard not to suck in an audible breath then: what was this Amantius saying – that he was going to decide who would be emperor when Anastasius passed away?

'No man will deserve it more than whosoever you have chosen, for no one within these walls can surpass you in your wisdom.'

Again it was hard not to react to those words from Petrus, so silky and to the ears of one who knew him well, utterly insincere.

'The rewards must be in place before the Emperor dies but cannot be distributed until the very moment our loss is announced.'

'It would be to our advantage if that could be precipitated, Petrus.'

'Too risky. Anyone trying would perish in the attempt.'

'Justinus,' Amantius hissed, as if the name referred to some kind of plague.

'What would you have him do? My uncle will serve you and your man faithfully once he is enthroned for he has pledged himself to protect the imperial person. But you must accept he will do likewise for Anastasius while he still breathes. Consider this, that a man who would betray one emperor, would do like to another.'

'Is he so much the paragon?'

It was Flavius who answered. 'He is, sir.'

That brought a look of doubt to the cadaver-like countenance. 'What if your paragon orders you to stand aside?'

'Amantius,' Petrus purred, 'leave my uncle to me.'

'He may commit himself to another.'

'He will never commit himself to anyone until they are wearing the diadem. To do otherwise would mean intriguing and that he avoids, which is why the way is open for the proposed elevation of your chosen successor. The younger officers of the Excubitors will ensure that the route to the imperial apartments are sealed off and their men will have orders to use force to ensure that you have a clear field. It will take a brave fellow to challenge them.'

'And if they have their reward, Petrus, what of you?'

'You know what I wish, that my uncle shall either hold his present office or, with your grace and if you so desire, that he be elevated to another higher appointment. My task is to be in his service but perhaps, in time, when matters are settled and all is secure, I will seek something for myself.'

'And this young man?'

'He too will be patient.'

The eyes fixed on Flavius again. 'I am about to entrust you with a great deal.'

'Not just Flavius, but me too. How can we repay such trust with anything other than blind loyalty?'

'Where will you store the treasure?'

It was as well Amantius was not looking at Flavius when he asked that question: the word 'treasure' had the eyebrows shooting up and they stayed there as Petrus responded.

'It must be within the palace for it cannot be brought here when the time is ripe. The only secure place is within the working apartments of my uncle, who will never know of its presence.'

'And they are hard by the imperial chambers. That, God rest his soul, is where Anastasius will expire, given he is now too weak to move from his bed.'

Amantius was nodding with vigour as he spoke. Lit by the candles his eyes seemed to gleam and that conveyed a sense of suppressed excitement, quickly masked as Petrus spoke again.

'I have chosen Flavius as the officer to take on the task of organisation because he has access to those apartments, being much feted by Justinus, indeed treated as the general would treat a son. The officer in charge of the detachment set to guard the imperial suite will go to their general first with the news of the Emperor's demise, which is his duty. You, of course, will know what has occurred at the same moment.'

A nod accompanied by a more thoughtful look was the response, as if he was seeking ways such a thing could go wrong.

'I will be made aware, too, because it has been arranged, alert to the point at which you will need to get your candidate through to the imperial chambers, while I send Flavius to ready his fellow officers, those to whom I have imparted what is to take place. They'll then take up the stations and only those you designate will be permitted to pass through them.'

The croak that got hinted at real dread. 'You have not used my name to these people?'

'All they know is that a high and deserving person aspires to the diadem and it is one considered to be well suited to rule our empire, also that he sees the need to reward loyalty as have emperors in times past to those who have aided him. They do not know any names and will not until they are called upon, when I fetch you to them, to acclaim your candidate. At that point your chests of gold, brought out by Flavius, will be opened and distributed.'

'If we fail, if this is discovered, Petrus? Loose tongues.'

'There are only two tongues about which you have to worry and they're both in your presence. No one else knows your name and since you have been guarded, even I do not know who you propose to make emperor.'

'Who else is plotting? Who has a plan that will thwart ours?'

'The imperial nephews are seeking support and finding none, while those with ambition meet only like minds. No one senator will stand aside for the other so they waste their words on plans that will never mature. None has seen the need to befriend the Excubitors, believe me I would know if they had, for I meet with them constantly. Only you will have a clear path.'

Amantius stepped forward to clutch at Petrus's arm. 'If you are true to me and mine, you will not regret it.'

'My uncle?'

'Will have much to thank you for.' The sunken eyes turned towards Flavius. 'And you too, young fellow.'

'Do show some gratitude, Flavius,' Petrus purred when he did not respond. The result was a croak as hoarse as the voice of the man at whom it was aimed, this with Petrus still talking. 'Flavius will come to your villa tonight and fetch away the funds we need. We dare not delay.'

'It is sinful to wish death upon another, but I swear I will not sleep till Anastasius has breathed his last.'

'It is true we cannot pray for such, but if God is merciful it is not impious to wish a body in pain and a soul in fear of damnation to be released into peace. We will leave now, Amantius. I trust you will be wise enough to wait awhile before doing likewise.'

Flavius had his arm taken and again he was ushered back out to the corridor, his face now with a thunderous look aimed at Petrus and a stride that obliged the intriguer to walk fast to keep pace.

'Your anger does not shock me, Flavius. Conspiracy is not to your liking, I suspect.'

'It is not and especially one of this magnitude.'

'All I ask is that you go to the villa of Amantius tonight and fetch his gold.'

'You go.'

Petrus sighed. 'Which would be like waving a red lantern. Why do you think we met today in such a place? Would you have me do it openly in this palace, where, for every two courtiers who meet there are three conspiracies and a dozen pairs of eyes and ears? I have not been near his home and nor will I ever be, for his ambitions are not the secret he hopes them to be, for all his seeming wiles he struggles to dissimulate. The only one of those still extant is that I have undertaken to aid him, which would no longer remain if I was seen in his company.'

'Is the man he has in mind worthy of that which you wish to gift him?'

That received a snort. 'Who is that? That old skinflint expiring as we speak, who only got the imperial title through his handsome face and the bedchamber of an empress who outlived her husband. Zeno before him, who left things in such a pass as to allow his widow to choose his successor? Flavius, it is not about worthy, it is about opportunity and the taking of it. Amantius does not possess a great mind but he has massive wealth and is manipulative.'

'Why does he not seek it for himself, then?'

'Why do you ask?' Petrus demanded, just before enlightenment dawned. 'You have no idea of who Amantius is?'

'No.'

'He is the Emperor's chief eunuch, which bars him from the purple since he cannot breed. So he has chosen someone he considers worthwhile, yet a person he can manipulate.'

'For what?'

'It's not wealth, for he has that in abundance.'

'Power, then?'

'Let us say he faithfully serves a man for whom he has little true regard and he is not alone in that.'

Petrus kept talking as they made their way through the endless corridors to the central section that contained the imperial apartments as well as those of Justinus, all the while denigrating Anastasius and his policies, the worst of which was religious in nature.

'And what about the madness of that, how much trouble has the old goat caused there?'

Those words dragged Flavius back to the events of three years previously, a time when his life had looked settled and his future a vision easy and untroubling. A single event had changed that as his father, in command of an understrength force guarding the Danube border, had been tempted into a battle he could not win, one in which the odds had been set against him by a treacherous local magnate who should have been his support. Those thoughts were swept away as Petrus grabbed his arm again to spin him round, his eyes boring in, his look deadly serious.

'You must trust me in this, Flavius, you must believe me when I say I do it for the safety of all of us. I am not playing a game, I am playing with our lives. Will you go tonight and carry out what I have arranged?'

'Give me one good reason why I should.'

'I saved your life, Flavius, and got you revenge for your family, is that not reason enough?'

'When?'

The explanation, the way revenge had been facilitated on the man who had betrayed his father, was swift and had Flavius dropping his head, brought on partly by amazement, but just as much by his own blindness at not seeing what Petrus had set out to do and what a cunning weave he had made. If it was a conspiracy it had been clever, and more tellingly, it had been successful or he would not be talking now.

'If you owe me your life, it is not a favour I would ever call in. But I do need your help and there is no one else I can turn to. That is why you were recalled.'

'I will do that which you ask,' Flavius replied after a lengthy pause, 'and no more.'

'No more is required.'

'I will need aid from the men of my unit.'

'As long as they have no idea what will be in the chests that is not a difficulty.'

The cart he borrowed belonged to the Excubitors, the four men he fetched along were under his command and they showed a pleasing lack of curiosity about the task, as soldiers often do, accustomed as they are to the whims of their officers. He left them outside until he had spoken with Amantius, who disappeared before they entered the villa. The first pair took one handle each of a chest, not large, so the sheer weight surprised them and led to an exchanged look of wonder. This had Flavius, who had not anticipated what should have been obvious, reaching for a quick excuse.

'It's being taken to the imperial treasury via the apartments of the *comes*.'

'Detour would be nice, Your Honour,' joked one.

'Don't tempt me,' Flavius replied.

This too was taken as a jest, just as the grave manner of delivery was taken as contrived. He meant it, though not in the way these soldiers thought: he was inclined to drop the whole lot in the Propontis and Petrus and his conspiracies be damned. His mood was no better at the other end, even more so when the chests were delivered to the apartments of Justinus, timed to be after he had retired to the single-door cell and hard cot on which he slept.

'Don't be gloomy, Flavius,' Petrus crowed when he discerned his mood. 'Believe me, when this is over you will heartily thank me.'

CHAPTER FOUR

The heat of the city, in the grip of high and continuing summer temperatures, was enough to permeate the thick walls of the palace; even the marble flooring seemed to be too warm. Was it that which contributed to the increased air of disquiet or was what Flavius observed being given greater definition because of what he had become a party to? If the name of the man Amantius wished to elevate was unknown that did nothing to allay suspicion, quite the reverse. Now he was looking at everyone he passed, seeking by whatever senses he possessed to discern if they were the chosen one.

Matters were not aided by the manner in which Anastasius hung onto mortality, helped by teams of physicians who feared to lose their heads if he died while they were in attendance. Others put it down to tenacity, while the ill-disposed, and they were legion, subscribed to the view that the old goat feared the retribution he might face from an angry redeemer, for if the Emperor had been fired by religious zeal, it had been at the price of much conflict with half of his subjects.

No words were ever more true than that one man's heresy was another's route to salvation. In a previous imperial reign, after much dissension, matters on dogma had appeared to have been settled. The Emperor called into being a Great Council in the city of Chalcedon, where the dispute about the divine nature of God and the Holy Trinity had been disputed.

After what seemed like endless argument on arcane points and endless biblical references it had been agreed that Jesus could be both a man and a god, this flying in the face of those who believed that position both impossible and heretical. The seeming acceptance of the conclusion of Chalcedon by those in opposition was just that; soon they were once more pressing for their dogma to be elevated to imperial policy.

Anastasius had backed them, insisting on adherence to the more mystical and Eastern position. The bishops of Asia Minor and Egypt, known as the Monophysites, had captured the imperial soul and in his passion for their cause Anastasius had cracked down on the proponents of the settlement of Chalcedon, removing divines from their diocese and replacing them with men who shared his doctrinal beliefs. The result had been rebellion on a massive scale in the Imperial Themes to the west and north of Constantinople, led by a general called Vitalian who had three times invested a capital city too formidable to actually capture.

It was his first attempt to take the city that had brought Flavius, marching with General Vitalian and fleeing certain death at home further north, to Constantinople and the apartments of Justinus, his late father's old comrade, where if he had not found peace he had felt something akin to a home.

The religious dispute mirrored in many ways the fissure between the two great groups of the empire, those who clung, and they were often of barbarian stock, to the notion of Imperial Rome as it had been for centuries, set against the greater number of Greeks and Levantines who made up the majority of the population. These were people who seemed to take more inspiration from Persia than Rome, not least in the way the Emperor was seen as divinely chosen and a certain conduit to God.

To a committed Christian this harked back to and mirrored too closely the pagan ethos of the pre-Constantine polity. The Roman-inspired also deplored and fought the way Greek modes of behaviour continually wore down on what they called the Ancient Virtues, notions of behaviour more breeched than observed but held to be a better mode of living.

Their enemies scoffed at these pretensions, seeing them for what they too often were, a hypocritical method of asserting cultural superiority when in truth the reverse was the case; if the Romans had ever had any virtues they were those of Italian peasants and farmers. Learning and sophistication came from Attica, not Italy.

Justinus, Thracian by birth, as had been the family of Flavius, sought to act as he thought a Roman should: honestly and selflessly. When it came to religion, if he kept his own counsel in public, his view in private was unequivocal. He thought his master misguided and making difficulties where none should exist; let each man worship in his own fashion and if the bishops wished to dispute on dogma let them do so without troubling the public peace.

Flavius Belisarius felt himself to be solidly Roman, an attitude inherited from his late father. The events of his death, and that of the three elder brothers who perished with him, were now long past in the life of a boy turned to manhood. Yet they were, to the person who had witnessed the act of treachery, as fresh as if they had happened the day before. This was even truer at night, when dreams turned the man who betrayed them into a Nemesis, an ogre of antiquity, some pagan fiend sent by the Fates to ruin his peace of mind.

Dining with Justinus – Petrus was off to one of his dockside dens of iniquity – the subject of how Flavius had come to the city was one bound to surface and with it the present state of the still unresolved religious divide which pitted the western half of the empire against the east and south, doing nothing to aid the cause of border protection.

'You served with Vitalian, Justinus?'

'Many years ago in the Isaurian revolts. He was a doughty fighter.'

'Upright?'

'Yes, but too inflexible sometimes. Very good with barbarians. You have to admire the way he has kept fighting, having been denied success so many times.'

'You'd do likewise, I am sure.'

'I am not sure it is a fight I would ever have got into.'

'Am I allowed to ask another question?' That got a quizzical look but also a shrug that said go ahead. 'Who do you think will succeed Anastasius?'

'I am tempted to leave that in the hands of Our Saviour and grateful that he is there to oversee it.'

'I can understand your reluctance to be drawn, but you must have both hopes and reservations, it would not be human to be otherwise.'

'Has Petrus put you up to this?'

'No.'

'I'm surprised, it sounds so very like the questions he plagues me with, though yours is more forthright. His tend to go halfway round the palace before I can get the point.'

'And what do you tell him?'

'That I will do my duty to the office I hold.'

'It is not unknown for a succession to cause bloodshed.'

Justinus looked quite irritated then, as if he was being pressed, which Flavius had tried hard to avoid. 'That I will not stand by and witness.'

'Which will involve you taking action.'

'Change the subject, Flavius,' Justinus growled, showing in his obvious anger a side of his character the youngster had rarely seen. 'Or change where you dine.'

'Forgive me.'

'Granted,' came the eventual reply, when the older man

had contained his annoyance. 'You met Vitalian, Petrus tells me, and he was full of praise for you.'

'I'm not sure how he knows that, given he was not witness to it.'

'My nephew would not find himself in strange company in a burrow of ferrets. He seems to know a great deal that he has not actually seen, which makes me wonder if he does not occasionally indulge in sorcery.'

You don't know the half of it, Flavius thought, as he covered his mouth and half his face with his wine goblet lest that become obvious.

'I do not say, Uncle, that you are in any particular danger, only that times are perilous and precautions are wise.'

'Then spare me from the food your mother's cook provides.'

Petrus acknowledged that; the person in question was a woman who had come from Thracia with his mother and no amount of bleating about the offal she served as food would dent the maternal faith in an old retainer and slave who had been with her since childhood. Yet Lupicina, wife to Justinian, who avoided the palace and the condescension she was exposed to there, also resided in the Sabbatius household and it was only fitting that her husband should visit her as often as his duties allowed. Petrus was outlining the obvious fact that such regular excursions were no secret.

'You do not see that you have enemies.'

'Why should I, nephew, when you see them everywhere?'

'An escort would add to your dignity.'

'I am going to dine with my family and my wife, your family – and come to think of it, I am curious how you have yet again got out of attendance?'

Tempted to say he had more willpower than his uncle, Petrus restrained himself. Even true it would not be taken well and would only lead to the observation, also a fact, that Vigilantia, sister to Justinus, did not only overindulge her far from capable cook, she was too soft on her only son.

'You're adamant?'

'I have never needed an armed escort when I moved around the city before and despite your wild theories I do not need one now.'

'At least indulge me by taking a weapon, a sword.'

'Very well,' came the impatient response, 'if it makes you feel better.'

'I cannot persuade him that at times like the present all that is normal no longer holds.'

'If he is at risk, who is it from?'

'How many people, Flavius, do you think would like to get into the bedchamber of Anastasius and press a pillow over his face? How many alliances do you think are being formed to take advantage of the succession and what does time do to those as the Emperor lingers on and their secret gatherings begin to leak?'

Petrus was pulling at his hair and his head was well canted, proof that he was troubled, with Flavius reckoning he was the one most distressed by the fact that Anastasius refused to expire quickly.

'I am not the only mind that sees the need to have the

Excubitors either as allies or men who will stand aside. How, Flavius, do you ensure that?'

Getting a shrug, Petrus got all professorial. 'No, you cannot answer for you have not thought it through, but I have. What if there was a new Count of the Excubitors, one committed to your cause? He could order the imperial guard to stand down or he could be the conduit by which they could be bribed to acclaim your candidate for emperor.'

'And in order to do that you would need to remove Justinus?'

'The point entirely.'

'If you cannot persuade Justinus to take precautions, what makes you think I can?'

That surprised Petrus. 'No one is asking you to.'

'Then what are you asking?'

'I want you and some of your men to follow his palanquin, at a discreet distance. I have asked and had him agree that he should take his sword so if he is attacked and an assassination is attempted he may be able to hold off his assailants until you can come to his aid.'

'If he finds out he will crucify me.'

'If he is killed we will all face the cross.'

Accepting that as exaggeration, Flavius nevertheless agreed; he was off duty and had no concerns about finding a quartet of his rankers to go with him. They would need some duty favours in return, though they must have wondered, albeit silently, why their officer, twenty paces ahead of them, was clad in a cloak on what was a stifling evening and why were they carrying his helmet and spear?

Nor were they alone in that; dripping sweat, Flavius sought to keep the palanquin ahead in sight, while his men were in view to his rear, not easy in streets still busy with citizenry and hawkers. The garment had been unnecessary; Petrus insisted they must remain out of sight and in some senses that got more difficult as Justinus left the centre of the city and headed through the quieter streets that led to his brother-in-law's villa at Blachernae.

A hilly suburb, it was far enough from the stink of the city, providing the wind was not blowing due north, to render life more agreeable for the patricians and those tradesfolk rich enough to match their style of living. With ample water from artesian wells and good soil, the large gardens were a source of neighbourly competition while the houses they surrounded vied with each other in sumptuousness.

If it replicated anything, Blachernae was very like what Rome had been in the Augustan Age on the Palatine Hill. It was generally held, by those who could only gaze in envy at such luxury, that it also mirrored the arrogance of the rich senatorial class of those times and there was just enough daylight left as they passed by them to allow for an occasional sigh of wonder from the rankers.

Everyone but Justinus was hot and bothered by the time the palanquin deposited him at the gate of the Sabbatius villa, the men who had carried him probably even more than Flavius, who quickly found a small copse of trees in which to conceal himself so he could disrobe. His men joined him in what was now, under such a canopy, near to darkness.

To a look of enquiry he responded. 'We wait.'

'Am I allowed to ask what it is we're about, Your Honour?'

'We are looking after the welfare of our general.'

'Without him knowin' of it.'

'You're asking for a right lashing, Tircas,' hissed another soldier; in the imperial army you did not question officers.

Not long back from the east these men who had been allotted to Flavius did not really yet know him. More than that they did not know of his past serving with Vitalian, when he had been what they were now, a common soldier. Unlike his peers, he knew what they faced and the stoicism with which they generally did so and it bothered him not at all that his actions were being questioned for he had felt that same need himself.

'I will never use a whip to answer a question,' Flavius insisted. 'It must be plain to you that if we are concealed it is because Justinus does not wish to be escorted by armed men, yet there are those who fear at present he may be in danger.'

'With the old Emperor on his last pegs?'

'Times like these are far from normal. I hope and pray that we will return to our barracks having witnessed nothing to disturb the night.'

'Would I be allowed, Your Honour, to see if I can find a public well? A cooling drink would not go amiss.'

'Do so, Tircas, and do not rush. Our charge will be in that villa for some time.'

In truth Justinus emerged earlier than Flavius had reckoned – he knew nothing of the Sabbatius cook and nor did he know that the night had ended not as it should in connubial bliss but with a matrimonial row and an unexpected departure long before the palanquin was due to return. He was woken up with a sharp shake, as were the pair of his men he had allowed their turn to sleep. This time they had to dog the heels of a striding and fit older man, going mainly downhill under a sky carpeted with stars.

'Reverse your spears,' Flavius whispered, even if Justinus was too far off to hear even normal speech. 'The points will catch the starlight.'

The other problem was the noise of their feet, for all were wearing regulation sandals and they had metal studs. To avoid the chance of Justinus looking round, Flavius dropped back as far as he could while still keeping the general in view, albeit only as a sort of outline, fortunately aided by his light-coloured garments.

They were back in the more populous part of the city now, where the streets narrowed and the higher buildings created gullies of gloom, forcing Flavius to hurry in order to keep the outline in view. He was reasoning the whole thing as a waste of time; the city was dark, few of the citizens prepared to waste precious oil to stay out of their cots, though there was a glim of a lamp from the occasional window of some night owl.

'Is that a lantern, Your Honour?'

Flavius cursed himself; he had allowed his attention to wander, partly because of the stifling heat trapped in by the tenements but more by the thought he might look like an old woman and a misguided worrier to the men in his unit. Indeed they would chatter, and the escapade, even if it never came to the ears of Justinus, would be all over the barracks before the next day was out. He could not say this was not his idea!

'Where away?'

'Saw just a flash, low down at street height, quick doused.'

'Sure?'

'Not certain.'

Flavius did not have to order an increase in pace, he only had to move faster himself for his men to pick up their own. His spear, hitherto shaft uppermost, was reversed with the needle-sharp point forward. The first shout echoed in the narrow street and at the sound of that Flavius broke into a run, the noise of which also echoed and had Justinus turn to see the cause.

In doing so he failed to see the figures emerging from the black walls of the tenements, they being clad in the same dark clothing. Flavius yelled for his general to take guard and luckily Justinus did not hesitate, perhaps because he heard footsteps too close, perhaps because of the tone of alarm of the youngster's yell. Still running, Flavius cast his spear right over the head of Justinus, unsure whether it would do any harm.

What it did do was strike the cobbled roadway to send up a shower of sparks and the clang of contact. The other sight was the flash of what looked like a sword blade, he hoped that of Justinus, so he called to his men to cast, which they did at full pelt and being trained it was done with care and accuracy, evidenced by a couple of howls that Flavius hoped were wounds.

Justinus had the sense to retreat towards what he must

now know to be support, his sword swinging wildly with no other purpose than to hold at bay his opponents. Such creatures could not be blind or deaf, they could hear and no doubt see that those rushing to close with them were trained fighters and if their numbers were an unknown they would have to be many more to contest with such people.

That they melted away with the same speed with which they had appeared was initially to be expected – black clothing against dark walls – but as Flavius swept past Justinus he did so into a vacuum empty of humanity; those who had attacked his patron had disappeared in an area riddled with narrow alleyways. Panting, sweating, and angry, Flavius stopped his men and called on them to surround their general. It was inside a square of his imperial guards, with Flavius Belisarius out in front, that the *comes Excubitorum* returned to the palace.

CHAPTER FIVE

'Yes, I denied your express wish, Uncle, but you must acknowledge that my suspicions were correct.'

'I would be interested to know where these suspicions come from.'

'An ear to the ground, or what lies beneath it.'

'Home to your spirit is it not?' Justinus was angry, but Flavius as a witness to this exchange was unsure if the irritation was really aimed at Petrus or at himself for being wrong. Nor would he acknowledge to having been in any real danger, claiming to have been faced with 'A bunch of ill-bred vagabonds that I would have seen off without aid from anyone.'

'Flavius?'

'I saw little, just some shadowy figures and they melted away as soon as we made our presence known.'

'Cowards,' Justinus spat.

'It could be he saved your life!' Petrus rarely raised his voice to Justinus and that he did so now caused a degree of astonishment and he was not finished. 'What do you think would happen to me and my family if you are slain? What of your wife, the Lady Lupicina? Do you think we would be left at peace to mourn? No, Uncle, if we were not slaughtered like goats we would be hounded from the city to what? A life of poverty and ridicule?'

'I know everyone depends on my holding my place.'

Petrus dropped the angry tone, his voice becoming emollient. 'To those who care for you, that you hold on to, your life is of more account and I say that is still at risk.'

There was no need to ask if Petrus thought there would be other attempts on the life of the *comes Excubitorum*: that was implicit in the words he employed. It was what to do and how to guard against it that filled his thinking.

'You trust Flavius?'

'That does not deserve an answer.'

'Then as his commander, I request that you detach him and his men from normal duties to act as a personal bodyguard until the matter of the succession is resolved.'

'It ill becomes you, Petrus, to speak of the Emperor as if he is already dead.'

Flavius expected Petrus to mention Amantius but that was not forthcoming. Instead he spoke of the imperial nephews, insisting that each would have some support but the real danger came if any two of them combined.

'It cannot be anything other than a temporary alliance, but it will serve to get one of them the purple. After that, if the winner has any sense, he will cut the throats of his rivals.'

'They may all align behind one,' Justinus suggested, though without much conviction: as he said before, he had seen too much of them and their rivalry to reckon that possible but plainly the whole subject concerned him. 'What do I do if they begin to murder each other? Do I stand aside or interfere?'

'Be concerned about your own skin not theirs,' Petrus ventured, before his head canted to one side. 'Truly it would be a tragedy if the imperial succession was dragged into another bloodbath.'

'If Anatastius had chosen it would have been clear.'

'You wish he had anointed a successor?'

'I do, and I say that even if I think his nephews to be poor candidates. The empire can withstand a fool but not a weakling. If matters are as you say, is the whole thing to be decided in the Hippodrome?'

'It has happened before, Uncle.'

'And rarely has it given us good governance. An emperor created by acclamation of the mob is ever in fear of being deposed by the same creatures that forced his elevation.'

Flavius felt he lacked real knowledge of what was being discussed, though he was as aware as anyone on the number of successions that had been mob-inspired, either by acclamation of a favoured candidate or the repudiation of one put forward by the powerful. Justinus and Petrus had talked of it at table in a way that saw succession problems as normal. There was a certain level of conversation regarding the fickleness of the mob in the officers' quarters based on the very real threat that out of control at a time of imperial interruption they were a danger to everyone, Excubitors included.

Even well-armed, you could not hold off a fired-up mob of thousands intent on imposing their will, so a massacre of the military was far from impossible. Yet it was raised there too in such a way that it seemed to be accepted as a feature of life in the imperial capital, which to him bordered on the absurd. He wondered if it might take years to understand the ramifications of the various polities that vied for supremacy in what should be a stable state but was not.

If the Emperor had supreme power it was held on to only by his ability to balance the many conflicting interests of the citizens of empire and nowhere was that more manifest than in Constantinople itself. It was hard enough for a young man who had spent little time in the city to get a grip on even the most basic rivalries that excluded those of a religious hue, that between the factions known as the Blues and the Greens. Originally split by competition over chariot racing they had mutated into groupings more intent on the protection of their rights than watching their teams compete in the Hippodrome.

At its very simplest the supporters of the Blues tended to come from the old patrician families and the Equestrians while the Greens had their enthusiasts among the mercantile classes but these were, as definitions, too loose. What was true and disturbing was the ability of either faction to bring onto the streets or into the seating of the chariot arena a multitude of supporters too fevered by some cause or other to easily control.

'Then you would see that as undesirable, Uncle?'

That question brought Flavius back to the present, as did the reply of Justinus that lamented the way the military units based in the city often stood aside when the Blues or the Greens rioted, they too being split by the same conflicts over allegiance. He accepted that having been chosen, a new emperor needed the support of the people and that was, by tradition, granted to them in the Hippodrome. But the person being acclaimed should be presented to them as the choice of the higher officers of state, not someone who merely appealed to their most base passions.

'Then we must do what we can to ensure that such an outcome is avoided.'

'You'll need more than an ear under the ground to foresee that, Petrus, perhaps a celestial presence might suit the need.'

'Excellency.' Justinus swung round to face the messenger, a man whose doleful expression gave notice of what he had come to impart. 'The physicians attending upon His Imperial Highness fear the end cannot be far off, having heard the rattle.'

'I will come at once.'

Justinus gave both Petrus and Flavius a searching look then grabbed his helmet and placed it under his arm; he would need to be properly dressed to attend upon his dying master, a man he had esteemed even if he had thought his religious policies misguided. Anastasius and he shared an Illyrian place of birth and could, when the need arose, converse in their local language so the Excubitor commander had acted as something of a confidante. If there was a difference in age it was not so great that memories could not be shared of a life vastly more simple and rustic than that to which they had both risen.

'Uncle, take your sword too.'

That stopped Justinus; he had the right, unlike others, as the head of the imperial bodyguard, to bear arms in his master's presence. Was it fitting to do so now when he would be attending upon a soul parting from its corporeal body?

'Indulge me,' Petrus insisted, 'and if not for yourself take the precaution for your family.'

The hesitation was brief, before Justinus nodded and strapped on his weapon. Then he was gone. As soon as he had disappeared Petrus moved to key open a casket and produce a scroll, which he immediately held out.

'Flavius, please go to barracks and alert the officers listed here to take up their places at the entrances to the palace. See them carried out then come back here and rejoin your own *decharchia*.'

'Did Justinus prearrange this?'

'No, Flavius, I did.'

'And the instructions regarding Amantius, or rather his candidate?'

The look that got was one of a man wondering if the person he could see before him could be so dense. 'There are none.'

'Why?'

'Amantius is the Emperor's chief eunuch and will be

where his station demands at such a time, by the bedside as a witness to his demise.'

'But the man he has chosen—'

'May hanker till he draws his last breath. Do as I ask, Flavius, and if you have questions save them till later.' Seeing the younger man still hesitate, Petrus was firm. 'I say to you what I said to my uncle. Our fate depends upon this and I add that it would not be unbecoming at such a time for an Excubitor officer to be seen running.'

Too confused to argue, Flavius left the room, not running but walking fast. The officers' quarters of the Excubitors lay within the main gate that led out to the Triumphal Way and as he entered it was clear that some form of alarm had already been disseminated: there was no one lounging about as per normal, no sound of clicking dice or general banter.

Many were deep in conversation and some were, without haste, donning their armour, Flavius soon to realise they to be the very names he had listed on Petrus's scroll. The sight of him was telling; each nodded silently, hastened their preparations and without a word to anyone, departed. These were the fellows who were the boon companions of Petrus, men often to be found in his company in the low dens he loved to frequent and into which he had introduced Flavius. The next sound he heard, as he departed to join Petrus and his own body of ten spears, was of those same officers rousing out their men.

'Splendid,' was the response when he reported, spoken by a man agitated but seemingly relieved. 'If all do their duty the palace is sealed off as are the necessary apartments.'

'I would deem it a favour, Petrus, to be told what it is you are up to?'

'Sit.' Flavius looked at the doorway, really to what was going on well beyond it. 'Anastasius has not yet left us.'

'How do you know?'

'I have not heard his servants wailing.'

'Which they will do?'

'Of course.'

Flavius nodded. 'For the loss of their master, it is fitting.'

'For the loss of their places and the weight of their purse,' Petrus scoffed, 'and the privileges that go with it, not least the right to pilfer. A new emperor means a clean-out of slaves and attendants.'

'They cannot all be thieves.'

'They are.'

'Do you see good in anyone?'

'What I see is what I see,' was the enigmatic reply.

As if it had been preordained, that was followed immediately by the sound of wailing, low to begin with but rising to a keening crescendo over a very short period.

'Now the real adventure begins.'

Petrus stood and indicated that Flavius should follow him. With the armed men he led at their back, they made their way towards the imperial apartments, passing any number of sobbing slaves and servants, even the odd official, not that the sight of such distress seemed to affect Petrus, who now had a knowing smile on his face, as irritating as it was mysterious.

There was no doubt that a great deal of planning had gone into what was now happening, but to what end? The drinking companions of Petrus knew what tasks they had to perform without Flavius having to say a word, and what did sealing the palace imply? A threat, but from whom? At the great double doors to the suite of Anastasius stood two Excubitor rankers, spears at the ready, with eight more present and fully armed. It took a quiet conversation and order from the officer who commanded them to allow Petrus and Flavius entry and they had to part from their own escort.

'No longer needed,' Petrus said. 'The only armed man in here is Justinus.'

The set of rooms was spacious, many chambered and endless, but they were empty and silent, all the close retainers and body slaves of Anastasius having been ejected, the only sound to emerge as they passed through various rooms being that of the priests praying and singing for the soul of the departed, which rose to be clearly audible as they passed the imperial bedchamber.

They carried on until they were outside the private council chamber, the place where decisions were taken by the Emperor and his closest advisors in secrecy, in truth the room from which the empire was run, though the Senate was allowed to act as if they made the necessary resolutions. Petrus, sliding to the side of the open double doors, silently indicated they should take station out of view.

'They will pray now,' he whispered, 'but the bargaining for the succession will begin very shortly.'

'Would it not be blasphemous to act so soon?'

The equally soft point got a quiet snort and a hissed lecture.

'There can be no hiatus. Word will spread that Anastasius is dead, to a populace that has been waiting weeks for it to happen. All the factions who seek advantage in that will be preparing to act but they will hold back to see if first, those who should decide on the succession, the men of the council, do so.'

'And if not?'

'Prepare for riots, looting and murder as scores are settled. The Blues and Greens will be at each other's throats within days.'

'Why are they allowed to be as they are?'

'Why does the sun rise of a morning, Flavius?' Petrus whispered as the praying ceased and a commanding voice spoke out.

'Sad as this day is, it falls to us to have a concern for the public peace.'

'Urban prefect,' Petrus whispered. 'He will have to deal with any trouble.'

Next came another voice, hoarse but firm. It took a few seconds for Flavius to recognise it as that of Amantius, it being so very much stronger than what he had heard in that cubicle. He now knew the man's official title to be that of *Magister Officiorum*, the functionary who controlled access to the Emperor when he held an assembly to hear complaints and grievances.

As such he was a real power, for he could deny as well as grant an audience, which explained all that gold Flavius had collected from his villa. The best way to get through his screening was to bribe him. It also gave reason to his concern on who should succeed: he wanted to keep his place, and if anything, enhance it as the power behind the throne.

'We are all aware that to delay in naming a successor to Anastasius, God rest his soul, is to invite disorder.'

'The palace will be secure,' Justinus said, his brisk military timbre easy to recognise. 'The order would have gone out as soon as our loss was known.'

'Then we know it will be so,' said Amantius in what seemed a bit of a purr. 'There is not one of us present, who make up the council, who has not deliberated in private as to who should succeed our late master.'

That got a murmur of agreement from a goodly number of throats. The whole body that had made up the council of Anastasius, senators all and the holders of the great offices of state, the men who controlled the vast bureaucracy of empire, were in the room.

'It does not fall to me by right, but I now ask if any of us present have a candidate.'

'Hypatius,' came a loud cry, to be met by howls of derision, the names of Probus and Pompeius greeted in like fashion, with one weak-voiced senator pointing out that if their own uncle had not thought his nephews fitting for the highest office then who were they to disagree, only for Amantius to respond.

'He did not name them as his successors, that is true, and I can now reveal to you all what was imparted to me in confidence, which is the one quality he did not apply to his nephews. He had no faith in their ability to rule and feared for the empire in their hands.'

Various voices spoke up, other names were mentioned,

to be cast aside either in loud defamation or after a quiet and serious discussion.

'He's playing a fine game,' Petrus hissed, 'but he must declare soon.'

Which Amantius did, naming Theocritus, commander of the *Scholae Palatinae*, as a man not only fit for the office but, vitally, able to muster support from his own body of troops as well as the Excubitors, they having been canvassed by a person in whom he reposed great faith.

'How do you know that to be true?' Justinus demanded. 'I have no knowledge of this.'

'Trust me, *Comes*, I do.'

It was a telling point to Flavius, given what he knew about the Excubitors, for the men that this Theocritus led enjoyed scant regard from the body of which he was a part. Originally raised as an Equestrian bodyguard for the Emperor, and it had to be admitted at one time a potent force, the *Scholae* had over time descended into an organisation stuffed with privileged young men, the sons of the wealthy members of the Patrician and Equestrian classes, peacocks more interested in appearing martial than being effectively so. To anyone seriously military they were nothing but a mounted, prancing joke.

Not so to Amantius, who was praising them to the heavens, as if they alone had the power to save the empire, and naturally the man who led them was a paragon. After a long and heartfelt paean of praise, what he said to follow did induce surprise.

'I hope the council will not take it amiss that I have Theocritus standing by. I also know that he is willing to accept the diadem and he has assured me that what offices we hold now and who holds them will not be altered.'

The voice became louder and almost imperious. 'Order is too important.'

Even Flavius could see the sense of that last ploy; it would not only be slaves and servants wondering about their future prosperity; every high courtier, in receipt of great wealth, would be likewise troubled given their entire existence was by imperial favour.

'If it is agreeable to you present I would ask that he be allowed to attend upon us and make his case.'

'You have been presumptuous, Amantius.'

This full-throated objection from a man identified by Petrus as the Master of the Largesse – the official who disbursed the empire's income throughout the various Themes and Dioceses, it being interesting to measure the number who agreed with him, which seemed to Flavius a great deal less than the number present. The look Petrus gave Flavius then was like that of a lion who had found a fresh kill.

'It is about to get interesting.'

CHAPTER SIX

When he spoke again Amantius, having faced some very vocal opposition, was beginning to sound desperate; did his assurance of military support from the two bodies of troops tasked to defend the person of the Emperor count for nothing?

'Do not rank the *Scholae Palatinae* alongside my Excubitors,' Justinus protested. 'I will not have it.'

'I do not mean to denigrate your fine men, *Comes*, but to include them. Theocritus has promised to be generous to all who aid him.'

'Aid which I have yet to see proof of.'

'Believe me it is there.'

What followed was a plea for understanding for what

could only have been quite a complex conspiracy: to get upon his side two such military bodies had to take months of subterfuge and secret gatherings and it could not be done without the disbursement of a great number of bribes and even more promises of gold to come, a fact obvious to everyone present, even if none referred to it.

'Since I cannot aspire myself, I have sought a solution which will be swift and orderly. Do not deny to me that every mind in this room had pondered the problem and discussed it. If you cannot put forward a name it is because you cannot agree on one. Theocritus is my candidate, he has military backing and he is popular with the mob as well.'

'The Blues, certainly. The Greens will howl if he is raised.'

'Urban prefect again,' Petrus whispered unnecessarily; the man had a distinctive voice.

'It is not the prerogative of either,' Justinus insisted, his irritation obvious.

What followed was much disordered discussion, voices rising and falling, senators speaking over each other, the odd loud disagreement, with the tone of the *Magister Officiorum* growing increasingly desperate.

'A day to think upon it, Amantius?'

'You risk mayhem.'

'Better that than a terrible error.'

'Let Theocritus make his case.'

The cry of 'tomorrow' came from many a voice.

Petrus snorted a sort of laugh as he moved into the open doorway, partially followed by Flavius, to whom he said,

'They are now about to find out that they are not the people to decide.'

All that got was a confused look before Petrus spoke in a loud voice to the whole room which now lay open before him. 'Eminences, forgive me that I interrupt your deliberations, but there is a delegation waiting to make representations to you regarding who should hold the office of emperor.'

'What are you talking about?'

Flavius heard the furious question from Justinus but it was the murmuring from his rear that took his main attention. Turning he saw gathered in the antechamber all the senior commanders of the Excubitors, the four *tribuni*, a dozen *centurio*, while behind them stood a good half of their inferior unit commanders, all of whom had come to where they now stood in such silence they had not been heard.

Petrus turned and gestured forward the senior men, most looking determined, one or two looking troubled, which was as nothing to the faces of the senators, for these Excubitors were fully armed. The most senior *tribunos* and second in command to Justinus, Galataeo the Thracian, stepped forward to speak, to tell these senators that, respectfully, the Excubitors would accept no other person to be crowned with the diadem other than their own commander, the *comes Excubitorum*.

'And that is the view of you all?' asked Petrus, ignoring the shock this produced on the face of Justinus, to get as response a full-throated roar of approbation from a room full of Excubitors, that is except from Flavius and the man himself; Justinus now looked both confused and embarrassed as his nephew looked at him.

'Uncle? The diadem is yours to take.'

'I cannot accept.'

What followed was a military chorus of 'You must!' and one Flavius suspected had been rehearsed

'I demand you deny this, Justinus,' Amantius cried, his objection somewhat diminished by his hoarse tone of voice; he was about to say more but the sound of swords being half-dragged from scabbards stilled him and it was not only he who took a hasty step back.

'My Lord,' Galataeo said, addressing Justinus, 'there is only one honest man in this room and that is you. We will not follow another and I can assure you the people of the city will welcome your elevation, for it is not only those who serve under you who esteem your probity.'

'Fine words,' said Amantius.

'And true,' claimed the urban prefect, in a meaningful aside.

'Please,' Justinus protested, embarrassed at such praise, unaware that his reaction only proved it to be true.

'Where is Theocritus?' demanded the eunuch.

'In your quarters, Amantius, and safe.'

There was no need for Petrus to add it was there he would stay or that any attempt by him to leave or to extract him would bring about a bloody demise.

'Flavius,' he said as a quiet aside, 'take your men and fetch the chests of gold.'

Doing as he was bid, Flavius heard the opening of Petrus's declaration, which was that Amantius had sought to embroil him in a conspiracy to grant the throne to Theocritus. If increasing distance denied him the rest it mattered not, for the first declaration set up a furious buzz and this from hypocrites who had all probably been at the same game in varying degrees and with other players.

When he returned, the chests borne by four of his Excubitor rankers, Petrus was extolling the virtues of his uncle while destroying the candidacy of not only Theocritus but the imperial nephews as well, with his uncle standing in deep thought. The chests were placed before the *tribunos* and *centurios Excubitorum* and at a command from the nephew of their commander the lids were thrown open to reveal their contents.

'A reward from my uncle for your loyalty,' Petrus cried.

Looking from one to the other Flavius saw the shock of Justinus, but more telling was the fury of Amantius to see his wealth used to elevate a man he had not chosen to be the next emperor. He was being cheered to the chamber ceiling and beyond as he was hailed by his Excubitors for his generosity in a way that brooked no refusal. Petrus had gone close to whisper, though given the noise of the soldiers discussing their reward and how they were going to spend it there was no need.

'What better way, Uncle, than this, to secure the safety of you and yours? I think you will find the Hippodrome is full of the citizens and they will be eager to acclaim you. I took the liberty of fetching my Aunt Lupicina from my father's house, who will enter the imperial box alongside you.'

'It does not occur to you that many will ask how I,

supposed to be so honest, gathered such a sum to bribe my own men?'

'There is a tale to that and one which will make you seem both clever and prescient.'

'One woven by you.'

'For you.'

'There is a part of Lucifer in you, Petrus.'

'While you are too much the saint, Uncle.'

Many of the senators, cowed into silence and aware that to resist was to risk being killed – they would never accept that Justinus would not allow it for in their minds it would seem natural – had knelt to acknowledge the obvious. A trio, Amantius included, who no doubt feared for their heads even if they recognised Justinus, had actually prostrated themselves, which brought forth an angry bark.

'Get up off the floor! This is the Roman Empire not Persia, you're citizens not slaves.'

It was the first imperial command of Justinus and it was hurriedly obeyed.

'Eminence,' Petrus murmured, his voice silky, 'we must proceed to the Hippodrome and before that you must be properly garbed as befits your station.'

At a signal the crowd of Excubitors parted to reveal a pair of Justinus's own servants. One had across his lower arms a decorated gold and purple cloak, the other the high and jewel-encrusted imperial diadem, both so recently the property of Anastasius.

The reply came with a deep sigh. 'You have arranged even this. Robbed a dead emperor of his possessions.'

'To avoid bloodshed, Uncle, it seemed apposite.'

'And your aunt?'

'Will be wearing suitable garments. She and you must appear before the mob as an imperial couple. Flavius take the chests to my uncle's quarters. The distribution can take place tomorrow as long as this day is a peaceful one. Galataeo, is all secure?'

'Word was sent by the *praefectus urbanus* to his troops to secure the Hippodrome and streets around as soon as he knew Anastasius was dying and this has been done. But fear not, Petrus Sabbatius, we Excubitors will make sure nothing happens to our new emperor.'

'Good. Please send a body of men ahead to line the imperial box.'

'I will lead them personally.'

The whole of the capital had been on edge for days now and if many had continued to toil, others had taken advantage of the tension to become idle, and naturally it was they, surely the least trustworthy citizens of the empire, who got to the Hippodrome first, to fill in anticipation the best seats as news of the death of Anastasius seeped out.

By the time a still reluctant Justinus, accompanied by Lupicina, who had also pressed him to accept, entered the covered passage that led from the palace to the imperial enclosure the place was packed to more than capacity and the noise of the gathering was like some buzzing swarm of distant hornets.

Petrus had been master of ceremonies from the very beginning of the day's events and he was not about to relinquish the lead position until he had to. He organised the way matters would proceed, and anyway, nothing could happen until the Patriarch of Constantinople, done with saying prayers for the soul of Anastasius, was informed of the new dispensation and sent ahead to bless the crowd.

When all was ready, Petrus, a man usually indifferent to his clothing, went ahead wearing a costume of shimmering black silk covered with silver devices that, once he encountered sunlight, flashed its reflections in all directions. His task was to prepare the multitude through rhetoric. The Excubitors, parade dressed and spick with it, marched out to take up guard positions at key points, a clear message that any dissent would be met with retribution.

Others lined the covered way, all eyes raised so as not to impiously stare at their new imperial master, each spear cast to the salute as he and his consort passed. Behind them came Flavius Belisarius, his sword in one hand, full infantry shield in the other, his task to act as personal protector of the imperial personages, a signal honour.

Justinus now wore a purple cloak sewn with a ransom in gold thread and on his head sat a wreath of laurels, the sign for centuries of a conquering Roman hero. The nerves he had evinced earlier – these emerged when he had finished berating Petrus for his devilish machinations – seemed to have morphed into a sort of stupor of acceptance. Lupicina, despite an encouragement that might have carried the greatest weight with her husband, was trembling like a leaf in the wind, for if her spouse had been close to imperial ritual and understood it, the same clearly terrified her.

The panegyric of Petrus, as he sang the praises of his uncle, was often drowned out by the sound of mob approval, for what had been said in the council chamber was not false.

Justinus was seen by the citizens of the metropolis as less venal than those alongside whom he carried out his duties. The reign of Anastasius as far as the city was concerned had been relatively peaceful, even if General Vitalian and his Rebels of Chalcedon had visited a trio of ineffectual sieges upon its walls.

As in every polity there were the ever-malcontents, those who hated imperial rule whoever was the occupant, prepared to make their opinions known with loud booing and catcall insults. But they were a minority amongst a citizenry that wished for order so that prosperity could be pursued. Only when these citizens were troubled did an emperor have concerns about the public peace; if they became riotous, then apprehension turned to deep alarm.

They wanted an emperor and if the men who had served Anatastius had, as far as they knew, agreed on a candidate quickly, as well as one of whom they could openly approve, then they were happy. There was, too, the knowledge that old Anastasius, who had taxed vigorously and spent sparingly, would have left full coffers and some of that would surely be distributed to the populace.

Behind the imperial party stood all the high officers of state, Amantius included, and if his face was that of a man who had swallowed a wasp, others were inclined to keep hidden any feelings they had, of either joy or the reverse. Given how they must have so recently schemed, Flavius wondered if such a trait could be put in abeyance when matters were seemingly resolved. That he doubted it made him feel sympathy for the man he was now protecting.

The next act overseen by Petrus involved the production

of the imperial diadem, gold-encrusted with diamonds, as well as the consort's less splendid crown, both borne onto the imperial viewing podium on a pair of purple cushions to be raised and shown to the audience. They fell silent as the Patriarch began to intone the prayers of blessing, their loud noises replaced by whispered and individual prayers. That done, the diadem was presented to the *comes Excubitorum*.

It might be the right of the citizen of empire to approve of an imperial candidate and it might be the task of the Church to bless it. But when it came to coronation it fell to the person taking office to see himself crowned and that was a moment to test the resolve of any man. To be the Roman Emperor, to have total sway over half of its territories and a titular supremacy over the old western polity, to be the focus of all law-giving and the arbiter of religious dogma, was a burden to be considered before being accepted.

Flavius watched the hands reach out then stop, the crowd falling into utter silence as the thought occurred that the man so gloriously clad in purple and gold might in fact deny that which was being offered to him. Some may have thought it to be merely dramatic show, a deliberate heightening of tension. Flavius knew the hesitation was genuine: Justinus lacked the pride to be sure of his right but he was still of strong mind. Decision made, those hands reached out, lifted the crown high, and then slowly he placed it on his head.

Had there been a roof on the Hippodrome it would have lifted at the roar which greeted the new Emperor Justin – his Roman rendering was held by Petrus to be too unpleasant to the ears of a population mostly of Greek extraction. Nor was it to be the Empress Lupicina, a name that identified her barbarian roots, her Roman leanings and was redolent of the pagan cult of Lupus, her crowning met with cheering if at a less fulsome volume.

She was acclaimed as Empress Euphemia, taking the name of a well-known martyred saint and seeking to imply, to those who would bow to her from this moment on, her aim was for their welfare. She personally venerated Saint Euphemia, something they would come to know by her actions and pronouncements. That she was a good choice would too become widely accepted for here was a woman who hated imperial pomp as well as patrician condescension, hence her refusal to previously take up residence in the palace. Deeply religious she would use her office to carry out good works.

Justin the First stepped forward to speak of his desires of peace, harmony and prosperity, the common tropes of any ruler seeking to ingratiate himself with his subjects. He wanted the empire's enemies thwarted and her friends cossetted, none of these causing excitement by folk expecting largess. But there was to be no distribution of gold; instead public works too long held in abeyance would be commenced, a better supply of water and a more swift removal of the city's filth would be put in hand, for it was not his policy to bribe those who were in anticipation of it but to improve the way of life for all.

It was instructive to watch Petrus. His smile, as his uncle spoke, went from full and genuine to a sort of rictus, an indication perhaps of his disagreement with what was being proposed or just that it was being done at present.

The smile disappeared completely when the peroration ended on the subject of religion.

'We have had a decade of conflict over that which should not divide us, for I believe each man should worship according to his own conscience. I will therefore reverse my predecessor's edicts on the Council of Chalcedon. All bishops displaced for their adherence to that creed shall be reinstated but no divine or citizen holding to Monophysitism will face denunciation or removal.'

It was time to observe the Patriarch, primary exponent of the latter and a major cause of the religious split, which had dogged the reign of Anastasius. He showed a mixture of anger for his views being denied followed by relief that he was not to be eased from his office.

'To that end, a message will be sent from me to my old comrade in arms, General Vitalian, telling him of my decision and seeking that he, now that his cause is no longer in existence, will lay down his arms and come to be by my side, where his counsel will be of more value than his present quest.'

The lips of Petrus Sabbatius were moving but he was talking to himself and not happily so. This statement had come out of the blue and it was one he clearly hated the thought of, not on grounds of religion, for Flavius knew that was not a matter of great concern to him. Was it just that his uncle had acted without consulting him, had shown that when it came to ruling he intended to do it from his own heart and not from the head of his nephew?

His peroration complete, the newly crowned Emperor Justin took the plaudits of the crowd and with a wave, departed the imperial box. But he spoke over his shoulder to issue an order.

'Petrus, write the message to Vitalian. Flavius, you will take it to him and you set off tomorrow. This matter has to be laid to rest quickly.'

'Uncle—'

Whatever Petrus intended to say was immediately cut off as his uncle stopped and turned to face him.

'You must address me properly, nephew, I cannot have you call me "uncle" in public when others are obliged to call me "Highness". And if you are going to question my right to make a decision, let me tell you that I am not beyond banishing my own family for the good of the empire. You have engineered this, and I am not full of joy at what you have done, but I hope it is not an act you are given cause to regret.'

'Highness,' Petrus replied, adding a deep, slow bow, which went some way to hiding his confusion.

CHAPTER SEVEN

Flavius Belisarius rode out the next morning at the head of a *decharchia* of cavalry, each of his men having an extra pack mount, carrying the despatch Petrus had written, or rather had dictated to him, the contents checked by another clerk before the newly named Justin the First used his freshly created imperial stencil and the Great Seal of his office that he had inherited to render it official.

As a messenger on imperial business Flavius had the right to command even senior officials to facilitate his passage, not that he anticipated the need. The roads of the Roman Empire, if not always in as good a repair as they should be, were very often straight for several leagues and lined at regular intervals with comfortable *mansiones* specifically for the use of people on official government business.

Sprawling as it was the empire depended on these roads to function, routes where riders bringing despatches could change mounts and if the news was desperate, ride on without resting to sound the alarm. Most officials travelled more slowly and comfortably in a slave-carried litter, staying overnight to bathe the dust off their bodies, to have their clothing brushed and cleaned and to be fed in a fashion that suited their rank. If they had needs of a sexual nature, these could be discreetly catered for.

Luxuriating in a bath, attended by two young slave girls and well beyond the point of gratification, Flavius was thinking about Petrus and the way he had reacted to his uncle's behaviour. No amount of logic seemed to be able to shift his sense of grievance.

'He resents the manipulation,' had been the explanation Flavius had volunteered for the new coolness between them.

'And where,' Petrus had demanded, with a well-canted head and a look of superior knowingness, 'would he be without it?'

'Perhaps if you had confided in him—'

'Confided in him!' came the shout, before Petrus had suppressed his vocal anger, well aware it could be overheard, giving a clear indication that his newly constrained status was troubling him. 'We would have been nowhere, or in the depths of the dungeons.'

Feeling the need to be emollient, Flavius advised that time would ease matters but he knew well, as he sat in this bath, that Petrus would not see it that way. He had focused particularly on the pardoning of Vitalian to vent his spleen, worried that the rebellious general would be a schemer – being one himself he hated that anyone else should employ such methods – and that once within the palace he might wonder at why a man who once served him as a junior military commander should now lord it over all he could survey.

'But how can I advise caution,' had been the plea, 'or even a special guard against the secret knife if the man will not listen to me anymore, tell me that?'

Climbing onto the warm tiles, to be dried by gentle towelling, Flavius deliberately forced his mind to concentrate on his task. How would he be received by a man he knew and had fought both under and alongside? Vitalian was a fine soldier, an excellent commander of his barbarian *foederati*, fighters mainly from north and east of Germany and fierce with it, men he would have to find a way past before he ever got to their general.

Once he had ensured his soldiers were likewise being catered for it was an unfortunate thought to take to bed, or was it the oversized meal he had felt obliged to consume? Someone had gone to the trouble of cooking it and the man who ran the *mansio* put such store by appreciation. The night was warm and humid, his stomach was full and thus his reveries were wide-ranging and finally deeply disturbing.

Flavius had a recurring dream-cum-nightmare in which he was fighting hard alongside his family on the banks of the River Danube. Yet he was simultaneously not part of the contest, able to hover above it and scream hopelessly that a blow should be parried or back should be covered, useless because no actual sound seemed to emanate from his mouth. Neither his father nor his brothers reacted to the aid he tried to give them and if the details varied the ending was ever the same as a horde of devilish fiends, slavering four-footed beasts able to ply swords and axes as well as their fearsome teeth, cut into his family and dismembered each one by one.

The limbs would struggle to rejoin only to be further mutilated and eyes would plead to the last remaining son to come to their aid. Flavius always woke up drenched in sweat and near to tears, the last image prior to wakefulness the florid, fat and grinning face of the villain who had betrayed them to the raiding Huns. Looking out of a window at an inky-black sky dotted with stars did not bring relief, only a wonder at a fate that had in reality allowed him to witness, if not the actual event, the way they had been overcome without his being able to have any effect on the outcome.

Then came the question to which there was no answer. Had his father realised why he had been abandoned to defeat and death along with the men he led? Had he told Flavius's brothers how close he was to bringing down his venal and wealthy nemesis, a senator of the empire and a lawbreaker of staggering proportions, but one who nevertheless had such strong support in Constantinople he had been able to frustrate efforts to bring him to justice for years.

After a decade of imperial inaction the Centurion Decimus Belisarius had finally got what he wanted; the promise of a high-ranking official commission to investigate the crimes and misdemeanours of his adversary and one kept secret even from the Emperor's own court officials. Somehow Senuthius Vicinus, the rogue in question, must have got wind of it and his reaction was to contrive a plan that removed the messenger and thus the threat.

Lying on his cot Flavius reprised what happened next; he had been forced to flee from his family home in the company of his father's aged *domesticus* Ohannes. A one-time fighting soldier, he had ensured the last surviving child did not suffer the same fate of the rest of his family, for Senuthius saw security only in the wiping out of the entire Belisarius clan. It was a blessing his mother had been absent visiting relatives when her family was destroyed for she too would have faced death, and escape with her in company would probably have been impossible.

Now he recalled the visit he had made to her and the tears they had both shed as he recounted the details of what had occurred. Not that she was unaware; he had sent Ohannes to her with the sad news so he was at least spared being the first to say the words and by the time he met with her, grief had mellowed to stoic acceptance. Happily, despite being deeply religious, she had never hinted any disapproval of the way he had seen to the remains of her husband and sons, which was seen by many as blasphemous.

On the site of the deadly encounter Flavius had built and lit a funeral pyre in true Roman fashion, sure his father would have approved, for he was strong for the virtues of the great millennial empire. That brought his ruminations full circle; it had been Petrus who had created the circumstances that got Flavius his revenge, Petrus who had given him the means to bring down Senuthius.

Rising from his bed and falling to his knees he began to pray for the souls of his lost family and he decided to include Petrus. Surely, given his nature, his way of living and his scheming nature, he required much intercession with the Almighty. Only when his supplications were concluded was it possible to sleep.

It was refreshing to be back in the saddle, spotting places and landscapes that had marked his passage south serving as a ranker under the rebellious Vitalian. Ohannes had been by his side much of the way, chastising, moaning and occasionally praising his young charge. There was a warm memory too, underscored with guilt, regarding a girl he had met, one of a group of camp followers; the warmth came from his first introduction to physical love, the guilt from a feeling he had abandoned her to pursue his own cause.

Their route, the *Via Gemina* ran along the shores of the Euxine Sea, which, when it was in sight, brought with it a welcome breeze that took some of the heat out of the air. Reaching Odessus they turned inland toward Marcianopolis, the landscape changing from an open vista to one often enclosed by thick woods, dotted with areas where these opened out to show fields of corn stubble. Often there were small groups of dwellings around a set of farm buildings and a villa.

They were now in country over which Vitalian exercised total control, for the imperial writ did not run in these parts, a region where, Flavius suspected, there would be no meaningful law. The man he had come to see was a rebel and his interest lay in ensuring the security of his fighting men; enforcing order on the surrounding countryside was a secondary consideration and would only concern the security of supply.

Nothing drove home more the state of affairs than the lack of traffic and when they did come across anyone moving towards the coast the party took time to assess them before coming on, passing with the minimum of exchange based on caution. Rebellion brought on lawlessness as the worst elements of the citizenry sought to profit from disorder so it was necessary to be guarded; no more resting in comfortable *mansiones*, no delightful and gratifying baths and no more changes of mounts.

What they rode was what they had so the animals had to be husbanded and cared for. Now it was a half-riding, half-walking progression with two men up ahead looking out for trouble and swords and spears to hand. Even divested of their fine Excubitor armour these ten men and their officer presented a tempting target if spotted by a large band of brigands, albeit one that could fight.

In the high heat of midday it was necessary to find shade and a stream, to unsaddle the mounts to let them drink as they wished and graze while Flavius and his men likewise rested. Where possible, when they camped for the night, it was within sight of one of those villas-cum-farms and their presence was not usually welcome, they being quickly identified as imperial soldiers and thus dangerous folk to be seen to be helping. Any objections had to be brushed aside; such places had feed to sell for both horses and humans and wells to access for much needed water.

The hilly country closer to Marcianopolis made more manifest that which they had already encountered; in the wooded valleys there was no farming and in high summer no trails of woodsmoke in the sky to hint at dwellings of any kind. The trees were taller, and being in full leaf and untended they formed a canopy that joined above their heads to create a tunnel. Likewise the actual pave was in poor repair, with blocks missing and in some cases whole sections gone, looking to have been washed away in winter storms.

The feeling you are being watched, once it takes hold, is impossible to shake and Flavius had felt it for the whole morning. There were signs, though they could be animal not human; sudden rustlings in the undergrowth not far from the road, the occasional startled bird that cawed as it was disturbed and flew to safety, added to that the particular sound a frightened pigeon makes as in escaping danger its wings flap against a surround of leaves.

Even in such dense woodland, where the sun did not penetrate, it was hot, and worse, it was humid. So walking the horses so as not to tire them out increased the feeling of vulnerability. Also, the need to find a resting place just off this badly maintained road was just as paramount, the problem being that if they existed, and they did, they tended to be tight glades with trickling streams that made the feeling of enclosure acute.

'Leave the riding horses saddled,' Flavius ordered, looking aloft at the patch of sky afforded them by the surrounding trees. 'Lead them to water and let them drink in pairs. Likewise we eat and drink two at a time, with the rest to stay armed and alert.'

'I don't like it much either, Your Honour.'

'Too quiet?'

'That, and the itch in my neck.'

Karas, the *decanus* who had spoken, was no spring chicken; he was an experienced soldier with a face the colour of leather, eyes surrounded by wrinkles and he acted as second in command. Flavius had learnt to have great respect for his abilities on the ride north; he kept the rest of the men up to the mark and was not slow to remind them that they belonged to a unit that formed the elite of the imperial army, with a responsibility to behave like it.

'Thoughts, Karas?'

That made the *decanus* blink; he was unaccustomed to have his views sought never mind listened to. Before he replied his eyes ranged around the surrounding trees, given there was no need to allude to what was being asked.

'It's not bears or cats.'

'Human, then?'

A nod. 'If there is a threat out there it is not large or well-armed, nor is it mounted.'

'They would have attacked us on the road.'

Karas nodded. 'So it won't be blood they're after but what we carry on the pack animals, for they will have seen our weapons. A horse round here and to a peasant will be of value an' all, Your Honour, never mind their loads.'

'A night raid?'

Again the eyes ranged around the enclosing woods, forests that the locals could very likely move through without giving away their presence. 'It will be if we are camped and sleeping in a place such as this.'

'Then there will be eyes on us now?'

'There will, but I would not like to seek to find them. We're safer in the open than on the turf they will call home.'

Flavius smiled; this older man was probably just taking precautions against the impetuosity of youth, unaware that he had no need to issue such a warning: they were on a mission to find Vitalian and that was paramount. He mused that whoever might be trailing them had to be a native and that must constrain the amount of distance they would move from their hearths.

'They will not stay with us more than one day, will they?'

'No, which makes tonight they're only chance.' Karas grunted. 'Should have fetched along a hound or two.'

'We will post sentinels, Karas.'

'Who I have known to fall asleep, even facing the wheel. Dogs you can rely on.'

'I think it best we don our armour, Karas, let them see what they are up against. It will make whoever is out there think.'

That got a jaundiced look; in the last two days they had been riding and walking in loose garments that suited the heat and humidity. Armour meant the padded jackets that lay beneath it for the body and an extra layer on the thighs, arms and lower legs, thus a high degree of discomfort.

'I would rather deter than let them raid and steal.'

The order was not well received yet that was well disguised – insubordination was too risky even with what seemed to be a soft officer, so the Excubitors were fully kitted out and sweating for it with short order. Flavius did not want any risk that their uniforms should be stolen; that would leave them looking very unmilitary in a situation in which he required appearances to be correct. Thus clad, they unloaded the packhorses and piled their belongings in what was to be the very centre of their encampment, near a large and kept flaming fire by which they took it in turns to sleep on what turned out to be an uneventful night.

At dawn, and after a breakfast of hard biscuit and water, they remounted and got back on to the road. Finding a long stretch to be seemingly in good repair, Flavius gave the order first to canter then to gallop. That was held longer than seemed wise given, once he called them back to a trot, it left the horses with their heads down and their mouths flecked with froth. Nor did he then dismount and walk them, he kept up a pace that seemed excessive until, earlier than would have been normal, a halt was called at yet another stream-dissected forest glade, though this time of greater size than hitherto.

'Now,' came the next command, which was not the usual order to remove saddles and see to the mounts, 'since we will have outrun anyone trailing us, let us lay for them some traps before they can catch up.'

'If we've outrun them, Your Honour,' Karas responded, part in question but also in part acknowledgement.

As a boy Flavius had hunted rabbits and small game and so it seemed had many of his soldiers, but this was different: little snares would be no good against human thieving. Stakes were cut from the surrounding branches, sharpened and set in the ground. One of his men had the notion of swinging rocks that would cover the gaps between the trees, their release set off by someone disturbing the tie on the ground. Likewise saplings were bent and secured so they would spring back and wound if disturbed.

Only then could the horses be looked to, fed and watered before being hobbled in lines. Lastly, as would have happened anyway and before it became dark, another large fire was created on which the whole unit could cook their food and one which, if kept fed, would illuminate much of the ground on which the majority would at any time be asleep, albeit fully clad and ready to defend themselves.

Flavius knew he would not be one of them; even if Karas volunteered to do likewise, the responsibility fell to him as an officer to ensure that those set as sentinels stayed awake. Also they had to be replaced and from his pack he produced the required hourglass that would be allowed to run through twice as the whole was rotated to cover the twelve hours of darkness.

'I hope they have given up, Karas, and all this will be a waste. Now, *Decanus*, check on the horse lines then get to sleep.'

Having done the duty himself Flavius knew that those set to keep watch would have imaginings, especially when the sky clouded over, trapping the heat of the day and cutting out any star or moonlight. Regardless of how many times you do it no one can stand sentinel without seeing chimeras as they stare in to a wall of blackness. Sitting down is forbidden for that brings on sleep, an offence that could see you broken on the wheel in the days of the Roman legions, so a man must wander to and fro, aware that half of the time his back is exposed to danger.

Forests do not sleep at night; they have their own sounds as the nocturnal hunters emerge to find their food, this while the wind moves the branches of trees in full leaf and they do not always just rustle. Nerves would be stretched even more by the suspicion that there was some kind of danger lurking just outside the ring of light provided by the fire, not aided by the hooting of owls and the swish of passing bats.

Flavius did not know what set off one of the traps, but the cry as a snapping-back sapling hit someone had his entire unit coming awake and getting to their feet, following a previous instruction to fan out and cover the ground. Only by looking backwards could they see those hoping to surreptitiously steal for they were in their midst, the crouched outlines silhouetted against the flickering embers of the fire.

Flavius had reacted the fastest; sword out, he ran towards the horse lines followed by a couple of his men carrying the torches they had just set light to. There was no casting of spears: in the dark, what might you hit? – a horse you needed to ride or one of your own. His quarry was no more than a shape, while he was silhouetted against the fire, so that when he raised his sword to strike the blade sent forth a flash of glaring orange.

The scream that action produced was so high and piercing it caused him to hesitate long enough to register that what he was about to cut in half was the wrong size. Instead of striking, he leant forward to grab and got hold of a smock. Pulling raised up what was either a dwarf or a child and, judging by the sound, it was not the former, a fact confirmed when one of his men shoved forward a torch to show a grubby, small and terrified face.

Torches now illuminated the glade and a quick turn showed what looked like dozens of scampering children seeking to avoid the swords that threatened to lop off their heads. Flavius called out a command to secure the perimeter and not to seek to kill those caught inside it. As a response it was not entirely successful, given there was too much space to fully secure, but when things died down, not least the screaming of children, that was what he found he had to deal with, his men having caught hold of half a dozen intruders, while it was obvious most had got clear.

It would have been funny had it not then created another problem: what to do with them once the sun came up and he could look at them properly? Attempts to ask questions fell up against two hurdles: mulish silence and, when they could be brought to speak, an impenetrable local dialect. Had he put it to his men how to respond to these youngsters – he reckoned none had seen twelve summers – they would have been strung from the surrounding trees.

His solution was less harsh, albeit it was painful. He had his men cut flexible saplings and administer a sound beating. While this was in progress he stomped the perimeter and glared into the forest at the ones who had escaped, sure they were still watching, sure they would get his message as the cries of their compatriots turned from yells to whimpers. His last act was to put them on the road, and facing east, with a stern finger that told them to go back from whence they came.

'Am I allowed to say you're too soft, Your Honour?'

'Hang them, Karas? Urchins when they did not have so much as a knife between them? No, that would be blasphemy, so let us breakfast and then be on our way.'

CHAPTER EIGHT

The first manned outposts protecting Vitalian heartlands were more than a full league from the main camp, precautions the general took to avoid being surprised. That had happened three years previously when Anastasius had sent an army under his nephew Hypatius to both surprise and chastise the rebellion, this at the same time as he was talking peace and reconciliation, a melee in which Flavius had inadvertently become embroiled.

The small rough and wooden stockade was manned by *foederati*, large men, with long blond hair and fearsome bodily decoration who hailed from a far northern Germanic tribe called the Gautoi. Terrible in battle, such men could also be hard to control; once the killing began, their lust for blood made it hard for any commander to bring them to order and sometimes they had been known, when engaged in one of their epic drinking bouts, to slay people just for sport. Vitalian had managed to keep them under tight control in the past; was that still the case now?

Given the Excubitors were clearly military and not of the rebellious army it was not worth taking a chance, especially since the whole Gautoi contingent was hauled out with their arms to face them as soon as they were sighted. Ahead of Flavius lay a straight road leading to their small stockade. There was a barrier, too, where local trade would be halted and taxed for passage, this to augment the pay Vitalian must provide to keep what were mercenary soldiers both happy and loyal.

In reflecting on this long rebellion, while acknowledging it to have proved fruitless so far, there had to be admiration for the mere fact of keeping it alive, this in the face of repeated failures to force the Emperor Anastasius to modify his stance on Monophysite dogma. To march on Constantinople and be rebuffed the first time had taken a massive effort of will; to repeat that in the face of disappointment required a great deal of charisma, for if these *foederati* formed the backbone of his forces they were insufficient to present any threat to the far more numerous imperial troops.

Every time he marched Vitalian had been required to raise a sizeable army from within the dissident Diocese of Thrace, a few trained soldiers but mostly idle or angry peasants. If most of those men were fired by their religion it still took great ability to tap into that zeal and gather them together to repeatedly disturb the public peace. Flavius, marching in the first rebellion, had carried his own purpose – he sought revenge for his family – but he well remembered how many of his compatriots were willing to risk their lives for the right to worship within the tenets agreed at the Council of Chalcedon. There were, of course, others who marched in search of plunder, men quite willing to cloak themselves in pious fervour to gain access to possible booty.

Flavius halted his party well beyond spear-throwing distance and, handing over the reins of his own packhorse, he rode forward alone to give his name and his purpose, first dismounting then seeking permission for him and his men to ride on and deliver the message he carried to their general, that swiftly denied.

'No force bearing arms is allowed to approach the main camp.'

'I would not proceed without them.'

It was not just pride that had Flavius declare such a stance; once inside the perimeter created to protect Vitalian he would be at the mercy of the type of men before him and he was wary of trusting them. They might reckon to have more to gain by delivering his severed head than his whole person.

'Then I bid you carry a message that the *tribunos* Flavius Belisarius wishes an audience with General Vitalian. He will know that his old enemy Anastasius is no more. I come on behalf of the Emperor Justin to offer peace and an amnesty for past misdeeds.'

'I've heard that name, Belisarius,' was the response, delivered in bad Latin.

'Then you will know it as one who has fought at your side.'

'Who perhaps betrayed us and now wears the armour of our enemies?' There was no point in seeking to deny that so he sat in silence until the Gautoi spoke again. 'Peace?'

That question set up a murmur in the whole file this man commanded, leaving Flavius to wonder if the notion of peace might be unwelcome to men who earned their living by war. If this lot had any religious feelings they would be pagan, not Christian, so they would be indifferent to either dogma. He had no right to make promises on behalf of Justin but he needed to say something reassuring, even if the amnesty he brought applied only to Vitalian, his sons and his officers.

'It is time to welcome the Thracian *foederati* back into the imperial army.'

Which basically meant regular food and pay, as well as a chance of fighting and spoils, which they would not be getting now. If it was a loose commitment it was sufficient.

'Your message will be sent and you may wait within the stockade if you wish.'

'We will wait where we are and I require that the general sends back to me an escort from his *comitatus*.'

Which meant his personal guard, not Gautoi. Once back with his own, Flavius increased the distance between his men and the stockade by several *stades*, and if they dismounted there was no relaxation. Two men were sent even further back with the pack animals while the remainder stood to with their spears at the ready, mounts by their side to give the impression they were prepared to give battle. Not that Flavius would do so; they might be matched in numbers but he doubted his Excubitors could stand in close combat against such fearsome warriors. Their horses were left saddled and ready for flight.

If the response was not swift there was no way of telling why. Was the man sent to advise him of this request just taking an interminable time or was the wily Vitalian deliberating, weighing the odds of refusal against agreement. Having been previously the victim of much imperial underhandedness he was bound to be cautious about allowing armed men in to his inner defences. The key was the name of the messenger; he knew Flavius and had some reason, it was hoped, to hold him as trustworthy.

The body of cavalry who appeared – their noisy hooves had signalled their coming – were recognisably *comitatus*, personal troops committed to their general not just for pay but also bound by ties of blood or deep loyalty.

Originally a German concept it was another sign of the way the Romans adopted the habits of their enemies, so that now every general had such a body, men who would never leave his side unless expressly ordered to do so. They could also be the shock troops of his army, for they tended to a discipline and cohesion rare in mounted warriors and were often led or thrown into battle at key moments.

The barrier was to allow through a single rider and once he was close Flavius recognised Marcus Vigilius, the man who had been his tribune on that first march to the capital. The greeting was cautious rather than friendly but the message was welcome: he was there to escort them to the main camp.

'How will we be received?' Flavius asked, once he and his soldiers were both reunited and mounted.

'Guardedly.'

'He can trust the word of the man who sent me.'

The response was sharp. 'Vitalian no longer trusts anyone!'

Handsome and from a rich patrician family, Vigilius had aged since last seen. There were lines in a face that had previously lacked blemish and the skin around the eyes was now creased and the whole had a weary look. Flavius wanted to ask how he fared and what had happened since they last met but Vigilius's attitude did not invite enquiry.

If his old tribune had aged that was as nothing to his leader. Vitalian seemed to have shrunk; though not tall, his once square shoulders were slightly rounded, the face cratered and the cheeks sunken, far from the commanding visage Flavius remembered. Also, he displayed an attitude that spoke of a burden too heavy to carry, not of a cause full of promise. With an acute eye, as they rode into the main encampment, Flavius had sensed decline; there was no feeling of fervour in the dull looks he got from those armed men he rode past and even the segment occupied by the camp followers, gimcrack huts and tents, seemed to be on the perish.

He was afforded no chance to address Vitalian alone; the rebel commander met the dismounted messenger flanked by two of his sons, Bouzes and Coutzes, now grown to full manhood and obviously, by their attitude and bearing, now raised to positions of command. This trio was surrounded by Vitalian's senior adherents, each of whom led their own groups, men Flavius also remembered from his last visit to this camp and it was evident that these were fewer in number than hitherto. Yet when Vitalian spoke, it was with a well-recalled strength of voice; if he looked diminished he did not sound so.

'So, my old comrade Justinus has grabbed the diadem?'

'Justin was the choice of the old imperial council, then presented to the citizens and acclaimed emperor in the Hippodrome.'

'By a mob that would be as quick to tear him limb from limb.'

'They were ecstatic, General. He is a good man and will make a fair-minded ruler.

'Justin?'

'His Imperial Highness wishes to be seen as the ruler for all citizens of empire, Greek and Roman.'

'Barbarians too?' Flavius nodded for it was a pointless question. 'Just as well, given his bloodline. You've changed, Flavius Belisarius, grown up.'

'If I may come to my purpose?'

There was a pause before Vitalian acceded to that, giving the impression that he knew what was coming – it could not be otherwise – and it not being fully welcome. A new emperor would only send a messenger on one resolve, to secure an end to this rebellion, and Flavius could understand the feeling that acceptance of such could be seen as capitulation.

But any impressions he had were of no account; he had his instructions and he delivered them as he should. The dispute on dogma was laid to rest, there would be no further repression of Chalcedony and any bishops or priests deposed from their diocese or churches by Anastasius would be reinstated forthwith. Vitalian and his officers should come to Constantinople where Justin would offer them the hand of amity as well as an amnesty for past misdeeds.

'Or lop off my head?' Vitalian grunted, his head turning to make the point to those around him. 'To be set on a pike atop the Golden Gate, perhaps.'

'If you believe that, then is it not my head that will adorn your gate? The Emperor wants this rebellion to end and not just for reasons of dogma but also of a remembered friendship. He desires to welcome you back into the fold where he assures me he would welcome your close counsel.'

'Assures you, Flavius? My, how you have risen, and of such tender years too.'

He's playing a part, Flavius thought, pretending to this gallery that there is an alternative when the whole impression of this encampment is one of a failed enterprise, it being nothing like it had been before, with boundless enthusiasm for a righteous cause. Even *in extremis*, when Hypatius and his army threatened, there had been an air of purpose. If he had inspired rebellion before, could Vitalian raise himself to do so again and for a fourth time? Flavius felt in his bones he could not.

'And if I decline?'

'General, I carry no threat. I have not been ordered to deal with such a consequence for the every simple reason that Justin cannot conceive it would be necessary. He invites you to the capital and will meet you in person.'

'Outside the walls?'

Flavius knew where that question came from; on the first investiture of Constantinople, Anastasius had invited

Vitalian and his officers to enter the city to treat for an accommodation. His subordinates had agreed and emerged impressed, safe and loaded with gold, as well as committed to the lifting of the siege. Vitalian had not, on the very good grounds that had he done so none of them would have emerged alive.

'That is for His Imperial Highness to decide.'

'It shall stick in my craw to address him so.'

That was a relief, for if it was not couched as such, it hinted at acceptance. 'I think you will find it easier than you suppose, for he wears his station lightly.'

'And when am I to be afforded this privilege?'

'It is at your convenience but it is hoped that you will return with me and my men.'

'Like a prisoner?'

He was playing to the crowd again and it was time to neutralise that. 'The offer of amnesty applies to you, sir, and those you choose to lead your men.'

'To counsel him?'

'Perhaps to fight for the empire and not against it.'

'Posts for all.'

'Possibly.'

'I would want that assured.'

'Then I repeat, meet Justin and let him be the one to convince you, since I cannot commit him to anything other than my mission allows.'

'You come in peace, Flavius, and will be treated as an honoured guest. But you must wait for your reply till I have discussed the offer with those who counsel me.' His head spun to one side. 'Vigilius, you have played host to this young man before, oblige me by doing so once more.'

'My men and their mounts? They must be catered for before I am given comfort.'

That got the first smile; he was a good general who took care of his own men and he was clearly happy that Flavius felt likewise. 'Vigilius, make it so.'

That his Excubitors were nervous was natural; they were ten men wearing imperial uniform, surrounded by what were still enemies and numerous, men who might not wait to ask what dogma they subscribed to before cutting their throats. Vigilius, once their horses had been fed and watered, with a couple of willing, young camp followers brought forth to groom them, led them to a communal tent, close to a long, low, wooden hut that was the general's own quarters, then surrounded that with guards. Once food was brought to them and that dished out Flavius could do no more.

It spoke a great deal that Vigilius then led him to a tent of his own, albeit a beautifully appointed one, richly furnished, he being the son of a wealthy senatorial family, already with guards outside as befitted his rank. To still be under canvas after all this time drove home how temporary the whole rebellion was. Vitalian might hold sway over much of Northern Thracia, he might be able to tax its citizens and recruit its men, dispense justice and enforce its edicts, but there was no permanence. What he had here counted for little; what he needed lay in Constantinople and try as he might he could not get at it.

Food was brought to this tent as well, to be eaten off fine plate and washed down with good wine. Flavius found himself subject to gentle interrogation and if there was some genuine interest in his time fighting on the Persian frontier that was only a mask to allow Vigilius to probe into his reasons for being here and what he had left behind. The tale he told of the rise of Justin to the purple was only partially true; the devious machinations of Petrus were not mentioned so it was made to sound as if there had been no opposition to the elevation and no alternative candidates.

His host had never met Justin/Justinus and had, it seemed, barely heard of him, so much delving arose related to the imperial character, and as Flavius described him he was aware that it sounded too good to be real. Yet the man was a good and successful soldier and so honest he had difficulty in telling a lie without blushing. He had been loyal to Anastasius when he was alive and revered his memory now, even if it was plain he had never agreed with the policy against Chalcedon.

'You make him sound like a paragon, Flavius.'

'If I do, then it is because I cannot do otherwise, which is what I expect you to tell Vitalian when he questions you as you have queried me.'

That got a wry smile. 'Are you going to tell me what I should say?'

'If I was it would be to this effect. The general who commands you has served with Justin before. If he remembers the man from then, you could not say better than that he is the very same now.' With that he stood. 'I must make a last visit to my men.'

'Then I must accompany you. The *foederati* will have been at their brew and that makes them dangerous.'

119

The vague noise of singing, which had penetrated the walls of the tent, became louder as they made their way through the encampment and being wistful it could hardly be reckoned as threatening. Vigilius explained if the Gautoi began their recitals with mournful ballads of their homeland, it would later turn to raucous renditions to the deeds of heroes and death to their foes.

'If it gets out of hand, then Vitalian must personally soothe them, for they are fiercely loyal to him as their leader.'

'No wonder he looks weary if he must attend to that every night.'

'It is not every night.'

The sound was a backdrop to the carrying out of his final task for the day. When Vigilius suggested he return to his quarters to sleep, Flavius politely refused; he would stay with those he led and share their cots, this before he commanded his men to keep their weapons close by them throughout the night, as would he.

If the passing of the hours of darkness were noisy there was no threat of danger. Flavius woke to the sound of the guards being changed. He rose from his cot to observe that being carried out and to reassure himself that it was men of the right kind. Morning brought food, the means to wash and shave as well as a message for him to attend upon Vitalian when he was ready.

Again the general surrounded himself with his inferior commanders, making Flavius wonder if there was a lack of complete trust. It was something of a thought to hold on to and possibly pass on as Vitalian, having rehearsed his grievances and theirs, finally got to the point.

'No man has the right to fight without just cause, therefore it is incumbent upon me to test the goodwill of my one-time comrade and see if his sudden rise has altered his character.' There was yet again that inclusive turn before he came back to look Flavius hard in the eye. 'But I will do so not only in the company of my sons and my officers but with my army at my back, and I will not accede to anything that favours me yet does not do likewise for them.'

'So be it,' Flavius replied.

Vitalian seemed to grow then, to become something of his old self, as in a loud and commanding voice he ordered that the camp be broken. 'We depart at dawn!'

'Which means that he is not at liberty to make a peace of his own. If he does, I think his officers will kill him.'

His audience with Justin was a private one; not even Petrus was in attendance, though Flavius had found enough time to relate to him what had occurred before being called into the private imperial chamber. He gave his report still with the muck of several days march upon him, having come south with Vitalian to only part company when the rebel army was outside the walls and setting up yet again a siege camp, albeit their numbers made such a notion risible.

'Should I go out to meet him?'

'I doubt he will enter the city, but if you do so, Highness, I would take as many archers as you can muster.'

'No,' Justin mused. 'I can see why you think it wise, Flavius, but I am a soldier still. To get what I want means the taking of risks, though I will make sure I am on a fleet-of-foot horse.

If there is trickery, it is best shown without the walls. Once inside it would be impossible to detect.'

That took Flavius back to that hurried conversation with Petrus who, if he had listened, was also full of enough worry and barely suppressed anger to speak. Justin was having trouble imposing himself on the officials he had inherited from Anastasius and the palace was seething with scheming, his nephew certain that some were openly plotting against the imperial person, furious that he would not do what was necessary.

'He will not remove them?' Flavius had asked.

'That is not how you deal with treachery. When you are faced with a snake, the best way to rid yourself of it is to cut off its head, but what does my uncle do? He wants to introduce another reptile into his presence and promises to hold him close.'

Justin did not go out to meet Vitalian entirely naked; he deployed the gloriously accoutred *Scholae Palatinae*, a unit that revelled in the opportunity to display themselves and appear as what they should have been: an effective imperial mounted bodyguard, to which Petrus remarked, 'God help us if it all if goes wrong, because those overperfumed oafs will not.'

They were halted halfway between the walls and the point at which Vitalian waited, while Justin rode on with only Flavius Belisarius and a *decharchia* of Excubitors to protect his person. When close he dismounted and Vitalian responded likewise, the two closing to engage in a private conversation. No one was sure of what was being said for there seemed no physical sign of either amity or dispute.

Finally, Vitalian took a step back, to spin round and stride out to close with and face his troops. The distance meant the words he used to address them were rendered indistinct to the likes of Flavius, but the final effect, if it was some time in coming, was stunning. As one, the entire rebellious army withdrew their swords then knelt, each one held out in submission. Vitalian did likewise until Justin closed the gap and raised him up to be taken in a tight and brotherly embrace.

The cheers were from the walls as well as from those Vitalian had led there and they lasted all the way through the Golden Gate and up the Triumphal Way as, on foot, Justin led his old comrade to his palace. It hardly seemed to matter that his army, officers included, was left outside.

CHAPTER NINE

It was two months before Vitalian's men were deployed on the Persian frontier, eight weeks in which the first two were spent outside of the walls of Constantinople. If allowed to enter it was in small groups and that applied even to the officers, so it was some time before Flavius was able to return hospitality to Vigilius. Not that he had him to himself; his colleagues in the Excubitor officers' quarters were keen to quiz this guest who had campaigned for nearly three years in a less than perfect army.

More impressive was the way Justin treated the one-time rebel commander; Vitalian was raised to senatorial rank and granted a pension, his sons Bouzes and Coutzes promised favour and advancement in the offices of empire. For those

125

who attended the meeting of the imperial council it must have been strange to find him not only present but listened to when he spoke, often to disagree with the Emperor, a way of behaviour most reckoned by long experience to be hazardous. They voiced their disagreements elsewhere and in private.

Vitalian's army was fed and paid as would be any unit of the imperial army, in this case the only difference being that it was prompt in delivery for it was overseen by Justin personally and not left to officials who seemed to behave, when it came to paying soldiers, as if they were disbursing their own money. The Emperor wanted no trouble from disgruntled *foederati* outside his walls.

'So you are to come with us, Flavius?' Vigilius asked.

'I am.'

'And we are now of like rank?'

'Does that cause resentment?'

'Not with me but I daresay there are those who see how young you are and wonder how you can achieve the title of *tribunos* so quickly.'

'Precocious ability,' Flavius responded, though with enough of a grin to ensure it was not to be taken seriously.

'Our newly elevated ruler obviously has great faith in you?'

'Why do you never call him Emperor? I have heard you use every other possible word to refer to Justin but not that.' It was the fact that Vigilius blushed and was plainly uncomfortable that made Flavius press the point. 'Is it that you think him unfitted to the office?'

'There must be many who do.'

'Must?'

'Where has he come from, Flavius? And is it fitting that a man who cannot read or write should rule over men who are trained in the arts of composition and rhetoric?'

'Arts which they employ to confuse.'

'These are matters that are beyond me.'

Sensing a desire not to get embroiled in a discussion that must, by definition, be insulting to his host, Vigilius changed the subject and began to talk about possible trouble on the frontier. If he was aware that he left Flavius feeling uncomfortable it did not show; perhaps his patrician upbringing had provided him with a carapace of protection against discomfiture.

'The Gautoi will not react well to the heat.'

'We are past high summer now and by the time we reach the border we may face rain and even snow so they are more likely to be at home than you or I.'

'No fighting for a time, then?'

'Not unless the Sassanids change their ways.'

The subject that Vigilius was keen to avoid was one Flavius took up with Petrus later the same day. The patrician class had never really supported even Anastasius, who had come to his eminence through the bedchamber of his predecessor's widow, but they were probably even less enamoured of Justin. What worried the nephew was the increasingly open way those who held positions at the palace were making their disdain known.

'A situation I could end within a day if he would allow me to.'

'He will take you back into his confidence soon I am sure.'

'Don't patronise me, Flavius,' Petrus spat back.

'I didn't mean it that way. If your uncle is foundering he cannot but be aware of it and who can he trust except you to remedy that?'

'Perhaps he will elevate Vitalian,' was the equally jaundiced response. 'From what I am told he allows that stoat much licence.'

There was no point in even seeking to refute that description or to say that Justin probably reposed more trust in the views of a fellow soldier than he did in men who had risen to prominence through the known to be corrupt imperial bureaucracy, a body he had been unhappily observing for years.

'He certainly trusts you now more than he does me.'

'For which I do not accept any blame. And can I say that I was not pleased to be some cog in your scheming, either.'

'Could I have trusted you to stay silent?'

'You will never know, Petrus, because you never tried.'

'You're too like my uncle.'

'Thank you for that. If it is a fault to you it is a compliment to me.'

Flavius was afforded another private audience with Justin before he departed for Asia Minor and one in which, given he had a licence to speak granted to few, he decided to plead the case of Petrus, not because he had forgiven him but because if Justin was having difficulty then his nephew was, even as a habitual intriguer, the person he could most rely on.

'Not an opinion my wife would share.'

Tempted to respond by pointing out that pillow politics were a bad idea, Flavius asked instead how the lady was adjusting to being the Empress Euphemia.

'She never took to living in the palace before, as you know, but she seems content now that we occupy the imperial apartments and no one dare look down their nose at her.'

'Apartments within which she proffers to you political advice?'

'Careful, young man! That is not a territory to stray into.'

Flavius did not know Euphemia well but he was aware she was strong of mind, a person not afraid to express her opinions and she would be doing that to her spouse regardless of his new eminence. She was also deeply religious, with a particular fondness for the saint whose name she had adopted. Her lack of regard for her nephew sprang from a deep and genuine piety; Petrus appeared too cynical for her, a man who used religion rather than adhering to it.

Justin too was religious but without being so fervent as to be blinded. He came across as one who trusted God to see into men's souls and make his decisions as to the rightness of their beliefs, hence his pardoning of Vitalian, not to mention the way he had embraced him, and not only physically. Was he too trusting? Did he, Flavius, have the right to pronounce upon such a matter? If Justin had become like a surrogate father to him it was his real parent that counted now. Decimus Belisarius had been adamant that a true Roman never wavered from the need to speak truth to the powerful.

'It must be confusing to go from *comes Excubitorum* to where you are now, Highness.'

'Such formality, Flavius, when we are alone?'

'Would it trouble you to know that I have concern for you, for the burden you carry?'

Justin favoured him with an avuncular smile. 'If you have a worry, Flavius, make it that you survive another bout with the Sassanid.'

'I would not presume to advise you—'

'But you are about to,' came the sharp interruption.

'Petrus?'

'We are back to that?'

Aware that he was either causing discomfort or sailing very close to the wind, probably both, Flavius spoke with some haste. 'He is committed to you.'

'He is committed to himself.'

'Do they not complement each other?' That got a grunt. 'He served you well previously and he would do so again if you will allow him.'

'A period in the wilderness will do him no harm, it might even temper his behaviour, especially in the matter of his social life.'

Justin did not have to say where that objection came from but it did confirm to him that the Empress was putting her stamp on the way in which things were run.

'He fears for you.' The look that got obliged that he add something. 'And he has said so.'

'Let him fear for himself for I am not beyond behaving in a manner he would approve of.'

Flavius took that for what it was, an empty gesture;

Justin would never threaten or harm his own blood. 'Can you test him, give him a chance to show you what he can do to ease your burden, to take the weight off your shoulders?'

'They are broad enough.'

By the tone of that response Flavius knew that to plead more would achieve nothing. He had done his best and adding more might risk his own standing with a man he had come close to loving.

'I hope you will bless me as we set out on campaign.'

'I will bless you, Flavius, even as I will miss you. Petrus does not know what he has in his advocate.'

It was often the case that when trouble began to brew the cause was hidden from the people destined to deal with it. Messengers had come from Constantinople warning of the need for extra preparedness so the frontier army knew that the Sassanids were stirring, not that they were entirely unaware. Lacauris, the *magister militum per Orientem*, had his own informants, mostly traders who criss-crossed the borders and no doubt gave similar service to the Kavadh or his satrap in Nisibis regarding the Romans.

Discussion of such matters did not filter down to the rank of *tribunos*; they were given orders to march and could do no more than obey. Once more the pillars that marked the boundary of the empire set the point beyond which Lacauris had no desire they should go, which was military folly to more than Flavius, granting as it did their potential enemy the time to choose when to act. It was the general opinion that, if they were not to cross into Sassanid territory, it would have been better to stay at Dara and invite an attack on ground they could easily protect.

The Roman army were encamped on an open plain severely lacking in the kind of features required for a defensive battle. There were few hills and no river on which they could secure one flank. Added to that they were facing the rising sun, which meant any attack at dawn would come with the sun at the Sassanid rear and be blinding to the Romans. If Flavius chafed at having no part in the higher decision-making, he was at least sure the cavalry he commanded would behave well for he had trained them rigorously.

As a military force, mounted soldiers had several inherent problems as well as certain advantages. In the latter case they could move from one point in a battle to another quickly, and if so desired visibly, thus disrupting enemy plans. In addition they could be sent in as shock troops to break up an attack. The problem lay in the truth that once released into the fight they became impossible to control and were usually lost as a continuing fighting force, so a wise general husbanded his horsemen until he knew they could be effective.

There was a certain stateliness to the way the Sassanid army deployed; it was done without haste, a great cloud of dust, as if they were rehearsing to fight rather than preparing to engage in one, this based on the certain knowledge that the Romans would not advance into their territory, for if they had determined to do so it would have happened already. As usual messages were exchanged, the Sassanids inviting their foes to quit the field and admit the battle lost before it had even begun, and in addition demanding promises that Constantinople pay high sums for their folly.

Lacauris might hold the office of *magister militum* but it had long been a tradition in imperial armies to split the command between two generals on what was seen as the sound reason of nullifying the kind of risk that had been inherent when emperors personally led their forces. One strong-headed leader could lose more than a battle, he could risk the empire, but in addition to that there was the knowledge that a too successful fighting man could become a threat.

The history of Rome was replete, from the days of Julius Caesar onwards, of men who had finished a successful campaign only to turn on those on whose behalf they had been fighting in a bid for personal power. To protect against both, control was split, which meant that any tactics employed had to be agreed upon as a wise course of action.

Thus Lacauris had to consult with his co-commander, Restines, as to how to draw up his forces and that took time. Eventually the army deployed with the mass of infantry in the centre, the archers behind them and the cavalry, Flavius included, holding the right wing. The left was allotted to the forces once led by Vitalian and at the front of that body stood the Gautoi *foederati*. If they had arrived in Mesopotamia and relished the winter they were less comfortable now in late spring rapidly turning to hot summer, and Vigilius, who commanded them, had arranged for great urns of water to be added to their baggage train so they could use it to cool themselves as well as quench what seemed a permanent thirst.

Perozes, the Sassanid general, had greater numbers but

not in such strength as to easily overwhelm the Roman position, so he sent forward his centre to engage and fix the Roman infantry. If the battlefield was devoid of hills it was not without rising ground and Flavius was sat on a mound that had a view of the way matters were developing. It was his impression that the enemy were not pressing evenly along their whole front; the greater pressure seemed to be on the point at which the infantry adjoined the *foederati*.

It was testament to the ability of Vigilius that he sensed this and began to reinforce his own right until obviously commanded to cease the manoeuvre and return to his original formation, at which point Perozes released the weapon most feared by the Romans, his horse archers. These men, Armenian mercenaries, rode short and agile ponies and operated as a fast-moving mobile force.

They were no more disciplined than any other mounted troops but they did not have to be: their task was to so harass enemy formations by stinging attacks with flights of arrows that they began to lose their cohesion. That was what began to happen to the *foederati*, who were assailed not just from their front but on their flank, which left any man holding a protective shield in doubt as to from where the threat was coming.

Now the pressure on the right of centre began to tell for the Sassanids as some of their spearmen began to break into a gap that had appeared on the left of the Roman infantry, which led to an order that half the cavalry should move across the rear of the army to shore up that flank and if possible drive into the enemy infantry and break up their assault. Flavius being part of that deployment felt the surge that comes to any young man at the prospect of actual battle.

The problem was the movement was visible to the enemy and Perozes moved his own cavalry to mitigate the threat. By the time Flavius and his compatriots were able to deploy they found themselves facing their own kind, and to drive into the flank of the enemy infantry would expose their own left to a counter-assault, while to merely charge might drive back the enemy but it would deprive the Romans of one of their major assets.

That was when the Armenian horse archers reappeared, their quivers replenished and their ponies still eager to run. Facing them were the drawn-up and static Roman cavalry, which presented a wonderful target to disrupt, especially since many of their arrows wounded unbarded horses, not men who had shields and mail armour. Those struck naturally became hard to control, some bending to their knees while others reared up and began to run amok, with their riders more intent on maintaining their seat than their fighting positions.

'We should charge them,' Flavius said.

This was addressed to no one in particular, for he could sense that to stand and just receive this assault was the worst of two evils and if it continued the Roman cavalry would lose all cohesion and be rendered ineffective. Lacauris and Restines must have realised the same and they moved their archers to back up the *foederati* who, furious at being so stung, were ordered to advance at an angle which would press in on the flank of the enemy infantry, the very tactic that Vigilius had been forced to abandon.

Suddenly the horse archers, quivers empty again, were gone and with much shouting and the occasional slaughter of a screeching horse the Roman cavalry got into some form of fighting order again, just in time to advance and block the mounted Sassanids who had begun to advance on the *foederati* flank.

Diomedes, the man in command of this portion of the mounted Roman forces, made no attempt to impose order and it was with some difficulty that Flavius avoided his own three-hundred-strong *command* from joining in the melee of a general charge. This was what he had trained for and his aim was simple: to keep his men in some kind of order so that when they made contact with the enemy they did so as a body and with maximum impact.

In this objective he was only partially successful but at least he fared better than his fellow tribunes, many of whom seemed to behave as though the wild yells they were uttering as they urged their men on would be enough to destroy their opponents. It was as well the Sassanid cavalry commander had as little control as the Romans, the result being that when the forces met it was usually one on one. Only the group led by Flavius had any great impact and he knew it to be marginal for they were far from the formation he had sought to create.

What he did have was a core of his troopers who had fully imbibed his ideas and they formed a phalanx of cavalry that drove into the enemy with great effect, each man able to protect at least one of his fellows and, should the lead horseman be held up – it was not always their commander – to drive forward and break the logjam. In the end it was too effective as Flavius found he had led his core right through the enemy, which left them in danger of being isolated.

It was necessary to wheel and fight his way back to rejoin his own side, now breaking off the fight on blown horses and with many wounded to retire over a field littered with dead or dying men and horses. The horns were blowing furiously from both sides of the battlefield as an action which had reached stalemate was discontinued, both sides later arranging a truce so that their casualties could be collected.

That night, around blazing fires, Flavius Belisarius listened to much boastful talk of the deeds his fellows had performed and what they would do on the morrow when the fight was resumed. If they were truthful in that they were disappointed – for Lacauris had decided that it was better to talk than fight and once they had commenced a parley, no doubt on instructions from Constantinople, it was decided that it was better to pay a bounty in talents of gold to Kavadh for peace rather than to engage in all-out war.

Flavius, along with the rest of the Roman army, retired once more to Dara to what was, in essence, boring garrison duty.

CHAPTER TEN

Flavius only found out why the border had flared up into that desultory campaign on his return to the capital: he also found Petrus once more acting as a close advisor to Justin in a relationship with as many strains as agreements. The star of Euphemia had waned and his had risen as Justin found the task of ruling the empire, especially the greedy and fractious bureaucracy, increasingly difficult; as Petrus pointed out, with his uncle being subjected to all sorts of obfuscation and downright intrigue in pursuit of personal gain, his pious wife was ill-equipped to deal with it and had been for some time.

'But most of all he needed sound advice to respond to the offer from Kavadh, for it was clear some of his other advisors had been bribed by the Sassanids to favour it.'

'An offer of what?'

'Eternal peace.'

'How many times has Rome been offered that, Petrus!'

'Scoff if you will but it may be this time he meant it. Kavadh does not easily hold his throne, you know, and he came by it by deposing another. He had lots of enemies, some very powerful, as well as allies to keep loyal.'

'Both of whom he pays off with the gold we gift him.'

'It works.'

'It's a wound dressing not a solution.'

'My, Flavius, have you become the wit?'

'You know I'm right.'

'What else would you have us do? Fight Kavadh to a bloody finish and take control of lands we cannot hold? What would we then face, the same troubles he has internally and on his eastern and southern borders? It is too big a meal to swallow.'

'Alexander not only swallowed Persia, he crossed the Indus too.'

That got a wry look from Petrus, implying it was meaningless to look back to the glories of the ancient Macedonians, that Flavius should know the truth as well as anyone. The Eastern Roman Empire lacked the resources to inflict a complete defeat on the Sassanids of Persia, indeed it was a task that had been beyond the Roman Empire at the height of its powers. All of the fighting on the eastern border had been and was, at its root, defensive and that had really been the situation for centuries. Frustrating it might be for an ambitious soldier, but it was a fact.

'What else did that devil offer, eternal peace being so common when his coffers are bare?'

'His son and heir, Khosrau, as hostage. The boy is coming up ten and it was suggested he would benefit from a Roman education here in Constantinople.'

That made Flavius sit up; if true it was serious, not as had been the case from what he had heard on the border and indeed before he ever got there; the Sassanids made peace for money and only for a period until they needed more.

'We refused.'

'We?'

'I advised my uncle, he finally agreed.'

'But surely if Kavadh's heir was in Constantinople?'

'He would not break the peace?' Petrus asked, but it was not really a question. 'Part of the offer was that Justin should adopt Khosrau.'

'That confuses me.'

'It did my uncle till I pointed out the flaw.'

'Which is?'

'Justin has no children. To adopt Khosrau would technically make him the imperial heir as well as the Sassanid. It was that advice that got me back into my uncle's confidence, given most others counselling him, and I include his wife, were too stupid or too compromised with gold to see where it might lead.'

'No one in the empire would accept a Sassanid to succeed Justin.'

'How naïve you are, Flavius. How many of the men around my uncle secretly harbour a desire to take the diadem when he, God forbid, dies? And if they cannot have the purple for themselves then the promotion of another and a chance to be the power behind the throne will serve. Do you really think to them it matters where the candidate comes from when we have had upstart Isaurians with Zeno and now an Illyrian whom they hold to be a barbarian.'

'From within the boundaries of empire.'

'Do you really think that would matter?'

Flavius got no chance to respond, Petrus was off tugging at his hair as he paced back and forth, cursing the ambition of men who he would not admit to being his rivals, just as he would not admit to his own aspirations. Justin was correct when he insisted his nephew was out for his own ends; the one unknown was how he would deal with it, for being childless and, barring a second marriage to a much younger woman, something he had never shown any signs of contemplating, he would remain so.

'How is the health of the Empress Euphemia?' Flavius enquired, mischievously, for if he could deduce what was needed to create a succession, namely her demise prior to a new consort, it was certain Petrus could too.

'Robust, God be praised,' came the fulsome reply.

Petrus was obviously on the horns of a dilemma with that lady, part of him wanting her and any influence she might still have out of the way, the other the fear of a sudden illness carrying her off and leaving the field clear for someone to replace her. Not that he would have eschewed precautions; there was probably some young and fertile woman already listed in the Sabbatius mind to take on the role. On second thoughts, she would be young and infertile.

'When my view finally prevailed and the suggestion was formally rebuffed, Kavadh started to assemble his army once more to counter the insult.'

'And got his bribe again,' Flavius sighed. 'It should not be so easy.'

'Perhaps, one day it will not be so.'

Looking for further explanation Flavius was left in limbo; all he had was that look on the face of the imperial nephew that hinted at plans laid that would be long in coming to fruition, that quickly masked by another more calculating.

'Come, Flavius, we must go down to the docks and some entertainment. Back from the wilds of Mesopotamia you will be in need of comfort of a kind I hardly believe can exist out there.'

'Don't be so sure, Petrus,' came the reply as Flavius stood to comply. 'If you have not known the sweetness of an Arab concubine do not dismiss it so.'

'You savoured some?'

'Of course.'

'Flavius, you're as big a rogue as I am.'

'Petrus, no one is as big a rogue as you.'

'Have you met this dancing girl of his yet, the one I am told he is so very enamoured of?'

Justin and Flavius were walking together on the sward that filled the area between the imperial palace and the walls abutting the Propontis, a place where the Emperor regularly took exercise. And he was striding out, still fit even in his eighth decade of life and the fourth of his reign, with an expert eye cast at those Excubitors exercising their military skills in the open spaces between the trees, swordplay and spear work accompanied by much shouting from instructors.

The way the question was posed underlined it was an awkward one. Flavius thought for a moment to say no, not sure if an admission of the truth would lead him into deep waters. Yet on reflection he could not easily lie to this man and he doubted his denial would be believed. Justin had any number of sources of information and he might well know of any visits both he and Petrus had made to the dockside fleshpots.

'Theodora?'

'I am told that is her name,' came a jaundiced response.

And not one you like to utter, Flavius thought. He had met the lady, if she could be called that, in the company of Petrus in his favoured dockside tavern-cum-brothel, one run by a singularly corpulent and debased Egyptian. Theodora was one of his troupe of entertainers, a quite athletic dancer, able to juggle, good with snakes and a fine singer. She was striking to look at, the flesh she readily bared much admired by the customers of the place, and bold in her person.

If she lacked education, which Flavius had to suppose would be the case, Theodora did not lack for wit or a kind of devious charm and she had certainly worked her wiles on the imperial nephew. Enamoured was too soft a word; Petrus was besotted to the point of being indifferent to possible flaws as well as the allure of any of the other dancers, and these were women he had regularly bedded, either alone or in various combinations some of which, he suspected, would have included Theodora. The lady was not regarded for her chastity.

She resented the clear regard Petrus had for him; if it was subtle, the way she sought to diminish him had become apparent at the time, even more in recollection. In the morning light Flavius had remembered the small, seemingly humorous asides that were on the cusp of being affronts, looks and words with double meanings that bordered on the salacious, designed, he thought, to make her smitten paramour jealous, not attempts at seduction but wedges to drive them apart.

Even aware of that it was hard not to be tempted for she was a beauty – and it was not just the stunning looks that made her attractive, it was her quick wits and a degree of presence and natural grace not normally afforded to those of her background, which was much chequered. Petrus was not the first man to have her sole attention; she seemingly had been the paramour of more than one other man.

'He has asked if I would permit him to marry her.'

'What!'

'You're right to be shocked. If the Sabbatius name is not amongst the most elevated it is high enough to make such a thing unthinkable. His mother would crucify me.'

'Quite apart from his being your nephew.'

It was the measure of Justin the man that he blushed at that; he never wished to be thought of as grand, even when clad in purple and gold. 'I suppose it will pass. We have all been struck by that singular arrow called lust at some time, and such a passion usually burns out.'

'Of course,' Flavius replied, his tone guarded.

He was far from sure that Justin was right, either, about everyone being subject to such a thunderbolt; he never had and it gave him cause to wonder when and who had struck his mentor, an event that would have had to have preceded his marriage. Nor was he convinced regarding Petrus, and it was not just the way he was behaving; the Theodora he had met and recalled on waking was not one to extract her claws once they were firmly in the Sabbatius flesh.

'Anyway, that must be left to time. Tell me about your adventures.'

'What adventures? We marched up and down the border, we trained and we fought one battle that ended with no fanfares for anyone.'

'How do you think the men in command behaved?'

'Well,' came the immediate response.

'Do not confuse loyalty to those you have served under with your duty to me Flavius.' There was no mistaking the change of tone; Justin had gone in a blink from surrogate father to imperial master. 'Was it a battle we could or should have won?'

The reply came after a lengthy pause. 'Not with what we possess.'

'Explain.'

'We lack a weapon to drive off their horse archers, who have a bad effect on any body of troops exposed to their fire. Yes, they can be compelled to retire by cavalry but once they have gone in pursuit of these Armenians, then they are as good as lost to the men who command them and they must continue the battle without one of their main components. I did formulate a way that might be countered but I hesitate to suggest it to even you.'

'Who else would you suggest it to?'

'The military commanders.'

'Who would have to come to me, so you may as well bypass that and speak up.'

'It is not a wholly formed idea.'

Justin stopped abruptly, forcing Flavius to do likewise, and given he was half a head taller, the way he was looking down as his young protégé showed he was irritated and that was amplified by his tone of voice.

'If you have thought on this Flavius, you will have done so assiduously. If you do not know to avoid dancing around the bushes with me then I wonder if you have any knowledge of my person at all.'

'It may be foolish.'

Justin began to walk again, forcing Flavius to scurry to catch up and match his longer stride, speaking over his shoulder. 'If it is, I will let you down with gentleness.'

'In everything we have done we Romans copy our enemies.'

'No arrogance there, eh?' Justin hooted. 'A thousand years of success in war dismissed in a sentence.'

'Did we not follow the Huns when it came to fighting on horseback?' That got a nod. 'Yet it is the Sassanids who have taken their bows and allied them to horsemen who can use them and move simultaneously.'

It was necessary for the sake of clarity that Flavius explain the effect of those tactics in an actual battle – the confusion and the effect it had on formations ready to do as required by their commanders – not because an old soldier who had faced the same enemy needed it but to set up his argument for a different kind of mounted force.

'One that needs to be both disciplined and flexible.'

'Are those two aims not mutually exclusive?'

'What if the horses were not ponies and swift but heavier beasts, with barding on their chests and flanks to protect them against arrows and spear thrusts.'

'Which would slow them.'

'Speed is not the only aim. Cohesion and impact are. I think we can improve on the Sassanid cataphracts with the use of speedier and specially trained horses.'

The younger voice took on the air of a preacher then, as he added the details of what he had in mind. 'A unit of heavy cavalry armed with bows as well as spears, well protected both in themselves and their horses, able to attack enemy infantry like a wall of flesh and bone, and drive into their formation having assailed them first with arrows.'

'And a mounted foe?'

'They would have nothing to fear from ordinary cavalry and, if need be, they would have the ability to engage and drive off enemy horse archers without indulging in a furious chase that takes them out of the battle.'

'Numbers?'

'One *numerus* to begin.'

'Horses?'

'There are many of the kind we need in the Cappadocian herds, as I found out on the way home.'

'Armour and barding?'

'Specially designed, again lighter than the cataphracts to assist with speed. I can show you some drawings I have made but I would need to go to the imperial factories and talk with those who will be required to make what is needed. Weapons we have already and all they will require is to be adapted.'

'And you think, Flavius, this will win us our battles.'

'I would be happy, Highness, to start by not losing one. The only reason we did not do so recently is that the Sassanid general did not press to do so. Had he attacked the second day I suspect we would have been obliged to flee for the safety of Dara.'

'What you suggest sounds to be heavy on cost. Three hundred men, twice as many mounts, and special equipment and I think I can assume that is just the beginning—'

'Whatever it costs must be less than the talents we send as subventions to Kavadh.'

'How long will you require?'

'Perhaps a year of training. As to proof, that is in the hands of others. Only an enemy can validate what I believe.'

'Many will see it as no more than a chance to enrich yourself.'

The response was too sharp to be addressed to an emperor, regardless of how high the speaker was held in esteem. 'I hope that you are not amongst them!'

'We are alone, Flavius, which is just as well, is it not?'

'Forgive me, Highness, if I speak too boldly. It is not an accusation I can lightly accept for it besmirches not only my name but that of my family.'

The mention of that seemed to mollify Justin. At least

it produced a wilful smile. 'Did your father ever tell you of how we came to Constantinople?'

Decimus had, many times, but his son felt it politic to imply he had not and because he did so Justin began reminiscing; how they had fled a serious barbarian invasion of Illyricum, four stalwarts who thought they had the world at their feet, entering a city where the streets were paved with gold and one in which such paragons must both conquer and find wealth.

'Not even lead did we find, Flavius. We encountered indifference and near starvation, for the people of Constantinople are not kind to strangers. Joining the army was a way to survive and, if I am now the only one left alive, it served us well.'

'I found the same indifference myself when I came here.'

Justin stopped and looked back towards the Great Palace, at the cream stones of the outer walls and at the eastern end the earthquake-damaged dome of the church of St Sophia.

'And who would have thought it would end like this? My wife and I say prayers every night for those we have loved and lost, but I tell you that your father holds a special place in mine. We were as close once as brothers.'

Seeing the eyes of the young man before him begin to well up, Justin added, to mitigate his obvious anguish, 'Gather your men and horses, Flavius, and let us see if we can forge the weapon you describe.'

It took more than a year; there seemed not one member of the military or imperial bureaucracy inclined to aid him, quite the reverse. They set out to obstruct him by diverting the funds he needed or holding up his new equipment in the imperial arms factories, standing proof that most men of high rank were more concerned with their place and their own purse than with the needs of the empire.

Only when Justin interceded did matters improve, but the travails of one young man did not figure large in the cares of the state and when he appealed to Petrus he found him to be indifferent to the task upon which he was engaged and overdistracted by his private affairs. Still enamoured of Theodora, Petrus had removed her from her less than salubrious circumstances as an entertainer and more besides.

She and some of her companions were now accommodated in a wing of the palace well away from the imperial apartments and the Empress Euphemia, a lady now in poor health but still strong in her piety and never one to be inclined to welcome the less than chaste daughter of a circus acrobat into her presence.

Not that Flavius saw much of either; all of his time was now spent on the task at hand. The horses had been gathered and broken in, as had the men he needed, of a size and muscular ability to command exceptionally strong and often stubborn mounts. The armour and weapons were coming, if slowly, while ideas that had seemed sound at first needed to be modified, not least the bow used by his shock cavalry, the Hunnish model being refined to be more balanced in its construction.

Even with everything in place the training had to be instituted in the open fields outside Galatea, put to the test and refined to the point where every man in charge of a *decharchia* could both command his own men and act in concert with every other group, to either combine or act independently as circumstances demanded in response to a set of horn-blown commands. Time spent on the other side of the Bosphorus was rare.

The news of the demise of Euphemia, of a wasting fever, brought him hurrying back to Constantinople for the ceremonies of burial and attendance at the Masses said for her soul. It was a testament to her innate goodness and the many works of charity she had performed since becoming empress that he found not just a household in mourning but a whole city. He brought his new cavalry with him, to join in the parade that followed the catafalque to her place of interment, a spacious sarcophagus commissioned by Justin, his beautifully caparisoned men a wonder to the assembled crowds, who might have cheered on a less solemn occasion.

Naturally, Euphemia's nephew was well to the fore amongst her mourners, just behind his parents and his uncle; more surprising to Flavius was the fact that he was accompanied by Theodora who, if she was overawed by the company in which she now found herself, managed to hide it well. He was sure he could see in her eye that she felt she was where she belonged.

CHAPTER ELEVEN

If Theodora had been a presence in the palace she had, up until now, been a discreet one. But from the day that the senate met in all its panoply – most guessed what was coming – she moved into the light. As soon as the necessary document was signed, Petrus, now to be known as Justinian in honour of his uncle, had married her, which meant on the day she observed to the anointing of her husband as co-Emperor and acknowledged Imperial Heir, Theodora was the sole occupant of the office of Empress.

The ceremony, albeit glittering, was relatively brief and entirely lacking in objections – that came as no surprise: it had been ever thus since the time of Augustus. The Senate never argued with the *Imperator*: they had only one recourse to action that would bring about change and that was bloody elimination of a man who always had soldiers to do his bidding.

There had to be speeches, first from Justinian promising to act for the good of all, to praise and reward virtue while bearing down on evildoing and deception. That he was not believed made no difference to the men who followed, to praise the sagacity of Justin in ensuring a peaceful handover of power while welcoming the elevation of his nephew as not just the continuation of a golden age but an opportunity to enhance and extend that rare occurrence.

Watching Petrus/Justinian was an entertaining game with which to stave off boredom as Flavius, heading the imperial guard detail, sought to discern behind that new imperial mask what the man was really thinking. If there was expression, it was so well hidden that a moving eyelash acted as evidence of feeling, even when men who saw themselves as rivals spouted paeans of praise that in their hypocrisy were grotesque.

The three nephews of Anastasius, who had some claim to the throne that Justin had occupied, were just as loud in their praises, with Hypatius speaking first, followed by his two cousins, Probus and Pompeius, who sought to outdo him and each other in grovelling. If anything indicated that all power in the empire issued from one source it was this fawning display; this trio, indeed everyone in the chamber, wanted positions from which they could enrich themselves and that could only come from imperial favour.

Vitalian excelled even them when it came to flattery, which led Flavius, once a soldier in his rebel army, to wonder how such a previously plain-spoken fellow could become so corrupted by merely spending a few years at court. He was, of course, motivated by the same concern, both for himself and his family; his two older sons now enjoyed the rank of *dux* in the two Phoenician provinces and had become prosperous because of it, while the youngest had been inducted into the *Scholae Palatinae*.

Halfway through the ceremony it was plain Justin's mind had clouded; once more he had the air of someone at a complete loss to know where he was or what was happening and that lasted through many a sycophantic peroration, with Flavius now wondering why his nephew did not curtail the speeches until the truth dawned on him. This public demonstration of Justin's affliction suited the new joint ruler very well; let those who occupied the great offices of state see where they must come if they required permission to initiate anything or even act on present procedures.

Only when Justin came back to lucidity did Petrus/Justinian whisper to him and the import was plain, since his uncle called forward Theodora so she could occupy the throne formerly used by Euphemia, which was a perfect way of announcing that one particular Law of Constantine was repealed, the one debarring marriages between patrician and those from a lower class. His voice seemed to gather some of its old strength as he put that into words.

'For too long men of talent have been unable to create a life howsoever they wish, for too long able people of the wrong class, apart from eunuchs, have been blocked from advancement. From this day on my nephew and I will wish to see ancient rank play no part in the selection of the officials of empire, military or civilian. Opportunity will thus be open to all.'

Given the nature of his audience, the fact that such an announcement sent up a hum of protest was hardly surprising; high-born men accustomed to competing with each other for lucrative offices were being told that from henceforth they would have to also contend with those outside a class that had husbanded its rights for a millennium.

'In discussion with my heir,' Justin continued, 'I have agreed that no precipitous changes will be made to the imperial bureaucracy. But we will, from this day on and in consultation, be seeking to find ways of introducing new blood.'

Justinian had a triumphant expression on his face now and it was not a benign one. He sat forward on his throne, reaching out at the same time to take Theodora's hand, his thoughts so obvious they might as well have been spoken. It addressed his feelings about these men gathered: you have tried to run rings round my uncle – do not be so foolish as to attempt the same trick on me!

Justin stood, his nephew and his wife doing likewise, which obliged the whole assembly to bow, probably just as well given the looks of hate being directed at a person they saw as no more than a low-born whore. Time spent like that allowed them to compose their features before they once more raised their heads, to gaze upon the imperial trio with looks of fabricated respect. As they departed, Flavius and his Excubitor bodyguard fell in behind them, to escort the party back to the now expanded imperial suite.

'So now, how do I address you?' Flavius asked, once his men had been deployed and he was alone with the new imperial couple.

The response came with a sly smile. 'Does Highness stick in your craw, Flavius?'

'I admit it will be hard, but I managed with your uncle, so I daresay I can abide the usage with you.'

'Just as long as you do not use his given name of Petrus!'

Flavius turned to face Theodora, to come under the gaze of a pair of near black eyes which were well short of affection, a reflection of the tone she had just employed.

'A right, I am sure, Lady, you will reserve to yourself?'

'What I choose to reserve to myself is no concern of yours, Flavius Belisarius.'

'My dear,' her husband interjected, 'he is my friend. I was merely jesting, he may address me as he wishes.'

The response was cold. 'You are a ruler now and an emperor can have no friends.'

'I fear you are in for a lonely existence,' Flavius responded, favouring Petrus with a sympathetic smile.

'I will take care that is not so, thus it does not fall to you to concern yourself.'

The dilated nostrils sent a physical message to add to the biting verbal one, a trait that took her nose and sharpened it in a remarkable and very obvious way. Flavius did not know, but his gut feeling was acute: Theodora, striking to look at and seemingly full of purpose, even after what had just taken place, felt vulnerable and that might extend to a deep-seated fear.

That the upper classes would hate her elevation, she must know; even many an ordinary citizen would shake their heads at such a woman occupying a position that could be, as it had in the past, one of great power and influence. Had not the late Emperor Anastasius got the diadem through the bedchamber? To reach such a pinnacle, as she had, brought with it risks and it did not take too vivid an imagination to see that should she fall, her end would not be a pleasant one.

Were such concerns justified? If she did not command her husband it was plain that he rarely did anything without consulting her. He was still as besotted as he had been when Flavius first sat with them in company, the time at which he had sensed her resentment of him; Theodora wanted to be the sole fount of advice and comfort, the one person the newly coined Justinian would turn to and she resented not only that Flavius was able to bypass this, but also, it seemed, that he did so in such an easy-going manner. Sensing the need to broker a peace, Justinian spoke up.

'I will not object, Flavius, if you call me Justinian in private, since I have never been truly enamoured of the name Petrus. But I would ask that you acknowledge my dignity in a public space.'

'You're too soft, husband.'

'No, Theodora, I owe Flavius much and so do you.'

That open repudiation, sternly delivered, was not well received: those nostrils dilated even further but the sight of that was brief; Theodora abruptly spun round and left the chamber, leaving Flavius to wonder what price her husband would pay for such a public rebuke.

'I fear your good lady does not care for me.'

'She will come round in time, Flavius. She has been betrayed too many times in her life, lied to and even abandoned, to repose much trust in anyone.'

'I can assume she trusts you?'

'Let's hope so, for if not I am in for an imperial nightmare.'

'Then I request that you send me on some service so that I do not have to share it.'

'Flavius, it is my intention to lead you. My uncle has granted me permission to attempt to remind the Sassanids that they have a power with whom they must contend. No more sitting and letting them do as they please and just soak up our subventions to their coffers.'

Full of enthusiasm, Justinian began to outline the plans, which involved a two-pronged assault, one in the north under his personal command, another further south in Mesopotamia to attack towards Nisibis under the command of one Libelarius. Flavius, examining the proposal, did not do so with as much confidence as that of the man outlining it, not least because of the utterly unproven military ability of Justinian. But the other factor which worried him was the excessive level of ambition.

Given such thoughts, there would have been a time, and a recent one, when Flavius might have responded with a jokily delivered 'God help us'. Now that seemed inappropriate; if Theodora was wrong in saying an emperor could have no friends, such companions were required to show care in bringing them to their senses.

*　*　*

Justinian led the forces that invaded Persian Armenia but it was not from the front; he took up residence in the city of Theodosiopolis in the Roman province of Armenia Inferior and acted as commander from there. These ancient lands, the cockpit of so much Persian, Greek and Roman conflict over the centuries, had been acrimoniously split between the two empires and that meant raid and counter raid, the odd siege of a border fortress. But there had been no major incursions by either side for years and that was a situation Justinian was keen to exploit, given there should be little organised opposition.

Flavius Belisarius was given the leadership of the cavalry under the command of one Sittas, thirty years his senior, invading a region lacking a force with which to contest. He was part of an army of several thousand local levies that barely qualified as proper infantry, *milities* happy to partake in the destruction of any of their neighbour's goods which could not be carried away. This did not include the various municipal treasuries taken from unfortified towns or objects of gold and silver and the coin-filled chests of the wealthier inhabitants. These, along with huge herds of horses and cattle, were brought back into Roman territory, while the crops that could not be eaten or brought out were burnt.

A cock-a-hoop Justinian, having seen the profits of what he saw as his masterful strategy, determined on another major raid, which was to be launched with high hopes and many a flowery prayer for an assured victory, this despite attempts by Flavius to suggest to him that such an incursion might run into trouble if it was pushed forward too aggressively.

He was right: this time they did not get far from the border marker posts of Armenia Inferior; the Persians were alert and awaiting them in superior numbers, which obliged Sittas to order an immediate withdrawal, though his reaction proved to be too slow. The Persians, as ever strong in their mounted arm and with a host of horse archers, moved too fast.

The Romans were forced into a post-noon battle in which their enemy chose the ground, open and waterless, with no protection on either flank, where the Sassanids could deploy two weapons which the Romans had ever struggled to contend with. First the horse archers wrought havoc, and by breaking up the various untrained *milities* units they destroyed any hope of holding the field. Then the Sassanids sent forward a body of their cataphract cavalry, lance-bearing armoured horsemen on equally protected substantial mounts, small in number on this occasion, but extremely effective.

Flavius was denied the chance to send forward his cavalry, who had taken the name of *bucellarii* from the hard biscuit that made up the base of their rations, in reality to test them in battle, which might not reverse matters but would buy time. Sittas feared to lose the one arm that might save him and nor did he seek to hold until nightfall, when it would become possible to slip away, albeit in broken groups.

He ordered an immediate retreat, one in which his already distressed units fell into chaos to become no more than a terrified rabble. Only the mounted force under Flavius, with Sittas in their midst, was able to ride clear. They returned to Theodosiopolis to find Justinian no longer present and if, at first thought it was to avoid blame for the defeat, that proved wrong.

The message of recall had come from the capital: Justin was dying and the designated successor had to be in Constantinople to claim his inheritance. Flavius was ordered to follow at once, it being obvious his friend would want close to him all those who would protect his person. Leaving the *bucellarii* to follow as fast as they could, he used many changes of mounts to ensure he arrived in time to pay his dying mentor his due respect.

In that he failed; Justin had passed away in a fog of debilitation, babbling of a life very far removed from that to which he had risen. The old man had harked back over sixty years to a rustic youth spent trying adult patience, scrapping for the means to eat at constant risk of a barbarian incursion, the very event that had driven him from his home and hearth in the company of his friends, one of them Flavius's father.

Justin was not alone in sloughing off his mortal coil; by the time Flavius reached the imperial palace Vitalian too was dead, but not through age or infirmity. He had been strangled as soon as the news of Justin's demise was promulgated, proof of just how much Justinian feared him. He would not have done the deed himself for he was not capable, but it had the Sabbatius imprint all over it; had he not advised Justin that the man be killed years before?

On meeting his now sole Emperor, it was not a subject

to be mentioned, even if Flavius suspected Justinian wanted him to enquire so he could either boast of it, explain or deny culpability. Such matters, when they came together, were best left unspoken but a message had been sent to anyone inclined to trouble the new reign and that included the nephews of Anastasius.

Matters in the east had not gone well and not just in Armenia. The incursion meant to threaten Nisibis had ended in fiasco, without even a pretence of a fight and the man in charge had been dismissed. Not that Justinian seemed chastened, if anything he was more determined than ever, even when the news came that Timostratus, the *dux Mesopotamiae* had died at Dara, leaving the forces there without a commander.

'I have sent word to Kavadh that, even if he must be feeling sure of his superiority, there will be no more talents coming his way. The imperial treasury is not as it should be, my uncle was too lax and too generous, as well as failing to punish those who freely lined their own purses.'

'I am sure you advised him on that.'

'Advised,' Justinian replied, imbuing the word with deep and unpleasant meaning. 'If I had a *solidus* for every time my advice was ignored, that to punish one of these thieves would only stir up more trouble, we could buy the Sassanid Empire wholesale.'

Flavius chuckled at the joke, which died in his throat as he realised it was not meant to be one. 'It will mean war. If Kavadh cannot pay for peace within his own domains then he has no choice but to threaten Rome.'

'And he will be well supported by those to whom he has

passed our gold over the years. Could we pay them directly and undermine Kavadh?'

'You could try, but the various tribes are weak individually as well as mutually lacking in trust, which bars them acting together. They would be left at the mercy of Kavadh and we would not be able to aid them if he sought to impose his authority.'

'So he will attack us once more?' Not waiting for a reply Justinian continued. 'Why can we not beat him?'

It should have been unnecessary to cite the reasons but Flavius did so anyway; his numerical advantage, given by territorial proximity, better tactics and poor leadership on the Roman side, the last wrapped in caveats lest, after the loss in Armenia, it imply Justinian himself. There was also his own part in that flight back to Roman territory, though it had been made plain to him that Sittas was the man who bore responsibility.

'But it must be possible, though it will be far from easy and luck must play a part as well as generalship.'

'Then I hope you are gifted with both.'

The Emperor was looking at him, head canted to one side in that manner Flavius knew so well, a slight smile playing on his lips, yet one so faint it was hard to decipher the meaning.

'Are you toying with me, Highness?'

'No, I am not,' came the terse reply, meant no doubt to infer that emperors did not jest.

'You have heard of the fate of Timostratus?' Flavius nodded, as Justinian added, 'I do not see it as much of a loss, for he was not aggressive.'

'Sometimes that is a good strategy.'

'It is too often employed. You will replace Timostratus and I know you will be more active.'

Flavius was tempted to mention his lack of years and a corresponding absence of experience in high command, indeed to decline what was clearly being offered, yet he struggled to find the words, having spent the last ten years wondering at how some of those who had been given leadership of the imperial armies had ever secured their place.

He had never met Timostratus but he was one whose appointment smacked more of politics than military judgement until you remembered that Justin, who put him in place, had wanted nothing more than to keep the peace. That, under the new reign, was set to change, so the demise of the man had been fortuitous.

Was he fit to replace him? If he had been asked by anyone other than Justinian, Flavius would have replied in the affirmative. He had much to boast of: had he not been promoted to the rank of *decanus* in Vitalian's rebel army, given command of men twice his age and more, when no more than a callow youth and after only serving for a short period?

With every action he had engaged in since, the pacification of insurrection, the question of the effectiveness of his personal leadership had never arisen and if he had been forced into an ignominious retreat in Armenia then that had been under the command of Sittas, who had never once sought the opinion of his junior commanders.

Justinian obviously sensed the unspoken concerns. 'I trust you, Flavius, that is all you need.'

'Highness.'

'I do think it would be fitting,' Justinian said in a slightly wounded tone, 'to thank me.'

The arrangements made for the eastern border seemed to be a mix of pragmatic moves and political expediency. Hypatius was named as *magister militum per Orientem*, giving him overall authority for the borders of Asia Minor, no doubt necessary to quiet what might prove a troublesome faction within a senate testing out the will of a new emperor.

The sons of the murdered Vitalian, who had on the accession sent immediate pledges of loyalty without reference to the fate of their father, would be not only kept in the offices but would be afforded a chance to distinguish themselves under the leadership of the new *dux Mesopotamiae*.

The overall strategy was offensive. Since Dara had proved advantageous in holding the central part of the border, it seemed to Justinian sensible to seek to construct more forts, albeit funds did not exist for the construction of places of the same size and strength. Flavius was given orders to begin construction at Minduous to the north of Dara, the first of a planned string of fortified and garrisoned places by which the empire could hold its territory without the need for the constant raising of armies.

But first the Lakhmids had to be dealt with; allies of Kavadh, they had been raiding to the south of Dara, issuing from their own tribal lands to burn and plunder, and they required to be stopped, which had the added advantage of distraction. With an army entering Kavadh's domains, threatening to chastise a confederate tribe, the Sassanids would be obliged to face that threat.

CHAPTER TWELVE

On taking over at Dara the new man discovered how different it was to command an army than to control a smaller military group. This was obvious from the first day and one that deteriorated as the men he was set to lead began to arrive, for Justinian had sent him to the frontier with no staff. Flavius had assumed the need would be met by those people who had served his dead predecessor but he had controlled only a static garrison that engaged in occasional patrols, not a force that aimed to blunt a Sassanid incursion and that was a very different beast.

Feeding and seeing to their supply requirements while within the confines of the fortress was burden enough, given their numbers: what wore him down was the need to plan for the forthcoming march, which being partly across desert meant ensuring a good supply of water, for the men certainly, but even more so for the horses. They required water by the barrel load and if it was lacking they would soon become useless.

Added to that there was feed for several thousand mouths, equine and human, which if it would be provided inside imperial territory, still had to be purchased and stockpiled. Once over the frontier the same supplies required to be transported and that meant hundreds of mules – wheeled transport on soft sand was never going to work – which only added to the nightmare.

Being so busy afforded him little time to assess the men he would lead, and in the short time he could spare in evaluation, what he observed did not excite him for it seemed far from being a cohesive force. The contingents arrived in piecemeal fashion from all over the southern provinces of the empire and as was normal with such bodies their leadership was personal. Each unit of men looked to their own commanders for instruction and he was too occupied to devote enough time to altering that.

His duties granted him even less of a chance to explain to these leaders his objectives and preferred tactics but with the time of departure approaching, and most of the needs of his army met, he finally called on them to confer. Flavius was very much the man in charge but, fresh to command, he was wary of treating them with too lofty a tone, so much so that it was not orders he issued but a set of guidelines that sought to achieve consensus on what manoeuvres to adopt that afforded the best chance of success.

The most important point was that this was no invasion; the object was to check the Lakhmid raiders and force them back over the frontier. That changed when information came in that they had been reinforced by a proper army; clearly news of the Roman response had forced Kavadh to act to protect his allies. Now the task became to eject that force from Roman territory, which might occasion a proper battle.

Flavius suggested, given the altered circumstances, they take up a position in the hope of drawing the enemy onto them, in short to choose the battlefield, not least because they had no idea of Sassanid numbers and it was definitely folly to attack an enemy of unknown strength. The feeling that those listening were merely paying lip service was one he could not put aside. He was sure he saw in their smiling agreement a hint of indulgence; they were as aware as he of his inexperience and probably saw in what he said the fear of defeat rather than a hope of victory and he decided that had to be addressed.

'I doubt any host has marched without a certainty of impending success and too many have paid in blood for being overzealous. I would want it to be no different with us but we must acknowledge realities.'

The response came from Coutzes, who led the largest contingent of cavalry. 'It is possible to be too cautious, Flavius Belisarius, and that is not a feeling it is wise to allow to pervade an army. Our men look to us to display confidence. We must ever appear certain of victory otherwise the spirit will not be there when we need it.'

A son of Vitalian and the *dux* of *Phoenicia Libanensis*,

Coutzes ruled his satrapy from Palmyra. He came across as a man full of confidence and one who saw no need for excessive respect to his titular superior, both obvious in the cast of his look and the tone of his voice, though he was never openly impolite.

That there was an undertone in his attitude was only to be expected; Coutzes knew Flavius was close to Justinian, just as he must be aware that the Emperor had been behind his father's murder. That fact alone made Flavius wonder how he could continue to serve the Emperor and placed a mark on his character. Yet to show any disrespect would not serve, so the response had to be one that took account of his obvious self-esteem.

'I know what you mean, Coutzes, and I accept it as valid. But men who cannot see further than the end of their lance rely on the likes of us to do so for them, to make sure we do not waste their blood. We are about to traverse a desert, which imposes supply problems not least with water and that tells our enemies the direction we must take to have access to the wells.'

Atafar the Saracen spoke up this time. 'Where they will wait for us.'

Of all the junior commanders he seemed the most receptive to what was being imparted and it was easy to understand why, for his men were entirely infantry. He was an experienced leader and came showered with honours from previous battles in which he had acted with bravery and distinction, so he knew what he wanted. Fluid battle and rushed movement was not the forte of the kind of levies he led. They were more suited to stout defence on suitable ground followed by a mass attack once the conditions for victory had been attained, namely the enemy been rendered disordered when they were still in proper formations.

'Perhaps. If they want to avoid battle they will block access and force us to withdraw, for we cannot remain an effective force without water. If they want a fight, then the position they will take will be beyond the wells in the hope that with thirst fully quenched we will attack them.'

'You seem to know their mind, Flavius Belisarius.'

'Let us say, Coutzes, that I know my own and it is what I would do.' That got a look that disconcerted him, given it smacked of scepticism. 'In the second case we will have ample water, a good line of supply back to Dara and enough cavalry to screen against being outflanked and surprised, so we can wait them out.'

'Hardly glorious.'

'You will have all the glory you wish, Coutzes, when we beat them.'

'You seem very sure we will.'

'You cannot hold both arguments, now can you? You reproach me for too much caution then question my confidence.' Flavius smiled to take the sting out of the next words. 'Which is it to be?'

'Just as long as we fight.'

'We shall, but think on this. The field of battle could be desert and that means sand. How much harder will it be for your horse, Coutzes, to stay strong on soft ground? The Sassanids rely on horse archers and their speed to cause havoc, to so affect our levies that they will wilt when attacked by the enemy infantry. Well, I have seen them and if I say to you I want them riding on that same sand I hope you will understand why.'

'It will slow and tire them,' Atafar said.

'I will wager my horsemen will do as well as any other,' Coutzes insisted, 'never mind the ground.'

Watching them the following morning as the men he was to lead fielded and paraded, Flavius concentrated his attention on the cavalry. There were two contingents, that of Coutzes and another from Palaestina led by a young Equestrian called Vincent, and he could not but compare their discipline to that of the *bucellarii* when he observed how hard it was for them to form up into the required files, efforts accompanied by much shouting and blowing of horns.

This told him he had command of a mounted force of the kind that had failed so often before, men on hard-to-control mounts chosen for speed, full of fire and with only one aim, to charge at and destroy any perceived enemy. The Saracen infantry were equally full of ardour for battle but at least they seemed able to arrange themselves in some kind of order within a reasonable time and this he put down to Atafar and his long experience.

Every inch the Arab, with his hooded eyes, hooked nose and full greying beard, Atafar was the man who most impressed Flavius. He would have liked to have anointed him as his deputy but the feelings of Coutzes, with his imperial rank of *dux*, made that difficult.

Flavius had his verbal instructions from Justinian and they brooked no delay and that was backed up by a constant stream of missives once the nature of the threat became known; this Sassanid force must be expelled, which led his anointed general to impious thoughts. With no one to restrain or check him, the new Emperor, after one marginally successful campaign in Armenia, seemed sure he was possessed of a hitherto undisclosed military genius.

Did he not see by his insistence on instant action he was leaving no time for training or the chance to impose his will on the force he led? However many times the despatches were read, Flavius knew the message: he must make do with what he had and act at once.

The first part of the march was relatively easy as they passed through an imperial territory rich in agriculture but just as long on indifference. There was no gathering of citizenry to cheer them on, no flowers cast at their feet and no paeans of praise aimed at the finely clad man leading them, which led Flavius to wonder, as he had in the past, at the nature of the men who ruled these far-flung provinces.

Far from Constantinople, provincial governance was carried out on the personal whim of the man in charge, and experience told him, something he had found in all those duties he had undertaken for Justin, that most of those cared not a whit for the welfare of the Emperor's subjects.

A province of empire was there to be bled for profit, the kind of sums that could then be employed to buy an office within the higher bureaucracy, something the ruler seemed incapable of changing. Justin had tried and failed in the face of obdurate officials. Knowing Justinian, Flavius felt he would be more inclined to use it to gain his ends than seek to alter it.

Even here he had a cavalry screen out in front of the

main force, this led by Coutzes. There had been an awkward moment the previous night when he had sought a private interview. After beating about the bush, there being many references to his father and his abilities, the *dux Phoenicia Libanensis* had hinted that when the time came for battle to be joined, he would wish to be granted a leading role and that should this be forthcoming it would be to the advantage of Flavius Belisarius.

The inference, however subtly it was put forward, was obvious: Flavius was being offered a bribe, which told him that this man knew nothing of him and had made no effort to find out. How many times when engaged in pacification had he been offered talents of gold to bend one way or the other? The mere suggestion always made him think of the fat and venal Senuthius Vicinus, the man responsible for the death of his male relatives as well as the men they led.

He could not do then what he had done in the past, string the miscreant up by his thumbs and invite those whose money they had no doubt pilfered to chastise him as they wished, either with rotten vegetables or, as had happened in some cases, with stones enough to leave a bloody pulp. He needed this man, which obliged him to think on his motives.

Coutzes clearly wanted glory and the sole reason for the need was to impress Justinian of his loyalty and secure himself against the same fate as his father. The notion nearly made Flavius laugh, which would have been just as insulting as a downright refusal to take his gold; Justinian would not kill Coutzes, he was not important enough and nor was he, as Vitalian had been, a perceived threat.

'It is to be hoped that we will all be eager to engage with our enemies when the time comes, Coutzes, and should glory beckon it will likely favour you as much as anyone.'

'I can arrange—'

Coutzes got no further as Flavius abruptly cut him off. 'No arrangements are necessary.'

The way that was taken showed that this cavalry commander was not yet the fully formed courtier, for he could not mask his anger, hard as he tried. It was with a stiff expression that he inclined his head, before spinning round and leaving the chamber. The memory of the encounter stayed with Flavius and was with him as he rode; a man in search of personal glory could pose problems.

Encamped that night, Flavius called another meeting at which he sought to cement his views. Then, having eaten, he took a tour round the tents, seeking to make his presence and his face known. He wanted, even if it was only with a look, to imply to those he led that he cared for their welfare and to ensure they knew that as they ate the supplies he had arranged for them, it was he who had worried for their bellies. It was an impossible task given if anyone spoke with him it was as rare and respectful as to have little effect.

The following morning, after the priests had said Mass and the men had broken their fast, they formed up again to head due east into the arid desert of Thannuris. This was done under a blazing sun that, with the sand dragging at their feet, took a heavy toll on the foot soldiers. Nor were those mounted spared; they spent as much time walking as riding with frequent stops for water taken from the loaded carts Flavius had sent ahead.

That would not pertain on the following day; the carts would follow the army not precede it, for they would be close to where they expected they might find their enemy. If they were west of the wells Flavius would have no choice but to order an immediate withdrawal, which would do nothing to enhance his standing here or in the capital. To give his infantry as little marching to do as possible he had sent the cavalry ahead to find the Sassanids and give him warning of what he faced.

His orders had been explicit: locate and wait unless they are west of the wells and seemingly set up to do battle, in which case we will make a display of force then retire out of the desert. Personally, he longed for them to be beyond the wells and his mood was a mixture of eagerness and anxiety as to what would be the outcome of his first battle as a general if that wish was granted. The history of fighting against the Sassanids was not one of success for the Eastern Empire but if he could deploy as he wished, then he had a chance to alter that.

How good it would have been to have someone close enough to him to confide in, to share such thoughts, like old and crabby Ohannes, long gone to meet his maker, or even his mentor Justin, to say that if he knew he faced failure he would embrace that, anything rather than risk men's lives for his personal aggrandisement.

'Rider coming, Your Honour,' came a call from one of his escort, 'and fast.'

'From Coutzes, no doubt,' Flavius replied.

He rose in his stirrups to cast a look to the front, shading his eyes against the glare of the sun. The messenger was closing at a flat-out gallop, the tail of his horse near horizontal, which had the Belisarius heart feel as if it was suddenly in his exceedingly dry mouth. That went to positive leather when the missive was delivered by the breathless rider, one of the *numerus* commanders that Flavius had met briefly.

'*Dux* Coutzes sends me to tell you that he has halted behind a ridge that overlooks the wells. The Sassanids are drawn up between us and water but he can see few in number and they seem unprepared to defend their position.'

'Few in number?'

'He has counted the tents and puts them at less than a thousand.'

'Cavalry?'

'None within sight.'

What followed was a verbal sketch of what this fellow and Coutzes had seen. An array of tents within which it was expected the enemy were sheltering from the sun and a calculation put Roman strength well above theirs. For security, the Sassanids were behind a barrier of pointed stakes buried in the ground but had left avenues through which their own men could come and go.

'My Lord feels it is possible to mount an attack and catch them unawares using those gaps between the stakes.

'Your lord has his orders.'

'I am to impress on Your Honour the point that matters no longer fit those orders. The enemy, *dux* Coutzes asks me to inform you, are at our mercy.'

'What of the other captains?'

'They are eager to back up his calculation.'

'They are obliged to follow mine.'

Flavius fell silent as he examined what he had been told while at the same time conjuring up a mental picture of what lay before his cavalry. If true, it was indeed a golden opportunity but would an enemy commander be so foolish as to leave himself so exposed? He must know that a Roman army was on its way; no force five thousand strong could move in such a region without news of its presence getting ahead of its progress. There was, of course, the obvious solution; he must see for himself.

He spurred his horse and took off, forcing the messenger to jump to one side, in which he was nearly trampled on by the hooves of those *bucellarii* who now formed his own *comitatus*. The dust cloud they sent up as they raced across the desert, thankfully not deep sand in this area, perhaps sent a message ahead to Coutzes, or was it just the hunt for valour that animated him?

By the time Flavius had sight of his mounted men they were lined up on the skyline, having ridden to the top of the ridge behind which, he had been told, they had previously been hidden from the enemy. All Coutzes had to do was look over his shoulder to see the man to whom he was bound to defer approaching. Did he do that, Flavius did not know for the sound of the horn, floating across the intervening space, saw the whole of his cavalry disappear down the slope before to leave an empty skyline, though they could hear the loud yells of over a thousand throats.

By the time Flavius and his escort crested that rise Coutzes, right to the front with his banner-bearer by his side, had closed the gap between the ridge and the line of forward-pointing and sharpened Sassanid stakes. The rest had echeloned into ragged arrow shapes and were, following that *dux* banner, heading towards those gaps that had been described, while to the rear Flavius saw what seemed like panicked defenders seeking to get to their stacked weapons and prepare to mount a defence.

From their elevation Flavius and his men could see what happened, a sight denied to those who rode in the wake of Coutzes. As soon as he chested through the gap, his body fully extended in his stirrups, his sword raised and swinging, the sand-coloured ground disappeared beneath him. He and his horse had charged into a deep, concealed ditch and those following him did likewise, the noise of screaming men and terrified horses filling the air as riders and their mounts piled on top of those already fallen.

'Back to Atafar. Tell him to turn round and march to the west as fast as he can.'

Order given, Flavius spurred forward, for what was before him now was a melee of his mounted units, riding in circles with no set purpose, while he could see the seemingly disordered Sassanids were anything but. In the distance, probably having been camped at the wells, bodies of mounted men, horse archers by the size of their mounts, were cantering forward to take part in the fight, proving that this had been a carefully designed stratagem.

Worse, disciplined units of foot soldiers, many more than the tents they had abandoned should have contained, were formed up for battle, preparing to advance over solid ground to first finish off those in the ditches and then to take on what was now a completely demoralised force of cavalry.

In amongst them was their general, waving his sword and yelling for them to retreat, a command hard to get across until he found the horn blower was still alive and could sound the right call in a way that would reach those who needed to hear. Some did not follow Flavius as he raced back towards that ridge, either out of loyalty to their *dux* or sheer confusion and they would surely die.

There was little doubt of his fate and those who had followed him. If the horses and riders falling on top of Coutzes had not killed him there were enough slashing Sassanids in the ditches to carry out the deed. So busy was he trying to get his remaining men clear of danger, it was an age before Flavius Belisarius came to realise the truth. In his first battle as a commanding general he had been soundly defeated.

CHAPTER THIRTEEN

The wait was frustrating: how would Justinian respond to what had occurred? Fast the imperial service might be, but it still took time to cover six hundred leagues there and back and that was before you factored in the period taken to assess not only the reverse the force from Dara had suffered but how to react to it. Even considering all those particulars it still seemed to drag out to an interminable wait during which, even after a month, Flavius could not get out of his mind the scale of the defeat.

Half his cavalry had perished either by rushing headlong into those concealed ditches or in the ground between them and the ridge from which Coutzes had attacked. They had been victims of the infantry but it was the enemy cavalry that posed the greatest threat. Leading the remainder of his own mounted forces away, Flavius had sought to distract the pursuit by drawing them off from Atafar and his retreating foot levies, who needed time to have any chance of avoiding a massacre. The ploy failed; the Sassanids had declined to follow him on a more northerly route and kept their mind on the primary task.

It had occasioned no tears when in his despatch he named Coutzes among the dead; that was not the case with Atafar and even less with the men he led. Many had perished, this he knew from a later examination of the body-littered field where they had sought to stand and fight, so many having fallen to arrows. The old Arab had died leading them, but there was another grim reading of what he observed: there were fewer bodies than Atafar had brought to Dara. How many had been taken as prisoners to endure a life of slavery?

In writing the full report Flavius had the memory of Vincent to aid him. The Equestrian was able to pass on the exhortations that Coutzes had employed to persuade his fellow captains to disobey what was a direct instruction from their general. Even if these were included and the outcome described Flavius made no attempt to shift the blame; he was the man in command and if he had entrusted part of his force to Coutzes he bore the responsibility for such a poor decision.

That he would be removed he had no doubt and he was resigned to his fate. Being a friend to Justinian would not count for much when every voice around him would be questioning his appointment of Flavius Belisarius to so important a post in the first place. They would do so with caveats to his imperial sagacity, of course, but these courtiers had spent a lifetime honing their oratorical skills. They were well versed in getting the message they really wanted to impart over to even the most deaf of rulers.

It hardly aided his mood when Flavius heard that the castle building he had set in train at Minduous had been abandoned in the face of a Sassanid threat. There had been no battle; all the enemy had to do was show enough strength in numbers to make the effort untenable and force the men Flavius had sent to carry out the construction running for the safety of Dara.

The day the messenger rode through the gates brought on that which Flavius dreaded, yet the despatches he brought were far from censorious. Instead they warned him that following their successes, the Sassanids were now emboldened enough to make an attempt to invest and capture Dara itself and that Kavadh was busy raising the necessary forces, which would take time and allow Flavius to prepare.

There was no hint of dismissal; the despatch informed him that fresh and better troops were on their way to support him and that he was now charged with making sure the fortress did not fall. As well as levies from the province of Phoenicia he was promised mercenary cavalry from both the Huns and the Germanic Heruls, who were numbered among the best mounted soldiers the empire possessed.

There was no point in asking if the information regarding an attempt of Dara was correct and even less did he have time to do so. The Romans had spies everywhere and in the past some of their intelligence had proved to be either wishful thinking or downright invention to secure their stipend, but he had no choice but to act as if it was true.

There was a second message, a private communication from Justinian in which the Emperor chided him for what had happened, but that was leavened by his point that when it came to defeats Flavius Belisarius was in some exalted company. How many of his fellow generals had failed as he had over the last decades? When he wrote that he still had faith in him it was couched in words that told him there were many voices assailing the imperial ear with contrary advice.

Justinian went to some lengths to address his concerns and showed some insight into the problems facing the man in the field as opposed to the people at court. When it came to organisation he was sending out Hermogenes, the *magister officiorum*, to oversee matters of supply and organisation. Surprised at the appointment of such a high-ranking bureaucrat Flavius wondered if it was a case of Justinian removing an irritant from his council. The other point was more personal; he urged him to appoint a *domesticus*, someone committed to him personally with whom he could discuss those matters that had to be kept within the bounds of discretion.

'Perhaps such a sounding board would have allowed you to see Coutzes for what he was.'

The letter ended with the kind of good wishes that one friend sends to another, only marred by the fact that it was purported to come not just from Justinian but from Theodora as well.

Mulling on it Flavius took to the idea of a *domesticus*. Ohannes had come under that designation in his father's household but a servant was not what Justinian was proposing. What he had in mind was a higher sort of position, filled by a man who might sometimes treat him as near an equal. If he was to have a person in that role then he too must be a soldier, for he needed someone with whom he could exchange ideas on his military and command responsibilities.

It was a few days later, when out studying the ground outside Dara, that he found two things: the field on which he wanted to fight and the man who would fulfil the role that Justinian had suggested. A eunuch called Solomon, he was a middle-ranking official of the Mesopotamian council who had, at one time, been a soldier. Such functionaries aided Flavius in his role as *dux*, given he was responsible to Constantinople for whatever happened in the whole province.

One of Solomon's duties was the recruitment or drafting of labour to keep the fortress in good repair, the roads, too, and any of the other tasks that were needed to maintain buildings, sewers and the like. It was, for the *dux*, an office easy to abuse by inflating costs or hiring out the labour to private individuals, and this had happened under his predecessor.

Expecting the same rapacious overlord, Solomon had shown some surprise when it became obvious that this Flavius Belisarius was not out to fill chests with gold; he wanted only that the necessary works be carried out without excessive expenditure and nothing for himself. If their association had not been of great length it had been mutually agreeable and based on doing that which was right, unlike that of others the *dux* was obliged to deal with, who took his insistence on honesty badly.

Solomon was along for a very sound reason: Flavius would be in need of much labour if the plan forming in his mind came to pass, so with him was the man who would have to see part of it implemented. When he alighted on the possibility that Solomon might well fulfil the role of *domesticus* it was because the combination was suitable, a knowledge of civil affairs married to a military background, these facts pointed out to him. But would he accept?

'At least you cannot, with such a name, be challenged for your wisdom.'

'It will be your wisdom I am supposed to challenge, Your Honour.'

The man was far from young, well past four decades, lugubrious in his nature, with a long, thin face, sad eyes and a lantern jaw below a wide mouth. If not a beauty that reply showed he was made of the right material.

'Tell me what you think of this place.'

'Do you intend to fight here?'

'Perhaps.'

'Hard to take Dara by siege, Your Honour,' came the reply, as Solomon looked over his shoulder at the massive walls plain to see from where they sat.

'Hiding behind those is no way to defeat the Sassanids and I want to soundly beat them.'

'For pride, would it be?'

'No, and I know from where your question springs.'

'Hurts to be bested.'

'I doubt you know how much, but I would not risk men's lives for my reputation.' That such an assertion was not questioned, even by the look on Solomon's face, cheered him. 'If Kavadh's armies invest Dara with us defending, it will drag to our aid every soldier the empire can spare for they cannot be sure it will hold. The Sassanids have not lost the art of siege warfare. Odd that we Romans taught them how and we have forgotten ourselves. There's not a ballista in the whole imperial army.'

'Nor the men skilled in their use. Kavadh has them too.'

'So his generals will have the means to keep us locked up in Dara, this while any forces marching to relieve us will be in the open and that is where we have always failed against our enemies. Say they are beaten, where does that leave us and our garrison? This time I want to fight them on my terms and all I need to know is, is this a good place?'

'Well,' the older man mused, 'you have a good-sized hill to secure one flank and you can be sure if the Sassanids come this far they will attack you as they must to get at the city.'

'You sense I will be defensive?'

'You would have to be and you'd best make sure no one panics and closes the fortress gates if matters look to be going against us.'

'Us?'

'If I accept your offer I would be by your side.'

'You should have remained a soldier, Solomon.'

'Fewer aches and pains with quill and parchment.'

'Less exhilaration.'

'I might be past that.'

'Yes or no?' It was a while before the nod came but come it did. 'So, let me outline my intentions.'

'I'm told there are men on the way. Best consult with their captains, do you not think?'

There was no cordiality in the reply. 'This time the men I lead will do exactly as I require.'

The least welcome of the men who came to lead his forces was Bouzes, brother of the late Coutzes, now sole *dux* of *Phoenicia Libanensis* and Vitalian's eldest son. From the first it was obvious, even if it was never mentioned, that he knew of the way Flavius had castigated his brother in the recent defeat and that was demonstrated in his resentment when required to obey an instruction. It was in this situation that having Solomon to talk to was an advantage.

'Who are those who would support him at court?'

'A wise question, to which I do not know the answer, such a place ever being a mystery to me.'

'One it might be wise to solve, Your Honour. Best to know who you will offend before you threaten to send him home.'

'Is that what you would suggest?'

'I sense it is what you wish to do, and yes, I would come to the same conclusion with greater confidence if I had some inkling of the trouble it will bring you.'

'I cannot think on that. Send to Bouzes asking him to attend upon me.'

That his arrival was long delayed sent a message to Flavius, which did nothing for his mood when the man who might be his senior cavalry commander eventually arrived. But he was not going to let himself be checked for tardiness.

'We are of equal rank, Flavius Belisarius, are we not? So it ill becomes you to be angered that I do not run to your side like a faithful dog.'

There was much of his father in Bouzes, the same stocky build and wide shoulders, most tellingly in the hard stare. But there was also his brother there, the same sureness of mind and no hint that listening served as well as talking.

'Do you blame me for your brother's death?'

That shook Bouzes, being so unexpected, but he quickly recovered. 'You led him.'

'The trouble is no one led him, for he would not have it. I will not bore you with an explanation of his folly, nor how expensive it was in the blood of those he had command of. Suffice to say I will not bear a repeat of the attitude he displayed.'

'Repeat?'

'Do not pretend you have no idea of what I am saying. Coutzes disobeyed a direct order from me. You, Bouzes, may be lucky to get the chance.'

'What do you mean?'

Flavius changed his tone then to make sure his point went to where it was needed. 'At the next sign of disrespect I will send you away from here.'

'You need my men.'

'And they shall stay, which will give you two choices, to slink back to your satrapy or go to the Emperor and plead your case.'

That took the blood from the man's face; he had the

same fears as Coutzes, that Justinian was just biding his time before having him killed, and his need was similar: to take part in a battle, to behave with distinction and prove that he was a loyal subject.

'There will be no repeat of this warning, Bouzes. Anger me once more and you will find my *bucellarii* escorting you out of the western gate.'

The face was thunderous and indicated a desire to argue but the mind must have been working behind that. Here before and berating him was a man who had failed in battle yet had suffered no censure that he knew of. Just how much was he Justinian's man? Could disputing with Flavius Belisarius be the quickest route to a dungeon or a fate even worse?

It hurt what he said then, that was obvious by the strangled tone. 'If I have offended you, it is not by design.'

'Good, and if you want my good offices that is easy. Just do as I command and kill our enemies. Now I think we are done.'

The digging of the ditches was overseen by Solomon, Flavius being too busy seeking to imbue his cavalry with some manoeuvres other than the charge. His own fifteen-hundred-strong *bucellarii* had to put aside their bows and lances to show how they wheeled, advanced and retired to the various horn commands as well as the purpose, the other cavalry being harangued about the need to maintain some control so as not to forfeit their tactical use.

The arrival of Hermogenes, with a pair of assistants, heralded a split in the command but he turned out to be a man quite satisfied to be merely consulted. It was not deference; if he disagreed he said so. But that was an attitude rarely displayed and when Flavius outlined his plan in private, the old bureaucrat readily assented, with a minor caveat that should the battle go badly some way must be found for the cavalry to screen and protect infantry retiring to the safety of the fortress, which received a caustic response from Flavius.

'If it comes to that the only use we will have for horses is as food.'

Hermogenes took on the task of supply procurement, scouring the surrounding countryside until the fortress storerooms could hold no more, the double advantage of that being the denial of the same to the enemy. While Flavius concentrated on his training, three great trenches were being dug to his design, not in a line but with the central ditch set forward.

Infantry preparation was undertaken as well, but this was not about movement, more about how to stay steady under fire from horse archers as well as a ground attack. At the same time the scouts were out to give prior warning of the enemy. In fact it was Perozes, the Sassanids' commander, who confirmed their approach; he sent Flavius a message ahead requesting that he prepare for him a bath.

'He will bath in blood,' Bouzes spat when this message was relayed to his officers by the recipient.

'He will satisfy me if he retires unwashed and smelling of disgrace, but what I need now are numbers, so get those scouts doing what they should and counting.'

The replies that came back put the strength of Perozes

very close to that of the Romans at some five thousand effectives, which his opponent knew was insufficient for the task the Sassanid general had been given. Apart from that there was no sign of siege equipment.

'There must be more coming in his wake. Keep men out and watching for reinforcements.'

'They may be caught and give your dispositions,' Hermogenes mused.

'The enemy will see my dispositions soon enough and I hope they will cause him to wonder. Right now we must get the army fed, blessed and rested.'

'Battle on the morrow?' Bouzes asked in a jovial voice, seeking to ingratiate himself.

'Pray for that,' Flavius replied, 'and pray for Rome.'

They heard the flutes and drums of the Sassanids as the sun rose to reveal a landscape covered with a mass of movement, with Perozes to the fore under a red, blue and white Sassanid banner. When he stopped it was to direct the various contingents to their positions before riding forward to examine what he could see of the defence Flavius had set out to create. There had been no attempt to hide the ditches and, watching him, his opposite number hoped that he was confused by their layout.

Following that nothing happened; the only activity in the morning hours was Perozes redeploying some of his men to take account of what he had observed, but he had few options if he was to avoid a frontal assault on the Romans whom he would have to destroy if he were to take Dara by main force.

The hours went by with no activity other than the arrival of the supply carts and the feeding of the Romans, overseen by one of the aides Hermogenes had brought with him, a young fellow called Procopius, a fellow of slim build, high forehead and a somewhat intense manner, an advocate by training.

Then once more it was hiatus until Hermogenes said. 'They want us hungry.'

This suggestion confused Flavius. Both were sat on a low mound, which gave them a clear view of the field before them, not that there was much to see and it was obvious that the younger man was at a loss to understand.

'We feed our men before noon, the Persians take their sustenance later. If they wait till mid afternoon they will hope themselves stronger for having been late fed.' The older man smiled. 'If you read the reports of Trajan's secretary this you would have seen.'

'What do we do?'

'Nothing. We have distributed our rations for the day.'

'We could have waited.'

'Allow me to advise you for once, Flavius Belisarius. Hold hard to habits, for to break them will upset large bodies of men more than you or I could imagine.'

It came to pass that the old bureaucrat was right; with the sun well past its zenith Perozes did sound the advance, pushing forward with his cavalry on his right wing. It had to be head on since he could not go around the Romans without presenting to them an opportunity to attack his flank, which had his horse archers riding forward to discharge their arrows from the other side of the ditch. This put them at the mercy of their Roman counterparts, on foot and concentrated as soon as the attack began to develop, able to send a hail of missiles so intense it drove them off.

Next came an advance by the Sassanid cataphracts, the layered armour covering both horse- and rider-proof against arrows. They thundered forward as if to take on the ditch, and in crossing it hit the lighter cavalry on the Roman left with force. Bouzes, in command, had begun to give way in order to minimise his losses from archery but, just as reinforcements were being assembled, the Sassanids declined to seek advantage from that retirement. They withdrew, which had Flavius chewing his lower lip, wondering what that portended.

'A gesture, no more,' Hermogenes suggested. 'The light is fading.'

'If I die in the battle,' Flavius responded with a sigh, 'it could be of boredom.'

'I think you may have a warmer day tomorrow.'

CHAPTER FOURTEEN

The old man was wrong; dawn brought the first movement of the day, a feint on the Roman right then another on the left as Perozes sought to get a sense of the Belisarius plan and some notion of how quickly he could shore up sections of his defence. Not that he saw anything; Flavius declined to move any of his units, content to wait until actual contact and some kind of pressed-home attack before he would react. Once more the morning passed without much further activity.

Nor did the Sassanid commander achieve his other purpose, which was to provoke an attack, to draw Flavius Belisarius into the chance of quick victory while the forces were evenly matched. Sat on the same hillock, with a good view of the gentle slope that trended away to the flat plain to the south, he had a better view of the Sassanid dispositions and movements than Perozes had of his, so he felt it safe to be passive.

The next event was an entertaining commonplace and came after the Sassanids had taken their afternoon nourishment; an unarmoured, well-built rider came forward to challenge Flavius Belisarius to personal combat without weapons, in order that battle could be avoided and the matter could be decided without an unnecessary effusion of blood.

Flavius sent forward his chosen champion to meet the one picked by Perozes, a Greek called Andreas, probably the strongest individual in his army and a noted wrestler who had never been known to lose a contest. Soon every man in either army was craning to see the outcome of the bout, one that lasted such a little time that it brought forth groans from the audience – the breaking of the neck by Andreas was too swift.

Perozes sent forth a second fellow, or maybe he had volunteered and he lasted even less time than the first, allowing the Greek to bare his arse to the Sassanids while simultaneously acknowledging the cheers of his comrades. Next came a well-accoutred rider with the Perozes banner and a letter to which Hermogenes, being the most literate, replied, declining the invitation to quit the battlefield and admit defeat, instead, in flowery terms suggesting Perozes, clearly at a loss to break the Roman resolve, take his army back to Nisibis.

'His reinforcements must be close,' Flavius said as he

signed what the older man had dictated to Procopius.

'Does Your Honour know how many?' asked the writer.

'More than he has now – double, maybe treble.'

'Why not bring them all at once?'

'You ask too many questions, Procopius.'

'Not for me, Hermogenes. I wish some of the men I led would ask more.'

'Would you answer them?'

That got a very wide grin. 'Not always. I would avoid anything my enemy might want to know.'

'And mine?' said Procopius.

'Perozes hoped I would seek to take advantage of his lack of strength. He wants that I take the initiative and launch an assault.'

'Would that not serve?'

'Possession of the field is not enough and we hold it. Perozes cannot take Dara unless he crushes us so comprehensively that the fortress is denied a defence. Even if we did attack and succeed he would be back here with twice the numbers in days and we would have bled men and horses for nothing.'

The scouts came in overnight to confirm what was suspected; a huge force was on the way to join Perozes, more than double his present strength. There would be no more feints once they were deployed; these were the anvil on which the Sassanids intended to wreck the Roman defence, a point he made to his assembled inferior commanders.

'The last two days have been about our resolve. Perozes wasn't sure if the dispositions we made were bluff or if we were determined to save Dara from without the walls and prevent a siege. Now he knows that is the case and his needs are obvious. We must be swept aside and he wants no pursuit to the city gates so he will seek to get behind us by breaking one of the flanks.'

'We stand where we are,' Hermogenes added, to shore up his own standing.

'Now you must be told how we plan to thwart them,' Flavius said with a gesture to include Hermogenes, which brought a wry grin to the man's face: any plan to be followed was not his. That smile stayed with him as Belisarius outlined what each commander must do and what he wanted to achieve, concluding with a warning.

'We must look to the point in the battle were Perozes has made a full commitment. Then I will know how to react, but each of you must be prepared to obey what I have just set out. Do not think to make decisions on your own that go counter to my instructions.' Bouzes got a hard and meaningful look. 'I have suffered one lost battle through insubordination, I do not intend that I should lose this one to the same fault.'

'Gentleman,' Hermogenes added. 'I suggest rest, ready for the exertions of tomorrow.'

Sleep being impossible Flavius once more went through the lines, with one eye cast towards the many more numerous fires now dotting the site of the Sassanid camp. This time he was greeted by men who had come to know him and an army that had been well catered for in both food and equipment, the credit belonging to Hermogenes and his able assistants, though Flavius took it anyway rather than seek to explain.

If some of the talk with the Huns and Heruls was stilted by dint of their indifferent Latin there was bond enough between cavalrymen to make for friendly exchanges. Promises of hard fighting went down well, for these men were mercenaries and they lived for combat. As the sky began to grey he passed through the lines of the mainly slumbering *bucellarii*, men who had served with him for years now so when he did exchange words with the sentinels it was like talking to old friends.

These were the fighters he was going to have to rely on, the body that he hoped would strike the killer blow that ended the Sassanid attempt on Dara; if they failed so would he. And before that what he had planned must come to pass, which even the dimmest soldier knew was not always the case. Back at his tent Solomon was waiting with bread and cheese laid out as well as a goblet of spiced wine.

'I never thought to sense it again, having laid aside my weapons.'

'Join me, Solomon, in asking that God grant us the chance to experience it many times in the future.'

Praying, Flavius had no idea of the supplications made by his *domesticus*. He was, as usual, invoking the memory of his father and brothers, and while seeking repose for their souls, he also wished for their good opinion and that his thinking be guided by their celestial hand. Was it a response from God that the walls of the tent shook? If that were the case then it was a message sustained as the wind began to blow steadily and strongly from the north.

Dawn brought the sound of horns and daylight exposed the level of movement as well as the vastly superior numbers now deployed to attack. Mounted and back on his slight hillock he and Solomon were joined by Hermogenes and Procopius, who asked to be allowed to observe the battle from this vantage point.

'By all means, and let us hope that when you come to write your letter to a certain person in Constantinople it is a joyful one.'

The man did not blush as he might, given Flavius was hinting he suspected Procopius to be an emissary from Justinian sent to observe and report privately on both he and Hermogenes. This was a supposition arrived at because, having watched him over weeks now, the man was too skilled and too sure of himself for the position he held.

The sound of hooves took his attention and he showed some irritation that Pharas, leader of the Heruls, had left his station between the infantry and the cavalry led by Bouzes. He was greeted with a frown, one that quickly evaporated when he made his quietly delivered suggestion of how and where his men could be better deployed.

'It fits with your plan, Flavius Belisarius,' he added softly, 'but I hope improves it. If I have overstepped the line, I apologise.'

'Move your men, Pharas.' Flavius issued another order after only a moment's consideration. 'And tell Bouzes to extend his front to cover your absence.'

Realising he had not done Hermogenes the courtesy of inclusion – the older man had not even heard the exchange – he turned to him looking apologetic, to receive in response an immediate and reassuring affirmation.

'A tactical alteration, perhaps?' Flavius nodded. 'Such

a decision falls within your competence, not mine.'

A gesture sent Pharas on his way, with Flavius moving his horse close to that of the Hermogenes to impart in the same quiet tone his exchange with the Herul. 'They are hardy fighters and I trust Pharas to do as he has outlined.'

'Meaning you would not trust another?'

'I best speak with Bouzes.'

The *dux Phoenicia* was not happy about the extension of his line, given it thinned out the forces he needed to repel an assault by the Sassanid cataphracts. Tempted to include him in what Pharas intended, Flavius demurred. He would act more properly in ignorance.

'You will do well, I am sure. Emulate your father, who would have relished to be here today.' Flavius looked skywards. 'His gaze will be upon you, I'm sure.'

'My whole family will be looking down on me!' came the crabbed response, which got a sharp rejoinder.

'No doubt to ensure you act according to my orders.'

The sound of the enemy horns cut off any response and had Flavius spurring back to his position in time to see the Sassanid horse archers deploy against Bouzes. He hoped this was no diversion but an assault Perozes would push to its limit. Behind the archers came a whole host of running men, infantry with large shields and behind them even more carrying long lengths of freshly cut boards, wide enough for a horse and rider and slatted for purchase.

Yet more followed with the shovels which would be employed to take out the leading edge of the ditch. Well to their rear sat the heavy cavalry, the sun glinting on their polished armour, waiting for the time when they could cross that obstacle and get at the enemy.

The archers were less effective than previously, given the strength of the opposing wind – it was blowing right into their faces – and this time they were clearly under instruction to press home and provide cover for the non-combatant diggers, all of whom had begun a furious assault on the soft and yielding earth that formed the outer bank of the ditch, their heads covered from counter arrow fire by a wall of held-aloft shields.

'The horse archers are suffering so that the work of destruction can proceed,' Flavius explained, when again Procopius asked for clarification. 'They do not often stay to take casualties and also they are less fluid in the role they have been given. Once enough damage has been done to our works then they will withdraw. It will be time then for the heavy cavalry to join in the fight.'

'Can our men not cross the ditch and drive the diggers off?'

'No, Procopius, they can't. They have orders to stay, for if they break their line it will never be put back together again.'

The Sassanids were making rapid progress, as the edge of the ditch turned from a wall into a slope. Perozes seemed to have an inexhaustible supply of horse archers for as one *numerus* dispersed, their quivers used up, another came to take its place. They were drawing so much counter fire that a message came to the hillock to tell Flavius his archers were running out of arrows.

'Tell them to desist and save some for what is yet to come.'

Such a decision allowed the spade men to work with impunity and that sped their progress. They soon had what they wanted, a traversable incline the horsemen could use to get at Bouzes and his men. Now the task was to get those wide boards forward to the other side and jammed into the rear wall and that required another level of protection.

'Cataphracts,' pointed out Hermogenes quietly as the armoured warriors, so numerous they must constitute the entire Sassanid force at the disposal of Kavadh, began to advance.

Flavius had seen the movement and he had also seen the spade men discard their tools and take up their boards, to then kneel behind a wall of shields and wait for their premium fighting men. At a command they opened ranks and the cataphracts set their horses at the slope, the first line slithering down the newly dug and loose surface to cross to the rear and engage the Romans, who were well above their heads.

It was admirable if troubling the way they created the gaps needed to get those wide gangways laid, just as it was to see how quickly a second line of horsemen took advantage of this to get to their enemies on even ground, clattering up the wooden boards and pressing forward using their horse and human armour to avoid being checked. So heavy was that linked metal it afforded few gaps by which an assailant could land a telling blow, even the faces and chests of the horses had a layer of metal, with only their eyes showing. Yet press as they did it seemed they made little progress.

'He holds,' said Procopius, admiration evident in his voice.

'For now,' came the toneless reply.

Bouzes would have struggled on the first day had the attack been pressed and now he had more of the line to protect. So when the cataphracts increased in numbers it came as no surprise that his front began to buckle. But it did not break and Bouzes was riding to the rear yelling and screaming, though he could not be heard on the hillock, clearly urging resistance before he dashed into the melee with his personal *bucellarii* to shore up a weakness, which brought a feeling of reluctant admiration to his general.

'Orders to Bouzes, Solomon. He is to allow the pressure to tell. Let him give ground but slowly and if he enquires why say to him we need him and his men whole for what is to come.'

In truth Bouzes was not going to be gifted with a choice; Flavius had sent the message to allow him to do that which was being forced upon him anyway, the sound reason that with permission to give ground he would keep his men intact as a fighting unit. The lighter cavalry he led were struggling to hold the heavier cataphracts and if they began to break up completely they would open a huge and irreparable gap in the Roman line and allow the enemy to begin an encirclement.

If he was enraged by the command it was clear Bouzes was obeying, but with commendable slowness, as if trying to send a message of his disapproval. Flavius issued his orders to the left central unit of cavalry and waited for the moment of decision, which lay not with him but with Pharas and his Herul cavalry. If it was agony it was necessary as he saw even more lines of cataphracts pressing forward towards the ditch till soon those at the rear were crowding the men at the front.

Pharas chose his moment well. He had led his men round behind the hill that formed the left flank of the battlefield, one so steep that it defied any horsemen the chance to overcome it and would have been hard going on foot, and this had been carried out unseen. Now that the Sassanid cataphracts were entirely committed he and his men emerged at the charge from the southern side of the hill and hit them in the flank, their lances taking horses mainly as well as knocking from their saddle the odd rider. Once a man so heavily armoured was on the ground he was as good as dead.

At the same time the centre-left Roman cavalry, light but fast, emerged from behind the middle ditch and took them in the other flank, the confusion caused by the twin surprise assaults immediate and obvious. The Sassanids, who were thrown into a muddle as some turned to face the new threats while others kept up the assault on Bouzes, who realised that he too had an opportunity and stopped his retreat, sounding the horns to advance.

The cataphracts were thrown back into a cluster in which they struggled to employ their weapons, pressed on all sides by Romans stabbing with spears and swords, with knife-carrying skirmishers in their midst seeking to cut their stirrups while from their rear a hail of arrows rained down on the crowded centre.

Assailed on three flanks the cataphracts lost all cohesion and broke into individuals seeking to save themselves, and within a blink the attack had turned into flight. Flavius

Belisarius had abandoned his hillock and was working to get ahead of his Romans with his mounted *comitatus*. He and his personal troops had to form a line that stopped the victorious cavalry from indulging in a pointless and dangerous pursuit.

At the same time Solomon was calling forward a mass of citizens from Dara armed with a variety of tools, their task to repair the ditch and re-form the defence as soon as Flavius forced his own men back to the right side of the line, working to get them to re-form, for the next attack could come soon.

Procopius beamed at him when he finally got back to his position of command. 'Would I be allowed to offer my congratulations, General Belisarius?'

'Save them until we have beaten the Sassanids, which we have not done yet!'

Chapter Fifteen

Even through the cloud of dust Flavius could see how many of those heavy cavalry had got clear. Driven off they might be but they would re-form and the Romans would have to face them again. All around him those that had fallen were being stripped of their armour while the non-maimed horses were being shepherded back towards Dara. The Roman archers reclaimed arrows that had missed flesh to end up stuck in the ground.

They were not to be left in leisure to carry this out. A line of infantry began marching right at his centre, to their fore men who would adopt the same obstacle-destroying tactics that had just been set in reverse. Once the ditch was rendered crossable, the assault would become a trial of strength as the front lines of each army fought a close-combat battle, one which allowed for little skill and much muscle and so it proved.

In places his line bent, in others it was the Sassanids who were forced to concede ground, yet that was not translated into a Roman advantage, as whoever commanded the central attack moved his reserves to shore up a position. As had now become common, Procopius wanted it explained to him. Flavius pointed out that the highest number of his cavalry were behind the fighting infantry, including the *bucellarii*.

'The object is to fix them in place before he launches the main assault, which must come soon as there is only so much daylight left.'

'Where will it come?'

'If it were me it would be in the same place. We can't surprise him from behind that hillock twice and the ditch repairs have to be easier to break down than what they had to destroy the first time. Against that we are able to move reserves without his being able to see it and it would have to be guarded against, which might blunt what happens to the front. Pharas is now back alongside Bouzes, so from where Perozes is looking that may seem a more formidable point to attack than previously.'

'And if he breaks the centre?'

'He won't!'

There are times in a battle when a sort of hiatus descends; it is not that nothing is happening, more that little is changing, though it is also a situation that cannot last forever. For Flavius the advantage of being in defence was bearing the fruit for which he had hoped. It was his opposite number who had to make all the tactical decisions, which allowed him to be reactive. But there was another string to his personal bow and one, if Perozes obliged him, that would prove decisive.

He was thus pleased to see that the central infantry attack was not being too ardently pressed, it was exerting just enough pressure to keep his men engaged and now Perozes had sent forward his ditch destroyers on the Roman left, while behind them once more the cataphracts had formed their lines in preparation to follow. It was what lay to their rear that gave the plan away; there were the Sassanid light cavalry, put in place to pursue a beaten foe once their more puissant comrades had created the necessary space.

Hermogenes pointed out to Procopius that this would be the main assault. It may have been decades since he had soldiered but he had seen enough to make sense of what lay before him, which was just as well, given Flavius needed to hand over tactical responsibility.

'I will need your good advice, Hermogenes, for staying here you will see what I cannot. If you think my plans are set to fail I need you to tell me.'

The older man just nodded as Flavius Belisarius rode off, his *comitatus* in his wake, to take command of the *bucellarii*. Once with them he would only see that which lay right before him.

In the letter Procopius wrote to Constantinople he outlined how the Sassanids had pressed on the right in the same manner as they had on the left against Bouzes. Even he, a non-military man, could discern the reasons for Perozes throwing his men forward on his left wing; there was no way they could be surprised by a sally from behind a hill for there was none, just the meandering stream in a deep gully that fed water to Dara and formed the right-flank defence of the Belisarius position.

Before long it appeared to be an attack that was on the verge of success; the same tactics produced the same result: a destroyed ditch, planking used to get onto even ground and equal terms, the pressure from the heavily armoured cataphracts forcing back the Romans, but once more it was with an unbroken frontage. What neither of his forward tactical commanders could see was the way that was going to be countered, for Bouzes and Pharas, those they could see and not already fighting, remained in place.

Flavius Belisarius had horsemen lined up at the right-hand edge of the central ditch and there they stayed until the Sassanid assault was well past their position, as apparent flank guard. From what the enemy could see it was but a thin screen; Procopius and Hermogenes could see the truth. Behind that seeming crust Flavius had moved his *bucellarii* as well as every other cavalryman who had been placed behind the central ditch.

Timing was crucial and that was a decision which could only be made by the man on the spot. For Flavius it was more of a feeling than what he could discern visually, the point at which a commander senses the moment has arrived to act. The horns blew and the forward Roman screen swung their mounts, giving the impression they were abandoning the field. The effect on the enemy was instantaneous. The man

Perozes had put in command sensed impending triumph and took some of the men driving forward, sending them to attack to their right, calling forward his light cavalry to provide support.

As they swung onto their new line of assault the heavy cavalry that Flavius Belisarius had spent years training came barrelling forward at a fast canter to hit an enemy not yet properly organised, it being a mixture of two different elements. The consequence was instantaneous as that part of the Sassanid force recoiled on their comrades. As the Roman heavy cavalry made inroads they were followed by a whole host of men on lighter mounts who got amongst their enemies and began to initiate carnage.

Armies can be like a single body in their minds; once a sense of panic arises it spreads quickly and that is what happened to the men Perozes commanded. Suddenly the Roman infantry contesting the central ditch saw the opposing line sway and seriously buckle as the Sassanids' will to fight began to waver. To their left the whole attack had become a nightmare as Flavius Belisarius, having formed his *bucellarii* into an arrow formation, drove right through the rear of the Sassanids to cut the attackers off from support, before wheeling to drive them on the renewed assault of the men they had previously forced into a retreat.

With that stream at their back these Sassanids found themselves fighting on three fronts, their very numbers ceasing to be an advantage. Perozes did send men forward to try and break through but even his best cataphracts were faced by a body of men who could match them in battle, led by the Roman general who had engineered the downfall of his plan.

To the rear of those *bucellarii* the rest of the Romans were engaged in a massacre that turned that meandering stream a deep red, running through a gully rapidly choking up with bodies. Flavius knew he had won when he heard the enemy horns recalling the men he was fighting. Perozes was now engaged in seeking to limit the damage to the Sassanid army and in short order the enemy ceased to engage the *bucellarii* and abandoned the fight.

The slaughter went on as the light of the day faded. The citizens of Dara, keen that it should be complete, came forward with lit torches that ensured it did not cease, they too engaging in the killing of any of their enemies seeking to surrender, before stripping them naked so their womenfolk could mutilate them.

Flavius was back on his hillock, the clothing under his armour stiff with blood, watching the first Roman victory in decades as the men Kavadh had sent to take Dara were destroyed.

'We have won a battle not a war.'

These words from the victorious Flavius Belisarius had not been an attempt to dampen celebrations but a mere statement of fact and that came true with a speed that surprised even him. By spring Kavadh had raised another army and sent it marching into Roman territory by a route never previously attempted. Entirely mounted they were now streaming along the banks of the Euphrates fifty leagues to the south of Dara.

There could be no immediate reaction, given there was suspicion it was a feint to draw the Romans away from their main base in order to denude it of a defence; Dara was still the key to holding the frontier but there were other fortress towns requiring garrisons that could not be moved so Flavius went to work to raise a force large enough to counter the threat, calling in contingents for all the territories he controlled. As the recently created *magister militum per Orientem*, he was now the undisputed military master in the region.

By the time it was decided this was a true incursion and dangerous, Flavius set off to counter it and if his intelligence was correct he outnumbered the enemy by a factor of just less than two to one. His forces were bolstered by five thousand Ghassanids, half mounted, half infantry, they a numerous frontier tribe often allied to Rome but just as ready to treat with Kavadh if that seemed wise and Constantinople appeared to be weak: after the victory at Dara they were sure they were now choosing the winning side.

Hermogenes had returned to the capital so he took with him Procopius who would act as his secretary as well as his quartermaster. The enemy commander this time was Azarethes, the senior military satrap of Kavadh, the most lauded general of the Sassanid Empire, who did not seem to be showing much in the way of guile or war craft.

Booty and sheer destruction seemed more important. He and his men were ravaging the rich and fecund Euphrates valley, burning crops, slaughtering cattle, killing the local citizenry and taking treasure. They had to be stopped and that ceased the moment Azarethes was appraised of the fact that the Romans were closing in on him and he was seriously outnumbered. He then began to retire towards the frontier.

Flavius Belisarius had force-marched to this point and he put on an extra spurt to get within a day's march of his enemy, intent on forcing a battle, getting so close that the fires in the Sassanid camps of the previous day were still warm when the Romans came upon them.

Aware that he might struggle to get away, Azarethes decided to turn and fight at a place of his choosing, just to the east of a city called Callinicum, while Flavius came on and set up his camp within sight of the Sassanid fires. He then took a tour of the probable field of battle to formulate his plans. Never entirely happy to let others decide where to fight he was not disheartened by what he observed, even if Azarethes had chosen well, a plain with the River Euphrates on one flank and some high hills to the south that projected to his left. While not narrow, it was not a space in which the Romans could deploy their superiority to advantage.

The disposition of his troops conformed to the best way to use the terrain, which being flat between the river and the steep hills favoured a central attack by cavalry. The river flank Flavius would protect with infantry, while he took personal command in the centre with the mass of his horses, Lycaonians on his right and the mounted element of the Ghassanids holding the right flank. Again he wanted the Sassanids to attack him, which they might do given that if Azarethes tried to escape he faced the possibility of being caught by the pursuing Romans in open country where the numerical advantage would be decisive.

The victory at Dara had imbued the Romans with a feeling of invincibility, one their general did not share. He could not doubt their desire to get at the enemy and begin the task of destruction and nor could he fault it; it was the timing of such where commander and the troops he led disagreed. Flavius counselled patience, given it would be Easter Sunday on the morrow and that was a day of fast for Christians. It seemed folly to him to fight on an empty stomach in a battle that was probably going to last from dawn till dusk.

The disagreement, albeit infusing the ranks of his army, was presented to him by his inferior unit commanders and very forcibly so, his objections being seen as too cautious. On the march to catch Azarethes the Romans had, as they passed through the ravaged countryside, seen the destruction this invasion had caused: the men decapitated or swinging from trees, the despoiled women wailing over their loss. Children had been tossed on spears in a hideous sort of sport, while in every field lay dead livestock or burnt crops.

To their certainty of success was added their fury of grievance. These apostates must be punished, every man of them made to pay with their own blood for that which they had spilt in Roman territory and the notion of waiting a day for their justified revenge was anathema.

'Is it not impious to fight on Easter Day, *Magister*?'

Procopius put forward this point in a break between conferences. Flavius had sent his captains to plead with their men to trust him; was he not the Victor of Dara and did he not know when to best bring about the destruction of Azarethes and his band of murderous marauders?

Flavius clutched at the notion. 'Solomon, get men out to spread the word that it would be displeasing to God to so act vengefully on the day of his resurrection.'

If it seemed a good idea it fell on deaf ears; to the men he led it seemed Easter Day was as good as any other for slaughter and despite his reservations Flavius gave way on the grounds that, if he did not, some of his troops might decide to act independently and if they began to fight piecemeal it would be a disaster.

A plea to the accompanying priests to allow his men to eat ran into a religious hostility every bit as vehement as the lay one; this was the holiest day of the year and God could not be denied his fast under any circumstances.

'Then God better be on hand to aid us,' was the sour comment in response.

Naturally such a day began with a Mass all along the extended line, as his men, high and low and including himself, were shriven and promised that what sins they had committed in this life would be forgiven in the next for they were engaged upon God's purpose. The priests were just as keen on retribution as the men over whom they prayed and it was made plain that in killing the Sassanids they would be doing holy work.

'Odd word,' Procopius whispered, more to himself than to Solomon kneeling beside him, 'regarding a divinity who insisted we turn the other cheek.'

'Hardly ever met a priest who knew truly the message of Jesus Christ. There are some good men who have become priests but too few. Most care more for their bellies than their faith.'

'Best not let your master hear you say that, *Domesticus*. He's a pious man.'

'He's too soft, Procopius. What happened was mutiny and he would have done best by stringing up a few and letting the rest wonder at sharing their fate.'

The trumpets blew to end the devotion and the army in their various dispositions turned from that to facing the enemy, who within a glass of sand set about them with a burst of arrow fire at a density few had previously experienced. Counter fire evened out the rate of casualties so Flavius could be reasonably happy that no sense of balance had been achieved – he still outnumbered Azarethes.

If he preferred the defensive, Flavius reasoned that with men who were going to be increasingly weakened from hunger, the longer the day went on the weaker they would become; best he launch an attack just in order to force a response. He was busy putting this in place when the discord on his right wing alerted him to a threat and had him riding hard to find out the cause.

It gave him no joy to observe that Azarethes had moved a huge number of his cavalry to the Roman right wing and attacked the Ghassanids. Even worse was to see that they were beginning to panic and their line was not going to hold, which would destroy that flank completely. That was spreading to the Lycaonians who were next to their left and that would result in half of his line being rolled up.

'Solomon, get as many cavalry to this wing as you can, while I try to shore up the defence.'

'Best send another, *Magister*. If you fall we are lost.'

'If the Lycaonians give way I reckon us lost anyway, now go.'

Flavius and a small contingent of his *bucellarii* rode

into what was the beginnings of a collapse and it was one at which he was at a loss to prevent. These mounted Ghassanids had not fought under him at Dara; the sight of him did not have the effect it would have had on the men he had led to victory, so his attempts to rally them failed. These were the men who had so wanted to fight. Now they desired nothing more than to set their mounts to the west and gallop to safety.

A messenger came to tell him the Lycaonian commanders, who had managed to keep their men in place, had both been killed. That gave him a feeling of dread; men rarely held their ground when they lost their leaders and that was the case now. If they went the Huns would be next and then the whole cavalry line would crumble, which would leave the infantry at the mercy of Azarethes.

If there is a moment when a general can sense victory then there is another that hints at defeat. Even worse is the feeling that can come which presages catastrophe, one only an arrogant numbskull would face up to and not react. Flavius recognised now that he very likely could not hold; fear would negate any generalship he could bring to bear, so the task was to avoid what had happened in his first battle.

There was only time to conclude that fact before the Lycaonians broke. Now they were following in the wake of the Ghassanids and there was no time to redeploy the rest of his light cavalry to face the coming threat, while his *bucellarii* were too few in number to fight on alone. This had him riding hard away from the mayhem around him to order his cavalry to quit the field, his own men included.

Collecting Procopius, he put Solomon in charge of

getting his men out of danger, sweeping aside the suggestion that he too flee. The waggons that carried the Belisarius possessions and those of the men who attended to him were harnessed up and driven towards the river. Before he followed he ordered Solomon to get to Callinicum and make sure it could be held, dismounting and passing the reins to his *domesticus*.

'Get every boat you can find and bring them upriver as soon as you can. If God has any mercy, you will find us still alive.'

There was no need to say who the 'we' were. The infantry could never outrun the Sassanid cavalry so their only one hope was to stand and fight with the river at their back and Flavius Belisarius was determined to lead that defence. Peter, the man who commanded the infantry, was from Justinian's Excubitors. Flavius had no knowledge of his reading of history but he knew what to do for he had learnt much at the knee of his father.

'Form the *testudo*. We do battle like the legions of old.'

Peter proved an asset, quick to follow orders and not one to waste time in asking for clarifications; he speedily had his men adopt the famous tortoise shape that gave them a round frontage and flat sides while Flavius organised the archers to take up a position in the centre of the protecting body and to be prepared to fire over their heads.

They got everything in place just in time; the first Sassanid attack came almost as they completed their dispositions. But with shields locked and nowhere to which they could run it was a hard defence to break and this time the Sassanids had no cataphracts in their force to make the needed breakthrough. Azarethes had only light horse, and faced with a wall of shields and protruding spears, as well as slashing swords if they got too close, the attackers were driven off a dozen times.

Being spring the heat was tolerable and there was no shortage of water. The fight went on all through the day, but what was running short was arrows as the archers sent salvo after salvo into the advancing ranks of Sassanid cavalry to break their organisation. In attack after attack the horsemen hit the shield wall piecemeal and with a lack of coordination. By twilight the arrows were exhausted, but so were the Sassanids, while the boats Solomon had organised began to arrive.

The defence was collapsed in an orderly manner, the lines shortened until Flavius, having got away the content of his waggons as well as the majority of his men, stood among the very last of his infantry. Azarethes rode forward in the gathering gloom, to raise his sword and kiss it in a form of salute. Flavius and Peter were the last to board a boat, to be carried downstream on the current of river full of spring meltwater.

If they had succeeded in extracting the infantry it had not been everyone; the field they left was dotted with many dead members of the Roman forces.

CHAPTER SIXTEEN

The capital city to which Flavius Belisarius returned as a partially successful general was one in turmoil and the target of the unrest was the Emperor Justinian, the cause being his well-intentioned efforts to effect some very important changes to a system that had become ossified. The law codes were stuffed full of statutes that no longer had any relevance while the treasury was not as full as it should be, meaning that to pursue his aims and prosecute a war in the east Justinian needed to get in all the taxes owed from a population well versed in avoidance, none more so than the richest patricians and merchants.

The problem the new Emperor had was not in the policies but in the people he chose to implement them. The recodification of the laws was handed to a senator called Tribunianus, famed for his knowledge of jurisprudence. Initially his reforms were greeted with approval, but slowly it began to be obvious that as the man in charge of judicial judgement too many of the cases were being decided in favour of his friends. Even less palatable was the suspicion that bribes were involved, for Tribunianus seemed to be a very much richer fellow halfway through the recodification than he had been at the outset.

Such matters tended to concern the upper reaches of Roman society but to that class the real trouble lay in taxation. The task of ensuring collection was allotted to John the Cappadocian and in that breast the population found a degree of venality that, as it went on, became increasingly intolerable: too much of what he soaked from their income was going into his coffers and not the treasury. John inflamed feelings even more by flaunting his increasing wealth in a way that was both crass and dangerous.

John had also been ordered by Justinian to cut the number in what was an exceedingly bloated bureaucracy, which meant separating men, mostly nobles, from their means of earning a living, as well as removing from them their status as imperial placemen. Given many had bribed their way to their occupation, this struck at the very heart of the class of people the empire relied on for support.

Disenfranchised men tend to foregather and these nobles were no exception; what held back the growing tide of anger was that they did not actually all combine into one group. Some gravitated towards the Blue faction, much favoured by the imperial couple, in the hope of reinstatement by ingratiation. Others joined the Greens, the party of the merchants and seen as the opposition to imperial fiscal overreach. The fact that they went their separate ways tended to hide just how serious was the discontent, given they had a habit of directing their resentments at each other.

If Flavius had heard rumours of it – no one could avoid the criticisms of John the Cappadocian for they were so loud they even reached the provinces he ran – he had no idea of the depth of feeling into which he rode into Constantinople. Unlike previous visits he came to the city at the head of the *bucellarii*, their armour and accoutrements shiny, they following behind their general and his personal guard unit.

The victory at Dara gave the Belisarius name lustre; the defeat at Callinicum was hailed as a miracle, given the losses were so few and he could be hailed as the man who had saved the day. His campaigns could be seen as a success; the Sassanids had made no more incursions since that last battle, it being conveniently put to one side that, his treasury now better supplied, Justinian had concluded a treaty and reinstated the payment of gold to Kavadh.

So he and his six-hundred-strong force entered the city to the cheers of the populace, or at least those not too occupied to notice. When they reached the plaza before the imperial palace Justinian was there to greet him, a signal honour. If it was noticed that Theodora was absent no one had the ill grace to make mention of it.

'The conquering hero is home.' Tempted to reply, one success, two failures did not a conquering hero make, Flavius merely smiled. 'You have bloodied the nose of Kavadh.'

The answer was too soft for anyone nearby to hear. 'While you have lined his purse, Highness.'

There was a moment then when Flavius thought he had gone too far. It was no secret between himself and Justinian that he disapproved of bribing the Sassanids to remain supine, indeed the Emperor had railed against it as an imperial nephew. But the look those words engendered, a flash of irritation, told Flavius that if he was still held in regard, the man was now well and truly at home in his imperial state and it was not for the likes of him to question policy. It was as brief as a small cloud obscuring the sun, for Justinian then smiled.

'Few would dare challenge me so directly.'

'You know I cannot be otherwise.'

'Just as you should know how much I miss dispute.' The voice rose from what it had been in that exchange to its normal level as Justinian added, with a scowl at the members of his counsel come to join him in the welcome, 'Everyone agrees with me now, at least to my face. Behind my back they conspire to hide from me the truth of their peculations.'

'Your lady wife is well, Highness?'

That change of subject did not go down well either: Flavius had no desire to become even tangentially involved in court politics. Or was it the way he referred to Theodora, not giving her proper title?

'My imperial consort is in very good health.'

'It pleases me to hear it.'

'Come, let us retire to a place where we can converse more freely, without so many ears seeking words that might be used to divide us.'

'My men?'

Justinian looked past him to the *bucellarii* lined up on parade; the point was obvious, some gesture should be made, like a close inspection, but Justinian was not to be drawn. He merely waved a dismissive hand.

'Will be looked after by the Excubitors, I'm sure. But they will, of course, be required to depart the city and move to the Galatea barracks.'

'My *comitatus*?'

'May stay within the confines of the city.'

Linking his arm, Justinian led Flavius past the guards at the palace entrance and into the cool interior, talking away like an old acquaintance, ignoring the deep bows that attended his passing as well as those of a more lowly station who knelt as if in an act of worship. His topic was the burdens of state, which were of course something he would love to put aside, a proposition that his companion took for what it was, window dressing. Justinian loved his role and only the Grim Reaper would separate him from the exercise of power.

'The real problem is that whatever the court officials do that is taken badly, I get the blame.'

Flavius was tempted to reply 'poor you', instead he pointed out the obvious. 'You do have the power to remove those who thwart your will.'

'Flavius, they are not the problem, it is those carrying out my express wishes that do that. John the Cappadocian removes a whole raft of people drawing stipends for doing nothing, but when they combine it is me they curse.'

'I have heard he is doing well.'

If Flavius was seeking to say he was corrupt it was not very well hidden, not that he intended it to be, but the reply from the Emperor answered several questions.

'Theodora has great faith in him.'

'Ah.'

'I can afford to buy off Kavadh only because John has seen to my coffers. If he looks to his own needs in the process then he is no different to anyone else I would employ in that task. The notion that any of my officials refuse to take bribes is one only the likes of you could hold.'

'Since you do not compliment me often, Highness, I will accept that one with gratitude.'

Justinian grinned like a naughty child, before a quick glance at the now closed door of the private chambers. 'We are alone, Flavius, you may call me by my name.'

That had the recipient look at the same door and pulling a face, the inference being plain: in this place they were never alone. Justinian began referring to the unrest, of which Flavius had received an inkling prior to his entry into Constantinople, the imperial view that it was not as bad as was being reported by the urban prefect.

'There are always grumbles in the city and that crescendos if you deprive lazy bureaucrats of their places. Besides, what one of my predecessors did not have the odd upheaval to contend with?'

'So it can be contained?'

'The city regiments are available to put a cap on any trouble.'

The entrance of Theodora stopped the conversation. A quick look established that she seemed more comfortable in her imperial status – there was an aura about her now as there was in her husband – but whereas Justinian had let that soften, there was no reduction in her manner for the sake of old acquaintance. She produced a smile, there was a greeting, but neither could be said to convey any warmth. Flavius then found himself on the receiving end of a series of rapid-fire questions that bordered on an interrogation, she demanding an explanation for the defeat at Callinicum, brushing aside the proposition that Flavius had said all that had to be imparted in his despatch.

'They are never enough,' she insisted as her husband nodded. 'The written word cannot fully describe what . . .' There was a pause then, before she added, 'The truth.'

'The truth is I failed, Highness.'

That being brushed aside, Flavius looked to Justinian to keep his wife in check, only to be reminded that it was not something he either wished to do or perhaps was capable of, which left his favourite general exposed to an uncomfortable period of explanation, one in which he refused to allot the blame for the defeat to any other cause than his own incompetence.

'Such nobility,' was the parting shot as Theodora reminded Justinian, just before she left the chamber, that there were other matters requiring his attention, things more important.

'We shall talk again,' the Emperor imparted quietly, adding the kind of smile that conveys a lack of liberty to do as you wish. 'And do not mind Theodora, she fears only for my well-being and that of the empire.'

'The good Lord help you if you do not do as you are told.'

That being said to an empty room had no consequences and he left the palace to lead his men to Galatea and see them safe to their barracks under the command of Solomon.

Over the next week, Flavius, who had returned to the city, sensed the growing unrest for, divested of his military garb, he was at liberty to walk the streets and overhear what was being said, to sense the febrile nature of the feelings of both factions, the Blues and the Greens. It was a mystery to him how rival chariot racing teams could morph over time into what they were now: political forces and sworn enemies.

From time to time he came across Procopius – their coincidental meeting seemed frequent – who had the same understanding of what was happening as he: Justinian was stoking passions as he sought to introduce edicts curbing the disturbances: limiting numbers permitted to gather outside the Hippodrome, higher fines for misbehaviour and a curb on too overt a display of allegiance. Such efforts to calm things turned out to have the absolute opposite effect and matters came to a head in the one place where the two polities gathered to vocally cheer on their charioteers.

The Hippodrome was packed, the early January weather was clement and the races were in progress when the trouble started. As reported it was small to begin with but it spread like a bushfire until the whole stadium seemed involved and the groups looked close to killing each other. The urban prefect, Eudaimon, asked and was given permission to enter the Hippodrome and not only quell the disorder but to arrest the leaders of both, people well known to the authorities. Seven men in all were taken up and a special court was set up which condemned all of them to death.

Such a show of force did not calm things, quite the reverse. Locked up in the urban prefect's gaol until the following day, their plight drew a crowd to protest at their impending fate, which continued into the morning as they were taken to the newly constructed scaffold to be hanged. The point at which the ropes began to choke then set off great lamentations, yet still the parties remained separate, one side cheering the drop of an enemy while keening and praying at the fate of one of their own.

Satisfied that the deed had been completed, Eudaimon led his men away, which allowed the mob to cut down the victims, whereupon they found two were still alive. Monks from the monastery of St Lawrence took both survivors to their cloisters which, being sanctified ground, they hoped would keep them safe. Eudaimon, unwilling to make a forced entry, posted guards outside to deny the whole monastery food until the monks surrendered the two miscreants.

This situation continued for months with no sign of the monks complying with the Prefect's demands, this while the atmosphere within the city walls went from bad to worse: the two surviving leaders, it transpired, consisted of one from each side, a Blue and a Green, and both having similar grievances they decided to combine.

Flavius, observing the mayhem that followed, took cognisance of one glaring fact: the regiments stationed permanently in the city were as factional as the general population. This was a factor which had kept them useful since they would only ever be employed against one or the other and only when called to contain a situation out of control.

Now that the Blues and Greens were acting in concert, what then? The answer came on the next occasion Justinian and Theodora entered the imperial box, to hear the entire assembled crowd in the Hippodrome, a stadium which held thirty thousand spectators, chanting in unison and their anger was aimed at him. The cry on which they combined was 'Nika', the Greek word for 'Victory', and it was plain the person they saw as the enemy needing to be defeated was Justinian.

Sat close to him Flavius watched as he tried to maintain an expression of unconcern – Theodora looked thunderous. If that worked at a distance it was certainly possible to observe the tenseness of his jaw and the odd furrowing of the brow in close proximity. Seeking to make a joke he made much play of laughing, which inflamed the crowd even more.

These protests should have ceased once the races began and the crowd became distracted; they did not, if anything they increased with shouting spectators flowing onto the competition area to get closer to the imperial podium. With the chariots unable to run the races were abandoned and the crowd, flushed with what they saw as success, poured out into the streets and headed for the palace of the urban prefect, killing the guards and, once they had freed the prisoners there, setting fire to the building.

They then rampaged through the city, setting alight to two churches, including St Sophia. Next the Senate House went up in flames as well as the Baths of Zeuxippus and

Alexander, all very close to the imperial palace. Nightfall brought some relief as weariness took over but the following morning the Hippodrome was once more packed with a fractious, screaming mob, audible to the gathered and frightened council.

The demands of the rioters' leaders were discussed. Flavius was present in his capacity as *magister* but did not seek to participate, merely to observe. The mob insisted on the removal of John the Cappadocian, of Tribunianus and Eudaimon, all of which, to the dismay of Flavius, his councillors advised Justinian to consent. The temptation to step forward and damn this as unwise was strong; no good would come of seeking to placate a mob, it had to be resisted, but he saw the feeling was so strong in favour he knew he would not change minds.

There was, however, one action he could initiate himself and he left for a brief moment and collared his old comrade from the Excubitors, Domnus Articus. 'I need you to send a message to Solomon to bring the *bucellarii* within the walls. Justinian needs protection. Send word to my *comitatus* as well.'

'The city regiments?'

'Have not moved and nor will they, in my opinion, which is a blessing, for with the Greens and Blues united they would be more of a danger than an aid.'

'The Excubitors will do their duty.'

'I don't doubt it, Domnus, but you might be too few.'

The proof that concessions only feed a mob was proved when Justinian returned to the imperial box to address them, offering to grant an amnesty to those who had misdeeds to their name, including their still condemned leaders. Having seen their previous demands met the crowd yelled him down and vocally called for a new emperor, naming Probus the nephew of Anastasius as their candidate, which rendered the presence of the incumbent superfluous.

Justinian re-entered the palace, his first demand being that both Probus and his cousin Hypatius leave the city. Never a man noted for his bravery and well aware of how fickle a crowd could be – mobs who create emperors can just as easily destroy them soon after – Probus immediately did as he was ordered, which resulted in the burning of his house.

But the rioters found a less than swift Hypatius trying to flee and took him as a virtual prisoner, escorting him to the Hippodrome where in the absence of a crown they declared him emperor by placing a gold necklet on his head, the news of this quickly conveyed to the imperial council chamber, causing Justinian to lose his nerve.

The mob were against him and it transpired that, despite the claims of Domnus Articus, the Excubitors had decided their best course in this crisis was inaction – to neither aid nor hinder the man they were tasked to protect, which implied that powerful forces, senators and perhaps some of those dismissed officials, were conspiring with the rioters.

There was a fast galley waiting in the private palace harbour and the notion was to get to the imperial armies in Thrace and seek their aid. If Flavius had mixed opinions of Theodora, they were tempered now as she stepped forward to address not only her husband but those gathered to counsel him, in a voice as strong as it was passionate.

'Run? To where? Wherever we go will we not face the same? We will be found and if not killed be dragged back to be torn limb from limb by that mob in the Hippodrome. Those who have worn the crown rarely survive its loss and I have no wish to see the day when I am not saluted as Empress. If we are to perish, Husband, let it be standing and facing those who would harm us, not skulking off like thieves in the night. Remember the old saying. Royalty is a fitting burial shroud.'

'Your men are in the Excubitor barracks, Flavius Belisarius,' whispered Domnus Articus, who had sidled into the antechamber as Theodora was declaiming to pass this on. 'Also, Mundus has fetched his Heruls, three hundred in number. I am with you too.'

The aid of such a fine warrior, a Gepid nobleman and *magister militum per Illyricum*, was very heartening yet it would be foolish to think the odds to be substantially altered.

'We may all die, Domnus.'

'A soldier's fate.'

The arrival of Narses, the elderly eunuch who had at one time been Flavius's commander, threw another voice into the discussion and had some positive information to impart. He had gone into the Hippodrome carrying a bag of Justinian's gold with which to bribe the Blues, also reminding them that both Justinian and Theodora were supporters and that Hypatius was an enthusiast of the opposition.

He could now definitely report that the mob were not as united as they had once been. Many of the Blues were aware that things had gone too far and they certainly did not want Hypatius as emperor. He had distributed the gold as gifts to those more inclined to waver, with promises of more from Justinian. They were now slipping in groups out of the Hippodrome to go to their homes.

'So most of those remaining will be Greens,' he concluded, 'and also those who relish in making trouble, whatever the grounds.'

The sound of studded boots on marble floors had Flavius pulling out his sword. Normally forbidden in the presence of the Emperor it had seemed to him sensible to be armed. He relaxed as Solomon and Mundus appeared, fully armed. Justinian was looking at Flavius with something approaching fear, his eyes darting between the face and the weapon. Was he about to be betrayed by one of the few people in whom he reposed trust?

CHAPTER SEVENTEEN

Observing that look of fear offended Flavius and some of that feeling was in the nature of his less than respectful explanation, the fact that neither the city regiments nor the Excubitors could be relied upon and that this being so he had thought it wise to bring the men he had led in battle into the city to join his personal guard.

'On your own word, without seeking permission.'

'Sometimes it is necessary to act without that.' Justinian looked at Mundus, far from reassured. 'Mundus has brought his men as well, because he is loyal, as I am, to your person, though I think you must thank Solomon for his presence.'

Theodora spoke up, the voice unfriendly. 'And what,

having done that, do you recommend, Flavius Belisarius? You have yet to offer any advice and I have never before known you shy of telling us what is right and what is wrong.' Her black eyes narrowed and the tone changed to one of sly innuendo. 'Perhaps you have your own reasons to have the *bucellarii* to hand at such a time.'

Tantamount to an accusation of perfidy Flavius responded with scant respect for her rank. 'He is not only my friend, Lady, he is the Emperor to whom I have sworn allegiance.'

Eudaimon asked for and was granted permission to speak: removed to satisfy the mob he had not yet been replaced as urban prefect. 'We must take control of the city.'

It was Flavius who replied, earning a black look from Theodora. 'We do not have the means. The city regiments may well oppose us, but if we can capture Hypatius that could remove the focus of the revolt.'

'We must consider whether that will that not make matters worse?'

Justinian got a look from his wife then that made him blench, though her words, carefully calculated not to diminish him, belied the feeling behind them. 'How much worse can it get? I have already said I will not run away, so if I am to die, let it be here and let it be soon.'

Justinian had a look on his face that seemed to imply he wished the decision be made by anyone but himself, so Flavius, for the lack of anyone else proposing any action, took up the baton.

'Mundus, you take the outer gates in case they try to

smuggle Hypatius out. I will try to get into the Hippodrome and find him.'

'He will not come willingly if you do.'

'If I find him he will come. I think him no more willing than Probus to be in the situation he now finds himself.'

'And if he refuses?'

'Then his reign will be brief. Solomon, place our men to cover the inner gates.'

Narses was quick to object. 'There will still be Blues there who wish to leave. They must be allowed to do so.'

Flavius had no time for such considerations. He raced along the corridor that led to the imperial box, which as usual had Excubitor guards at the gate. His demand that they stand aside was refused and so the door to the imperial box remained locked. Frustrated but determined Flavius gathered up his *comitatus* and headed for another and lesser known way in. This took them through the still-smoking ruins of the Baths of Zeuxippus to a point just beyond one of the entrances, to a postern gate and a small staircase that led to a service door which opened on to the imperial box.

There he was faced by another set of armed men and they were vocal in their loyalty to Hypatius. The option to attack them was there but in such a confined space it was full of risk. If the crowd got wind of their presence and exited through the nearby gangway, he and his men could be trapped in the passageway, a too confined space in which to fight. Yet the presence of those guards told him Hypatius was where he expected him to be, on the podium where he had very likely been crowned.

'Find Solomon. Tell him to bring the *bucellarii* to this gate.'

That took time but Flavius had no intention of going into the stadium with only a hundred men at his back. Once Solomon and his six hundred *bucellarii* had arrived he had only one order to give.

'Weapons out,' he commanded, 'we will have to fight our way through the crowd to get Hypatius.'

'And if they oppose us?' asked Solomon.

'Then they pay whatever price is demanded.'

The noise within the stadium was so loud that, even with studded boots striking the stone staircase, no one heard Flavius and his men until they were almost upon them. One or two turned from their cheering to see the proximity of these men in armour, weapons drawn, and they panicked, seeking safety by pushing forward and that impacted on those on the terraces before them, causing the whole crowd to surge.

Even with that there was no space to give quarter; once in amongst these rioters Flavius and the *bucellarii* would be massively outnumbered and that was seen by those who were the first to face them. Their screams of fear drowned out the cheers of others and soon the ripple of dread filled the stadium as Mundus, on the other side of the Hippodrome, entering by what was to become known as the Gate of Death, sent his German mercenaries into action.

Unbeknown to Flavius, Nárses had gathered up enough armed men to seal the gates to the stadium, including the one he had just employed, trapping inside the entire

240

audience who had been so recently cheering the crowning of their new emperor. Once the killing started it became impossible to stop for those seeking to flee were trapped. The men Flavius led were fresh from bloody battle in the east, and hardened by what they had done they were not about to extend mercy.

Mundus and his huge and bloodthirsty Germans, armed with long swords and axes, were soon in the element they so loved, slashing left, right and centre at whatever stood in their way and nothing was going to stop them once their bloodlust was kindled.

Even if Flavius, having captured Hypatius as well as his brother Pompeius, had wanted to call a halt he would have been shouting at deaf ears. All he could do was lead his two captives out of the Hippodrome, through the now open door to the private corridor, through which were now pouring Excubitors to join in the slaughter, they having seen which way matters were going.

There was not enough sand on the racing track to soak up so much blood and given there were no open exits – the men Narses had put on the gates killed those who tried – the slaughter went on for hours until the stone tiers of seating were littered with dead bodies and slippery with gore, men mostly, but also some women and the occasional child.

When the citizens of Constantinople were dragooned into clearing the stadium, the body count was established as the capacity of the Hippodrome: thirty thousand were dead. Also, executed on the orders of Justinian, were the two nephews of Anastasius taken by Flavius, even though they had been given no choice but to go along with what the mob demanded. Several senators and former officials were likewise executed even if nothing could be proved against them; suspicion was enough.

A pall now hung over the city and it was not only made up of smoke. For a long time emperors had been obliged to placate the mob in the Hippodrome, often called to plead with them to be allowed to continue their rule. The charioteer factions had become too powerful, sure even as they competed with each other that they had a divine right to approve or disapprove the actions of the wearer of the purple. That was now gone, though there was no certainty it would not resurface.

That so many had died was a cause for repentance, but underneath the display of that lay the knowledge that the present incumbent had achieved a level of personal and unbridled power that had not existed since the days of the early Caesars. If he had not done the deed or even set it in motion, Justinian garnered as much credit for the actions of others as he had previously attracted blame.

He would never be loved – he was not gifted that way, regardless – but he was feared, which suited him. Theodora was held in even more dread, for it was soon common knowledge – she made sure the tale was disseminated – of how she had refused to flee and how she had sworn to revenge herself on the population of the city.

To those who supported the imperial couple she was seen as the real person who saved the empire as well as a co-ruler and she delighted in the caution with which even the most patrician senator now treated her. There was no more condescension directed at her lowly birth, while she made no attempt to hide her contempt for their pretensions.

One person not exposed to any of her malevolence was Flavius Belisarius; it seemed as if her attitude to him had swung round and he was now cosseted by her, invited into her circle of friends, many women and men who formed a sort of court separate to that of her husband. A loose lot, they reminded Flavius of the company he had enjoyed with Petrus in those dockside taverns-cum-brothels for, involved as he was with court matters, it was good to relax among people who seemed not to care one whit for the progress of the empire.

Even dining with Theodora and Justinian together was rarely overly formal and it was on such occasions that he really began to understand the nature of their political relationship, which really came down to a sort of joint rule in which Theodora was free to say as much as she wished about the future actions needing to be taken, advice Justinian either took or ignored.

Her abiding cause was that people from the lower classes should be advanced in official circles for the very good reason that they were less greedy than the senators who thought they owned these highly rewarded sinecures by right.

'Only until they learn how to steal, Flavius, and then they will be as greedy as their predecessors.'

The woman who whispered this to him –Theodora was off on her hobby horse and did not notice – was Antonina, one of the Empress's oldest friends and not for the first time sat next to him. Flavius had first met her years before at a gathering in the Sabbatius villa, taken over by Justinian not long after his accession as a place where he could escape the dull protocol of palace life, his father having been given the province of Illyricum to run, a sop to the sister of Justin who hankered to rule the part of the world from which she had sprung.

Being away in the east Flavius had been afforded only that one occasion in such company but it was enough to demonstrate to him the protocols: imperial grandeur was set to one side, everyone being encouraged to act as if the rank of the host did not exist, impossible to ignore of course, but it was a situation in which there could be a pretence that the life lived before Justinian's elevation could be recalled and that nowhere applied more than in sexual licence.

Neither Justinian nor Theodora saw much virtue in fidelity; both had come to the present estate through a world of much moral laxity and had acquired habits and desires difficult to put aside. By the time Flavius returned from Dara the villa had been abandoned and such gatherings had moved to the palace, the original venue being unsafe for a highly unpopular emperor. Indeed the whole arrangement had been in abeyance due to the troubles Justinian was labouring under.

Now that the Nika riots, as they had come to be called, had killed off the bacillus of impeding revolt both Theodora and Justinian felt safe to revive these events at which the pious and God-fearing face the imperial couple presented to the world was cast aside in the confines of the imperial palace. It was ever in the nature of rulers to expect virtue from their subjects while paying no attention to such constraints themselves.

Emperors lived in an enclosed world and much effort was extended to ensure that what went on inside was not common knowledge without. There was a strata of courtiers who were aware, how could there not be, and there were servants. The former were as debauched as their rulers and thought of their purse if they were not. The latter were chosen for their discretion and there was always the threat of strangulation if it was suspected they were telling tales to the outside world.

Added to that, much was done to present a devout aspect. Justinian had recently set in train the rebuilding of the Church of St Sophia, to a design that would make it the greatest basilica in the world, rivalling and outdoing anything in Rome. Everyone looking at the plans was staggered by the dimensions: a good way to get on the right side of Justinian was to mention this building and praise him as the genius behind it. The architects did the work, the Emperor took the plaudits.

One of the things Flavius liked about his present dining companion was her amusing indiscretion. Though careful to whom she spoke she was wonderfully scabrous about the band of hangers-on that made up the immediate social circle of the imperial couple and not afraid either to describe herself as the greediest of them. In short, she made him laugh.

'Why do I always seem to be seated next to you? This is the fourth time.'

Antonina raised a pair of already arched eyebrows. 'Do you object?'

'No, I am just curious. I observe that others move from neighbour to neighbour, we do not.'

'The consequence being that it is to my bed that you retire. But if you would prefer another . . . ?'

Flavius felt himself blush; Antonina was older than him and was much worldlier in so many ways – she had been married before and was now a widow with a young son – while she had shown in the bedchamber a wonderful ability to invoke in him a deep pleasure he had never before achieved. He had often been tempted to ask where she had learnt her dexterity but he feared the answer might distress him. Theodora had not been beyond multiple bed partners prior to marrying Justinian – he had been a party to it – and Antonina may well have behaved in the same manner.

He did not want that to be the case, not out of piousness but out of regard, in short he liked her. In any event, to take a moral position with a woman you had bedded more than once was the height of hypocrisy. Given she was a widow that was likely to be the source of her experience but there was another possibility: she came from a background not dissimilar to Theodora.

Antonina was the daughter of a successful charioteer, a member of the Blues whose luck had run out in the Hippodrome when a removed wheel, taken off by a competitor, saw him chucked from his chariot and thrown under the wheels of those following behind. Such men might make great fortunes but they came from lowly backgrounds, not the higher reaches of society, and so did she.

To even consider such things made Flavius feel like a scrub; who was he to judge anyone by their background? That was one area in which he fully supported Theodora. Let a man, or a woman for that matter, rise to the level their abilities would take them. No one had the right to prominence by mere birth.

'Do you like me, Flavius?'

Caught in a welter of thoughts the reply was hurried. 'Of course.'

A hand caressed his cheek. 'I believe you, for you are not one to lie. In fact, I think you incapable of being deceitful.'

'No man is that.'

'Look down the table and what do you see?'

'People taking their food and enjoying themselves. Servants pouring wine – and Justinian pondering, of course.'

'Is he enjoying himself? He looks worried.'

'Do not be fooled if you see a pensive expression, Justinian loves being emperor.'

'I should not like it, would you?'

'Not a question that requires an answer, since the opportunity would never arise.'

If it was implied that imperial protocol was set aside on these occasions it was never entirely true; when Justinian stood everyone followed suit, for to sit in the presence of a standing emperor was never to be allowed to anyone other than the seriously lame.

As a group they retired to another well-furnished chamber, with any number of couches on which the guests could disport themselves. There was wine and sweetmeats but no servants, for the double doors were shut behind them to ensure complete privacy. Theodora liked to play robust games, which over time became more and more risqué, often competitions which saw items of clothing being paid as forfeits.

In time, those couches would be used for various couplings and that was a situation Flavius Belisarius did not enjoy. Public copulation he found embarrassing and the same applied to the pleasure Justinian took in watching others perform. One of the other factors he liked about Antonina is that she had seen his discomfort and had taken care to rescue him, choosing a discreet moment when, unobserved, she could lead him from the chamber by a secret door to the suite of rooms Theodora had provided for her within the palace.

He woke the next morning feeling sated, and in the dawn light he sat up and took to examining the sleeping Antonina. Her greater years did not show; the skin of her face was still good, the flesh of her body firm and the cast of her mind seemed to him to be more youthful than mature. There is an innocence to a person asleep and even if they had made robust love during the night Antonina looked very much that in her slumbers.

Looking closer Flavius saw the full lips twitch slightly as a dream registered on her features. Strong nose, tightly fleshed chin and a swan-like neck leading to a fine bosom. His hand reached out to caress her breast which made her stir slightly and murmur. Next he pressed soft lips to her nipple, then a gently flicking tongue, which made her writhe and brought forth a moan of pleasure.

Sliding down Flavius pressed close to her to be rewarded by a willing companion who turned her body towards him, eyes still closed, a hand reaching out to take one of his buttocks and pull him close. Their coupling was not furious, it was slow and languid as befitted the time of day and, if it was possible that it could be so, it was even more pleasurable.

Later, in a shared bath, the way they spoke to each other seemed to him to take on a different dimension, not a pair who had come together to provide mutual gratification but a sort of intimacy he had never before felt. Then there was her son Photius, an engaging boy of twelve who seemed to accept him as a proxy for his dead father, a man he had been too much an infant to know, though the lad was wary of his strict mother.

Flavius was the opposite, positively indulgent: playing games with the boy was a pleasure, seeking to hone his skill with sword and spear took Flavius back to his own childhood and his father Decimus doing the same with him at a time that preceded the stuff of his nightmares and seemed so blissfully innocent. There was no reserve, no seeking to avoid interrogation as Photius sought the answer to every question that entered his young mind, or feeling harassed by his attention.

As a trio they seemed like a unit and over the following weeks that feeling deepened, so when Theodora hinted that Antonina might make for him a suitable wife it was not a suggestion he dismissed out of hand. In fact, the notion entered his thoughts often as he took a full part in

Justinian's plans for the future, which harked back to a conversation they had engaged in years before, nothing less than the reunification of the Eastern and Western Empires, and in order that he should be of aid Flavius set himself to study both the history of recent events as well as the present problems.

CHAPTER EIGHTEEN

Flavius was explaining to his paramour Justinian's ambitions, emphasising it would not be a simple task. 'With the east paid for and quiet he feels the time might be right.'

'And it involves you?'

'He wants me to command the armies. What military man, Antonina, would not want to undertake such a possible conquest?'

That she was interested at all surprised Flavius but also pleased him; he would have suggested it was hardly a subject to engage women if it had not been for Theodora, who seemed equally keen. They were sitting on a grassy bank overlooking the Propontis, their horses grazing at the pasture, reins trailing the ground. The sun was warm, the sea was blue and all seemed right with the world. It was good to get away from the palace and the constant need to be ready to jump to the needs of the imperial couple. It was just good to be alone in each other's company.

'So I plan how to fight and hopefully to win but that would, I am sure, bore you.'

'No, Flavius, I wish to hear what you are doing.'

He touched the back of her hand. 'I do too.'

She let out a peal of laughter. 'You mean you do now know what you're doing?'

'I didn't mean that, I meant you.'

'I know, my dear, just teasing. Now, enlighten a person who is ignorant.'

'The politics are the province of the Emperor and he is sure they are favourable.'

'The military problems fall to me.'

When examined, certain matters appeared obvious. Italy was the bigger fish needing to be caught but there was a discontented and oppressed population in North Africa, which might prove an easier place to begin, not a statement allowed to pass without explanation.

'In the past, the Vandal rulers made no attempt to make peace with those they had conquered. They forbade intermarriage and imposed their Arian religion on a population who looked to the Bishop of Rome for spiritual guidance. They were also inclined to kill people who sought no more than to worship in a different rite.'

'So there's many a martyr to avenge.'

'Hilderic changed that policy and treated, I'm told, with Justinian for an alliance.' Anticipating a question – her face told him – he answered before she could ask. 'He was overthrown three years ago by his brother, Gelimer, who has seized the throne and is persecuting the Catholics and Trinitarians again.'

'What names,' Antonina opined, not with approval.

'They sound as they are, barbarians. Justinian insists the time is propitious for an attempt at reconquest. This Gelimer faces not only a hostile population but those who revere the memory of his brother. Added to that, he has Moors to the west of his possessions who might ally with us, and insurrections in Sardinia and Byzacium.'

That had to be explained; Antonina had never heard of that particular province; neither had Flavius until he had begun to study the problem but he kept that to himself, an air of knowledge suited him.

'The difficulty would be to get an army transported to Africa that is large enough to retake the land and free the majority of the people.'

'Is it worth it?'

'They are our coreligionists, and besides, it's an old and valuable province that once helped to feed Rome.'

'You sound hesitant, Flavius?'

'It's Justinian. He thinks we should seek to take Italy and he's a hard man to dissuade. Attack there and Gelimer will make an alliance with the Ostrogoths, because he knows if we succeed in Italy he will be next. We cannot fight them combined and it is going to be far from easy to fight them piecemeal.'

It was difficult sometimes to contain Justinian; his desires ran ahead of the ability to meet his expectations. The east was kept quiet with gold; the west was now less peaceable thanks to the death, after a very long reign, of Theodoric, the man who had ruled Italy for thirty-three trouble-free years. But with him gone, as far as Justinian was concerned, Italy was an equally possible target for reconquest.

But it could only be invaded by sea; to seek a land route could not be kept secret from the enemy and the room to manoeuvre in the land between the Alps and the Adriatic was constrained. Not that the gathering of forces for a seaborne attack would go unnoticed, but the landing place on an extended shore calculated at having over six hundred beaches made the point of invasion too hard to fix.

'Having said that, Sicily would be a primary target. All history tells me it would be easier to invade the mainland from there.'

'All history? Would it trouble you if I said I have no idea what you are talking about?'

'No. Would it trouble you if I explained?'

Antonina rolled on to her side and looked directly at him. 'I insist you do. Being in ignorance does not cheer me.'

'Surely you must know something of this?'

'Why would I?'

'It's a long story.'

A hand caressed his bearded jaw to tickle the hairs. 'And we are in no rush.'

'Theodora will wonder where you are.'

'No, Flavius, she will know I am with you.'

He was about to mention her suggestion that they marry but he hesitated too long, so to cover a degree of confusion he began to talk of the events of the last fifty years and indeed beyond, all the way back to the division of the empire in the year 364, with an enthusiasm that had to be constantly checked against her reaction. He was only too aware that what was of interest to him was not always seen in the same light by others. What he saw in Antonina's eyes was firm interest.

If Flavius had not been at the centre of things in Constantinople he had been raised by a parent who took a keen interest in both the history and present state of the Roman Empire. Decimus Belisarius had seen himself as the heir to a thousand years of glorious expansion, the successor to legions of fighting men who had spread civilisation around the Middle Sea, defeating everyone who stood against the civilising influence.

All this had been passed on to his sons; they were Romans and the history of the empire was there to be studied and learnt from, and not for the first time Flavius was in conversation with a person who did not know the past of the polity in which they lived.

The empire had been split by Valentinian because it was too vast to administer; he gave half to his brother Valens and as long as they lived there was harmony. But, supposed to provide better security, it had not worked as it had been hoped, not least because of rivalries between those who succeeded them.

The Eastern Empire, with a huge land border, had struggled many times to repel serious barbarian invasions. They had as often inducted their enemies into the imperial fold as defeated them, for Constantinople had as its core great revenues with which to bribe the invading tribes to either depart or settle, hence the composition of the army.

'The empire in the west has fared less well since the time of Julius Nepos.'

'Him I have heard of, but only the name.'

'He was raised to the purple by the Leo in 474 in place of a man the Emperor thought a usurper. Sadly, in less than two years Nepos was deposed by Orestes, his own *magister militum*.'

'Now that is a nice name, Orestes.'

Flavius smiled indulgently and continued. 'Nepos retired to Dalmatia, where he had previously acted as *dux*. Legally he still held the imperial title, but it was one only in name. Orestes was in all respects like the King of Italy. Then Orestes tried to raise his own son to the purple, treating after Leo's death with the Emperor Zeno, but that failed. He in turn was killed by the leader of his *foederati*, a German mercenary called Odoacer and now he became the ruler of Italy.'

'Not Nepos?'

'He was murdered by the officers of his own *comitatus*.'

'There are Greek plays that tell stories such as this.'

'There's been no Western Emperor since, but stability came with the rise of Theodoric.'

'The famous Theodoric. I have heard they are calling him "the Great".'

'He may deserve it. He governed Italy with our consent and governed well.'

Theodoric had originally been a thorn in the flesh of Zeno – he had ravaged imperial territory and even threatened Constantinople before being diverted to Italy to fight Odoacer.

'That war lasted three years, but finally he defeated Odoacer and captured Ravenna. Then Theodoric strangled him, killed him with his own hands at a banquet designed to cement a peace.'

That got Flavius a finger in the chest. 'There are some people it is better not to dine with.'

'Theodoric settled his followers in Italy, showing great care in the way he dealt with Zeno, then Anastasius and finally Justin. He never sought the title of emperor, content to be *magister militum* and to be raised to the rank of patrician.'

'That makes him sound modest. I may not know as much as you do but Theodoric didn't strike me as that.'

'What's in a title? He acted as he wished and we in the east valued harmony more than anything else. Theodoric gave us that and neither did he seek expansion. In all his dealing with Constantinople he was careful to always show respect. Better still, he made no attempt to convert the Italian citizenry to Arianism, allowing them to worship in their own faith. He's been a bulwark against other threats, marrying three of his daughters, one to the King of Franks, another to the ruler of Burgundy and the third to a previous Vandal king of North Africa.'

'No sons?'

'No.'

'And now he's dead,' Antonina whispered, with a yawn.

'He is, and there was a great deal of conflict in Italy over his inheritance. Ripe, Justinian thinks, for us to intervene.'

She sat up and looked around; outside the gates of the city and well away from any dwelling they were not under any scrutiny. So when Antonina rolled towards him and began to kiss he could not find it within him to resist what followed. It was on the slow ride back to Constantinople that he asked her to marry him.

Theodora was delighted for a woman she saw as one of her closest friends; immediately on being told the news she announced that Justinian would give Antonina away and that she and he would be there to witness. The ceremony would be conducted by the Patriarch and the wedding feast would rival that of any Persian despot. Flavius was not consulted; he was too heavily involved in the expedition he had proposed and Justinian had agreed to.

Antonina was given a larger and grander set of apartments prior to the nuptials and it was to there the married couple would retire. The children of her previous marriage, Photius and Phoebe, acted as cup-bearers and the men who made up the imperial court, several hundred in number, as well as their wives, thought it politic to attend. Antonina insisted it was not out of regard for either her or her intended but a mark of their fear of Theodora.

All the pomp that the imperial establishment could muster was given to them gratis; a servant behind every chair, the best food the imperial kitchens could provide with wines from vineyards planted long before Constantine made this city his capital and it was a glittering occasion marred only by two things.

The clear doubt expressed by Flavius's mother, fetched all the way from Illyricum, that this was a suitable match, and the behaviour of the mother of the bride, a raddled-looking woman who took to the contents of the imperial wine cellars with too much gusto and made an exhibition of herself by being both sick and unable to keep her feet, leading to her being carried from the feast.

It was at the conclusion that Justinian, having given his blessing to the newly-weds, announced that his trusted general Flavius Belisarius was about to be given sole command of an expedition to reconquer from the Vandals the provinces of Africa and the great city of Carthage. That raised a few eyebrows; Flavius had only recently been cleared from blame after an enquiry into his conduct as *magister per Orientem*, in which out of four battles he had lost three, though the lustre of Dara was undiminished.

And sole command was rare, but when Justinian had first proposed the task Flavius had insisted that he would not accept unless that condition was met. The army he led would be on its own once it landed, with nowhere to retreat to, barring its own ships. In such a situation there would be no time for conferences to decide what to do. Quick action would be required and that meant a single controlling hand.

Given that everyone had eaten and drunk well, the news – to many it was far from that – was greeted with loud cheers from the majority of guests, which allowed Justinian to bask in the glory of something he would only watch from a distance.

'You can stay in Constantinople, Mother, we have room in these apartments for a dozen people.'

'No, Flavius, the city does not suit me. I prefer the countryside where I now live and besides, you are not going to be here, are you?'

'It is to where I will return.'

His mother was looking old and frail now and he wanted to say to her that if she went back to Illyricum this might be the last time they would spend together. Yet that seemed too final. He would have been hurt to hear her real reasons; she did not like his new wife and if the doubts she had expressed had been carefully couched they were a great deal deeper and more profound than she had ever let be known to her son.

'If God permits, you will find the time to come to me. Now let us pray together for the memory of your father and brothers as well your success in battle and your safe return.'

There had been a great deal of diplomatic activity while the expedition had been in the planning stage, an area where Justinian was in his element; playing one person off against another, holding all the cards while his correspondent could see only one, was meat and drink for he was still the master intriguer. This was an area in which Flavius did not interfere but he knew that nothing would have been attempted if his emperor was not sure that all possible trouble would fall upon Gelimer.

The Vandal usurper had sought an alliance with Constantinople, one he wished to use against his own rebels. Those same insurgents were treating with Justinian for support against Gelimer and the Emperor was promising much and delivering very little in return. Finally Gelimer, sensing he was being pulled as would be a puppet, broke off his correspondence; those rebelling against him did not and the time had come to proceed.

Since the announcement, Flavius had been inundated

with requests by high-ranking soldiers and courtiers on behalf of relatives with requests to take them as his inferior commanders. These same people had tried Justinian first, only to find that such a decision did not rest with him. The fact was there had come about an occasion of disagreement that came as close to an argument any subject can have with a sovereign.

'I do not want people who will even think to disobey me.'

'And I am being told that I cannot reward loyal service from one of my council by giving an opportunity to his son.'

In reality, what Flavius was trying to avoid was backstabbing correspondence being sent back to the capital, this from his inferior commanders seeking to undermine him in the search of advancement for their own careers, a commonplace in the imperial army. Every letter from such creatures was far from a report on matters as they happened and nor were they the truth: they were political statements and too often a tissue of inventions. Yet such missives could do much damage and Flavius wanted none of it, and eventually Justinian gave way.

Apart from inferior officers and the men he had already led into battle, Flavius required a secretary and that led to an interview with Procopius. Ever since Dara the man had been a constant in the Belisarius life, always seeming to be close by, full of praise for a man he saw as a brilliant general, yet with wit enough to puncture anything that smacked of vanity.

In enquiring about him Flavius had found that he was a native of Caesarea and had studied law, coming to Constantinople with a glittering reputation. He was a fine speaker and had proved at Dara an able assistant to Hermogenes, who had trusted Procopius enough to give him many of the duties that fell to the older man, tasks in which peculation would have been easy. Hermogenes was of the opinion Procopius had not mislaid as much as a *solidus*.

Also, the suspicion that he had been in correspondence with Justinian seemed to have been mistaken. That he wrote to someone Flavius was sure, but having mentioned Procopius to the Emperor the response, that he had no idea of whom his friend was talking about, seemed genuine, Theodora likewise, and hints to certain court officials convinced him that the aide to Hermogenes was not a familiar figure either in the palace or the offices of state. Fiscal honesty was important and as to wealth, success in North Africa would take care of that; it was the other matter that required clarification.

'Tell me, Procopius, who did you write to from Dara? At first I thought it might be the Emperor but that I now know is not the case. But you did correspond with someone of standing.'

'What point would there be in denying it, General? I was charged to give my views to a certain person, a powerful person, and I did so. My loyalty to that commission forbids me from naming him but I can say if you read my letters you might be brought to the blush.'

'I need a secretary as well as an assessor, and an efficient one. You proved yourself that at Dara. But I also need utter loyalty. I know you to be the former but I wonder at the latter.'

'What words could I use that would overcome any doubts. I will say that I am happy to serve you, and flattered as well. If I take the offer I will bind myself to you and your future to the exclusion of all else.'

Flavius was looking him right in the eye and Procopius did not blink or seek to avoid the contact. 'Let me think on it, I will let you know in the morning.'

'Not now?'

That got a slight smile. 'Do you not know me yet, Procopius? I do not make instant decisions.'

It was Antonina that really fixed matters, when the subject was raised in post-coital murmurs. 'He worships you, can you not see that, Flavius?'

'Worships?'

'You do not see the way he gazes upon you when you are not looking, but I do. If he is a lover of men I would say he was enamoured of you.'

'He's not, is he?'

That got her up on an elbow and looking down at him with shaking head. 'Only you would be in ignorance of his desires.'

'I have no ignorance of yours and they please me.' That got him a poke in the ribs. 'Is Procopius . . . ?' Typical of the upright Roman he could not bring himself to say the words, only to wave a wrist.

'I would say he has a Roman name and Greek leanings. Do you not find that you come across him frequently?'

Thinking on it, Flavius could see that Antonina might be right; there was a prissy quality to Procopius, an excessive tidiness and a manner that placed great store in things being right. Recalling him at Dara there had been those endless questions, which might in the light of Antonina's opinions appear more like attention seeking than genuine enquiry. And it was true; Procopius had seemed to be around too many times for it to be coincidence.

'Perhaps I should fear to be alone with him.'

'Then you will not mind that Theodora has insisted I accompany you to Africa.'

'What!'

'Does such a prospect alarm you?'

'You cannot come on campaign, Antonina.'

'Because it's dangerous?'

'That and the distraction of worrying about your safety.'

'Safety? I look forward to you telling Theodora, which will be full of risk. You might have bested Justinian in the article of who you will take as officers, but she is a tougher nut than he.'

'But do you want to accompany me?'

'I certainly don't want to be left here when you are gone.'

A hand cupped her breast, 'Then Theodora can have her wish.'

'And Procopius?'

'Him too. What he is matters as nothing against what he can do.'

CHAPTER NINETEEN

The organisation necessary to prepare and carry an army across five hundred leagues of sea was vast and complex, made more so by the sheer number of horses required and these had to be of the right type for both fighting and carrying for, once ashore in North Africa, everything might have to be transported by hoof.

The *bucellarii* required heavier mounts than contingents like the Huns and Heruls. They, like the Roman cavalry who would make up the bulk of the force, required fleet ponies and not only those they already possessed. Both types required enough spares to account for losses to illness, accidents at sea, breakdown by overuse and casualties in battle. These animals also required a massive quantity of feed and grooms to care for them, adding to the burden of transport.

In numbers, if the expanded *comitatus* of Flavius was included – they now mustered seven *numerus* of three hundred men each – he was to lead an army of near seventeen thousand effectives, accompanied by all the necessary support arms to ensure against failure: armourers, carpenters, cooks, servants and sutlers.

He took from the barracks at Galatea six hundred Huns led by a chieftain called Blasas, a noted warrior said to be utterly fearless in battle, as well as Pharas and the three hundred Heruls he commanded, men who had been so effective at Dara. From Thrace came a strong contingent of Gepid *foederati*, one part of which Flavius gave to Solomon to command. He was no longer just his *domesticus*, he was now a fully committed soldier and leader. Ten thousand infantry and half that number of cavalry from the *praesental* army of the Emperor were marching to meet him at Methone in Thessaloniki under a general called Valerianus, the man who would be his second in command.

Transport to the North African shore required over five hundred vessels and while the transports carrying humans could be packed full of men, the same could not be applied to equines. They required special stalls to be built, with strapping that would keep them from falling in heavy seas, and they had to be exercised on the decks as often as the weather permitted.

The ships were manned by thirty thousand sailors and the provincial seaports had been combed to gather those with the necessary skills as well as the man who could command such a huge fleet, which was now crowded in two deep bays and loading stores. In addition there would be an escort of a hundred warships, single-deck galleys with fighting men at the oars to protect the transports in a sea that suffered much from piracy.

Flavius would be aboard one of the larger vessels and so that everyone should know where their general was in such a vast argosy he had his sails and those of the ships carrying his staff dyed with red stripes. He also worked out a special arrangement of lanterns that, set on the upper mast, would identify their leader at night. Unintended dispersal had to be avoided, though, as was common, they would rarely be out of sight of land.

To supply and keep fed such a force required skills that had nothing to do with fighting; Flavius recruited Archelaus, acknowledged as the best quartermaster in the empire and it was he who arranged for the necessary horses to be gathered from the imperial Thracian herds and brought to the port of Abydos. He also had to fetch to the embarkation ports food and wine as well as weapons, the same being required along a route that would take them first across the Aegean then south to weather the southern tip of Greece.

In this task Archelaus was required to deal with John the Cappadocian and the frustration of that wore him down, for the man who held the purse strings of supply was not going to release funds or empty the imperial storehouses unless some of the value came into his personal possession. Flavius complained to Justinian: he promised to act, but nothing changed.

Of course the Emperor was busy on other matters. He had secured peace in the east by withdrawing the administrative centre of *dux Mesopotamiae* from Dara and paying Kavadh a fortune in gold for what was called an Eternal Peace. Rapacious as the Sassanid ruler was, he had to be bought off; the expedition in the west could not be launched without him being passive on the eastern frontier and with enough money he would concentrate on controlling his own borders further east where he always faced difficulties with nomadic raiders.

There were other and equally vital diplomatic moves to attend to, not least the need to deprive Gelimer of allies by the sending of a set of demands he must refuse, such as the release of his brother Hilderic from prison and the despatch of him and his supporters to Constantinople. Since to comply would be fatal – Hilderic would seek support to oust him – it was no surprise he declined.

Aid and promises had to be despatched to those rebelling against Gelimer in Sardinia and Tripolitania. The expedition needed to land in Sicily for supplies and this could only be achieved with the permission of the present ruler of Italy, Amalasuintha, Theodoric's youngest daughter, mother and regent for Theodoric's grandson and heir Athalaric, who was many years away from his majority.

Far from secure in her position, Amalasuintha had been seeking support from Constantinople to shore up her position, she being surrounded by Goth warlords who could, if too many of them combined, overthrow her and murder her son. Besides that she had a personal grudge against the Vandals who had badly treated one of her sisters.

Thus Sicily was open to the forces from the east. Letters had been sent to the King of the Visigoths in Hispania, seeking an alliance that would debar the Vandals from seeking their aid, but as yet no response had come.

With all in place Flavius, Antonina beside him and with Procopius in attendance, waited on the harbour mole at Constantinople for the imperial couple to bid them farewell. Justinian and Theodora arrived with the kind of pomp more suited to an eastern despot, in a gilded four-horse carriage, gorgeously canopied to keep out the sun and escorted by a troop of the *Scholae Palatinae*. Their presence, as if it were not already obvious, was announced by blaring trumpets that had many on the quayside kneeling in obeisance.

Flavius stayed on his feet and waited for the pair to come to him and it was noticeable that whereas the Empress seemed unfazed by the purpose upon which they were engaged, the blessing of an expedition that carried the hopes of the empire, her husband was pallid and fidgety which had Flavius whisper to Antonina.

'He is like that. The plotting and scheming make him happy but the prospect of fruition brings out his nerves in case it all goes wrong.'

'Theodora seems not to care.'

'She cares, Antonina. If what we are about to embark on fails, the blame will not only lie with us.'

'Us? How can I be blamed?' she pouted.

'Only for failing to keep me happy.'

These were the last words he could impart before Justinian was too close and he greeted him with due but not excessive deference, a sharp drop of the head that got a cold response from Theodora.

'You carry the hopes of the empire in your hands, Flavius Belisarius.'

The formality jarred slightly and it was not the first time he had been exposed to it since the day of his marriage, much as he told himself it was imagination. He had ceased to be merely Flavius and he was no longer treated to those warm encompassing smiles. It was as if she had reverted to her previous demeanour, where her reservations about him were very thinly veiled.

'How can you think her jealous of you?' had been Antonina's response when he hinted at it.

'I did not say jealous,' he had protested. 'I just don't think she likes Justinian having me as a friend. The ways she looks when we talk to each other is, for Theodora, too familiar. The lady wants Justinian to herself.'

Antonina had a quick reply. 'Fear not, Flavius, she will cosset you because she loves me.'

Which got the rejoinder that it was perhaps he who should be jealous.

'I have dreamt of this as you know, Flavius,' Justinian croaked, signifying a dry throat.

'The first step, Highness, one, to be hoped, of many.'

'The hardest to bear,' came the quiet reply. 'I find it hard to sleep, so many of my dreams being full of disturbing images.'

Rumours abounded that Theodora had suggested he lead the army himself, that she could mind the empire while he garnered the kind of glory that had not attended the throne since the days of Julian the Apostate. The same sources told that Justinian had insisted he had chosen the right leader, which seemed not to sit well with his wife.

Justinian stepped forward to embrace Flavius, something he had not done even prior to assuming his title. He had never been a demonstrative fellow, all his intimacies had been with the other sex and Flavius had often wondered if he would have benefited from being more at home in male company. He had been an Excubitor officer once but made no secret of the fact that he found the barrack room camaraderie not to his taste.

As if not to be outdone, Theodora likewise embraced Antonina before kissing her on both cheeks. Flavius, now free of the imperial clinch, felt the presence of Procopius at his side and he effected an introduction, not without close examination to see if there had been previous contact. Justinian practically ignored him; all Procopius got was a nod before the Emperor took the arm of his commanding general and led him towards the gangplank that would take him aboard ship.

Neither man saw the furious, though hurriedly suppressed reaction of Procopius, who felt slighted by being treated in such a peremptory fashion. He was still seething when they were aboard the ship and the cables had been cast off, it being poled clear of the harbour wall as the sails were lowered to take a decent wind.

'Having seen the Emperor close up, General, I wonder at how someone so seemingly anxious can achieve such a high office. His nerves are very obvious.'

'Do not underestimate him, Procopius,' came a distracted

response. 'His mind is sharper than you or I could manage and the anxiety only whets that.'

'Of course, one would need to be in his company for some time to see the whole man.'

That there was a certain amount of pleading in that passed by his still distracted superior, but it got Procopius an arch look from Antonina, so much more acutely aware when ambition surfaced. The talking did not last long; as soon as the ship cleared the mole all three fell seasick and were soon prostrate and being attended to by servants in no better condition.

It was no consolation to be told that half the crew, experienced sailors all and including the master, who was also the man who commanded the fleet, were also afflicted. It was two whole days before Flavius could walk the deck without discomfort and once his secretary was on his feet his employer began to discuss with him the Vandals – Procopius had sought to find out what he could from the citizens of the capital – and what Flavius heard was not a great deal.

'They seem to be a very insular people.'

'They trade, do they not?'

'With Italy, yes, but very rarely with Constantinople. When I asked of their methods of making war there was no one who could tell me anything for no one has fought them.'

'Let's hope the Sicilians are better informed.'

'We do, of course, have their history.'

That was one solid Roman virtue; they always sought to understand their enemies and books existed that told of their emergence on the frontiers. The Vandals were another one of those tribes that had come out of the deep and endless forest that stretched east from the Rivers Rhine and Danube, a migratory people who had been pushed westward by the Huns.

In Gaul they ran up against the Franks, fought one battle and lost, then another which they won, going on to plunder their way south and west through the abundant region of Aquitaine, finally crossing the Pyrenees to enter a less-than-well-defended region of Hispania from which Rome lacked the power to dislodge them.

No one knew what had caused them to move to Africa but they had done so successfully and from there they had launched raids into Sicily and mainland Italy, on one occasion sacking Rome itself, as well as becoming for many decades the scourge of the western Mediterranean. Their kingship now extended to Corsica and Sardinia, though the latter island had risen against them and was awaiting support from Flavius.

The Vandals would have ships; how else could they keep their possessions intact as well as threaten their neighbours? If they were waiting for him to arrive they would meet at sea and that, Flavius knew, had to be avoided. The notion induced near panic among the men he commanded and it would likely be the same with those he was about to combine with.

Few of the sailors could swim, which seemed to be tempting providence. But the Huns, Heruls and *foederati* he now led lived in terror of a sea battle. Men who would face a fully armed cataphract and fight to the death, even if disadvantaged, viewed the notion of drowning with horror.

Even being at sea when the wind strengthened, which it had done soon after departure, was enough to induce nerves so it was a blessing that they raised Abydos and dropped anchor in the calm waters of the bay.

It was not a blessing that the blustery weather fell away and they were becalmed there. There was not enough wind to get them back out to sea and to keep soldiers cooped up aboard ship was a bad idea, especially when he had disembarked the horses loaded at their first port of call so they could graze pasture. So Flavius let the men go ashore to be told the bad news the next morning.

'A fight,' Procopius reported. 'Two Huns killed one of their comrades, all three drunk and that after they had molested some of the local women. The leading citizens of the port are demanding something be done.'

'And it will.'

He had everyone brought back aboard their ships and had himself rowed around the fleet to pass on his message that this was a Christian army going to the aid of a persecuted people who shared their faith and who were suffering persecution, ignoring a wind that had sprung up to allow departure.

'We cannot prevail if they turn against us, but I would demand they be respected even if they were pagans. It is pointless to take land then oppress those who live off it for then we become their enemy. We are charged by our Emperor to bring back under his sceptre a province of the Roman Empire. I promise any man that transgresses against those we are about to free will feel the full force of my wrath, as you will see.'

Back aboard his command vessel the two miscreants stood, their hands bound in the middle of the deck with their leader Blasas present but declining to intervene to save them. From each end of the mainsail spar hung a rope, noosed at the end. The men who had murdered and molested were led forward to have these placed round their necks. Within what Flavius hoped was sight of the whole fleet, a running body of his *comitatus* officers hauled the pair, legs kicking, into the air, there to writhe and jerk until their last breath departed their body.

'We leave them there,' he told the commander of the fleet, Calonymus. 'Let all see what their fate will be for transgression.'

The bodies still swung from the spar as, three days' sailing later, the fleet entered the harbour of Methone. There the task of loading the regular troops of the empire began and it did not go well. Units marched onto the quay in no order whatsoever and got in each other's path, ending up as a rabble. He seemed to have command of a mob not an army, and it got worse as each hour passed.

'If I have another moment of this disorder, Procopius, I will cut my throat.'

'I am not a soldier, General, but land this horde and we will perish.'

This time, when the wind dropped and becalmed the fleet, Flavius was grateful and if it led to men being disgruntled he did not care. Just come aboard they were disembarked and led out of the small port to open fields where he could begin to form them into the fighting force he wanted and needed.

He had a dozen men who held general rank and understood what was required, even if they had never tried to impose it. To change that he bypassed them and spoke directly to their middle-ranking officers to tell them what he required. In addition to that there were the outright mercenaries and his own well-drilled *comitatus* to demonstrate the necessary drills.

There was no time to ask if they could fight, that had to be a hope, but they had to be taught how to manoeuvre, more so the cavalry than the ten thousand infantry. The education they required was in holding their ground against a horse-led assault, for if he knew nothing of Vandal tactics or weaponry he had to assume them to be mobile and mounted. The cavalry arm had to be able to move as individual units, had to be shown how as well as when to combine, and most importantly how not be tempted into useless pursuits.

In the face of a degree of mild resistance from his inferior commanders – they were all long-serving military men – Flavius had several assets to employ. First he had chosen them and he knew them to be good commanders. What made their movement poor was not stupidity or a lack of ability, but an absence of the experience of operating as a large body. Second, he was the Victor of Dara and none of these men had fought a major battle let alone won one. But greatest of all was the plain fact that he had the trust of Justinian and sole command. He had no need to include another in his deliberations or seek support in a discussion of tactics.

'Pharas will tell you that I am no martinet.'

The crowded tent was full of men with their eyes fixed upon him and Flavius was pleased by their acute attention. If they were ruffled they still wanted to know his plans for they wanted, like him, to succeed.

'Ask for the right to act on your own notions and I will listen – and if I agree? Well, as I said, ask Pharas, who did just that at Dara and aided me in the victory we achieved. But another man who owed me obedience was Coutzes and because he disobeyed a direct instruction thousands died. I have no need to tell you that is not what I desire. Give me cause to think you will do so and the next ship home is what you earn.'

He smiled to take the sting out of the threat. 'Let us hope for a wind on the morrow, but if it fails us again then it is to these fields we will return, for my friends, I tell you there is no amount of training that constitutes too much. What the enemy will do I have no idea. But I must know what we will do, and I must have the confidence to confound any move they make.'

It was not wind that came on the morrow but something close to a calamity. A whole *chiliarch* of his infantry were unable to parade when called forth by the horns at dawn. Of the three thousand men afflicted, a high number succumbed during the day, dying in an agony of severe stomach pains. This was a situation in which the suspicious and superstitious made merry with rumours of either conspiracy or evil portents.

Flavius had to gather the local priests to go amongst the army and institute prayers, as well as to scotch any wild imagining, and those same priests were to later bury nearly five hundred men. Those who survived, indeed the entire army, needed to know what had happened and the common cause was narrowed down to infected bread baked to look as it should, but with some ingredient within that was potentially deadly. Archelaus was summoned for an explanation.

'All I do, Flavius Belisarius, is indent for supplies. In the case of bread it is the imperial granaries that provide them and they do so on the instructions of the Cappadocian.'

'It was not inspected prior to distribution?'

'Why would it be, we are still in imperial territory?'

Flavius knew it was no good laying blame on Archelaus; the bread had been consumed and the aforementioned John was back in Constantinople, where it would be impossible to prove that he had a hand in what was clearly an attempt to cheat and save money by using questionable and less costly ingredients.

'It must be disseminated that John is responsible.'

'He might not be, he would have asked the provincial governor to provide.'

'He is a villain with enough guilt to spare for his many thefts, so let him carry the responsibility for this. It cannot be you, Archelaus, or the men will lose faith in our provisions.'

The wind came the following day but that had to be ignored; many were still too sick. It was another two days before they could think to depart and they would be leaving behind a mass grave of their unlucky comrades. The now overcrowded argosy finally raised sail and dropped oars, heading due south in sight of the Greek shore, heading for the twin capes that formed the south of the Attic mainland.

Flavius, with little to do, was happy in the company of Antonina and the closest officer members of his *comitatus*, while she seemed delighted to entertain a group of young and admiring men who set out to flatter her, that is till the weather turned foul and she found herself once more confined and retching to her cot.

Procopius succumbed too, but Flavius kept a steady stomach and was often on deck, his body whipped by the wind, easing and stiffening his legs with the role of the ship. These were the very waters Odysseus sailed through on his return from Troy, and if it was fanciful of him to think himself on a similar odyssey, it was pleasant listening to the breeze singing in the rigging and imagining it to be the voice of the siren Circe.

CHAPTER TWENTY

No matter how good a general a man is, no matter the state of the army he leads, good fortune must attend his efforts and Flavius Belisarius was lucky. Crossing the Adriatic, the only time the fleet was out of sight of land, a contrary wind, not anticipated by the vastly experienced Calonymus, meant that the journey took many days longer than he anticipated. That meant a shortage of water, for to carry enough for both the men and the horses was too taxing even for such a large quantity of transports, and it became brackish and undrinkable. Even then men consumed it until it ran out, adding illness to a raging thirst.

The results would have been catastrophic had the wind not swung round just in time; the horses were in a bad way and the soldiers and sailors Flavius led were worse: it takes very little time in mild weather to suffer from thirst. At sea, with a hot wind and a scorching temperature, confined between stuffy and crowded decks, an hour of deprivation became critical and the time was approaching where the only sustenance for the humans would be the blood of the equines.

Flavius sent the fighting galleys ahead in the hope they could make a landfall and return with enough water to stave off disaster. The abiding sound before that change of wind was of men praying to God, mixed with the neighing of distressed horses and then Hosannas, as they felt the breeze shift and saw the sails swing and the water before the bows begin to cream. They raised Brindisi with little time to spare, glad to find that their galley captains had barges setting out to save them.

There was no pumping to fill barrels, just a stream of pumped water aimed at the crowded decks which the men took at full force into grateful faces before filling buckets for their mounts. From now on and all the way to Sicily, they would again be in sight of the shore, only when they crossed from there to their destination would the same threat occur, a lesser one given the shorter distance between islands.

Restored, it seemed as if everything went in their favour as a fair wind took them round to the Straits of Messina. At Syracuse they found a special market had been set up for them by the Queen of the Goths where they could cheaply buy fresh produce to supplement their rations. The locals were Catholic coreligionists, likewise ruled by Arians, though the Goths allowed them the freedom to worship. They hated the Vandals not only for their persecutions but for the memory of raids and depredations all along the coast: rape, theft, the taking of slaves and murder, so the thought of chastisement of these barbarians was welcome, the people set to carry it out treated as champions.

There had been a constant stream of news and encouragement from Constantinople: Tripolitania was still in revolt and the province of Byzacium was on the verge of an uprising, intelligence supplied by disaffected Christians. There was a message from the leader of the revolt on the island of Sardinia saying he needed scant help in terms of soldiers and certainly no one to command him, which meant little diminution of the forces Flavius would have available.

Procopius went investigating again. Left behind once the fleet sailed on, his task was to interrogate anyone who might provide intelligence on the enemy. Again luck played a part; Procopius ran into an old acquaintance with whom he had studied law. The man was now in the seaborne trade and had recently had a ship and cargo return from Carthage. The master of that vessel was summoned and he was adamant that the Vandal capital was peaceful.

No one there behaved as if an invasion was imminent and Gelimer was not even in the capital city, he was rumoured to be in the eastern province of Byzacium to cow the disaffected populace, which fitted with what had been heard from home. Even more important was the information that he had despatched a force of five thousand of his soldiers, under his brother Tzazon, to quell the rebellion in Sardinia.

The sailing master was taken to be questioned by Flavius, now anchored off the southern tip of Sicily.

The other information he provided was just as valuable. As a regular visitor to Carthage he knew how the society of the region was constituted and that again fitted with what was already known. The Vandals had done nothing to integrate with the indigenes until the accession of Hilderic, and with him now in prison they had reverted to old habits and renewed religious persecution.

The barbarians held themselves separate from those over whom they ruled and were very much in the minority, using fear and oppression to keep a grip on the country. They also maintained their migratory traditions: there were no Vandal farmers; every man was a warrior, expected when called upon to heed any call to arms to maintain ethnic supremacy. Only when it came to tactics when fighting was the seafarer at a loss, never having seen them do more than harass people in the crowded streets of the old city, which left Flavius still uncertain of what they would face when he landed.

'I have carried out a calculation,' Procopius said, producing a scroll which he opened on his lap. That fluttered in the welcome breeze coming in through the open cabin shutters, it still being hot. 'Based on what we know of Vandal numbers.'

'Not a great deal, I suspect.'

'More, possibly, than you think, General. They have a well-stocked library in Syracuse and I went there to see what I could find, and I found books, mostly Greek but quite a lot of Roman as well, a lot of them military histories going back to and beyond Caesar's *Commentaries*.'

'I'm impressed.'

'Better still, those who first treated with them in North Africa wrote accounts of the difficulties and I found one that sought to assess their population when they departed Hispania and arrived in Africa at some sixty thousand souls.'

That got an appreciative nod from his employer; Procopius was carrying out calculations that were of some importance and ones that had not even occurred to him.

'Prior to the last migration they were at war with every one of their neighbours as well as Rome, so were much diminished by casualties in battle. In North Africa they have had peace at home excepting some losses in their piracy. But they have been settled for some time, inhabiting a fertile province which provides them with ample food so they should have procreated by some measure.'

Antonina, who had been walking, taking air on the deck, entered the cabin as Procopius was talking and, waving a fan to ward off the heat, she threw herself on a divan, her eyes on him, her expression a frown directed towards the seated secretary.

'So you think they will have increased in numbers?' Flavius enquired.

'I do, but a figure of double their previous strength is only a guess.'

'War is that in a lot of ways.'

'Take out the elderly, the women and children and accept what our ship's master says about everyone being a warrior and at my reckoning we face at worst some thirty thousand warriors in total.'

'Less the men sent to Sardinia.'

'Which still leaves them numerically superior.'

Antonina spoke up, her tone firm. 'Then it comes down, Procopius, to who is the better general.'

'Who has the better army, surely,' her husband corrected her, with a kindly look that earned him a very brief scowl. 'So it will have to be us.'

'Anything else?' Antonina asked, though it was far from her place to do so. 'I have invited the *comitatus* officers to dine with us and the cabin must be got ready.'

'Again?' This Flavius said with just a trace of impatience and one that was brushed aside.

'How else are we to entertain ourselves, Husband?'

About to respond with a salacious remark Flavius had to bite his tongue. Procopius was still present and he spoke again, his face pinched.

'I have drafted for your approval a final despatch to the Emperor.'

Antonina sat forward then. 'I will have a letter for Theodora to go with it.'

'I'm sure you will,' Procopius responded in a sour way that made Antonina bridle.

'What do you mean by that?'

'I don't understand,' the secretary replied in an unconvincing aside as he stood up, laying the scroll on the desk. 'It's an innocent remark.'

'I do not like your tone.'

'Antonina, please,' Flavius said in a firm voice. 'Fetch

the draft, Procopius, and we shall go over it together, which will give you, my dear, time to use our private quarters to compose the letter you wish to send.'

Antonina did not budge until Procopius was gone. 'You overindulge that fellow. I have said it before and it is worthy of repetition.'

Flavius left his chair and came to sit beside her. 'He does his job well and he does not steal.'

'He does not show you sufficient respect. What is he doing sitting in your presence?'

'I invited him to do so.'

'As I said, overindulged.'

She exited, leaving Flavius to contemplate the problem of the mutual hostility between his secretary and his wife, which if it was awkward in itself was made ten times worse by being cooped up in the ship. This abrasion had manifested itself not long after leaving Constantinople and it had not abated since, if anything it had got worse, the only relief being when Procopius was absent at Syracuse.

He was a tidy fellow, evidenced by his own cubicle in which he both worked and slept. Procopius had a desk in which his writing equipment was neatly arranged and so were his possessions and it was known to Flavius they were not rendered so by his servant. His attention to detail was reflected in everything he did.

It would be unfair to suggest Antonina was the opposite but she was one to leave things to be cleaned up after her, which they were. The Belisarius servants, of which there were many thanks to her presence, were competent. The truth was they were chalk and cheese and he was caught in the middle. He had no desire to play the master with Procopius and no chance of doing so with his wife.

Thank God they would soon be ashore.

The day came when these red-striped sails were raised to take the northerly wind and for the ship commanded by Calonymus to lead the argosy south-west past the islands of Malta and Gozo, on to tiny Lampedusa where the water was replenished, before finally sighting the coast of Africa within the confines of a single day. The shore was far enough off their quarter to be just visible as a streak on the horizon, which Flavius wished maintained. Before the final dash to shore he called all his commanders to join him aboard his ship for a conference.

'You may have wondered why I have left it so late to say what I intend. Do not think I insult you when I say wagging tongues can do us much damage. The information I have tells me we are not expected by the Vandals but that is the word of one man, recently a visitor to Carthage but no soldier, though I will say I believe what he told me. My silence was a mere precaution to maintain what I hope is the true situation.'

He reminded them that another Roman expedition had been destroyed very close by where they lay, nearly a hundred years previously, and in reading of that campaign he had seen several things that needed to be altered to avoid the failure that was their lot.

'We shall not reside aboard our vessels for a moment longer than is necessary, which will ease discomfort. More than that, it gives our enemies a chance to attack us, which they will certainly take in a situation where they would have the advantage. Well-manned ships, more manoeuvrable than our transports, and the time to choose a propitious moment.'

Valerianus, the general who commanded the *praesental* infantry, spoke up to say he was sure they could beat the enemy off.

'At what cost, Valerianus? I have no idea of the size of their fleet and I would hazard I am not alone. Apart from a battle I have no desire to fight, we risk bad weather as well, but that is not why I wish to rapidly disembark. If our presence is unknown it will not remain so. A fleet this size cannot beat up and down off the coast without word getting to our enemies, if only from fishermen. If we anchor inshore the same applies and it seems to me if there is Vandal ignorance we must move swiftly to take advantage of it.'

It was necessary with men of this calibre to pause and let them acknowledge the acceptance of his points, one being that whatever forces the Vandals possessed must of necessity at present be dispersed.

'But are we deceived?' Flavius added, entering a note of caution. 'Is Gelimer waiting to strike, knowing full well where we are and the likely spot at which we will come ashore? We must guard against that, so the first thing to do on landing is to give ourselves a secure base. We will throw up an earthen rampart behind which we will be secure and we will turn that into a fortress, as well guarded as would be an old legionary camp. For the vessels anchored offshore the fighting galleys must be manned, and employed in rowing guard too. You know why.'

The expedition he had just mentioned had been destroyed by Vandals sending in among them fireships while they were at anchor. The losses sustained to that tactic ensured that the battle ended in defeat.

'Rowboats too, General,' suggested Calonymus. 'As far from the anchorage as they can without losing sight of our masts. An early warning if they have torches and flints with which to ignite them.'

'A good idea. Gentlemen it is time to pray. We land at dawn.'

With the sun at their backs they hit the open beach just south of a settlement known as Caput Vada, the infantry disembarking first. Half set to digging and throwing up the earthwork Flavius wanted, the rest hauling the horse transports beam on to the beach and securing them with ropes and stakes so their wide gangplanks could be lowered over the side. Both the horses and those landing them took pleasure in the time spent in the warm sea, the animals, even if they had been continually groomed, carrying the filth of accumulated travel and confinement, causing a great amount of splashing that turned the sea light brown by disturbed sand.

Much shouting in various tongues ensued as the commanders sought to organise their troops of cavalry and it was far from smooth. But it was heartening to Flavius, watching from the deck of his command ship, to see it being less of a melee than had attended any of the previous disembarkations. Not long after, midday patrols were out scouring the surrounding countryside for any evidence of an enemy but there was none. Belisarius and the Roman army were ashore and secure, now with a wooden stockade under construction and a fleet to which they could retreat at will behind them.

Next he must go ashore himself and lead the march on Carthage. If Gelimer was not in his capital it made no difference where he lay, for with a Roman army on the way to besiege it he must hurry to secure his base. He who held the city held the region and that had been the case since the time of Hannibal and Scipio Africanus. The only worry was the lack of knowledge of the whereabouts of any forces out in the countryside and that dictated his tactics from now on.

The Vandals, once they found the Romans had landed, would not be organised into a composite army ready for battle and thus, being dispersed, they must coalesce in groups of varying sizes according to previous arrangements at certain key locations. There had to be another plan for them to unite and his aim was to prevent such a union so that he would always outnumber whoever he faced.

There was one other consideration and it was important, the attitude of those the Vandals ruled: what would they do when they encountered the Roman army, welcome them and provide aid and intelligence, or stand aside and wait to see who was more likely to triumph? The nearest town of any size was called Syllectus, a place large enough to have both a local forum and an amphitheatre.

Flavius selected one of his best *bucellarii* commanders to go there. Boriades had a cool head and a shrewd mind, but more importantly he was, like his general, a native Latin speaker, for that was the language of the province. The instructions were clear: whatever happened, no harm was to come to the indigenes.

'Even if you lose men in the process you are to retire in the face of any resistance.'

'Not an easy order to obey, General.'

'But obey it you must.'

The day was spent in more organisation, though the troops were given some freedom to roam and that led to the first flogging, administered to a quartet of infantry to drive home that it was not acceptable for any of his men to help themselves to food and drink without payment, which was what had occurred, though in this case it was merely picking fruit without asking.

That had him call his entire force together and harangue them; the local population had been under Vandal rule for a century but he thought them still to be Romans at heart. Such people could be their friends or, exposed to unprincipled behaviour, at best indifferent and at worst actively resistant. Treated well they might provide valuable information on the Vandals, for whom they should have no love, treated badly they might join with the enemy. Then there was food, which would be abundant only if paid for; stolen on the march, those ahead of the army would hide their stored produce.

He reminded them they were alone on a hostile shore and without driving it home too forcibly, alluded to the vicissitudes the men had suffered just to get here; did they want to be forced back aboard those ships to return defeated to Constantinople? It was then made plain that any more incidents of such a nature would be more severely punished and the men were reminded of those two Huns publically hanged.

'Pay for what you need,' was the blanket command.

Boriades did not return in person but sent a small detachment back to the main camp to report that having bivouacked outside Syllectus the men had entered the town by just following in the morning carts proceeding to market; no violence and no parleying had been necessary. Finding Romans in their midst, albeit from the east, the leading citizens had bid them welcome and promised aid.

'Freely given or out of fear?' Flavius asked. 'Faced with a body of mounted fighting men they may be just being cautious.'

'Impossible to tell, Excellence.'

'Your impression will suffice.'

'I think them pleased, but with worries that should we not prevail their overlords will take a stiff revenge.'

While they were talking another messenger came in from Syllectus, to say that Boriades, with the help of the overseer of the local post house, had taken into custody a messenger on his way to alert Carthage to the landing, the fellow having stopped to change mounts. This revealed that the Vandals were still using the same method of fast-mounted messengers on the roads they inherited from Roman rule and that would be used to get their forces organised. Discussing what to do with this messenger, Flavius was politely interrupted by Procopius.

'Is our cause against Gelimer or the Vandals as a people?'

The man he served was quick to get the drift of that

suggestion, which seemed to confuse the other senior officers present. The messenger, sent on his way, might provide an opportunity to separate those who still supported the imprisoned Hilderic from Gelimer, and the majority of those would be in Carthage where such a message might have an effect. He spoke while Procopius wrote, saying who they were and more importantly whom they represented.

The message stated that the Emperor Justinian had no desire to make war on the Vandals as a people, just to see their rightful ruler, a man with whom he had corresponded and with whom he was about to sign a treaty of friendship, placed back on his throne. That accomplished, the invasion force would re-embark and sail for home.

'Justinian would brand us for such a falsehood,' Procopius ventured.

'The opposite is true; when it comes to spinning lies our Emperor is a past master. This is mean stuff to him and would scarce warrant a reward.'

CHAPTER TWENTY-ONE

The Romans having no idea of the whereabouts of their enemies or their mode of fighting, Flavius split the army into separate detachments prior to the march to Styllectus, their first destination. Three hundred *bucellarii* were placed under an experienced commander, John the Armenian. They were sent ahead of the main body at a distance of one league, that to be maintained.

Balas and his Huns were allotted the inland flank defence, there being no need for that on the shoreside of the advance; that was guarded by the fleet which would accompany the army and match its pace as long as they hugged the coast. Flavius brought up the rear with the remainder of the *bucellarii* as well as his own *comitatus*, these being his best troops. Gelimer had last been placed south of their landing place; being behind his main force their commander was well placed not only to protect them but to launch an immediate attack should the need arise.

They arrived at Syllectus to be greeted by a wary populace, but that caution evaporated in the face of the way the Romans behaved. Soon a delegation of the leading citizens were happy to inform Flavius that he had their full support and the first task he had for them was that these worthies should give him some indication of the methods of fighting he was likely to face.

Being non-military it could only be partial but that proved edifying. The first point established that the Vandals did not train as an army, each fighter was expected to work on his own skills but never in large bodies, more in small local detachments, and that boded well. Better still was their opinion regarding the Moors, the local rivals of the Vandals, nomads occupying the lands to the west all the way to the Pillars of Hercules and beyond, into which these northern barbarians were inclined to encroach.

The two protagonists had fought a battle not long past in which the Moors had triumphed by placing a screen of camels ahead of their army, which threw the mounted attack into disarray, the stink of camels being one equines cannot abide. They had then, from behind that screen, assailed their enemies with archery and volleys of stones fired from small ballistae, throwing the entire Vandal assault into turmoil and eventually obliging them to retire. The first lesson to be drawn from this was obvious: the

Vandals would struggle against any force that could disrupt their structure, for it appeared they lacked the ability to make swift tactical changes.

With the population of Syllectus on his side these elders were happy to send out riders to gather intelligence from the cities that lay in the Roman army's path. The reports that came back indicated that another brother of Gelimer, Ammatus, was in the capital with some five thousand effectives while the unconfirmed news was that Gelimer was hurrying north to join up with him, traversing the road between the capital and Hermione. His numbers were greater but that was yet to be established, so in essence it was a race to Carthage.

That allowed Flavius to alter his dispositions; the cavalry were to go ahead of the infantry, which he would command, keeping with him his mounted *comitatus* as a shock and protective force bringing up the rear until notice came that Gelimer may have reached his columns. There was no hiding the fact that this was a strategy that carried risks. The Vandals had morphed in North Africa from travelling in carts and fighting on foot into a mounted power and that was the kind of opposition the Roman infantry ever struggled to contain.

Like the Vandal messengers he would base his advance on the roads. The difficulty was that moving at the pace of a foot soldier imposed some restrictions: first there was the speed of penetration; Gelimer would not forever be in ignorance of the whereabouts of those he must fight and destroy. There would be scouts out soon if not already, so Flavius wanted any information he received to put the

Roman army well ahead of where it was in total, which would form the basis of his contrary tactics.

Strung out along a highway made the infantry vulnerable but with a strong cavalry screen and the fact that he had spent so much time in training them to manoeuvre, their commander was sure by the time any enemy came upon them they would be formed up and ready to defend themselves, very likely on favourable ground chosen by their general. At that point he would send out skirmishers and archers to disrupt the Vandal preparations in order to delay any attack.

The cavalry, operating in strong flying columns, would have standing orders to retire on the position Flavius took up, which might completely surprise the enemy in the first instance. But more importantly it would unite the two arms into a formidable whole in a spot where the Romans should enjoy the advantage. To any observation on the dangers Flavius Belisarius had his response ready: war was ever carried out in a fog of uncertainty and that applied to Gelimer just as much as it applied to him.

Never one to underestimate his opponent, he knew that his enemy would be seeking to surprise him, and putting the sandal on the other foot he sought to outguess him. There was one obvious point on the old Roman maps which told Flavius danger would very likely threaten, the narrow pass at Ad Decimum, some three leagues from Carthage, a place where, if his information was accurate, success depended more on how troops were deployed than the mere numerical supremacy he was sure he enjoyed.

Could Gelimer leave his capital city undefended? To ask

Ammatus to come towards him was to bring that to pass, which meant wherever battle was joined the Vandal leader must win for any other outcome would leave his capital at the mercy of the invader. But the Romans were between the two Vandal forces and Flavius could not see how they could combine without him being aware of their dispositions.

Truly war was carried out in a fog; for all his intelligence and the aid of the locals no one told the Romans that there was another road to the south by which Gelimer could join forces with his brother, other than the direct route from Hermione. That road met the main route from the coast and Leptis Magna, south of the very pass where danger threatened.

It had been the intention to draw the enemy towards him, and as was his way, fight a battle on his chosen ground. If his insistence on what amounted to a defensive tactic met with disapproval from his more fiery inferiors, that he was willing to suffer, so, on the fourth day, having found a suitable site for an encampment, on ground he knew he could defend, Flavius ordered it made secure before sending Solomon and a force of mounted *foederati* riding off to reconnoitre for the enemy as well as join up with John the Armenian.

Unbeknown to the man in command, battle was already being joined. Balas and his Huns were still to the west of the main force to guard its flank, albeit they had increased the distance somewhat, which brought them to the main road from Hermione to Carthage and there they encountered a force of Vandals outnumbering their six hundred by some three or four times. Sense indicated an immediate withdrawal but one of Balas's men rode right on to top a slight mound and gazed down upon the enemy, defying them to attack.

This piece of bravado caused the Vandals to stop, either because they feared a trap or they were merely nonplussed by such behaviour and it was at that point Balas saw an opportunity. Famously fierce and sometimes uncontrollable he attacked an enemy now static, which was a bad situation for cavalry under any circumstances and deadly when they lacked the discipline to properly react.

Before the Vandals could get into any sort of defensive formation, the fast-riding Huns were peppering them with arrows just before, swords out, they got amongst them, throwing the Vandals into utter confusion. To say they acted like headless chickens was only to anticipate the fate of many who ended up as headless humans, many more being skewered or dragged from their horses by whips in the hands of riders of great skill.

The enemy were routed, many of them killed, including their leader who, it transpired, was the nephew of Gelimer. The Huns also established that, two thousand strong, they had been on their way to defend Carthage, which was a solid indication that Ammatus had left the city to join his elder brother.

The next phase of the battle was as much a mystery to Flavius Belisarius as the first; at almost the same moment at Balas was routing his enemies, John the Armenian had encountered a force of Vandals scouting forward, one clearly a high-ranking leader with a small escort of no more than thirty men, and that led to an immediate engagement.

John suffered casualties, for the Vandals fought bravely and well, but for his dozen dead John could account in profit of the bodies of every man he had faced.

Sensing the road to Carthage might be open, John ordered his men to follow and sped along it, encountering on his way the army of Ammatus strung out in small groups along the roadway, these either fleeing or, if they stood to fight, dying. John kept going until he sighted the walls of Carthage itself where, knowing he was isolated, he turned to retrace his steps, the men he led looting his dead and dying victims en route.

Solomon, coming upon the site of John's recent victory, discovered one of the dead to be none other than Ammatus himself, but with no sight of John he was at a loss what to do. Reconnoitring to the west he and his men ascended a decent-sized hill and from there spotted a cloud of dust on the horizon; it had to be Gelimer and the main Vandal force, so word was sent back to Flavius Belisarius that an opportunity arose to smite the enemy, to catch them strung out on the march, as long as the main army moved swiftly.

If they had sighted Gelimer, his scouts had seen Solomon. Between the two forces stood a high hill that dominated the surrounding country. Possession of that would give a huge advantage to whoever held it and a race resulted to get control. The Vandals got there first and despite Solomon's best efforts he was up against too many to prevail and was obliged to retreat, not without a hot and threatening pursuit.

Halfway back to the camp he came across a force of eight hundred *bucellarii*, all from the Belisarius *comitatus*, dismounted and holding a strong position. They, on hearing of Solomon's reverse – it was not more than that – instead of standing where they were to provide aid, immediately fled. It was as well they encountered their general, himself out seeking news of his enemies and, though he would scarce admit it, getting himself away from the bickering of Antonina and Procopius.

Rallying them by sheer force of personality he was able to steady his troops and get them ready to fight, while the pursuit, seeing the formation of that stand, saw it as prudent to withdraw. Now Belisarius knew the whereabouts of his enemy and he also knew of the existence of the second road leading to the pass at Ad Decimum, which had him send a fast rider to order an immediate advance to secure a position that would cut Gelimer off from Carthage or, if the Vandal usurper got there first, force him to do battle before he could retire towards the safety of the city walls.

Luck, that indefinable quality, came to the aid of Flavius once more, for Gelimer delayed in his decision-making. He neither force-marched north nor seemed to be prepared for battle when the forces Belisarius led fell upon him. It was clear by the Vandal dispositions that Gelimer thought he had been beaten to the pass so that the arrival of the Romans at his rear threw his forces into complete confusion, a situation the better general was able to exploit.

There was resistance but it was fragmented and easily broken, which had the Vandals breaking off the battle and fleeing, not towards Carthage, but north-west towards the wide fertile Plains of Boulla, perhaps fearing that with the bodies of their comrades littering the road the route to the capital was already barred by substantial numbers of their enemies: they could never have guessed that the force of John the Armenian numbered a mere three hundred men.

The flat and grassy and fertile plain facilitated, for mounted men, a swift retreat and left the way open for Flavius to advance, but he halted, eager to gather in his disparate cavalry. John returned laden with Vandal booty, likewise Balas, and with the night drawing in sentinels were posted and the army settled down for a night in which the general who had won a victory sought to find out how he had achieved it, that after he had sent back to the infantry to join him at Ad Decimum, bringing with them his wife.

In assessing what he had been told Flavius knew just how fortunate he had been, not least in encountering that fleeing *bucellarii* and rallying them, for if the pursuit had made it through to the main encampment the whole army might have panicked. He had no illusions about such a scenario; the mood of his troops could swing from confidence to despair in the blink of an eye. It was not just true of his host, it was true of any and he understood why.

A fighting soldier could only see so much and for him, and often for the men that led them, what was happening over the extent of a whole field of battle was a mystery. In essence they were confined to the periphery of a very limited vision, thus they depended to a great extent on the mood of their comrades, which was why the wildfire sense of panic could so readily spread. One man fearing death can scare a thousand.

But Gelimer had played a good hand badly too, seeking to join his forces away from Carthage and splitting them even more than when they were already divided. Having got first to the pass at Ad Decimum he should have carried on and not allowed himself to be attacked, all of these matters discussed with Procopius so that he could write up an account which would be sent to Justinian, who would have no fingernails left with the amount of worry he must be suffering.

That also afflicted Flavius when news was passed to him that his ships, now out of sight of an army too far inland, had disobeyed his orders to match his pace and proceeded to round Cap Bon, nearly to reach the point at which lay the Vandal fleet. They might have been brought to battle and if defeated where that would have left him? As it was, nothing untoward had occurred so, reunited with Antonina, he could retire to his bed and celebrate the victory in connubial bliss.

The horns blew on a bright dawn and, with Antonina at his side, Flavius Belisarius led his army on the short march to Carthage, passing the locations of his predecessors who had fought there and humbled Hannibal and the rival Carthaginian Empire to make Rome the supreme ruler of the Mediterranean. There was an attempt at humility but it was hard; how could he not feel proud? How could he not recall his father Decimus, so much the Roman, at a time like this?

He came upon a city without a garrison to defend it and with walls in poor repair; migratory barbarians were not adept at building or maintaining fortifications, while inside the walls lived a population eager in the main to embrace them. Yet there was no rush to enter; the streets of the city were narrow, the Vandals if defeated, not destroyed. Despite the direction in which they fled how many might there be within the city waiting to ambush his men? Another day would make no difference.

Word had reached Calonymus of the victory so they were heading for the port, a move Flavius blocked; they were to stay away until he had secured the Vandal capital and all was safe. The sailors satisfied themselves by plundering every merchant ship they could find and many a shore warehouse too, in the ports close to the capital.

On the sixth day the citizens of Carthage awoke to find the Roman army drawing up in battle formation. If they were fearful they did not hear the conquering general admonish his troops to show the citizens respect, as well as their property. On demand the gates were opened and Flavius Belisarius entered the city, making for the palace of Gelimer to take up residence, eating the meal that had been prepared for the owner's return.

Two things frustrated him: Hilderic and his supporters had been murdered by Ammatus on the news of the Roman landing; also the treasury was empty and that was a great disappointment for it was legendary in its value. It was reputed to contain the proceeds of the Vandal rampage across Gaul and Aquitaine, during two centuries in which they had despoiled palaces, churches and the villas of the rich citizenry, stripping the county of every gold *solidus* they could find, many of them worked into fabulous decorative ornaments. Hispania had suffered the same depredations, a land that had within it the spoils of Carthage, Rome and the Celtic tribes who had inhabited the land prior to any imperial subjection.

It had been removed, no doubt on the orders of Gelimer, to where no one knew, but what it meant was that the man who had occupied the city previously had the means, in both manpower and money, to keep the war going. Flavius made plain, through the leading citizens of the city whom he called to consult with him, that his policy towards the Vandals who remained with Carthage was one of peace and harmony, the same as he was extending to the old Roman stock.

Most had fled to their churches and monasteries for sanctuary from the expected wrath of their enemies; he had to convince them that they had nothing to fear. Then he turned to other pressing matters. Defending the place!

'The walls can wait, surely, Husband,' Antonina protested, when he said his next task was to inspect them. It was unfortunate that it was Procopius who chose to respond, saying the same as would his employer but beating him to it.

'Gelimer is not yet beaten.'

'Then wave your stylus at him, Procopius. I am sure he will flee then.'

The reply was icy and delivered with a thin and waspish smile. 'Perhaps, Lady Antonina, he will encounter your good self and surrender to be spared from your tongue.'

'Procopius, enough,' Flavius barked. 'Both of you are commenting on matters outside your responsibilities.'

'As if I had been granted any,' pouted his wife.

'You have them now. I am the imperial representative here and you're my consort, which will mean many tasks devolving upon you to ensure that what we have gained stays in our possession.'

'And what will they be?'

'Ask Theodora,' Procopius suggested. 'I'm sure she will be able to advise you of your duties.'

'Just as long as you never seek to.'

'I am off to inspect the walls,' Flavius growled. 'They at least will not dispute with me.'

CHAPTER TWENTY-TWO

'The walls are in such poor repair, they are inadequate to repel an assault. One push and half the stones will fall.'

Valerianus replied to Flavius with something of a shrug. 'Then they need to be rebuilt.'

'We would struggle to hold them if Gelimer attacks.'

'Flavius Belisarius, there is no indication that he has the strength.'

The desire to tell him he was wrong was solid; they had driven Gelimer from the battlefield but he had not been destroyed. The relationship with his second in command was interesting, Valerianus being a patrician; it must be galling to serve under someone from the Belisarius background, the son of a centurion commanding the offshoot of generals.

His family had filled military and bureaucratic posts within the empire for centuries and, given his name, it was odd that when he spoke he chose to do so in Greek, a growing trait throughout the higher reaches of the old aristocracy. Flavius made a point of speaking to him in Latin, which tended to make the man think before replying, even if he had been reminded several times that was the language of the people they now controlled.

He never dared to condescend openly to his commanding general, nor was he overly questioning on his tactics, perhaps because he had good grounds to think that Flavius would not remain in Carthage, so there would exist a vacancy to succeed him in what would be a rich office in a province ripe for plucking. The man to whom he was talking always wondered if that was why he was studiously polite.

'I want a ditch dug around the land walls, that to be lined with stakes. Then, and only then, can we consider working on any masonry.'

'My infantry are looking forward to a touch of ease.'

'Then employ the citizens of the city, Valerianus; let them show in labour how much they appreciate our victory.'

'The Emperor?'

'I am sending Solomon to Constantinople to carry the news.'

There was a blink then, of what? Jealousy. The messenger to Justinian would be well rewarded. Was it a task for which Valerianus could put himself forward and one he might have a right to claim?

'Digging ditches. I doubt my family will be impressed.'

'No one is asking you to personally employ a spade.'

310

The task was completed within a week by obliging the Carthaginians to provide the necessary muscle. Flavius felt more secure, albeit there was bad news as well as good. Gelimer's brother, Tzazon, had reconquered Sardinia, killing the leader of the rebellion which would, once he was appraised of the defeat at home, bring him and his five thousand warriors back to North Africa. The only silver lining was that the four hundred Heruls under Pharas that Flavius had sent to aid the uprising had arrived too late to become involved and were coming back to rejoin him.

Next news came of a Visigoth refusal to aid Gelimer. The envoys he had sent to Hispania were slackers and arrived just as the news of the fall of Carthage reached the Visigoth ruler; he sent them home without bothering to tell them, thus they landed in Carthage and fell straight into the hands of the Romans. That at least shut off a potential route of escape for Gelimer, not that any indication came he was seeking one.

He had called all the remaining Vandals to his banner and was distributing gold to the indigenes who resided on the breadbasket Plains of Boulla to aid him. There was also a reward offered for the head of any one of the men Flavius led. This was particularly a problem inside the city, given the ease of committing murder. Delivery was harder and searches were introduced in which several villains were apprehended and hung from the newly repaired sections of the walls. Most of the victims turned out to be servants; the soldiers, armed, were too difficult a target.

'What will Gelimer do next?' was the question on everyone's lips.

'He must attack us,' replied John the Armenian, who since the departure of Solomon had become close to Flavius and had no fear of speaking out at the daily conference. 'He needs a quick win and that is the only way to get one.'

That opened a discussion on how to counter that; to exit the city and fight him in the open – favoured by the likes of Balas and the cavalry commanders – or to sit behind the walls and wait to be attacked. There might be much talking but the man in command was sure of his own course. He would act defensively for now as he had no need to do otherwise; Gelimer was the one with the problem.

'Has his brother joined him yet?' Valerianus asked.

'We must assume he has yet to arrive,' Procopius said, intelligence on the enemy being his responsibility. 'In my view he will move as soon as that happens.'

That raised a few eyebrows amongst the military men; what was this clerkish fellow doing commenting on matters that were their territory?

'The Moors?' John asked; that was the province of the secretary.

'They seem reluctant to give him aid. Some have joined Gelimer but not all they can muster. I have some hopes of making an alliance that will favour us, for I have made it plain that we Romans have no designs on Mauretania.'

'Yet,' Valerianus crowed.

'Probably never,' Flavius interjected, only for Procopius to tell everyone why.

'Move on Mauretania and you will have the Visigoths to contend with. They do not want us on the south side of the Pillars of Hercules.'

'We beat the Vandals and we can beat them too.'

'With the Moors fully on their side.'

'Well, it is plain,' Flavius concluded, 'that Gelimer is gathering strength and not only from Sardinia. He is collecting in every waif and stray he can find to beef up his forces. If he does not come to us, which like John I think he must, then we must go to him and before our army gets too soft from luxuriating in Carthage.'

It was agreed that as matters stood the Belisarius view should prevail: stay behind the ditch and the walls and wait. As the meeting broke up Balas hung back and it was plain he wanted a private talk. Procopius was permitted to stay as the Hun leader raised the discomfort being felt by his men.

'I hope, Flavius Belisarius, you see them as having acquitted themselves well.'

'Without doubt, a couple of transgressors notwithstanding.'

Balas shrugged. 'They got what they deserved but the rest of my soldiers are wondering when they can go home?'

'We are in the middle of a campaign,' Procopius protested.

'And they will see it through. But there's not one of them gives this Gelimer a chance and they are hoping you will say to them that as soon as he is defeated proper they will be boarded onto ships for Constantinople and the borderlands. They did not make a mark to serve abroad.'

There was no need to ask why this request was forthcoming; the Huns served as mercenaries close to their own homelands. They liked to do their service in a spot where they could easily visit family, often wives and children, or friends who lived just beyond the imperial border markers. If they campaigned away from that it was of short duration.

Flavius had always had an ambivalent attitude to Huns – it was men of that race who had massacred the cohort led by his father and if they had been bribed to do so that did not diminish the relish with which their murderous raid was carried out. Perhaps there were men now serving Justinian who had taken part in that incursion, maybe even in his army.

Not that he would enquire; the Huns who enrolled as mercenaries were wonderful fighters with a reputation that was respected throughout the known world. But their tribal comrades who did not serve the armies of Constantinople were more numerous and seen as homicidal, especially by imperial citizens. If any of that ilk were present it was best not to know.

'We must defeat Gelimer before anyone goes anywhere.'

'I have acknowledged that.'

'And if it takes time?'

'Then they will stay true.'

'True?' demanded Procopius, hinting at treason.

'An inappropriate word, Balas,' Flavius said in an emollient tone. 'Please tell your men that no one will be kept here beyond the need, but I have also to add I have no idea when that might be.'

'Strange to make the request now,' Procopius opined when the Hun leader had left.

'It's a cautioning. Balas is letting us know well in

advance of any difficulties that there might be one.'

Any concerns would have been eased if they could have seen into the mind of Gelimer. He too would have agreed with John the Armenian, for he knew that a protracted war was unsustainable and would only have been so with the aid of the indigenous population. But they were now firmly, thanks to the mildness of the Belisarian policies, firmly in his camp.

Thus he had a limited number of men and after they were gone there would be no more. To keep them in the field without fighting was not the way of their tribe, and even if he had wanted to play a waiting game their hot blood would not have permitted it. He needed to beat the Romans and quickly; that done, the spineless indigenes would soon bow at the knee again.

Flavius Belisarius was in Carthage, which is where Gelimer knew he must proceed and quickly. The walls were being repaired; it was getting stronger not weaker so it was time to march.

The first act was to damage the city aqueduct and deprive it of much of its fresh water. Yet Gelimer did not want a siege, he wanted the Romans to emerge from within and fight, so there was no attempt to cut off the city from supply, impossible anyway given the amount of shipping available and an open port. He moved his main camp back to a place called Tricamarum though he had many a patrol pass jeering before the walls.

In addition he had his agents seeking to weaken Belisarius; there was some hope that the Carthaginians, who had done better out of Vandal rule than their country cousins, might defect to his banner. Then there was religion; the Huns and Heruls were Arians and so easy to approach through the Vandal divines who still said Masses within the city.

The latter, being Germans, were quick to rebuff such an overture but it fell on more fertile ground with the Huns; the warning given by Balas had not been hot air, there was a genuine grievance and it affected the entire contingent. If Belisarius was beaten they could leave; if he won that was not certain.

One of the problems was that Flavius gave them time; he was not to be tempted to battle until the walls of the city were fully repaired. Then and only then, when he had an absolutely secure base to retire to in the face of possible defeat would he oblige Gelimer. Nor was he unconscious of the hopes of the Vandal leader. One citizen of Carthage was caught seeking to join the Vandals; Flavius had him impaled on the battlements and left to rot as a warning to others.

With the Huns he sought to seduce them with his attention, to perhaps tie them to him personally. There were gifts and banquets over the next two months which calmed the chance of any immediate defection. Yet asked if he had secured their allegiance he was only able to reply, while struggling to keep his personal distaste for the breed out of his voice, 'What I have secured is their indifference. They will be with us if we are winning, but will side with Gelimer if not. They care only for their own needs.'

Patience was aided by domestic harmony; that existed as long as Procopius was not around. Antonina had taken to being a suzerain with delight. The Belisarian apartments, lately Gelimer's, were full most nights of her husband's officers as well as the leading citizens of Carthage, who saw it as politic to shower her with gifts – the soldiers settled for flattery – both of which she took with both hands.

The only fly in this happy scene was Procopius, hinting that such gatherings were not as innocent as his employer supposed. Flavius was not always present – he had duties to attend to which could not be delegated. The secretary was careful, of course, never once accusing Antonina of anything untoward. But there was enough in his concerns to have Flavius wondering; she had, after all, led a very chequered life before their nuptials and he knew her to be a lusty lover with an appetite he was not always able to satisfy.

That was a consideration that required to be left for another time; three months had gone by now and with a stout city fortress fully repaired Flavius could contemplate giving battle. His first act was to send out John the Armenian with most of the *bucellarii*, his orders to approach the fortified camp of Gelimer, to bait the enemy with archery and probing attacks if the opportunity arose but on no account to initiate a full-scale battle.

The next morning Flavius left Carthage at the head of the infantry and the remaining cavalry, to cover the six leagues to where Gelimer had set up camp. But the Vandals had moved out and were now on the far side of a stream some distance from their camp. The Vandal leader used that watercourse and the dip in the ground that it created to draw up his own forces but he waited till midday before fully deploying; clearly someone had advised him of the same tactics once employed by the Sassanids: fight the Romans when they are hungry.

Yet he was preparing to attack and that caught the men John led by surprise, meaning they had to rapidly deploy to face Gelimer before their entire force was on the field. Flavius was still marching with the infantry, following well behind him, only in sight of John's predicament when matters had come to a critical stage. Knowing the Armenian would be forced to engage before he could be fully supported – the infantry were too far off and coming on too slowly – he sent forward the army standard and his own *comitatus* along with a message to say he had every confidence in his ability.

On the left wing John deployed the *foederati*, men armed for hand-to-hand combat with a section of archers, fighters who would work ballistae aided by spear-carrying cavalry. On the right were the bulk of the cavalry and Flavius ensured the Huns and their horses, who were with him, were held well to the rear to keep them out of the battle. It was noticeable that on the other side the Moors were likewise in a disengaged position, behind but not close to the centre of the Vandal lines.

John sought to tempt the Vandals by peppering them with arrows and missiles, to which they responded with not a single spear, a fact the Romans found peculiar. Tzazon would not be drawn; if he attacked to drive these skirmishers off he did not let his men cross the stream. He knew that to be the enemy aim, just as he knew that even if as an obstacle it was small it was enough to disorder his ranks.

The same aim was the tactic of John's next sally, leading forward the *bucellarii*. Again Tzazon mounted an attack to throw them back, again his men halted at the water's edge. Watching from an elevated position Flavius had observed that on each occasion the Vandal wings had not moved to support Tzazon and his Sardinian veterans. Fearing that John, into close proximity, might have failed to observe this he sent a messenger to advise him. But there were no accompanying orders; he had handed over tactical command, to interfere would be wrong.

John needed no instruction, anyway; he had noted that on both occasions there had been no sign of a mounted response to his pinprick attacks. If the Vandals would not move then he must. With that knowledge added to the message from Flavius he brought forward the whole *comitatus*, the very best troops he commanded, and attacked across the stream himself.

His general was right; the Vandal wings remained static, taking no part in what had become a fight of the centre sections of both armies. Once more it was noticed there were no Vandal spears employed, which meant the Romans got close up to the enemy and began to press them back. As is often the case it was the fall of a leader that decided matters. Tzazon was isolated and cut down, his collapse sending a deep wail of despair through the men he had led both here and in Sardinia.

When they broke so did the Vandal wings and soon it turned into a rout, one in which the Huns spurred forward to take part, cutting down their coreligionists with abandon in a retreat that took the Vandals back inside their fortified camp, one that was too strong to be assaulted by cavalry.

Flavius was harrying his infantry to get to the same spot, and once there he formed them up for an immediate assault, now once more in possession of his standard. It proved a waste; Gelimer knew he was beaten and with a few close followers, relatives and the like, he abandoned his men and fled. It was only moments later that the whole Vandal army did likewise – they would not stand where their usurper king would not – leaving their enemies to plunder their camp. This time it included a great quantity of treasure, including many of the priceless objects looted from Gaul and Hispania, fortunately secured by the more disciplined units.

There was no holding back the men Flavius led. They had found an abundance of wine too, as well as women; and were fired up for rapine, slaughter and plunder. Even if their general had wanted to pursue Gelimer it would have proved impossible. It did not occur to these rampaging fools that the Vandals might re-form and attack. If they had it would have been fatal.

It was daybreak before he could impose some order, halfway through the morning before he got a chance to harangue and curse his own troops for their behaviour, this after he had got John the Armenian away with two hundred cavalry to seek to kill or capture Gelimer. Women and children were rescued from being privately sold into slavery. Vandals who had taken sanctuary in their Arian churches were relieved of their weapons and sent to Carthage.

That done, Flavius formed up his army to engage in his personal pursuit only to come across tragedy. After several days and nights of a hard chase John had got close enough to the rump of Gelimer's forces to effect a capture or kill him as commanded. One of his bowman, in firing an arrow, let one hand slip as he loosed and the bolt swerved from true aim and hit John in the neck. When Flavius caught up with them it was to find them in mourning for their dead and much revered commander, none more so than the guilty bowman.

Yet on questioning them all it had to be concluded to be an accident, a fluke of battle but not a fitting end for such a fine warrior. The culprit was pardoned and John was buried at the very spot, with Flavius pledging funds to ensure it would be marked by a stone obelisk listing his achievements and offices, all in Latin as befitted a man deserving to be called a true Roman.

Gelimer was still free as well as alive and the pursuit had to continue.

CHAPTER TWENTY-THREE

To get at their quarry became harder than merely catching up with him. Gelimer had allies of which the Romans were unaware and they were now in a land where if the populace were known as Moors, that covered many individual tribes who would not have responded to that folkloric label, people who answered only to their own leaders in an area of Africa riven by fractious infighting. One such occupied an ancient hill fort and city known as Medeus, and it had been fighters from there that had been observed at the recent battle.

Situated on the slopes of a high mountain, the fortress looked unassailable and for one man, however elevated, it was not a place to employ a whole army nor could it occupy a person with a recently reconquered kingdom to run.

Flavius entrusted the task of capture, either by negotiation or other means, to Pharas and his Heruls, men who had been staunchly loyal to his banner.

Returning to Hippo Regius, the largest and most wealthy city west of Carthage, from there he began to make certain dispositions. There were Vandal outposts in the region of Mauretania to take possession of, one right opposite the coast of Hispania at the Pillars of Hercules and one in Caesarea, the old Roman capital when Mauretania had been an imperial province, one of which Procopius had a very fixed view.

'Justinian will wish you to take control of that too.'

'Then he better send me another army, for by my reading all we really ever held was the coast. The mountain tribes are impossible to subdue, the best that can be hoped for is that they can be kept from too much raiding. We have enough to swallow with the possessions of the Vandals.'

'I questioned one of Tzazon's captains, a fellow who was with him in Sardinia. His leader did such a fine job on the island the place is properly cowed. Seems he hung or strangled anyone who looked like a rebel. The locals will not believe he is dead and they will not believe that we have beaten Gelimer.'

Procopius got an expectant look then: Flavius knew such preambles usually led to a solution and he was waiting for one now. 'So since we have the head of Tzazon, I suggest we send it with whoever is despatched to secure the place.'

'We best send a strong force,' Flavius mused. 'Tzazon would not have left the place without a garrison of some kind who might fight. Whoever we send will have to secure Corsica as well.'

The other problem was the Vandals spread out all over their now defunct kingdom. Flavius was well aware that more than half of his inferior commanders believed they should be rounded up and slaughtered like dogs, Balas of the Huns particularly keen to be allotted the task, no doubt to prove their renewed loyalty.

But the man who had to decide wanted a peaceful province not a troubled one, and to do as was suggested would mean sending out bodies of troops to scour the countryside and root out the perceived enemy. What he had observed in Carthage made that questionable. If the indigenes that the Vandals had subdued hated them, they were yet Christians and would probably not, in many cases, welcome persecution. It was plain that if the Vandal touch had been heavy in the larger concentrations like the capital, out in the country he sensed they had been more benign; logic dictated they would have had to be, for the Vandals were so heavily outnumbered by the local population to be cruel invited assassination.

There was another consideration: bands of warriors roaming around out of his personal control might be lax in whom they chastised. The invading army could not have beaten Gelimer so speedily without aid, such as freely given supplies and intelligence of the enemy. Anything that might alienate the people who had behaved so well had to be avoided and that included unnecessary massacres that might kill the wrong people. The amnesty was to apply to all Vandals and only those who refused it would suffer.

'A messenger, Excellence.'

Flavius looked up from the papers he was examining to respond, grateful that his labours might be interrupted given he found them tedious. Old property rolls, census returns and taxation receipts for the region in which he now sat, the very stuff by which bureaucrats run empires, though these were out of date. They were not to his taste but they had to be studied so that he could put in place the officials necessary to run the province without handing them the keys to the coffers and an easy way to line their own pockets.

'A Vandal who seeks a personal audience,' the servant added. 'Well dressed.'

'A high official?'

'All I can say is his clothing is fine.'

Even knowing the fellow would not be armed, Flavius fetched his sword and placed it on the desk he was using, before sitting behind it and permitting the man's entry. Fine clothing did not do him justice and did not describe his person; well larded in a way that indicated a superior diet, he was clad in silks of exceptionally good quality, which had Flavius ask the man who had escorted him to send for Procopius.

The bow that followed was so low the man's head was near to touching the ground, an act that was greeted in silence. Given the position was held, Flavius reckoned through uncertainty. When Procopius entered he was greeted by a quite substantial posterior and he could not resist what for him was unusual, a joke.

'I think I know that face.'

'Bonifatius of Caesarea greets the mighty Flavius Belisarius.'

Being aimed at the marble floor and pronounced in perfect Latin gave this declaration an ethereal quality. 'And what does that signify?'

Flavius having spoken was obviously seen as a release for his self-imposed obsequiousness for this Bonifatius stood up to hear Procopius remark that it was a very Roman name.

'I have ever been a friend to the empire.'

'We have discovered so many friends to the empire since coming here,' Flavius replied, his tone deeply ironic, 'it is a wonder we needed to invade at all.'

'I hazard you will find me a true one.'

'Why?'

'I have a tale to impart you, mighty Belisarius, that will enthral you.'

There was no change in tone. 'I do so love a story.'

'This one comes with a reward in gold.'

'For you, no doubt,' Procopius opined, he having come to join Flavius and now able to examine the round and shiny red-cheeked face. His employer indicated that he should sit.

'You are, I suspect, Procopius, the mighty Belisarius's *assessor*. When you hear what I have to say you will have much to count.'

That slightly threw Procopius who knew the term as a legal one until he realised the Bonifatius had made a joke. Given he had so recently done the same the frown was inappropriate as he demanded the man get to the point.

'Upon hearing of you landing, King Gelimer—'

'The usurper Gelimer,' Flavius corrected, but softly to a reluctant nod.

'Lord Gelimer gave certain instructions.'

'To murder his brother, Hilderic, was one. Ammatus may have done the deed but it was Gelimer's hand.'

Seeing that posed as a question Bonifatius was quick to say that such acts were none of his affair adding, without too much sincerity, how much they were to be regretted.

'The Lord worried for the treasure of his family.'

'Which we took out of his camp at Tricamarum,' Procopius interjected.

That remark earned him the kind of smile with which a kindly parent indulges an errant child and it was not missed by the fastidious secretary, a man who reacted badly when condescended to. But even angry he did not miss the implication.

'Are you going to tell us there is more?'

'Naturally Lord Gelimer kept a portion with him, to be used to garner support.'

'Bribes.'

Bonifatius shrugged. 'It does no harm for a ruler, even a usurper, to have visible the means by which he might distribute rewards.'

'But it was not all.'

'I doubt your mind can encompass the success of generations of the Vandal people when it comes to the spoils of war. The main royal treasure was loaded aboard a vessel and I had instructions, should matters go against my king, that his property should be transported to Hispania where he was certain he could find refuge with the King of the Visigoths.'

'And you have disobeyed that injunction?' Flavius enquired.

'Far from it, mighty Belisarius—'

'Do stop calling me that. It irritates me.'

'A thousand pardons humbly given.'

'If there was such a thing and reincarnation, as some people of the east believe, this fellow would come back as a snail.' Procopius had spoken in Greek, but the look his remark received told him this fellow spoke that language as well as he did Latin. 'Go on.'

'I set sail on news of his reverse at Tricamarum but ran into contrary winds which have blown us back to our native shore and we are now obliged to throw ourselves on to the mercy of the mighty – forgive me – General Belisarius.'

'Where is this ship now? I cannot believe it is in the Hippo Regius harbour.'

'It was not felt such a berth would be secure.'

'For your head or what you carried?' That got a non-committal display of open palms. 'So you have come to treat, using the latter to preserve the former?'

'Wise as well as mighty. I am, as you will guess, not a sailing man. I also have with me not only the master and crew, people to whom I have become attached, but members of my own family. Naturally I would want assurances of their safety before surrendering so valuable a prize.'

'And, of course,' Procopius remarked, his cynicism barely disguised, 'you will hand over it all.'

'Why would I not?' came the reply, which was sophistry of the highest order.

Flavius had arched his fingers before his mouth, as if in deep thought, but really to hide a smile; this courtier, and he was that to the very end of his own fingertips, did not know of his intention to amnesty every Vandal or of the announcement he was about to make promulgating that throughout the old kingdom.

Procopius leant over to whisper in his ear that this rogue before them would certainly be in the process of hiding a goodly proportion of what he had been tasked to transport, which Flavius could do no more than acknowledge. But the man would have to show some caution; there would be documents somewhere that listed the plunder that the Vandals had accumulated over two centuries, as well as human memory. He would have to be careful what and how much he purloined.

'And the ship is now where?' A shrug that annoyed. 'I could have you racked to find out.'

'There is a limit to the patience the master will show should I not return.'

On considering that, it became probable that this Bonifatius knew that his late master was locked up in Medeus, or he may not be sure of that as a detail, but he was certain the Vandal hold on the kingdom was no more. If he had dipped his fingers in the pie of Gelimer's treasure it would be a hard hoard to find. What he was being told was that he, the mighty Belisarius, would not find any of it and he thought he knew what this Bonifatius was really after.

'You served your king well?'

The word 'king' was the clue to a sharp thinker, a long-serving courtier with a bureaucrat's mind. 'I would hope if he were present he would say so, and that would apply to the man Gelimer replaced.' Bonifatius crossed himself, which was not the Arian way. 'May Hilderic's soul rest in peace, for he was a good man.'

'I have taken over responsibility for the governance of what is now an imperial province.'

'In mere months. Who would have thought it possible?'

'Perhaps God,' Procopius sneered.

'It is to him we look for wisdom,' came the calm reply.

'There will be occasions, Bonifatius, when in dealing with those we now rule, matters arise that require a knowledge of how the province was previously governed.'

'I would see it as my duty to aid the peaceful transfer of power so that as little harm comes to those for whom I care as it does to my own body.'

'And if I was to offer you a chance to bring that about?'

'I could not bring myself to reject such a blessed opportunity, for God would never forgive me.'

'The ship?'

'Is anchored to the west in a shallow bay, awaiting my return.'

'Which you will make in my company, Bonifatius.' Sensing the bodily tension to one side, Flavius added, 'As, of course, the man who must make an inventory of what we find.'

'Flabbergasted' is a word that can only rarely be applied but it was apposite when the holds of the ship were opened and the numerous chests were brought on deck and opened. Not only were there objects of gold and silver studded with precious stones, there were chests of coin enough to pay for the whole expedition Justinian had initiated. Then there were the relics of Christian martyrs looted from churches and abbeys all through Gaul, South-west France and Hispania, more than enough in these alone for Gelimer to buy from the Visigoths a life of ease.

Procopius was tasked with the listing of the totals, with Flavius questioning Bonifatius about which object would be of most personal worth to Gelimer? The surprise came in the form of the bones of St Sebastian, looted from the Vandal sacking of Rome, now encased in a golden casket and personally venerated by the now deposed king.

Flavius put together a strong party from his *comitatus* led by Boriades – he could not risk their loss – with orders to take the casket to Pharas at Medeus, where it could be shown to Gelimer as proof that his last hope, to escape to Hispania and be in possession of enough treasure to mount a reconquest of the Vandal kingdom – Flavius was sure that would have been his intention – was no more.

Pharas had sat idly watching Medeus for weeks now, knowing that with no food getting in and none of the inhabitants getting out he was engaged in a war of attrition, a siege in which starvation would bring a result. It was a situation that did not suit him and was anathema to his Heruls, who saw the chance of slaughter and plunder in front of their eyes, albeit they needed to be raised to have sight of the city perched on a rocky outcrop, while they sat and cooked their food, drank their wheaten beer and told tales of Germanic bravery and deeds of heroism.

Unable to stand it any longer, Pharas mounted an assault and it was a total failure in terms of penetration. He lost a high proportion of his effectives – either killed or so seriously wounded as to be rendered useless – and was left once more staring up at the formidable fortified city, his frustration now double that which it had been before. In his heart he prayed that Flavius Belisarius would realise that this was not war to his Heruls and that he needed to be relieved.

The sight of the troop of his general's *comitatus*, unmissable in their distinctive uniforms, cheered everyone who saw their approach until it dawned on them there were no more and that these were never going to be enough to take over the burden. Being Arians, the sight of the relics impressed them, but that did not translate into what they thought a solution.

'Our general wishes you to show this casket to Gelimer.'

'You can show it to him, Boriades. I lost a hundred men against those walls. I was about to send to Flavius Belisarius to ask for more and enough so we could be employed elsewhere.'

'Then I require a truce flag.'

'What makes you think they'll respect one? They are Moors.'

Boriades let that pass; to Heruls no other tribe, even a Germanic one, was worthy of trust. He had his own men fashion a cloth of white and he made his own way on foot up the steep mountainside followed by two of his men carrying the heavy casket, which was covered to keep it hidden. Being a Latin speaker he had no trouble in getting one of Gelimer's supporters to the walls, if not the man himself, who declined to treat with a mere officer of his main enemy.

The first message was that Flavius Belisarius should come himself if he wished to talk of the terms of a Roman surrender, a jest that had laughing all of Gelimer's men who heard it. Boriades was up to trading jests; he replied that if surrender was on offer, Gelimer should take it from a pauper, if need be.

'Which he now is.' That got a curious look from a face which required a steep craning of the neck to see. 'Now that we have his treasure ship and Bonifatius too.'

'You speak in riddles.'

Which led Boriades to suspect that the transport was a secret Gelimer had not confided to even his closest adherents, his personal guard, men who had stayed loyal to him in disaster and would probably die to protect him. A poor reward that would be for such service.

'I speak to you, but I have, now, need to speak with Gelimer.'

'King Gelimer!' came the angry response and not from the man Boriades was addressing.

'I ask only that he comes to the battlements and looks. No words need be exchanged that impinge upon his dignity.'

There was a hiatus, Boriades waiting while he could hear but not see the murmuring of a conversation filled with dispute. The battlements were only the height of two men while the gathering of people was on the wooden fighting parapet. Odd that it seemed that one voice was arguing both positions.

Eventually a new face appeared but there was no speaking. Never having seen Gelimer, Boriades had no idea if it was really him, yet there was no alternative but to assume it to be the case. He called forward his two troopers and whipped the cover off the casket, that producing a gasp. Then he had it opened to reveal the relics laying on their velvet lining. After a wait he then shut the lid and recovered it as the head disappeared.

'That is a message from Flavius Belisarius who wishes Gelimer to know that, should he surrender, no harm will come to him, a pledge made on the bones of Saint Sebastian.'

More murmuring followed and the man with whom he had originally spoken leant over to talk. He insisted that as a king, Gelimer could only treat with someone whose rank did not insult his standing. Being told that the general was too busy in organising the new imperial province to make such a journey led to proposals made and offers rejected until it was agreed that the two should communicate by letter.

Told he would have to remain until this was complete, Pharas was far from happy. It took weeks of missives flying to and fro until the terms were agreed, and under a strong escort Gelimer was escorted from Medeus to Carthage, there to join all the other Vandals who had surrendered.

The war was over and it had taken six months to subdue a kingdom that had stood for a hundred years.

CHAPTER TWENTY-FOUR

Other problems required to be solved: the Balearic Islands had been a Vandal fief and they had to be secured for the empire, the man sent to effect the takeover, Hilderic's representative to Constantinople. But the most pressing difficulty lay in Sicily and the city of Lilybaeum, which lay at the very western tip of the island and had been a Vandal possession that Flavius now claimed for the empire, this dismissed by Amalasuintha on behalf of her son. Much correspondence ensued with no one giving ground, so the final suggestion was that the matter should be referred to Justinian to arbitrate.

That was a cunning ploy – he was unlikely to give up what was once part of the Roman Empire – given

Amalasuintha depended on the Emperor's support to hold her own position against her nobles. The notion came from Procopius who, having served throughout the campaign, had continued to impress the man for whom he laboured, the only problem being that Antonina was sure he was vying for influence in a way that was designed to ensure she provided none.

If the burden of winning the campaign had been hard, acting as a proconsul was even more difficult, though at least he could send the Huns home, which removed the running sore of their discontent. But for the others there were responsibilities to undertake in garrisoning the vital cities that held the whole polity together. Another problem was that not all the tax and census details for the whole region could be found, and fearing to be landed with the burden of repair he agreed with Procopius to hand the matter over to Constantinople; let them provide the people to right that loss.

The feeling that matters had changed since the conclusion of the war was palpable. In some senses it reminded Flavius of that which he had observed in the corridors of the imperial palace, sly looks and especially long silences when he held a conference of his commanders, he being left with the feeling they were not all entirely with him. Nothing manifested this more than the reaction to the oft-reiterated mantra that they must be seen to be different to the Vandals.

They had not come like them to live off the toil of others, to eat food they did not grow and to reward themselves with monies they did not earn so they could retain their martial purity. The population must be treated as Romans should, the Vandals willing to change must be integrated into the society in which they lived.

Procopius had a reason, 'I think you will find, General, that ambition is stirring in more than one breast. There is much to aim for.'

'I always get the impression that with Valerianus he cannot wait for me to depart.'

'He is an officer in the *praesental* and personally appointed by his emperor as commander. He would need a commission directly from Justinian to succeed you.'

'Meaning I could not anoint him even if I wanted to?'

'Legally, no.'

'He must know that, Procopius?'

The look Flavius got them told him that if one general did not know the statutes by which such matters were decided why should another? And Flavius had to acknowledge his understanding of the legal codes of the empire were sketchy.

'Maybe I should ask him outright.'

'That rarely provides an honest answer.'

Looking at him, tall, slim and by his movements somewhat fussy, Flavius wondered if even Procopius always told him the truth. The man was so clearly committed to him he had to hope it was the case, despite Antonina's insistence that he was the kind to always have up his sleeve a means by which he could protect himself.

'Those sort always do,' she had said more than once.

Was he that sort? There had been no evidence that Flavius could see, no lovers of either gender. It seemed as if Procopius had no need of such attachments, content to immerse himself in his toils to the exclusion of a private life. He certainly took little pleasure in the regular entertainments that, despite Antonina's clear hostility, he was at liberty to attend – gatherings of officers and officials to eat and drink, and others where the Lady Belisarius brought in singers and dancers.

They were far from being to her own husband's taste, being too frivolous at a time when he was engaged in a war. It seemed wrong to be entertaining oneself when what you were planning would see men die, and that might include your own self. Antonina would have none of that; if you could not relax, to her mind, how could you fight?

'Might I suggest, General, that a watch be kept on some of your officers?'

'Why?' came the guarded response.

'You have just alluded to what is at stake here in North Africa. A rich province far from Constantinople, ambitious men—'

'No, Procopius, let us see if we can just trust them.'

Yet what his secretary was suggesting did stay with Flavius; anyone seizing the province and declaring themselves as rulers would have many factors on their side. Distance, of course, the fact that it could not be carried out without troops but they, the Belisarius *comitatus* aside, would be bribable with slave-cultivated land if not hard coin. But to actually spy on them was not to his taste. In this he was circumvented.

'You must forgive me for acting without your express permission.'

'Against my express orders more like. What possessed you?'

'Is my skin not worth saving?'

'Of course.'

'Then accept that was my purpose.'

Tempted to argue with that, Flavius declined to do so. It might have been to save him that he acted. 'Are they fit for me to question them?'

'They will answer whatever you ask.'

The two specimens brought into his presence by Pharas and a couple of his Heruls were in a sorry state. Middle-ranking officers, they had been racked and had hot iron applied to their flesh. Their straggle of beards showed they had been long unshaven and in their eyes Flavius was sure he saw despair.

They had been apprehended boarding a ship bound for Constantinople, one of the many elements of the fleet that had fetched the expedition to these shores, returning to their home ports to resume their normal trading duties. Their owners had never liked the rate they were paid by the imperial treasury for their hire and had been clamouring for the return of their property.

'Fetch wine and bread,' Flavius said. 'These men need sustenance.'

'They need a rope round their neck,' Pharas responded.

'Have you tried kindness, Pharas? They may have told you what you wanted to know.'

That got a look of utter disbelief and not only from the Heruls; Procopius was equally unconvinced. The servants did as their masters required; the two miscreants were allowed to sit, Flavius watching them all the time while aware he was being likewise examined by those to whom he owed a debt of gratitude.

The pair had already confessed under torture to the mission on which they had been engaged, carrying a message to Justinian telling him that Flavius Belisarius, his most trusted general, was about to rebel and seize the old Vandal kingdom for himself. What they would not divulge was the identity of the person on whose behalf they were acting.

It took no great genius to see what was being hatched: a smokescreen for another's ambition, the chance to create, after a coup, the time to organise the province so that when it was declared free of imperial control it would have a chance of survival. Though it had not been extracted from their bleeding lips, because the question had never been put, there was another obvious point. For any rebellion to succeed he would have to be killed and very likely, given it would include anyone loyal to him, it would result in the death of Antonina as well.

It was Procopius acting on his own who had uncovered the plot and his point about his own skin was well made; he was too close to Flavius to survive. The recruitment of Pharas had been clever. Procopius knew how much faith his employer had in the leader of the Heruls just as he was aware that if asked he would keep the secret until the time came to reveal it and help to extract from the culprits what the general needed to know.

'So, Procopius, from the beginning?'

'Pharas came to me first.'

That got the Herul a sharp look. 'Not to me?'

His bad Latin worked for Pharas not against him; the question made him indignant not defensive. 'You would have sent me packing, General, and don't you go denying it. You are too ready to believe the best in folk.'

'I have faith in you.'

'And I had nothing but a smell, a few questions asked about how we Heruls might settle here and become part of the army of the province.'

'Which made you suspicious?'

'It wasn't you asking an' it should have been.'

'So Pharas came to me to ask if that was what you were seeking. It immediately struck me that anyone asking was not doing so for you, because I would have known of it.'

'I am at a loss to know how you worked out that messengers would be sent to Constantinople damning and accusing me.'

'It is sometimes necessary to think like a thief to catch one, is it not? The same applies to conspiracies. Now we have come this far I doubt I need to explain.'

'No,' Flavius replied, looking at the two downcast prisoners. The food seemed to have done little for their spirit. 'So you were on your way to blacken my name?'

One nodded, the other looked at his feet.

'Who is it I have treated so badly that they see the need for me to die so that they can prosper?' The tone, one of obvious regret, made the fellow who had been looking at his feet lift his head to stare with bloodshot eyes at Flavius Belisarius, making him repeat himself.

'Who?' When no reply came it was he who was almost pleading. 'It would ease my soul to know.'

'They refuse to say,' Pharas barked, 'but they will.'

'Perhaps they don't know.'

'General—'

Flavius held up a hand to stop Procopius talking and it had the desired effect. His mind was elsewhere, going back in time, several years to the elevation of Justin to the diadem.

'Conspiracy, yes?'

'A damnable clever one.'

'If it is that, then one fact that would be kept close is who these men were acting on behalf of. It shames me to say I once became involved in something of a similar nature, a deep plot and one that succeeded.'

The disbelief on the face of Procopius was not mirrored by that from Pharas. 'You can fool an enemy on a battlefield, General, can't see no reason why you would not off one.'

'The plot was not mine but that of Justinian.'

Procopius obviously felt free to comment on that. 'At least that makes sense.'

Flavius stood up and went to the nearest prisoner, gently lifting the head of the man who did not want to look him in the eye. 'Do you know who would have benefited from this intrigue?'

The head shook slowly and the question was put to his companion, the result the same.

'You do not have to believe them,' Pharas insisted.

'If they said a name I would doubt it to be the true one.' He produced a wry smile. 'I have been well trained, you see.'

'This plot of Justinian's?' Procopius asked.

'Another time, perhaps,' came the reply, as he went back to the first man to whom he had spoken. 'Was it just you two?'

No answer, not even a head shake, and that brought from Flavius a sigh. The second fellow was now looking at him, and in his eyes as far as Flavius was concerned lay an honest answer. He could not, in his weakened state, consider the notion had been arrived at by sheer deduction.

'Procopius, we need a list of vessels that have sailed for Constantinople in the last few days.' He was looking at the two victims again, one after the other and their bodily reactions were telling, not least their heads being dropped once more to avoid eye contact. 'Also, initiate a poll of middle-ranking officers, tribunes, and where they are, discreetly. Find out who is not where he is supposed to be. These two are of that rank, what's left of their clothing.'

'You think there were more?' Flavius nodded at the question, so Procopius added, 'Because it's what you would do?'

The smile now had no warmth in it at all. It was more that of a man cursing some error. 'Let us just say it is what my tutor in scheming would do.'

Pharas was quick to interject. 'We could rack them some more.'

'Why, when they have told you all they know?'

'Have they?'

'By their silence they have.'

'And what shall we do with them?'

The look was harder now. 'Given they care nothing for their lives you may as well kill them. You would expect me, knowing me as you do, to let them go. But that will only see them murdered by others for their own security.'

Now the bloodshot eyes were pleading and Flavius knew why. They might not know the name of the ultimate beneficiary of their mission but someone of lesser standing, maybe more than one, had suborned them to act for that person and under torture they had not revealed their names. Released, such men would suspect they had talked and might give evidence against them, the refusal to do so condemned them now. The pair were dead as soon as they were apprehended trying to board ship.

'Justinian will not believe them, so I have nothing to fear.'

'That may not be true.'

'In as much as he trusts anyone, Procopius, he reposes that in me.'

'I was not thinking of the Emperor,' Procopius said in a soft and somewhat sad tone. 'But Theodora.'

'She has influence, but how much? Enough to turn him against the person who aided him to the purple?'

'I would speak with you alone, General.'

About to say it was not necessary Flavius saw the look in the eyes of Procopius and it was a wounded one, almost like a man on the verge of tears. So he nodded, which had Pharas ask what he was to do with the prisoners.

Flavius came close to reply, his voice a low hiss and with no attempt to stifle his anger. 'I want their heads on pikes. Set them up outside the baths reserved for tribunes and above. Let the bastards who conspired know that if I find them that will be their fate too.'

The clanking of chains accompanied the departure of the Heruls and the prisoners, with Flavius staring at his secretary, who looked now like someone who had wished he had not spoken. But he had no choice and the look he was getting made that obvious.

'This obviously has something to do with the Empress?' A nod. 'So what is it?'

'As you know, General, your wife writes to the Lady Theodora as often it seems to me as you send a despatch to Justinian.'

'They are the oldest of friends, are they not, and have much that unites them.'

'I fear that it is you that does that.'

'Me?' Given Procopius did not immediately respond made Flavius deeply curious until the coin dropped. 'I am mentioned in these letters, a fact I find hardly surprising.'

'Would it surprise you to know that you are the main subject?'

'In what way?'

'Your lady wife writes to Theodora to report on you.'

'How do you know?' Flavius demanded, but it was close to futile: there was only one answer. 'You have read them!'

'I did so in order to protect you.'

'Against what!'

'The malice of Theodora. She does not trust you, General, even if Justinian does. If anything, she is jealous of your close association.' The 'why would that be?' was in the look he was getting, so Procopius added, 'The Empress is jealous of you.'

Flavius was thinking about the way he had been

embraced before his wedding and how cool she had become afterwards and that had him asking a question he would have dearly liked to have left fallow.

'These letters Antonina writes.'

'Report every word you say regarding the imperial couple, not least the insults.'

About to protest he never insulted them, Flavius had to bite his tongue. In a sense that was the truth, but he did complain about things and make sometimes silly jokes at their expense, especially Justinian and his foibles, when in bed with Antonina, who seemed to often raise the subject and who was much amused by his sallies.

It was not hard to imagine how these would be perceived in a written account. If Justinian could be sensitive then that applied tenfold to his wife, who was ever on the outlook for a slight.

'Every letter.'

Flavius knew he should shout at the man, tell him he had no right to open private letters and that he was misreading that which he had sneakily perused, no doubt fuelled by his own jealousies. Procopius was talking of the woman to whom he was married, a person who deserved his loyalty. Yet . . . !

'Explain everything, leave nothing out.'

Now Procopius was definitely close to tears. The deep nod was as much seeking to disguise his discomfort as to acknowledge the truth of what he was saying, for he must know that part of the mental world his employer had built for himself he had just forced him to collapse. Yet even he could not see matters as Flavius could. Procopius had just told him he was married to a spy and that it might have been the intention that she fulfil that role from the day they had met.

If it had felt bad before he knew, it was much worse after. Right now he was going to have to go and spend time with Antonina and he had no idea how he was going to cope.

'I made copies of some of the letters.'

'Bring them to me in the morning.'

The look of relief on the face of Procopius was obvious and it made Flavius want to slap him. He was clearly thinking that in his long tussle with Antonina he had emerged the winner. It was a stony face that passed the secretary and there was no bidding of goodnight.

CHAPTER TWENTY-FIVE

Flavius did not go directly to the apartments he shared with Antonina, he went to walk the battlements of the citadel that overlooked the packed harbour of Carthage. This was normally a view that brought a certain amount of contentment, it being busy by day and the place where the locals, and he assumed his soldiers, took their ease by night, just as they and he had done in the dockside taverns of Constantinople.

There were no thoughts of that nature now; his mind was in turmoil and that allowed his imagination to go in so many directions it was hard to control. It seemed he was reprising every conversation he had ever had with his wife from the day they met, and not just talk; he was thrown back to the dinners arranged by Theodora. Had they been deliberately thrown together, had their whole relationship been engineered by the woman Antonina was writing to about him?

From time to time he castigated himself as an ingrate; he had only the word of Procopius that such reflections were required but his secretary had not lacked confidence in his assertions and had mentioned the copies he had made. Then he was calling upon himself to wait! How could he know they were genuine? Antonina was always hinting that Procopius carried a torch for him, so was this whole thing being got up by jealousy?

It was dark now, the stars winking to match the oil lamps that illuminated the occupied ships' cabins as well as the signs and doorways of the watering holes that lined the quays. How he longed to go there, to drink wine and think, maybe even to talk of things not to do with his responsibilities as a proconsul or his marriage, but that was clearly impossible.

As soon as he moved he would be surrounded by a section of armed soldiers from his *comitatus*. Everywhere he went outside these walls he was guarded, on the very good grounds that it was unsafe not to be in a city where no amount of peaceful intention would satisfy everyone. The thought could not be avoided: perhaps the greater threat to his being was within. Aware that he could not walk the parapet forever, that Antonina would be waiting to dine, he reluctantly made his way to their public apartments.

The noise alerted him to the presence of others and

352

at first he felt a flash of anger that his wife arranged entertainments without ever bothering to consult him. How many times had he had to go back to the place where he oversaw the running of the province because his own audience chamber was full of her guests and he needed peace to work?

That anger abated; tonight what was happening would suit him for he dreaded a private conversation. Flavius held himself to be no good at subterfuge and in moments of self-regard, quickly beaten down as showing too much conceit, he was proud of his honesty. If he had to lie sometimes he took no pleasure in it and he was a soldier, occasionally finding it necessary to deceive his inferior commanders in order to ensure he beat his enemies. Tonight he would require the skills of Justinian to avoid an indulgence in recrimination.

'Husband, wherever have you been?' Antonina cried as he entered. 'I have sent the food back to the kitchens three times.'

Did his eyes give him away? Was his look a glare not a smile? It was telling that he could not be sure that the muscles of his face conformed to the needs of his mind but she had turned away from questioning him to a humorous berating of her guests for their inability to take the burden of running North Africa off her poor husband's shoulders.

'Do not blame us, Lady, Belisarius takes too much to himself and does not permit us to ease his encumbrances.'

The words with which he replied seemed to be coming from within another head. It was Valerianus who had spoken and when thinking on the acts of those two tortured tribunes his name had arisen as a possible instigator.

'In the time it takes me to explain what needs to be done it can be completed.'

'He does not trust us, Lady Antonina.'

Said in jest, those words could not but jar and Flavius had to bite his tongue to avoid an angry response as well as struggle to say something appropriate. 'What a poor general I am, keeping my troops from the trough.'

The faces swam before him, familiar all of them, officers of his *comitatus*, high-ranking soldiers and the bureaucrats needed to keep an army in the field and now to carry out the mundane work of administration. They looked like strangers, given he was seeking a culprit.

'I sense by that expression it is you that needs food, Flavius,' Antonina said, this before once more turning to her guests. 'I have never met his like when it comes to hunger, indifferent one moment, ravenous the next. Come sit.'

Flavius did as he was bid while she ordered that the food be returned. Her hand reached out to caress the back of his and he was aware of not responding as he normally did, though gratefully Antonina did not seem to notice, she being too busy playing the hostess. This he knew was her element just as soldiering was his. Could it be that her actions, always assuming they were true, were more ingenuous than driven by wickedness?

The food helped and so did the hubbub of talk, allowing Flavius to hide behind consumption and occasional agreement with some point made, or a smile at a sally from one of her guests good enough to make others, well supplied with wine, laugh. As a place to hide, such a gathering was perfect and it had the added attraction of distraction from depressing cogitations. By the time the evening ended and those invited were taking their leave, Flavius could feel he had carried off a difficult feat reasonably well.

He had not fooled his wife who waited until the servants had cleared the main room and they were on their way to their private rooms and their bedchamber before she asked him what was amiss, a question that had the oil lamp he was carrying quiver.

'Wrong? There is nothing wrong.' He managed a false chuckle. 'Except there is too much to do and no hours in the day to complete it.'

She took his arm and used it to stop him, which spun Flavius round to look her in the eye. 'Flavius, do not seek to play with me.'

All he could do was repeat the word. 'Play?'

Antonina slowly shook her head in the way a woman does when what she is being presented with makes no sense. 'Something is troubling you and if our other guests did not notice, though I cannot see how they failed to, I certainly did. It was as if you were elsewhere tonight.'

'The burdens—'

'Please, Flavius,' she snapped, albeit gently. 'Allow that I know you too well for that old saw.'

'I have extra concerns that weigh upon me.'

Her pressure on his arm was enough to move them on, and fortunately it broke eye contact. 'And they are?'

'Do you really want to share my worries?'

'I cannot see they can be so different from those I have shared with you before?'

Antonina said this in a confident tone and indeed it was true. How many times had he discussed matters that pressed on his mind, propped up on pillows of their bed while she prepared and applied her treatments? Then there were the post-coital intimacies, which strayed often into a discussion of personalities. How many times had his words and digs at Justinian been transcribed afterwards in letters to Theodora? It was as well Antonina was not looking at him as that thought occurred for his face, crumpled, would have given him away.

'So are you going to tell me?' she asked as her maid came forward to help her undress.

Was it the light from the oil lamps casting shadows or was he looking at her for the first time? She was still beautiful, but right now he could see lines that had not been visible to him before, the crow's feet around the eyes, the slight slacking of the jawline, a depth of crease where her cheeks met her nose and mouth.

'Leave us!' he barked, startling a maid to whom he was ever considerate.

The look he got from his wife as the girl fled was not allowed to last more than a blink. Flavius had hold of her shoulders and was soon ripping at what garments were left, before he pushed her so the knees hit the edge of the bed, knocking her back. Then he was on top of her, scrabbling at his own clothing before roughly entering her.

If the coarse act of lovemaking that followed – could it be called that being so fuelled by fury – was some satisfaction to him, the gurgling laugh from beneath him was a clear indication of the pleasure his wife was taking in this unusual behaviour. Sated he rolled away, only to hear her whisper.

'My Flavius, I enjoyed that.'

The fine cloth screen that covered the open embrasures might keep out flying insects but it did let in a bit of breeze and a modicum of light, enough to show the outline of Antonina's face. It was so easy to allow sadness to overwhelm him at such a time and in such a place, where the only distractions to disturb his thinking seemed to be the distant sounds of guards being changed.

No matter how much he thought on the problem, no matter how many conversations he imagined having with Antonina, no solution presented itself to what was an intractable problem. Accuse her and she would deny it, he was sure. Present her with evidence and that might turn a person meeting the demands of a friend – he had to believe Theodora had applied pressure – into an antagonist and he had enough enemies right now to think it unwise to add another.

He would take refuge in silence, though Flavius was not fool enough to think that would be easy. From this moment on, and for how long he did not know, his personal life would be an act and that was a skill at which he was not adept. He would have to learn to smile when he was unhappy, agree when he wanted to dispute, slither round subjects rather than deal with them and act as lustily as a husband should in the bedchamber.

Would Antonina perceive the change? He had to believe so. If she challenged him, that might mean his previous excuse of naïvety for her actions might be true, but if she accepted the way he had changed did that mean guilt? Sick of his endless and formless rambling peregrinations he left the bed, threw on a loose gown and went to his place of work, to find on his desk and at the top of the pile a series of letters.

The hand was that of Procopius, the words only too recognisably those of Antonina; gossipy, sentences badly formed in a way that his secretary must have winced at, misspellings abounding. Observing those was mere distraction and he had to concentrate on the contents which were damning. Flavius said this, my husband thinks that, none of it flattering to Justinian but even more critical of Theodora's influence on imperial policy. Nowhere did it mention he thought her braver than her spouse!

Had Theodora passed these on to Justinian? Why ask for reports if they were not to be used to bolster her own position? Flavius doubted if the Emperor would be much thrown by the description of him as an untrustworthy schemer; if anything that would bring a smile to his lips. What about his sexual preferences, openly discussed with a woman who had, Flavius had always suspected, shared in some of them.

Bed-delivered sallies meant for laughter looked very different on the page. They were not jokes but words that diminished the person referred to. He and Antonina had related to each other anecdotes about Theodora as well. In these copies only his comments appeared, underscored as if to convey shock.

Flavius Belisarius pressed his fingers to the corners of his eyes. The despair he was assailed by seemed to match that he had experienced when he had seen his family mutilated and dead, their open eyes staring to an unresponsive heaven as if they had been asking how this fate could have been visited upon them by a deity they worshipped.

'General.'

Looking up, Flavius saw Procopius standing in the doorway and he looked abashed, as if he was trying to share in his employer's misery. The hand that waved across the now scattered letters said it all, there was no need to comment but Procopius did so anyway.

'I regret that I did not bring this to your attention earlier, General.'

'I don't.'

'I feared to hurt you.'

'Hurt is not a word of enough force to describe it. What plagues me now is how I deal with it.'

'I cannot stop you confronting your wife with what you have read, but I can say it means that I could no longer serve you.'

'I have to admit that did not occur to me.'

'Untenable, I think.' That got a weary nod. 'What do you wish me to do?'

The reply was some time in coming, but when it did it was firm. 'Put these away somewhere safe. I may need them in the future, though it pains me to think like that.'

'And me?'

'I have forfeited any trust I have in my wife, Procopius. To lose you as well would not help me bear that cross.'

'Then I have another painful duty to perform.'

'Spare me, man,' Flavius pleaded.

'General, I dare not and please do not think I derive either pleasure or comfort for things that I am required to reveal that distress you. You are aware that the Lady Belisarius often entertains the officers of your *comitatus*?'

Sure he knew what was coming Flavius threw his face into his hands and groaned. 'Who?'

'Theodosius visits her when you are fully occupied. Only her maid knows of it.'

His own godson, the offspring of one of his *bucellarii* officers and a person he and Antonina had adopted, his frequent presence in their personal apartments was not something to remark upon; he was family.

'And I do not, do I,' Flavius moaned, 'the fool that I am.'

It hurt to admit to himself that such a statement was not strictly true; if he had never seen evidence of adultery Flavius had often wondered if it might be happening. Had he not thought on Antonina's past on more than one occasion, would he have seen the facts if he had looked closely enough?

As a man who felt that he had suffered many setbacks in his life – though he admitted to good fortune too – Flavius knew he could not give way to despair. If what he had been told was a weight on his mind it was one he would have to carry. Life might get very difficult from now on, but it would persist and all he could do was to silently pray to God to provide him with the strength to bear it and the Christian will to forgive.

'I must go back and talk with my wife.' Seeing alarm on

the face of Procopius he took a bit of delight in delaying the need to allay his fears; why should he not suffer some discomfort too? 'Do not worry, what you have told me remains a secret, though I will ensure that Theodosius is moved to where he can cause me no more grief.'

The question was not posed by Procopius; there might be others to take his place. 'And I will need to be more attentive, will I not?'

'I will happily aid you in that.'

Flavius produced a dry laugh. 'You should get to know Justinian better, Procopius, you and he would be firm friends. And before you take that amiss I mean it as a compliment.'

The first thing Flavius did was to apologise to a freshly wakened Antonina for his behaviour the previous night, which got him licked lips and a wet smile.

'The last part was wonderful, though I have never seen you so sullen over the meal and you have yet to tell me why.'

'I had just come from questioning two tribunes who had been apprehended on their way to Constantinople to tell Justinian that I was about to rebel, claim the province as my own and crown myself king.'

'Is that true?'

What a revealing response that was. Antonina did not decry it as nonsense, nor did she seem overly upset at the prospect that such a claim might have some validity. It took some effort to contain himself, to sit on the bed and stroke her hair.

'Would you like it to be true?

She pondered for a bit, as if thinking through the pros and cons, perhaps imagining herself a queen, before concluding it was impossible to give an honest answer.

'I doubt your good friend Theodora would approve of your hesitation.'

'What makes you think her view counts?'

'Nothing. And just so you can cease to wonder, I have no intention of betraying the faith Justinian placed in me.'

A most unladylike snort was the response to that. 'It is to be hoped he would keep faith likewise with you, but I would not wish to wager my head on it.'

The guts were churning, the desire to yell at her near to overwhelming. How could she question Justinian after what she had done? The control he fought to impose on himself was necessary but it took several seconds to achieve.

'As I said, two tribunes were stopped in the docks before they could sail, for which I have to thank Procopius.' That name made her frown and aged her in an instant, the fact that he noticed being upsetting. 'It was he who brought the conspiracy to light.'

'He is snake enough for that.' Seeing Flavius bridle she was quick to add, 'Which is as well if it is in your service.'

'There is, however, a difficulty.' The place where her eyebrows existed during the day – they were well plucked – shot up. 'These two were not the only ones. I suspect more have been despatched by whoever it is who wants to do me harm, to carry that same message to Constantinople.'

'And if that is the case?'

She had controlled her voice when asking that, but not

enough to fool a man who knew her so intimately. He had, of course, to let his observation pass.

'I should not be concerned, Antonina. After all, what possible grounds could Justinian have for believing it?'

His wife was not looking at him when she whispered, 'None.'

CHAPTER TWENTY-SIX

The best way for Flavius to ignore his problems was activity and that involved movement. He made a point of travelling the region, talking to the leading citizens of the towns and to any leaders of tribes that still held themselves aloof. That he did do in an elaborate almost regal caravan was so that Antonina could accompany him, and of course along came Procopius; watching them spar now caused less discomfort and more amusement, for it was to Flavius a game, one of the few things in which he could take pleasure.

Theodosius had been sent to the one-time Vandal fortress of Septem, right by the Pillars of Hercules, with instructions to keep an eye on the towering rock and the safe harbour it protected; if the Visigoths had any notion to take advantage of turmoil in North Africa while the Romans sought to pacify the province, that was where it would come from.

If Antonina was in any way affected by this posting it did not show; indeed she seemed to relish the travel even if it was the cause of some discomfort. Perhaps it was the treatment she received as the consort of the Roman-proconsul. Those who wished a good opinion from Flavius saw flattering her as a good avenue and Antonina lapped at it like a cat in a creamery.

The wait for word of a response from Constantinople was never mentioned between them; it was as if Antonina had forgotten. That was only ever referred to between Flavius and Procopius and the longer it was delayed the more troubling it seemed, yet the time taken to sail to there and back, notwithstanding the discussion and decisions such a message might entail, were subject to many variables.

There was the wind, which had Flavius making a rare joke that as much would be expended in talking about what to do as was needed to fill the sails of the ship carrying the imperial response. He could have no idea how that quip cheered his secretary, who saw it as a sign that the despair of what had been revealed, if not easing, was morphing into acceptance, albeit that must cause disquiet.

Thoughts on who had despatched the message did not mellow either, for Flavius knew he would have to be very much on his guard. Whoever was the traitor might move at any time and not wait to hear how their communication had been received, though Procopius thought that unlikely.

'The way I see it, General, is this.'

You have become more confident of late, fellow, Flavius thought, but nothing on his face betrayed that, leading him to wonder if he had become more subtle in his dealings. Certainly he had been that with his wife, whom he now watched as a hawk observes its prey, seeking to read her mind even if he had concluded long ago that it was somewhat shallow.

'The man who intends to rebel has a plan at the centre of which lies you.' Procopius had his nose in the air now, and his eyes were following it upwards, as if he was cogitating the meaning of the universe. 'He expects from Constantinople some kind of message either chastising you or ordering your recall. At that point he will move to kill you, then claim he has prevented your coup and he will pledge his loyalty to Justinian.'

'A smokescreen?'

'Precisely.'

Perfectly capable of working these things out for himself it pleased Flavius to indulge his secretary. The man had always been a touch self-satisfied; now he felt he had his employer's absolute confidence that had swelled. Flavius was pleased to let it be; it would be Procopius who would see the dangers that threatened, perhaps before he did, no matter how guarded he had become.

It was hard to face his inferior generals and not speculate, but even travelling he was obliged to return to Carthage to call a conference and ensure his policies were being implemented. There were stirrings everywhere, how could there not be, yet nothing so serious as to trouble the public weal. Odd that the place where he should feel most secure was the one at which he felt most at risk. Did they notice the increase in his guard detail? Would they spot that only those *bucellarii* he had raised before the Battle of Dara, men who were loyal and part of his original recruitment to the corps, made up his escort?

It was unfortunate that real trouble began to brew just as the emissaries from Justinian arrived, two high-ranking bureaucrats tasked with the job of assessing the new province for taxation with his own emissary Solomon a welcome returnee. They would carry out a new census, make certain titles to land were valid – much had been appropriated from the Vandals including the royal estate – and set the rate at which North Africa would pay into the imperial treasury after funds were extracted for local expenses.

'Justinian has sent a right pair of villains,' Flavius remarked when he saw their names. 'I know them to be adept at fleecing.'

'I doubt it matters who he sent, General. There is too much temptation here even for an honest man.'

'I hope my coffers only hold that which is my due.'

'Which is my point,' Procopius replied. 'You are honest and those coffers are overflowing.'

'With you being straightforward on my behalf, I know.'

That made Procopius preen and again that was let pass. The time had come to meet the representatives from Constantinople, for as well as their imperial edicts they carried those detailing how the province should be run and garrisoned, orders he would have to begin to implement. They also carried a sealed communication from the Emperor to him, which he opened in their presence, though much to their obvious frustration he did not divulge the contents.

'You will wish to read it, Procopius?' Flavius said, when they were alone.

'If I am permitted.'

The held-out hand gave the lie to that faux reluctance and his secretary took and read the letter, skipping over the niceties of greeting and praise for the achievements of Flavius to the nub.

'A trap?'

'Partly,' Flavius replied. 'It all depends on what I choose to do.'

'Am I allowed to suggest that the matter resting with you is a snare?' Procopius studied the writing before reading it out. 'After such an achievement, how can I not leave you to make up your own mind as to how to proceed? You are in Carthage, I am not. If you feel that you need to remain there to oversee those edicts I have promulgated then do so. If you think your work complete and it would be best to return, then your well-beloved friend is eager to welcome you home.'

'If I choose to stay he will think I mean to rebel.'

'And in order to guard against that his envoys will carry messages to more than yourself.'

'I can see Theodora's hand in this. Justinian knows me well enough to demand a straight answer.'

The doubt that such was true travelled across the face of Procopius. 'You must go home.'

'God above, do I not long to!'

'This undermines those who wished to depose you, and anyway, I fear they have waited too long to act. They must see you are on your guard.'

'Which means we may never know who are the miscreants, which I must say troubles me greatly. What will happen once I am gone?'

'Put it behind you, for it will not serve to brood on it.'

Preparations were put in hand to travel. A ship had to be equipped with a comfortable place of confinement for Gelimer, another less altered to carry his leading adherents and the remainder of his family. The treasure of the Vandals would travel with Flavius and Antonina and it required a deep-hulled transport to carry it, so great was the weight. There was a small fleet of vessels to accommodate his *comitatus* for they were his personal troops and went with their general.

A final tour of his units had to be hurriedly arranged so he could say farewell to those who had aided him to conquer, so obviously the news of his impending departure spread through the whole of the North African littoral, and if it stirred some emotion in his pardoned Vandals it was the Moors who saw opportunity, Flavius being sure they were egged on by the Visigoths making mischief. They might fear Hispania as a new objective of Roman reconquest.

It could not be classed as rebellion, the Moors were not under imperial tutelage, but it infuriated Flavius Belisarius for he could do nothing about their invasion of the western border. Stay and fight them and he could be seen as a traitor. He had to leave the need to chastise them in the hands of others and the one he trusted most, Solomon, was given the task and he was also given the *bucellarii* of Flavius's personal troops in order to accomplish it, but it was only a loan. As soon as the Moors were subdued they were to be sent back to serve under him, for he had no illusion that he would not be occupied elsewhere and he wanted his best soldiers with him when that came about.

There were, of course, ceremonies; the handing over of command to Valerianus, the regretful farewell to Pharas, which was tearful for both. But the time came to board ship, unmoor and sail out of the harbour, with the man who had conquered thinking, as he looked back at the fortifications of Carthage, if he had that to his credit, there was just as much debit in his personal life.

The route taken home was nearly the same as coming, the first stop being Sicily where they heard of the death of the Goth heir Athalaric, no more than sixteen summers old, his demise reputedly brought on by a bloody flux after an epic drinking bout. That must impact on his mother and her tenuous grip on power but if Flavius was curious as to what such an event would entail, he had his course to resume, once more crossing the Adriatic and hugging the coast of Greece.

The sea did not suit Antonina, who seemed to suffer from sickness on a daily basis and her affliction became so regular that doctors were consulted, only to tell Flavius Belisarius that he was about to become a father; Antonina was pregnant and since she had a child from her previous marriage she must have known what the symptoms portended. Why had she not told him herself?

'These things are a mystery even to the women who bear the consequences,' was her answer when he enquired gently as to her seeming ignorance. 'You can only be certain when you feel the first kick.'

If she claimed ignorance of what constituted a pregnancy that was more than Flavius knew and further probing suggested that the conception may have occurred on the very night he had been told by Procopius of her possible infidelity, which Antonina recalled fondly, but also with a wistful aside that there had been no reoccurrence of the passion he had then shown.

'Perhaps you require the threat of being killed to rouse you, Flavius.'

'I live with that, Antonina, every time I go out to fight.'

Even with the torture of uncertainty Flavius had to assume the child was his own and he wavered between joy and, in his darker moments, the contrary thought. But it was impossible not to become solicitous, to seek to ensure that his wife was comfortable, even if he was aware that his secretary saw him as perhaps being taken for a fool.

The first sight of Constantinople was the number of high domes of the many churches that dotted the seven hills of the city, looking vague in the smoke from the many fires that had been lit to ward off what the inhabitants saw as cold, this added to all-year-round fug from cooking charcoal. The wind being in the east there was the smell of the city too, highly unpleasant after time spent at sea, then the crowded approach to the main channel before their vessels peeled off to moor at the pier of the imperial palace.

The court had been forewarned and there was a signal mark of honour in the sheer number of high functionaries lined up to greet the returning hero. Gelimer was on the deck, in chains he had been free of throughout the voyage, this for show, likewise the other Vandal captives. It took longer to berth than was actually required, this to allow the imperial couple to be there on the landing stage – not for them a long wait even for an imperial hero.

The whole quay was lined with Excubitors in their finest regalia and if the trumpets were used to greet the presence of Justinian and Theodora they were blown again when the gangplank was lowered and Flavius Belisarius, his wife on his arm, came on to dry land.

'Is there a finer sight in all Christendom to compare with you, Flavius?'

'I can think of many, Highness.'

'How can you be modest at a time like this, a year away and you return a conqueror?'

Flavius turned and bowed to Theodora, a deep obeisance that disguised his thoughts that this woman might be his enemy.

'We welcome you,' was her regal response. 'And you, Antonina, whom I have much missed.'

His wife being led slightly away to converse with Theodora had Flavius guessing at what they might discuss amid the realisation that from now on he would be in ignorance. There would be no letters to read between two women who could now talk to each other. There was in any case another matter to attend to.

Procopius was behind Flavius again, he knew that

without looking, just as he was aware his secretary would be dying for another chance of an introduction that might gain him such recognition; attached as he was to Flavius Belisarius, Procopius was in the presence of the fount of all patronage, a rare event for a man of his standing and one not to be lightly thrown away, as he had hinted on more than one occasion since leaving Carthage.

'If I may be allowed to insist, Highness,' Flavius began, only to be interrupted.

'What could I possibly refuse you?'

Trust was on the Belisarius lips, but could not be uttered here, so he turned and brought forward his secretary, fulfilling what was to him an obligation. 'I ask you to acknowledge Procopius, who aided me much in my campaign.'

'A soldier?' Justinian asked, the air of confusion obvious; anyone senior he would have known of, anyone junior was another matter.

'My secretary.'

The Emperor looked confused for a moment but it was just a flash across his features. He obviously concluded this fellow was important to Flavius so he proffered a hand to be kissed, which was duly done by a bowing Procopius. The point at which he followed that up by trying to speak was embarrassing and not only to him. Justinian's hand was so abruptly withdrawn and so swiftly hooked into the arm of Flavius that the pair were moving past him before Procopius was once more fully upright.

'I am agog to meet this Gelimer and I am eager to hear what you think we should do with him.'

'I wondered if the treasure we brought home might be of more interest, Highness.'

'I am never able to fox you, Flavius, you know me too well.'

How often does he say that? How often do I doubt it to be true?

Antonina, less occupied than her husband, had seen the flash of anger on the face of Procopius at being so condescended to and she burst out laughing, which had Theodora curious as to the cause. Her newly returned friend leant to whisper in the imperial ear, words which Procopius could not overhear, but then he hardly needed to for the Empress laughed as well, this after throwing him a quick and sneering glance. Then they followed their respective spouses, leaving him isolated and unsure what to do.

'You have fought a free campaign, Highness.'

'So it would seem.'

Justinian had been much impressed by what he had seen aboard the ship carrying the Vandal treasure and that had only been a partial glance at the top layer of deep coffers. Gelimer he had chastised for the murder of Hilderic, asking how he could give orders to kill a man so committed to peace, a king who had opened the Catholic cathedral and appointed a bishop of that faith.

'A Germanic king is elected to fight, not to make peace or bishops. My brother could not lead our armies, therefore he forfeited the right to his liberty.'

'And his death?'

'Falls to you and your army. If you had not invaded he would still be alive. I had no desire to kill him but my brother carried out the deed because you might have reinstated him in my place. Then Hilderic would have killed me. Do not think him a saint.'

'I have read the terms of your surrender at Medeus and I wonder if Flavius Belisarius here was a mite too generous. Perhaps I should visit upon you that which you had visited upon your elder brother.'

'Kill me if you wish. I will not plead.'

'Flavius?'

'I gave my word, Highness, I would be unhappy to see it breeched.'

The silence was long-lasting enough to induce concern, for Flavius was prepared to argue if the surrender terms he had agreed with Gelimer were not met, given it impinged on his honour.

'We will decide after the triumph, in which you will be the most puissant prisoner. Then perhaps we will evoke those old Roman habits that my good friend here is so wedded to and invite him to strangle you. Come, Flavius, it is time to take you to my private rooms where we can lay out our plans for that event.'

'A triumph?'

'You deserve no less.'

That did surprise Flavius: no one but a reigning emperor had been granted a triumph for decades and no general leading the armies of the Eastern Empire had ever been gifted one. It seemed politic to claim he was hardly worthy.

'I will decide who is worthy, my friend. Now we must go, for we have little time before the banquet I have arranged to allow those rogues that surround me to welcome you back.'

They were walking now, back onto the quay, leaving Theodora and Antonina gazing lovingly at the Vandal treasure, with Justinian talking in his usual rapid fashion.

'Does that Gelimer think I will break your word? Does he really think we went to all that trouble to put his brother back on the throne?'

They passed Procopius who bowed once more only to be ignored for a second time in the sand of one glass. All he got was a sympathetic look from his employer and a quick aside.

'Stay aboard, Procopius, and I will send for you.'

It was a still-smarting secretary, sorting his scrolls before unloading, who got the message sent to him by Flavius, to say that he had secured for him a place at the imperial banquet and enclosing a pass that would get him past the Excubitors and into the palace. He was advised to wear his best clothing and to understand that if he would be very far from the imperial presence it was the best his grateful general could do.

The clothing in which Procopius presented himself to at the Watergate was splendid garb indeed. Honest he might be but the wardrobe of the Vandal royals had fallen to the Romans when Carthage was occupied and he saw no difficulty in borrowing their finery. It was pleasing so attired to be treated with deep respect, not only by the imperial guards but those he was sat next to, who took him for someone much more important than he really was.

When they found he had been with and close to Flavius

Belisarius his stock with those same people rose even more, he being a fount of information about the campaign which occasioned many a smile from a man in his element. There was only one person subjected to an infrequent glare and that was Justinian, though care had to be taken not to be too obvious in his loathing.

CHAPTER TWENTY-SEVEN

In all his previous sojourns in the imperial palace, even as an acknowledged confidant of Justinian, even as the Victor of Dara, Flavius Belisarius had not been seen as someone with whom it was vital to be on good terms but now that was utterly reversed. It seemed no courtier or official felt comfortable without some insight into his thinking on matters of policy and those included areas where he had no interest: taxation and the new code of laws being drawn up at the Emperor's behest.

Strangest of all the questions posed to him was his view on the rebuilding of the massive Church of St Sophia, set alight during the Nika riots and burnt to the ground. The new building was now well on its way to completion, when it would be seen by the citizens as a basilica that would proclaim the glory of God as well as the empire and dwarf anything that had gone before. It would certainly meet the aim of Justinian, to render insignificant the Church of St Peter in Rome, built by Constantine the Great.

'I am happy for it to be built, Highness, and I am sure it will be a thing of great beauty shorn of its scaffolding, but my opinion on its merits, what is that worth?'

'Do not think they really care about St Sophia, Flavius, it is merely a ploy to get you to converse with them. In time, the topic of conversation will not be my new church but me and the way I govern the empire, which they will suspect you and I discuss.'

'Then it will be wasted breath,' was his reply.

'But any act of a military nature I undertake will be led by you and everyone knows that. They also know that early knowledge provides a chance to profit from it.'

Flavius suspected that would be Italy; since the death of Athalaric there had to be turmoil and Justinian would be determined to exploit that, indeed it had been loosely alluded to. During this conversation the question Flavius wanted to ask died on his lips as he contemplated, and not for the first time since landing, asking Justinian if he had believed the tale of his plan to rebel, something that had not been mentioned and was clearly being treated as if it had never happened.

Flavius was not beyond a touch of reserve on the matter; he made no mention of having interrogated those tribunes in Carthage or what he had deduced, which had him wonder if he was absorbing the mores of the place where he now spent most of his time, the palace and the Senate House, and his being a full member of Justinian's council exposed Flavius to a community he would rather not have been part of.

He needed no telling that the palace was a fount of secret manoeuvres, of officials jockeying for a sliver of advantage, usually by damning their rivals. It was made worse because he had come from a task in which he was clearly the sole fount of authority and if he had been intrigued, against that was better than being a part of the morass he was now embroiled in.

Only in one area was he studiously alert; the relationship with Antonina he kept on an even keel and her being with child was an aid to that, allowing him to be solicitous without too much intimacy. Despite what he knew, the only thing that could flow from any accusations of bad faith would be yet further misery with a woman to whom he was bound by the most holy of sacraments.

Then there was the rapport his wife enjoyed with Theodora who might take any slight against Antonina as one against herself. They had resumed their previous intimacy and joy in each other's company as if there had been no gap in time, the only difference now being that he seemed to be excluded from a fellowship of which he had previously been a part. Whatever set the pair giggling no longer included him and the message he took from that was that his wife had a greater lever on imperial favour than he did.

Justinian was prone to waver even when he was dealing

with someone he insisted was a trusted friend, while Theodora had a constancy of purpose the Emperor lacked, which was made obvious by the way his promised triumph was whittled down from grandeur to an event that would not diminish the imperial standing. It had all started so well as Justinian enthused about what was to come, exposing a desire for pomp and ceremony that Flavius had never perceived before.

'We shall have a proper Roman triumph,' had been the Justinian declaration. 'You in a chariot painted blue, crowned with laurels, your prisoners dragged along in chains and your soldiers parading at their rear.'

Normally quite physically constrained, in discussing the plans he became quite animated so it was doubly noticeable when that stopped and he began to slice away at things, the first part of the ceremony to go being the chariot.

'It is perhaps not fitting for even a general as successful as you to take upon yourself that which is reserved for monarchy.' Justinian looked somewhat sheepish as he continued, 'You will, of course, be splendidly garbed.'

'On my horse?'

'Perhaps on foot.'

The prisoners he kept, and the chains, which were symbolic in any case. The notion of his whole *comitatus* marching in his wake was shortened by the *bucellarii* he had left with Solomon and was now further cut by Justinian to a mere *numerus* of his best troops. The embarrassment with which these economies were spoken of led Flavius to believe that Theodora was at the back of them and that was borne out by her continued behaviour.

She did not trust him. Not only was he too close to her husband, he was now too successful. Flavius guessed in her view that if there was any opposition to Justinian, and by extension herself, he would be the focus around which it would coalesce. To deny it would achieve nothing and he was aware that the way he was cornered by other senators, even if the talk was innocent, only fuelled her suspicions, given she had no idea what was being discussed. His own mistrust of his wife barred him seeking to use her as a conduit.

It is not pleasant to feel there is nothing you can do about a misperception. The idea Theodora obviously entertained, that he hankered after the diadem, was firmly rooted in her own fear of being torn apart by the mob. Emperors were rarely popular; they taxed, they punished and they built up over time a rising tide of grievances, but within that Justinian was not doing as badly as some of his predecessors. He had peace on the eastern border, albeit a bought one, and his favourite general had brought not only North Africa back into the imperial fold but a treasure so great it had been fought at a profit.

'Added to that, the mob have forgiven me for my part in the Nika riots and I am hailed wherever I go.'

'How she must hate that.'

Procopius being right did not make matters any easier, for there was always the fear that Theodora would allow her imaginings to get out of control and seek to dispose of him.

'I cannot see how you will be safe if you do not speak with Justinian.'

'And say what?'

'You are at risk,' his secretary insisted, before adding, 'Not that I would believe any assurances he gave me.'

'Then, what is the point?'

'It tells him you're aware of the dangers, and who knows, he may stay her vitriol because he needs you. He is the only one who can stop Theodora, and from what you say that might be necessary.'

It had to be done, Flavius knew it as well as Procopius, but there was the timing to add to the reluctance. The suggestion that Justinian might, as had his uncle of old, take a walk on the greensward with Flavius in company was not met with instant approval; the nephew was neither a lover of the outdoors or much in the way of physical exercise, which in truth he scarcely needed, given his frantic way of pacing the palace corridors. As usual, they walked past men exercising with weapons, but whereas Justin had shown interest his nephew eschewed none and nor was he fooled into thinking that this was just a friendly stroll.

'So, Flavius, now that you have me where no one can overhear what we say . . . ?'

'I need the answer to certain questions and only you possess them.'

'Need? I have ceased to be accustomed to that.'

There was a degree of annoyance in the imperial tone. Justinian had grown into his role; any nerves he had displayed, albeit in private, after his elevation or during the Nika riots had evaporated now. He was not open to his subjects demanding anything, never mind his inner thoughts.

'Then I am going to encroach on our past association to seek answers.'

'And I will use that past association to warn you to show some care.'

He would know what was coming: Justinian was not a fool, but it was clear the first query threw him. 'My triumph, which is rapidly becoming a sham.'

'Imperial dignity,' was the reply, a slow response and one that was as evasive as it was unsatisfactory.

'Yours, Highness, or that of your wife?' Getting no immediate reply Flavius continued. 'What was her reaction when those messengers came from Carthage to tell you I was preparing to rebel?'

Looking at him Flavius was sure he was going to deny that any such message had come to him, but it was an exchanged look and a flinty-eyed one from Flavius that told His Imperial Highness that would not wash.

'It troubled me, it was bound to.'

'Me?'

'I spend my whole life now having people declare to me how virtuous they are and not one of them is telling the truth.'

'And I do not count as an exception?'

'Yes, Flavius, you do.'

'Then why—'

Justinian cut across him. 'If I am counselled to show caution I would be a fool to refuse to take heed. When someone reminds you that it was Brutus who helped murder Julius Caesar then you will know that no ruler can ever think himself secure.'

'Theodora thinks I mean to topple you?'

'She will not cease to fear that the possibility exists and the oddity is, Flavius, that it is your upright nature that she fears most.'

'That makes little sense.'

'It does to her. You cannot rule without making enemies and we have made many and that does not begin to count the greedy. In addition to that we both have a bloodline despised by most of these with whom you share the Senate, Theodora especially.'

'Mine is not much better.'

That point was ignored. 'Who would those people turn to when they seek to overthrow the person they conveniently call a tyrant other than the man of shining virtue? Who would the mob proclaim in the Hippodrome if not the most successful general this empire has produced in decades, the paragon who is draped in glory?'

'I cannot help what people think.'

'Then apply that to my wife and take comfort from this. If she fears you, then you are far from alone.'

'Fears me enough to ensure I can be no threat?'

'I will protect you, Flavius, but there are occasions where I must bend with the wind she creates. I rule but she does so as my consort and we are, in all respects, partners.'

There was a terrible temptation to ask Justinian if he too felt threatened by Theodora – homicidal female companions were not unknown – but that would be a step too far, indeed it was next made plain to him that he had already overstepped the bounds of whatever friendship existed between them, an admonition delivered in a tone that left Flavius in no doubt Justinian meant the words he employed.

'This subject will never be raised again, for if it is, what you rely on for your freedom to speak will be forfeit. Do not ever seek to have me choose between a subject, which is what you are, and my wife, who is Empress and not just in name.'

'Would it help if I said I have faith you will keep your word?'

'Given it is all you have it better be so.'

Justinian spun away to walk back to the palace. Flavius could not help but notice how canted was that head of his, exaggerated by the gold circlet that was his everyday crown. Clearly he was deep in thought and it was far from idle to speculate what they might be.

If the triumph was bogus to the man celebrating it, the crowds that lined the Triumphal Way took it seriously. Even before that there was a surge of well-wishers by the Golden Gate, those who lived outside the city walls, in the farms and villages that supplied much of the capital's food, who had come to partake in the celebrations. Naturally there were the usual opportunistic vendors selling everything from false Vandal trinkets to Belisarius dolls.

Flavius had been allowed at least to partly dress in proper old Roman armour, a gleaming leather breastplate decorated with gold symbols, the white cloak that denoted his rank, and in his hand the fasces enclosing an axe that had once been the symbol of proconsular praetorian power since the Republic. The huge gates, hitherto closed, were opened to the sound of the imperial trumpets and the roar of approbation came bursting out from several thousand throats.

'Every shout a dagger in Theodora's vitals,' he murmured to himself before he crossed himself and stepped out. 'Cheer yourself with that, Flavius.'

To walk through these gates on such an occasion was a pinnacle dreamt of by his father, and not just him. Even if triumphs had long been appropriated by pagan god-emperors for their own aggrandisement – no mere mortal would be allowed to share their glory – it had stayed the dream of military men down the centuries and now, even if it was in a diminished form, he was taking what was his due.

Flavius had no illusions; this was as much a show for Justinian as it was for him. The crowd would applaud General Belisarius and shout acclaim, throwing flowers in his path so deep they would carpet the cobblestones. They would jeer and spit at the chained and shuffling Vandals, including Gelimer who came behind. The soldiers, even in such a small number, would bring back the noise of approbation, but it was the treasure the crowd really wanted to see and what they would talk about when the ceremonies were complete.

The carts, escorted by Excubitors, had been piled in such a way that every object of value was visible; the jewelled crucifixes of gold and silver so large half a dozen men would struggle to carry them, open chests of coins, with a fellow by them to dip in a hand and let the glistening objects fall back to rest on the heaped-up pile with that dull clunk only precious metal makes.

Every artefact of value, all the Vandal loot was on display, but last would come the relics, held out by black-clad monks and named as they walked, which would bring genuflection and much pious crossing as those observing thought of their sins and looked to the bones of saints and martyrs to absolve them.

The Triumphal Way ran for a full league and to traverse such a distance on foot and slowly, while acknowledging the cheers, took time. The *milion* monument came in to view, the obelisk from which all imperial distances were measured, as well as the high wall of the Hippodrome, and behind the edge of the Senate House there rose up the beautiful dome of the still scaffolding-enclosed St Sophia.

Behind the *milion* the imperial party awaited him and Flavius could not but wonder at the first time he had seen this view and the trickery he had used to get an audience with the man who had become his mentor: Justinus, the then *comes Excubitorum*, a high official who had no idea he wished to see him or even that he existed.

Now he was coming to face his emperor and to be acclaimed as consul for the year of Our Lord 535, a pinnacle of achievement he could never have dreamt of. There was no other image to fill his mind than that of his father, and he hoped that from the celestial paradise in which his soul must now reside he was looking down with pride on his youngest son.

It was the duty of Flavius to make his way up the steps to kneel before Justinian and there to offer to him the treasure he had brought and the captives he had taken.

It was a mark of tremendous respect that the Emperor left his throne and came halfway to meet him and to embrace his general, this to a roar from the crowd that had followed to fill the space before the palace, greater than any so far raised. The crowd did not hear, Theodora who had not moved did not hear and nor did Antonina beside her, the whisper from Justinian as he put his lips to the Belisarius ear.

'You have no need to bend the knee to me, Flavius, and if I spoke harshly to you previously, never forget that I do hold you as a friend whom I sometimes cannot put before my duty.'

'Highness,' was all Flavius could say, given, assailed as he was by memories, he was choking back tears.

'If my uncle could have been here to see this, his pride would be as great as is mine.'

Pushing Flavius to one side Justinian publicly hailed him and pronounced him Consul, the highest office in the land after the imperial titles, albeit more of a fiction of power than the real article. Then he listed the crimes of Gelimer – the defiance of his imperial will, the murder of his own brother, even if he was absent. The Vandal usurper had the wisdom to take these accusations and the haranguing from the crowd head bowed: he was, after all, not going to be ritually strangled, but was, as promised by Flavius, to depart for a life of comfort in a spacious villa in Galatea.

A monk already primed brought to Justinian the casket containing the bones of St Sebastian, to be held up for veneration before the Emperor announced that in the spirit which these relics were held, they would be returned to Rome, the place from where they had been stolen. That did depress Gelimer.

Finally, linking arms, he led Flavius up the remaining steps and through the portal of the imperial palace, passing Theodora who gave the hero of the moment a look from her black and steady eyes that would have frozen Lucifer.

CHAPTER TWENTY-EIGHT

The maps of Italy and Sicily were laid out on the great table round which Justinian, Flavius and a whole clutch of senior officers were gathered, while the Emperor explained to them what had been happening in that huge peninsula and how he intended that it should be brought back to be once more part of his empire. If the rest did not know it, Flavius did; this was a long-held dream and a personal quest.

'The death of Athalaric merely brings forward a plan long in my mind. He would have never made a king, anyway.'

His mother had tried to keep him out of the clutches of her nobles. She had wanted a Roman education for Athalaric and would have sent him to Constantinople if she had been allowed, but those around her were too powerful to ignore and they wanted the eight-year-old boy to have an education and upbringing fit for an Ostrogoth king.

Forced to surrender him into their clutches, Amalasuintha could only watch as, over the next eight years, he was debauched by men who hoped, when he reached his majority and took his rightful place, to control him. Introduced early to wine he became addicted and his death had occurred after what had been described to Justinian as an epic drinking bout.

'Probably choked on his own vomit. It matters not, Amalasuintha is utterly weakened by it and there is a fight going on amongst the powerful to seize the vacant throne.'

'She will have appealed to you for aid, Highness?'

'She has, Narses,' Justinian replied, his grin wolfish, 'which demonstrates how weak she is, given my demand that she cede Lilybaeum was refused. Anyway I have had reports of the Goths taking Roman property by force which they would never have dared to do under Theodoric so that indicates a breakdown in order, with nobles acting to suit their own needs.'

It was common knowledge that one of the thieving culprits was an unsavoury character called Theodahad, who was a cousin to Athalaric and had a strong claim to the throne, which he might have taken if he had not been so unpopular. Utterly unscrupulous he had offered Justinian all his Italian lands for a sum in gold as well as residence in Constantinople. This was a bargain the Emperor would have accepted if his machinations had not been uncovered and Theodahad forced by Amalasuintha to confess and make restitution of his stolen property. He was now telling

Justinian that he was no longer bound to his aunt in any way and was at his service.

'Remarkable woman, Amalasuintha,' Flavius opined. 'To lord it over the Ostrogoths.'

'Remarkable women are not as rare as you might think. Anyway there were three main rivals to take away her power—'

'Were, Highness?'

'She had them killed.'

'Risky.'

'I offered her a home here if she failed.'

Which was as good as saying she had not acted without Justinian knowing full well what was about to happen. But that was an aside as far as the Emperor was concerned. The woman had more problems than that, for she was plagued by aggressive neighbours to the north, the Franks and the Burgundians, who were encroaching on the Ostrogoth possessions and now she was in dispute with Constantinople over the old Vandal fief in Sicily. Justinian had demanded it, she had refused. At one time she might have had the Vandals as allies; that was now gone.

Only Flavius of the present generals knew the latest intelligence from Italy, imparted to him before this meeting. Amalasuintha was no more. She had tried to come to an arrangement with Theodahad by offering him the throne as long as she could continue to rule, the proposition being surrounded by oaths of a nature that would damn for eternity the man who broke them. At the same time Justinian was treating with her to come east and receive large estates in the hope that she would hand him Italy.

Caught between the two she had been taken by Theodahad and if it was others who did the foul deed, he did nothing to save her.

'They're an untrustworthy lot, Flavius,' had been the Justinian opinion. 'I was treating with Theodahad too for the same thing not long ago, and what does he do? Imprisons his aunt then stands by when she is murdered.'

'They could teach us a thing or two, certainly.'

The jest was taken well; Justinian reckoned he was being complimented on his own deviousness. He did not know that it was never meant as praise.

'My envoy declared war.'

'Does he have that right?'

'No, but he had only anticipated what I would have done. Italy is in turmoil and is as ripe as a ready-to-fall apple. What we need now, Flavius, is a plan to make that happen, and as luck would have it we are not threatened anywhere else and you are here after your success in North Africa. God, I would suggest, is with us.'

That was a point he made to all the commanders assembled, passing on the moves he had made to act in alliance with the Franks, who had claims on the north of Italy. If they acted, and he had sent them a fortune in gold as encouragement, it would split the Ostrogoth defence.

'Do they not compete with us?'

The question was posed by Peranias, another senior officer in the imperial army, but one without much in the way of active service to his name; Flavius suspected powerful relatives.

'In time they will, but I have laid claim only to what was

ours. Rome certainly, Ravenna given Theodoric made it his capital. Everything south of course.'

'Sicily will have to be secured first,' Flavius ventured. 'It would be madness to seek to take the mainland with that at our back, but I observed few Gothic troops on the island when we passed through it.'

Narses spoke after Flavius. 'And I would suggest a strong force on the Adriatic coast to keep them worried about a second invasion. That further splits their forces.'

That received general agreement; the first task was to get an army ashore and any diversions would aid that. The talk went on for an age, tactics were discussed as well as the overall strategy, obstacles identified mainly in fortified cities that would have to be subdued or bypassed. It ended on a note of high confidence, not least from the Emperor himself.

'There's a degree of hubris there, don't you think, Flavius Belisarius?'

Posed after Justinian had left, that got Peranias a bland look; no nod, no agreement or disagreement. That was the kind of remark which, from a placeman like this fellow, could be an opening gambit in what would become treachery. Flavius had decided the only way to deal with people like this fellow was not to respond, given he could not know to whom any reply would be repeated and there was at least one person who would, he was sure, set traps for him.

The idea of no other threats was illusory; an imperial messenger brought news that a Gothic army had landed on the Dalmatian coast and there defeated the forces under the son of Mundus and their young leader killed. By the time Flavius was making ready to depart for Sicily, news came that Mundus himself, a man so feared his name was enough to keep the province at peace, had also been slain in a second battle but that the Gothic army had been defeated. It did not bode well for future operations and changed the nature of the orders Flavius was given.

'Touch at Sicily and seek out how the population feels. If there seems to be resistance to us retaking the island you can sail on with no loss of face to Carthage, claiming that as your destination all along.'

And that he did, again securing sole command and leading his fleet to a landing near Catania on the east coast, his main worry the lack of force he had at his disposal, which was nothing like that with which he had beaten the Vandals. He had with him, too, Photius, his stepson, now that age at which he, Flavius, had first soldiered. A winning and willing aide it was a pleasure to have him along, especially as at the first sign of a threat the good folk of Catania promptly surrendered their city to him, which had Photius declaring that war was easy.

It seemed as if the youngster had the right of it: what followed was in effect akin to the falling of a set of gambling bones; every city on the island declared for Belisarius and Constantinople except one, Panormus, with a Gothic garrison and stout walls. The defenders were wagering the Romans lacked the force to overcome them and the truth was the man who led them agreed.

The problem he now had was altered: news had come of a mutiny in the provinces of North Africa and that, he suspected, would require his presence and that of a large part of his army. Subdue Panormus and he could claim Sicily conquered. Fail to attain that and he could not leave a force of Goths to reverse what he had just achieved; every city that had opened their gates to him would do the same to the armed garrison of Panormus.

'This, Photius, is where war becomes less simple.'

The pair were raiding round the extensive walls that went from the sea to the east then round the city to the other end of the deep bay and there were no gaps Flavius could see as well as much evidence of repair. Flavius was using the occasion to educate his young charge.

'If we attack we lack the strength to do so at enough points that we can hope to face an inferior defence by distraction elsewhere.' Flavius pointed out the towers that held up the curtain wall and helped Photius to understand that they were only a double-cast spear apart. 'So soldiers caught between them face annihilation if they use ladders, and boiling oil on their heads as they clamber. If they have archers it is suicide.'

'Do they have them, Father?'

Warmed by the respect but unable to answer Flavius spurred his horse straight for the walls and cried, 'Let's find out.'

Photius did not hesitate; he was right on the heels of the man he had for years thought of as his parent and he copied too Flavius's wild yell. The walls before them, hitherto empty, suddenly showed faces peering between the embrasures as the two came well within the range of archery. Flavius hauled hard to pull up his mount out of the range of a cast spear and sat there, the youngster at his side.

'Put your shield over your shoulders to cover your back. First sign of an arrow, pray to God and ride hard to safety.'

What they got were shouts of incomprehensible derision and even though they sat a while no one came to address or insult them in Latin, so eventually they trotted off to jeers, carrying on their inspection until the walls ended at the western shore, and there Flavius sat musing.

'It would be remiss not to examine the sea walls but I fear it will be to no purpose.'

Back at the point at which they had begun their inspection a fishing boat was commandeered. Flavius had them rowed out into the wide bay and then close into the sea-stained stonework, standing up to get a good look and lifting his head several times as if seeking a measurement.

'Photius, find a better boat than this and head back to Catania. Order the fleet to this bay. They are to make haste and spare no canvas or rower for time is of the essence.'

It was just the task for a keen youngster and he was given an escort of four experienced men to avoid him being tempted into an adventure that might be dangerous. With nothing to do Flavius went to his tent to join Procopius and to get from the messenger from Carthage, a senior tribune, some idea of what had been happening in the province since he left. There had been victories and defeats but the key battle was that of Solomon against the largest body of Moors.

'You will have heard tell, General, of the way they used camels against the Vandals, well they tried it on Solomon. They made a circle in which they put their women and children, being nomads even when fighting they travel with their families—'

That got a slightly impatient nod; Flavius had no need to be told that.

'The place they chose to give battle was cunning, a flat plain but with some high hills on one side. Solomon suspected that not all the Moors were amongst their camels.'

'He was at Dara, so he would suspect some of his enemies to be in hiding behind those hills.'

'Aye. We tried to attack those on the flat ground from the open, plain flank but the horses panicked at the smell of the camels. Not one archer of your *bucellarii* could settle them enough to fire a bow, so the horns were blown to retreat.'

The tribune could see in the face of Flavius that the thought did not please him, and that he could accept. It was the look Procopius was aiming at him that rankled. What did this jumped-up scribe know of what he was speaking, or any aspect of fighting?

'The order came to dismount and Solomon led us back into the fight on foot, but instead of attacking straight on he slid round to the other flank, the mountain one, and struck from there. The Moors had left that side short and those hidden, well whatever they thought, they did not engage and we broke through the line of camels as easy as kiss my hand.' That got a loud sniff. 'Easy to kill camels, Your Honour.'

'Moors?'

'Them too. A lot were slain, the rest taken as slaves and that included the whole crowd of women and children. Fetched a pretty penny, they did. Next Solomon and Theodorus the Cappadocian caught the Moors in a trap

401

in Byzacium and that was a grand slaughter I'm told, but for details I wasn't there, Your Honour, so I can't tell you much.'

'And the mutiny?'

'Where to start. Men ain't been paid, land that they was hoping for, having wed the Vandal widows, been taken for Justinian, may his greed send him to hell.'

'Careful where you say that, Tribune.'

That made the fellow sit up and he recounted all the problems that assailed what he had left in peace. Not just those mentioned, but also religion, for if it seemed right to shut the Arian churches and deny baptism, that took no account of the number of Arians in the imperial army such as the Heruls. Then there were Vandals stirring things up too.

'One piles on top of another and before you know it, mutiny.'

'Led by whom?'

'No one.'

That could not be true, but this tribune had no idea. The arrival of Solomon – who had fled Carthage – with the fleet fetched by Photius, brought the information Flavius required but that had to be set to one side since nothing could be done until he had dealt with what was before him. That required that he take to one of the larger transports and sail it as close to the walls of Panormus as was commensurate with safety.

'I may be too old for this.'

That was said as he began to climb the rigging that held the large central mast. It was not age that was against him but motion of a kind he had never before experienced, even in rough seas. The height exaggerated what on deck was light swell and Flavius felt his stomach churn as he swayed back and forth. For all his discomfort he had observed what he had come to see, though the descent he found was ten times more nerve-racking than the ascent.

Back on deck he spoke with the master mariner acting as the fleet commander and laid out his proposals, to which the fellow readily agreed, sending men off in a boat to go round the other large transports. Some were ordered to join with the vessel on which Flavius was still feeling unwell, others to send their most commodious boats.

'Photius, ashore as quick as you can with those boats and fetch me my archers.'

They came in small packets and some of them, even in a calm bay, were showing signs of being green at the gills. While they had been travelling, the transports chosen had lined up on the command vessel and were busy anchoring head and stern so they became as stable a platform as was possible on an open sea.

'Eight archers per boat was the command', and men who had got gratefully to the deck were put back from where they had come, with a cheerful Flavius commanding his stepson Photius, 'to wave to our enemies'.

This the boy did, a line of faces at the battlements that seemed to have no idea what was coming; hardly surprising, few did. The boats full of archers were now being rigged with lines, split to both sides so as to keep them even. That done Flavius gave the men on the windlass the order to haul, and slowly, one by one, the boats were raised till they were as near to the top of the mast as they could go.

'Choose your targets, no arrows to be wasted.'

It was hard to see from the deck but from aloft the masts were much higher than the sea wall defences, which were lower than the landward wall. The archers were firing down on Goths who had nothing with which to defend themselves for they had no archery with which to reply. The protection they relied upon was gone and the threat of what would follow was obvious. A seaward assault in which they dare not man their parapet.

'Photius. Take one of the other boats and offer the garrison terms. They may leave without their weapons and we will transport them to Italy. They have till the morning to decide.'

With that he called to the archers to desist.

The positive reply came back as required; the man leading the garrison knew he could not withstand the tactic which had been employed against him. A ship was arranged and the Goths marched out of their own watergate as the Romans marched in, the man Flavius was leaving in command given one order to be carried out straight away.

'Get the masons working, I want those seaward walls up to the height of a Goliath.'

CHAPTER TWENTY-NINE

Flavius had no time to hang around and watch those walls being built; he selected two of the fastest ships available, one to be sent off to Constantinople with a demand for gold. In the other, along with a hundred of his *comitatus*, he sailed for Carthage, a journey so short it allowed him limited time to assess what he would face on arrival.

Solomon had made certain dispositions before he departed; Theodorus was to hold the capital until aid arrived and a messenger was sent to Numidia and the far west with orders to seek to seduce as many mutineers as possible in these areas by bribes and promises, the aim to starve the rebellion of men because Flavius knew the most important factor was going to be numbers.

As yet he had no idea who he would face as an opponent or what kind of force he would lead, but it took no great imagination to work out that as well as disaffected imperial soldiers, any rebellion would bring out from the hedgerows those Vandals who had not accepted his amnesty and remained in hiding, while many more would revert to their previous allegiance: they might not get their own kings back but the notion of being free of the Roman yoke would be attractive.

The recently defeated Moors might help, but there was some hope that the wounds Solomon had so recently inflicted upon them went so deep they would still be licking them and in no condition to interfere. Reassuring was the fact that no senior officer seemed to have defected, which meant that when it came to command there was a fair chance the man who led the mutiny would lack knowledge, though it had to be accepted that some people took to command naturally.

The good fortune that had always attended his actions favoured Flavius once more. As soon as he sailed into harbour and his figure, standing in the prow, was recognised – his banner might be seen as a sham – the spirits of those holding the city rose and such a lift in their mood was essential. The day before, the leader of the revolt, a fellow called Stotzas and elected to the role by acclamation, had brought his forces, reckoned to be some eight thousand strong, to the walls of Carthage and demanded it be surrendered to him.

Theodorus had rejected that and to buy time sent a representative to treat for terms; it was an indication of the depth of feeling such mutinies generated that the poor fellow was killed and his crucified body set up below the walls for the inhabitants to see and ponder on, the message plain: this will be your fate if you resist.

'How has he mustered so many cavalry, Theodorus? His numbers well exceed what he could raise by just mutiny.'

'Vandals.'

'Even with those.'

'It includes men we sent to the east as mercenaries.'

Seeing his leader confused he explained they had taken over the ships transporting them and headed back home in time to join Stotzas.

'And he has recruited slaves, promising them freedom.'

'Foolish.'

It was not the notion of freeing such people that animated that response from Flavius: slaves would be too fickle to easily command and in a battle could be a hindrance rather than an aid; trained infantry were bad enough, slaves would be a rabble. He led the way up on to the walls to gaze over the mass of campfires that seemed to stretch forever, and his orders were simple. To gather every available man capable of fighting within the city and promise them great rewards to serve under his banner.

'We will not match them, Flavius Belisarius,' Solomon ventured.

'We don't need to, we only have to beat them.'

Said with confidence and an ironic smile it was designed to bolster what was a desperate cause and the same was true of what followed.

'My banner on the battlements so it can be seen at dawn,

and get the news to this Stotzas somehow that I am here and back in command.'

The effect of that surprised even Flavius. At dawn, either because of the standard flapping on the walls or the information of his arrival, the rebel army quickly began to decamp and head south, for his mere presence promised them a battle they had hoped to avoid. Stotzas had clearly expected the gates of Carthage to open because it was indefensible but with Belisarius defiantly there he could have no idea how many troops the general had with him and how many more were on their way.

Even less expected was that they would be immediately pursued by Flavius who knew he had a mental advantage; they were afraid of him but that would diminish with time and distance. The knowledge that he was on their tail would sow doubt into their whole endeavour for the common soldier was a fretful beast; how could they fight and defeat the empire's most successful military leader?

Moving faster than the cumbersome rebels he caught them outside the city of Membresa where they had camped. The place was unwalled and therefore offered no defensive advantage, so Flavius did likewise. With only two thousand effectives Flavius was massively outnumbered and his campfires sent that message to his enemies; he would need that famous good luck and more to achieve a victory, perhaps even to survive.

Dawn broke with dust in the air, caused by a strong wind coming off the Mediterranean. The sand was not blinding but it must indicate to any commander with a brain that it would put him at a disadvantage when it came to an exchange of missiles: archery, spears, or even slingshot. Those Belisarius deployed would have added range against his firing into the wind and it was obvious this was noticed and acted upon.

With the River Bagradas on his flank, Stotzas sought to turn that into his backstop, angling his forces so that the wind would blow south across both fronts, which would not only nullify any advantage but would force Belisarius to likewise manoeuvre, given his inferior numbers. It might even oblige him to withdraw.

But Stotzas was no great leader, he had been a member of the guard of General Martinus, now holding Numidia. He was seeking to control a ragtag force that lacked either good training or internal discipline. Given those drawbacks and his greater numbers he should have taken what regular troops he had and could have relied upon to create a body of troops that could defend movements that would render him vulnerable.

What he got was confusion: mounted Vandals mixed with the imperial mutineers, on foot and horsed who, as a body, had little cohesion in themselves, being from all over the empire and now very likely led by strangers. In amongst that were what Flavius had already estimated as a ball and chain in battle: the mass of slaves to whom a simple command was so easy to misunderstand and enough to cause muddle.

'Solomon, the cavalry. An immediate charge and do not try to hold them back, let them loose, it is time for fear to do its work.'

Even Solomon, a man who trusted Flavius Belisarius absolutely, hesitated to execute that command. The few horses they had were their best men.

'Do as I say. Now!'

Not all the dust in the air was now coming from what was blown off the land. As much was being generated by the untidy manoeuvres Stotzas was seeking to carry out, with men and horses stamping up a cloud. The sound of the horns seemed to cause the whole thing to freeze as everyone stopped to see what they portended, for not all knew. Those who did, ex-imperial soldiers, recognised the advance when they heard it and it was not coming from those close to Stotzas. Aware an attack was coming they sought to rush to where they had been told to deploy and that turned disorder into mayhem.

It was hard to see beyond his own cavalry lining up to charge, but there was a definite ripple along the line of the rebels and it presaged the flight of those who were not familiar with battle. They began to break and run, which spread to those who should have known better. But panic is contagious and that was what happened now.

Before the Belisarius cavalry had really got going the entire rebel force was in flight, the plain before his eyes a mass of fleeing men who, when they reached their encampment, did not stop to gather their possessions but carried on and abandoned them. When Flavius led his troops into that he found they had also left behind any monies they had sequestered as well as the women with whom many an imperial soldier hoped to acquire inherited land.

There could be no pursuit beyond that, Flavius lacked the numbers, but the work had been done; he had every confidence that once broken that force would not again combine, for there would be no end of mutual recrimination and Stotzas and his other mutiny leaders, if they had any sense, would be looking for a place where they could go beyond the reach of Roman revenge.

Hubris is quick to strike when any man feels too pleased with what he has achieved; as famed for his modesty as much as his military skill, Flavius Belisarius would not have been human had he not been aware that it was his name that had been as much the cause of success as any other factor. Had Stotzas not struck his camp and fled as soon as he heard of his return? So the man who rode back into Carthage was entitled to a little pride.

That lasted no more than the time it takes to get through the gate: there was now an uprising in Sicily, another mutiny, these with troops he had not long left and caused by much the same reason; a lack of pay. He was gone by the time the news arrived that Stotzas had managed to reform his rabble – clearly his tongue outbid his skill on a battlefield – and Marcellus, the man left behind in command as *dux*, feeling they were dealing with an enemy who would be easy to overcome, set out to finish what had failed to be completed by the departed Flavius Belisarius.

The name said a great deal. Marcellus was the offspring of an old patrician family that could trace its roots back to the Palatine Hill in Rome and even to the days of the Republic. His rise in the army had been as swift as befitted the influence his relatives could bring to bear and his pride reflected both his background and the feeling of natural authority that belonged to his class.

When they found and confronted the rebels, Stotzas

asked to be allowed to address the troops Marcellus led, which included *foederati*, *bucellarii* and Gepid mercenaries. Thinking the rebel was about to plead for forgiveness, permission was granted, for such a man as Marcellus, trained in rhetoric, could not conceive that someone so low born might have the gift of persuasion.

In a rousing speech Stotzas listed the grievances that had driven him to mutiny and these were matters as yet unresolved in any part of the imperial army in North Africa. He then asked that the men join him instead of fighting him. Those Marcellus led and Belisarius before him had declined to mutiny through caution, not out of love for Justinian or the empire, and they were swayed; soon the *dux* found his army melting away.

Aware that he faced annihilation, Marcellus and his inferior commanders abandoned those still loyal and took refuge in a church, from which Stotzas, now in command of both forces combined, offered them safe passage to Carthage. As they exited the church and left sanctified ground he killed them.

Back in Sicily, Flavius had managed to restore order through his personality, reputation for honesty, as well as his military prowess. He was aided by the arrival of a ship bearing that which he had insisted be sent from Constantinople: gold to pay his troops. His other demand had been acceded to as well; money was on its way to Carthage and with it came fresh troops that could confront any further trouble under an imperial nephew called Germanus, who naturally sought advice from Flavius Belisarius.

'You have money and soldiers. Use the first to bribe and the latter for battle.'

'Stotzas?'

'Is not a general, so if he feels he will face an army he will think of himself first.'

'It seems wrong to bribe a mutineer.'

'It is, but, Germanus, it is also wise. Detach Stotzas from his men if you can, kill him if you cannot and if you feel the need for support I am no more than two days away by galley.'

It was good to hear his advice being acted upon; Flavius was not sure that the news that he got was as cut and dried as the advice he gave but the thing was resolved. Stotzas had abandoned his army after his second attempt to take Carthage was rebuffed. Was it brought about by the amount of gold he received or the level of fear he felt for his hide? It mattered not; Stotzas acted as had been predicted and many of his followers returned to their duty once they were promised their pay. The rump were brought to battle and annihilated.

'I am free to act at last, Photius, all I await now is my orders from Justinian.'

Procopius had an opinion to air and he did so. 'Am I at liberty to point out, General, that you have many fewer soldiers at your disposal now than were sent with you to North Africa? And the situation in Italy is not as propitious as it was only months past, added to which it is a much larger task.'

'You can point it out to me, Procopius, but I am not the one to decide.'

Flavius knew he was at the mercy of events elsewhere, in Dalmatia and Illyricum. Then there were the Franks and the Burgundians; had Justinian managed to get from them the backing he wanted? The wisdom of leaving Sicily and landing in a hostile Italy were not hard to perceive. What he did not have was the whole picture; that only existed in Constantinople and the machinations of the Emperor.

Looking at Photius, Flavius naturally thought of Antonina, delivered of a daughter whom she had named Ioannina, acceding to his request. She did not know it was in honour of Flavius's old friend and the man he thought of as his saviour. Ohannes, his father's elderly *domesticus*, had protected him and guided Flavius when the entire forces of the most powerful magnate in Moesia were ranged against him and when he was no more of an age than the boy he was sat with.

Memories flooded his mind as they often did and he could not but believe, in reflections on his life so far and the fact he had survived, that God had spared him for a purpose and perhaps that lay across the Straits of Messina. Was it his destiny, albeit for the glory of Justinian, to reconquer the old heartland of the empire of which his father Decimus had been so proud?

If it was, and in memory of him, it was fitting.